The Wish Doctor

MARK E. SHUPE

The Wish Doctor
© 2023 Mark E. Shupe

Cover art: James T. Pantuso
Cover design: Rebekah Wetmore
Editor: Andrew Wetmore

ISBN: 978-1-998149-23-0
First edition December, 2023

MOOSE HOUSE
PUBLICATIONS

2475 Perotte Road
Annapolis County, NS
B0S 1A0
moosehousepress.com
info@moosehousepress.com

We live and work in Mi'kma'ki, the ancestral and unceded territory of the Mi'kmaw people. This territory is covered by the "Treaties of Peace and Friendship" which Mi'kmaw and Wolastoqiyik (Maliseet) people first signed with the British Crown in 1725. The treaties did not deal with surrender of lands and resources but in fact recognized Mi'kmaq and Wolastoqiyik (Maliseet) title and established the rules for what was to be an ongoing relationship between nations. We are all Treaty people.

Dedication

To Lana, the first time I saw you, I said, "I wish I could be with you for ever." It is a wish that has turned out perfectly for me, a one true power wish, where nothing went wrong. Your strength gave me the power to walk through the darkest times, when other wishes turned our lives awry. As we settle into WishLight cottage, this is proof that hard work and patience are more important than wishes.

If my first wish required a power wish, the next three were a set of pure wishes that came from within a wishing well deeper than any described in this book. Deep was the power to make you, K, R and A, the special three you are. I could not be prouder of you, my children. If my wish power had any part of making you who you are, I stand aside in humility, knowing you have surpassed those wishes.

To Andrew Wetmore, the grand Wish-Master who understood the Wish Doctor from the first taste of wishkey, I wish for you only the finest wishkey from the finest kegs.

To all of you who ever felt a little different, or felt the burden of responsibility too strongly, or could never find someone to truly understand you, I wish for you the bestest of the best, that all your wishes are power wishes, and that all your protection wishes hold true, and that the only wish you ever reverse is the wish that you were something other than yourself.

To all above and everyone else, let us all wish to be better people and work together more and fight each other less. If there must be criticism, let it be criticism with respect.

This is a work of fiction. The author has created the characters, conversations, interactions, and events; and any resemblance of any character to any real person is coincidental.

The Wish Doctor

The Wish Doctor

"I have got work to do, so much work on so many subjects that I want many more years of life to finish it all."

-Alexander Graham Bell

"A proper thank you, given freely and meaningfully, at the right time and place, can be more powerful than any wish."

- The Wish Doctor

"Hoy, Hoy!"

-Alexander Graham Bell and the Wish Doctor

Mark E. Shupe

1: Alma Faye

The doctor stared at his wish watch. It was shortly after sunrise but the watch had already struck thirteen. Thirteen wishes gone wrong in the world. Thirteen tragedies to cure. He grabbed his tweed coat and flying goggles, letting the front door slam behind him as he hurried out of the Lodge of Wonders.

It was going to be a busy day.

~

Alma Faye's job was to hold the magical orb steady on her lap. It would have been easy to do for a few minutes if she was in a comfortable chair in the living room, but not in the back of a ten-year-old jalopy that bounced and careened over potholes along backwater Canadian roads. And not for six hours as they drove from Halifax to Baddeck, the summer home of the man who invented the telephone.

Oh, and before they went any further could she just shake her head one more time? Of all the consequences of her personality disorder, why did her mother, Lavinia, have to believe she was a witch?

Alma's arms ached like she was in one of the challenges on *Survivor* where the contestants had to hold their arms out to keep a pail of water from spilling. Could she complain? Not if she didn't want to earn the wrath of her precious brother.

Her brother could not hold the orb, they had told her. He had to be in best condition to audition for the secretive magical school in Baddeck.

She sighed inwardly in frustration as Lavinia 'read' the runes of the land, finding omens everywhere that reinforced their course of action to come to this land of New Scotland.

Alma grimaced. She was not completely sure there was no magic in the orb. She had seen Lavinia predict things that seemed impossible, though nothing to Alma's benefit. Lavinia had predicted the COVID epidemic, but then she had predicted plagues every two years.

"How much further?" Alma asked as her arms screamed to set down the orb.

"Shh," Lavinia said. "Your brother is sleeping."

Sure enough, drool was oozing down Pierre's tilted chin.

It wasn't easy for Alma, being the second child with her mother always fawning on *him*. While everything he did was perfect, everything she did seemed inconsequential. If she got a "That's nice" from her mother, she felt lucky. The whole household revolved around, well portends, but also her brother. He was destined to do this. He was fated to do that. If Fates could see his drool, she wondered if they'd honour their choice.

He was half-decent looking, she admitted. Half her friends, which wasn't that many, wanted to date him. His dark hair and caramel skin framed a handsome face. When he bothered to put on his charm, he was hard to resist.

Deep down, she believed she could equal him in many ways. Her features were not as distinct, having inherited more of her father's characteristics, but her hair was nearly as shiny black. People often said it was her best feature, though she wasn't sure if this was a compliment or a consolation.

She was sure she could outdo him in algebra. Her scores in solitaire apps were always higher, which frustrated him. Though she could never match his skill in Fortnite. She could play the flute and he couldn't, though that excited exactly nobody. Even the couple she met who claimed they ran a flute-making company seemed bored when she told them.

Perhaps her time would come if Pierre went off to this school. She sighed. He would continue to be the centre of conversation. Her mother would certainly stare into the orb, wondering how he was doing, never mind that her iPhones 12, 13 and 14 sat unused. Truthfully, she could live without attention, but if she wasn't made to be Pierre's assistant most of the day, and didn't have to listen to his voice, her life would be better. Maybe worth the permanent damage the strain of the orb was causing her.

If only there was a way to entertain herself. Not like her family would enjoy talking with her.

She fought dozing eyes, then came awake suddenly, as the car bumped chaotically, her father desperately trying to regain control. She knew better than to say anything, but where the blazes were the portends that warned of possible car wrecks?

Her father, Jean, fought the careening car. He just missed an oncoming pickup and barely dodged the mother grizzly on the road. It took all Alma's concentration to keep the crystal steady. As her body thumped and bounced, she held it immobile, though she was ready to turn it in for one that had a better chance of predicting car crashes.

She almost lost her grip when Lavinia's eyes flamed at her. She renewed her concentration, and as they decelerated in a fishtailing, squid-jigging, screech of rubber, the crystal stayed as steady as the most valuable Faberge egg.

Pierre finally woke and, through the drool, said "What happened?"

"Flat tire," father said. "Everybody out. I'll have to jack the car."

Alma braced for the warning from Lavinia, and it wasn't long coming.

"Alma, make sure you protect that crystal."

"Yes'm."

She cautiously opened the door, stretching her legs one at a time, delicately balancing the crystal, while clenching her butt cheeks and shifting her weight. Despite her screaming arms, she held the orb immobile; no way was she going to upset Lavinia.

Jean opened the trunk, stirred through her brother's six suitcases, and pulled out a jack and spare tire. He set about placing the jack, tenderly asking his wife if she wouldn't mind pulling rocks out of the nearby ditch to use as blocks under the tires. "I'd ask Alma but she's holding that orb like she's found her true love."

Nobody smiled, least of all his wife, who was above any kind of manual labour. (The portends never recommended it.)

He silently cranked the jack, while his wife gruffly placed the rocks. Puffing heavily, Jean gave the tire iron a mighty tug.

And immediately screamed, clutching his spine. "My back!" he hollered. He swore not quite under his breath and danced around in pain.

It didn't take someone with a magic orb to know he was badly hurt.

When the dance stopped, Jean looked at Pierre, whose face drooped at the prospect of physical exertion.

But Lavinia had her hand up. "No, he's not doing it. He can't be dirty when we reach the school."

Jean tried to hand his wife the tire iron, but she shook her head. "Enough labour for me. Alma, give me the crystal."

Lavinia had a camp chair already unfolded, blanket on her lap, ready to receive it.

Alma was relieved to be free of the orb as it went to Lavinia's lap. But now everyone was staring, waiting for her to get to work on the tire.

She sighed, but grabbed the tire iron. There was no point grumbling. She knew her place in the family.

It took thirty minutes of listening to mother and brother asking how much longer. She did not have her father's strength but she had persistence and knowledge of leverage. Slowly the tire came off. She caught a glimpse of herself in the side mirror as she hoisted the replacement: dirt, mud, and rubber residue all over her arms and face.

As she put the jack and flat tire in the trunk Pierre laughed. She almost hit him with the tire iron.

"Little piggy," he sang. "Little tired piggy, covered in mud."

"Enough, son," Lavinia said. "Time to go."

They climbed back in the car, father sure he could drive despite his twinged back, and the crystal ceremoniously returned to Alma's lap.

"Keep the blanket on it. Don't get that crystal dirty."

Pierre laughed. "Piggy with a crystal, tired piggy with a crystal."

Alma tried to ignore him, but he wouldn't stop. The noon sun glaring on the crystal reflected into her eyes. She rubbed them and a grist of dirt brought a tear. She could feel the floodgates opening but held them.

She looked into the crystal as if it really had magic. *If I could wish anything*, she said silently to it, *I wish my brother gets accepted by this school and I never see him again.*

~

It wasn't the Wish Doctor's habit to come home for lunch. It depended on the wishes he had to fix. If he had to travel far, he usually stayed away. If there was a cluster of wishes, and that was often lately, he would fix the cluster. On his odd days off, he was so tired he usually slept through lunch.

Today, it might have been more efficient to stay out, but he had an odd craving to return to the Lodge of Wonders. He could consult his references. He could check on the wishes brewing for the next day but that made little difference in his workload, and sometimes put him on edge. Maybe it was a portend calling him home.

In any event, or at least in this event, he returned home for lunch in the tetrahedron, the travelling box kite his friend and host had perfected. He felt a little guilty about being the only person to have one, but until he had someone to replace him fixing wishes, he wasn't going to feel too guilty.

He wasn't sure which had allowed the kite to be perfected, the wish or the prayer, but in decades of use, the kite had not failed him. Not even on days with dangerous winds, so most likely it was the prayer. Or his friend's genius, which hadn't diminished in the least after his passing.

The sky was clear after the early rain, with low winds, so the kite landed gracefully. He stepped out, raised his goggles and started down the driveway.

He wasn't always one to notice the physical world, but something looked out of place on the long driveway. A vehicle had limped down it, forming an uneven rut.

He came around the bend in the lane to find a dusty old car that didn't belong there. He looked toward the estate he loved. There were four people on the veranda, then off, then pressing noses against windows, then knocking at the door. People not invited, but people not wanting a wish fixed. Not in the way clients normally wanted a wish fixed.

His mind really must be distracted. A score of years had gone. The summer was over. It was almost time for the training he put on every twenty years for possible wish doctors.

Maybe his last birthday wish was working. If so, he might be about to find someone to replace him.

There were several clever students from his last class using wish magic around the world. A few could possibly take over for him, but all were using their cleverness for other purposes. He could not blame them. Other than living on this great estate there was not a lot of joy in being a wish doctor. Not with so many bad wishes.

This year, his assistant, Selva, had done the recruiting. He wondered if the veranda people were family of one of the recruits, coming to check out the historical but private estate. Unlikely they would know this was where their child would be quartered, as *that* was a secret secret.

"Hoy, hoy," he said.

There were two children. They ducked behind a large man as if seeking protection on the top step of the veranda, the Wish Doctor rather awkwardly looking up at them. "Can I help you?"

The other grownup, a woman, stepped forward from the family cluster. He must have looked odd, given his goggles and mostly tweed clothing would have been at home in Scotland in the 19th century.

She cleared her throat as if uncertain how to proceed. "We have come a long way to talk to a special man who would likely know we were coming."

"Ah," the doctor said. "That certainly explains everything. Can you let me get past you into the kitchen while you wait? I'm slightly famished."

"You're not him? My fortunes said he'd be the first person we'd meet."

The Wish Doctor began to think he would miss lunch after all. Surely, they were not Selva's recruits. They would have better manners than to block the veranda.

"I don't know how special I am. I'm just a country doctor trying to help people. Now let's say I was the person you were to meet, would I know that? Just because *you* have a way to know, would *I*? I do have a lot to keep track of and I'm not as organized as when I was in my younger days."

"Your younger days? You can't be older than twenty-five. I'd say younger but if you're a doctor you'd need many years to learn your craft."

"Aye." It had indeed taken many years to learn his craft. If he had any vanity left, he'd be pleased at the compliment to his looks. *If only she knew how many years.*

She suddenly grabbed the arm of the boy behind her, pulling him in front of her. "This is Pierre. He's special too. It's why we have come to you."

The doctor nodded. If his Iwish Setter was here, he'd have her sniff Pierre for wish magic. He had a feeling this was what this was about.

Out of his side vision, he could see the daughter edging down the veranda as if to distance herself. She walked lopsided, with a balled sweater in her hands. She was carrying something heavy.

"Let's speak plainly, then. Who are you?"

"Lavinia and Jean."

"Nice to meet you." *Why is the name of the daughter missing from the conversation?* "Why are you here? Let's not hold anything back. I've found that rarely works. Except in chess."

Jean gave Lavinia a nudge. "For heaven's sake, we came all this way on your say-so. Get talking."

After an awkward pause, Lavinia sputtered, "We want you to teach Pierre."

"What is it you want me to teach him?"

"Wish magic, of course."

The doctor's eyebrows raised. "You know that sounds absurd."

"To the uninformed. But not to you. I'm only a half-blood witch, but I have a history of understanding future news, and knowing truths. Alma, show the doctor my crystal."

At last, the girl's name. The doctor slid his eyes toward the girl as she stepped closer and unwrapped the sweater. Underneath was indeed a crystal. And not a fake piece of parlour merchandise.

He looked at the boy. The lad had clever eyes. He was reasonably fit. Clearly, he did not spend all of his time playing video games or tormenting his sister. Still, the doctor didn't see the spark of eagerness he expected in students, nor any sign of ability to make sacrifices. He sighed. Lavinia had a tinge of authenticity. She probably could read the crystal and make minor predictions. But she was wrong about her son being special enough to take a slot in his school.

He was a little annoyed she had broken protocol. His training, like good wishes, came to people, the people didn't come to him. Had she wished her son to be part of the school? There was a wrongness in the boy but not a wish to be fixed today. It was just the misaligned hope of a woman with some small power. *Well, medium power. She's psychic, after all.*

It was the route of all magic gone wrong. People with enough knowledge to recognize power, maybe even to enact a spell, but unable to predict all the actions, reactions, and multiple order effects that led to the upsetting of the natural way of things. Which of course many of the creatures offering wishes hoped to cause.

He sensed no danger nearby. He still had wishes to fix and would now be very hungry for supper. He gazed at his wish watch again. So much to do and now this annoyance. No way was this lad ever going to be a wish doctor.

"Bring the crystal closer," he said.

At first the girl didn't move. He fixed her with a fierce look and finally she stretched out the crystal for him to grasp.

But he didn't need to. He had had enough of magics gone rogue. He didn't need a crystal stirring more trouble.

He motioned the boy closer, until he was standing next to his sister. "Do you know what this is about? Do you know why your mother brought you here?"

The boy said, "I came to be taught wish magic. I can do some slight readings and illusions. Mom thinks I can do wish magic."

"I see. Would you be willing to help people when their wishes go wrong?"

"If that was part of the training. But I want to be able to make my wishes come true."

"Ah. Making wishes for yourself is what causes the greatest trouble."

He turned to Alma, pretending for the parents that he was staring at the crystal. "And why are you here?"

The crystal didn't answer and neither did the girl.

The doctor's eyes commanded. From the corner of his eye he saw Lavinia making a shushing gesture.

Alma was looking only at him. "I'm too young to stay at home."

"I see. Yet you hold the crystal."

"It's too heavy for mom."

Her words were coldly bland, as if some force had peeled her personality away. She had not wanted to come but at this moment he could tell she felt not just different, but spell bound. In her eyes he saw what she couldn't say: the family did whatever their mother wanted, whatever the crystal thought was good for her older brother. She could not say she yearned to break free of that trap, but didn't want to upset her mother's hope for Pierre.

"Do you know Morse code?" the doctor asked suddenly, turning back to Peter.

The boy shook his head, but Alma involuntarily raised her hand.

"I see." He turned back to the girl. "Say what is in your head."

"Dot dot. Dash dot dot. Dash dash dash."

The doctor's irritation faded. "You'll say that again on your wedding day."

"If I have one."

So there is some spark of character there. "Here's a question. Have you changed a tire recently?"

"What does that matter?" Pierre said.

"I have," Alma said.

"Shh," Lavinia said. "He was asking your brother."

"I'm not sure I was," the doctor said.

There was a waiting silence from everyone. The Wish Doctor turned in a slow circle until he was facing between the two children. "Give me an example of a palindrome."

Pierre said, "It's...it's when..."

At the same time Alma said, "Nurses run. You can read it forwards or backwards."

The doctor nodded. "Tell me a pun, then."

"My brother is so lazy and biased, he has two butts."

The Wish Doctor nodded. "Indeed."

"My mother says puns are lazy humour," Pierre said.

"Well, then, can you read lips, speak backwards, talk in sign language?"

"No, but I can sing."

"That isn't important. I need someone who can talk to ghosts. And you, young lady?"

"I know a little sign language and I'd work hard to learn the rest."

The father, Jean, seemed to emerge with a start from a bit of a daze. "We can pay tuition. His marks are good. He can write an essay."

The doctor cocked his head. "But can he pull a rabbit out of his hat?"

Jean shook his head, visibly annoyed.

"My colleague is responsible for recruiting, but I can make a case for a candidate." He turned back to the girl. "Alma Faye, how hard does your brother work?"

"He is a...good student."

"Has either of your parents said they wished he'd work harder?"

The girl said slowly, "I never told you my full name."

Her mother was behind Alma now, hand gripping her shoulder. *More concerned about the crystal than her daughter.*

This Wish Doctor turned to Pierre again. "Pablo, do you like Renaissance Italy?"

The boy frowned.

"Ever heard of Michelangelo?"

"He's my favourite turtle!"

"Indeed."

For every question, the doctor's ears listened to the boy, but his eyes read the girl. How many questions would he need to ask before the parents realized the only offer he could make?

They had once made a wish about their son. Like so many wishes it would not come true as they had expected, but it *could* come true, in a positive, not destructive way. It would be a good result for a wish, if they could see beyond the end of their noses.

He nodded to himself, then gave the girl his full attention. "Alma, I can't promise all this will be fun, but you will learn more than you ever expected. There is no tuition as long as you supply intuwishin. You will learn to fly in a kite and how to speak backwards. You will learn to fix bad wishes and make good wishes. You will learn to manage risk and danger. I give you an invitation that only comes to a few students every twenty years."

Lavinia's voice was thin as wire. "What are you saying? She's too young, she's not special enough. My son is what the portends said I had to watch."

The Wish Doctor smiled, but not in a happy way. "The portends are right."

The parents looked at each other in annoyed confusion.

"I'm sorry," he said to Piers. *Sorry I cannot teach you, sorry for what the portends will bring and sorry I cannot remember your name.* "You will make your parents proud, but not without heartache. You would not be happy here. The dry snow that keeps you locked in would not appeal to you. The days when the old forces of this island block the airwaves would mean no internet, no video games, no sports scores, no funny cat videos."

Pierre said slowly, "No internet?"

"Are you comfortable knowing this is not right for you?"

The boy struggled to not look at his mother. "But she—"

"No, don't say it! Don't say you wish, not on this ground, not if you don't want nightmares."

The doctor didn't mean to be mean. The parents, now unsure, had sacrificed and driven so far, their faith in the crystal unshakable.

Pierre stepped closer to the doctor and spoke in a quiet, urgent flow. "This is not *my* dream. I wasn't sure about the crystal. I had three different tellers read my fortune. They all said I would face a choice and my sister would matter."

He glanced at Alma. "She's annoying, but I think Alma's schooling here matters more than me.

"Yes," the doctor said. "Alma's alma mater must matter."

"Besides I don't like snow."

The doctor pondered. Was the boy caught in some sort of wish trap? Was there something about the girl he could not see? Was she more trouble than the obvious trouble the boy would be? It'd been a while since he'd been wrong, but it did happen every century or two.

"I don't know," the mother said.

The doctor turned to her with a touch of impatience "Don't be wishy-washy. Your crystal drove you to me. I did not request that you come. The girl has talent. She will learn more here than anywhere, both of magic and non-magic. The risks you dared put your son under will be lesser for your daughter."

Jean looked at his wife. "Lavinia, the portends aren't always clear. They meant one of our children to come. We picked the wrong one."

Lavinia glared at her daughter. "You little brat," she muttered. "I hope you're proud ruining your brother's chances. All we have sacrificed. This is how you repay us?"

"Shh," the doctor said, using the leftover power of a wish to soften her hurt.

The child must not stay solely because she is running from her mother. "Alma," he said, "you must look inside to what you want. You will be far from your friends but will make new ones you will keep forever. There is danger. There is hard work. You will be challenged but, in the end, grateful. Everyone who has graduated has hated the place at one time while they were here, but all say were glad they attended. There is magic and science and truth and fiction. There is humour and history, imagination and life. And two ghosts. But above all else good wishes."

Her eyes were locked on his. She was shaking slightly, but not with fear. "Tell me truly, letting this be your last uneducated wish. Do you wish to study here?"

Alma tapped her foot on the veranda. Dot dot. Dash dot dot. Dash dash dash.

The doctor smiled. "Welcome, my little starfish to the School of Wish."

2: A boy and his bear

The Wish Doctor hated when teddy bears came alive.

Unfortunately, they came alive more often than you would think and the spells that brought them alive were more varied than you would imagine. Although you might think that most of these spells came from wishes of children whose teddy bears were their constant companions you would be in error. Many teddy bears came to life due to adult lost loves, loneliness, anger, or identity difference. Thus, it wasn't as easy to trace down the reason for a teddy bear coming to life as, say, a boy's wish to be a giant.

It wasn't always teddy bears that came alive from wishes. The doctor had seen wolves, unicorns, penguins, dragons, camels, gorillas, giraffes and squirrels (one of the most unbelievably mean creatures to come alive, believe it or not). He had seen toucans, frogs, hippos, starfish, seals and killer whales.

Not all of them turned out to be menaces. Some turned out to be kind and gentle souls.

Some even understood they had to be put back to their original form. Some had personalities and understanding of their place in the world. A rare few he let stay alive for a particular purpose, or let disappear into nature where they might balance things the human race had unbalanced. Two he even consulted for help from time to time. There was often nothing better to counter a wish creation than another wish creation.

Make no mistake about it, though. Those that came alive, were alive and alive for real. They were not copies, nor synthetic approximations.

Some of them were fully-created individuals with a claim on life just the same as you and me. Of course, those created from a poorly-constructed wish could be unstable, and a real danger. And don't get him started on stuffed superheroes. They were the worst.

Although trolls could be amazingly friendly, he had a hard time getting them to turn back into toys.

But there was something about bears, especially teddy bears. You would think them the cuddliest, tamest of creatures.

You would be wrong. They were almost as bad as gnomes.

He shivered. It was like everyone who owned a stuffed bear wanted it to come alive and be their best friend, or lend a paw when needed.

To be fair, stuffed bears that came alive were rarely violent. But they could be. They were often very ornery when awoken after hibernation. And not sarcastic and ultimately lovable like Boston Ted from the *Ted* movies. When they weren't ornery, they were troublemakers for the sake of making trouble, often pulling practical jokes that no one would laugh at. He remembered the one time the bear had asked the boy to pull his finger and it was a stick stuck into a hive.

Even the ones that just liked to sing, eat honey, or get drunk were troublemakers, stumbling awkwardly or getting stuck in doors where they shouldn't be.

Then there were the violent ones, violent because their habitat had been encroached on, or their babies threatened, or their owners had projected loneliness, anger, frustration upon them.

Since bear wishes were so varied, the doctor was often barely prepared. So, as he descended in the tetrahedron kite into the Highlands National Park, he was feeling just a bit apprehensive. He had saved this as his last wish reversal for the day and, without lunch, he himself was a little ornery.

It was getting dark, the last wish taking too long to undo. If he had his preference, he would stop all children from watching *Willy Wonka and the Chocolate Factory* and getting the wrong ideas.

Although the park was within driving distance, he preferred his kite to all the twists and turns of the scenic highway that led past the Canadian Cape Smokey. The kite settled gently in a small clearing that had once been a parking lot, now overgrown, and he got out to check his bearings.

This one wouldn't be hard to find. According to his wish watch, this was a strong wish, and thus easy to detect.

The doctor wandered along a gravel trail into the campground and stopped at an abandoned tennis court.

In the court was the largest bear he had seen conjured in eastern North America. It was a black bear, not as big as a grizzly or polar bear in real life but still dangerously gigantic compared to the cuddly bear it was likely conjured from.

It took him a second to relax and adjust to the scene in front of him. The situation was not as dangerous as his watch had first warned. The bear after all, was wearing a plastic mask and holding a goalie stick.

The bear was also standing between two ragged work boots that indicated where the edges of the goal should be, while a rather solid lad fired tennis balls with blinding speed, as if he was a tennis cannon.

If you did not know it was a bear deflecting the balls, you would immediately call a hockey scout to sign him (undoubtedly, he would fit right in with the Boston Bruins).

The doctor, slightly amused, watched as the boy finished shooting. The bear, for there was no doubt that he was a bear and not a hockey player wearing a fur coat, carefully gathered the balls with its stick and gently fired them back to the boy.

Before the boy could shoot again, the bear lifted its mask for a second and pointed at the Wish Doctor. The boy only gave the Wish Doctor a glance and then resumed shooting.

While before the bear had deflected every shot, this time two went by it, one between its legs, another past its left paw. The bear growled; whether from frustration or the presence of the Wish Doctor was not certain. It was clear the Wish Doctor's presence made the bear more nervous than the boy.

It was then that the Wish Doctor noticed the bear was wearing a bright orange jersey that was the team colours of the Philadelphia Flyers of the National Hockey League. As the Wish Doctor noted the nameplate on the back of the jersey read "Hextall," he knew it was time to take charge.

"Hoy, Hoy," he said. "Getting a little dark for hockey isn't it? One of you might get hurt."

"Bah," the bear said. "I've had three months of berries, fish, and honey. I'm nice and fat and protected. Tennis balls won't hurt me."

While the bear clearly seemed annoyed at the doctor's presence, the boy seemed neither surprised nor annoyed. Most people bringing a bear to life would be surprised at the odd dress and mannerisms of the doctor and likely wary that he might try to undo their work, but the boy barely seemed to blink.

It was almost if the boy had met the Wish Doctor before, but for the life of him the Wish Doctor could not place him.

The boy said, "We'll be finished in a few minutes. My mother's been over six times already asking me to come for marshmallows."

"Marshmallows!" said the bear, taking off the goalie mask. "You didn't mention marshmallows. I do believe it is time we finished."

"Alright," the boy sighed. "But after the hike tomorrow, promise you'll play with me again."

"If you let me have enough marshmallows." The bear smiled wolfishly but in a bearlike way, "I will play with you tomorrow and the day after that."

"Deal," the boy said. He gathered up the work boots, tying a knot in the laces and flinging them over his shoulder. The bear eyed the doctor cautiously, then ambled behind the boy, still on two feet.

Neither bear nor boy invited the doctor for marshmallows, though in truth he hadn't wished for such an invitation. Still, he felt his feelings hurt as he hadn't eaten lunch and fighting wishes was beary exhausting work.

The Wish Doctor coughed gently.

The bear replied by motioning his paw for the doctor to join them, then said, "I didn't suppose you were going to allow us to eat the marshmallows in peace."

"You are very astute, Mr. Hextall. Can I call you Mr. Hextall?"

"'Mr. Hextall' was my father," the bear said. "You can call me Ron."

The Wish Doctor had a sudden memory of watching hockey in the 1980s. No, wait, it must have been later, especially if he wanted to keep up the pretense of his age. Maybe it was an old game aired during the COVID time, when live events were cancelled. He was still more of a fan of the sport of Irish Hurley, despite his time in Canada.

The game was memorable for the rough play from the goalie, a Flyer with the name of Ron Hextall. The goalie was particularly vicious, and he remembered Selva telling him that his behavior was unusual for a goalie. And that, in real life, Hextall was a sweetheart.

The doctor mused. Most bears were sweethearts. It's what got them in trouble. Always looking for honey. Or marshmallows. Or, in rare occasions, better ways to stop pucks.

Unfortunately, their natural instincts could lead to violence.

Ron seemed quite pleasant now, but the Wish Doctor wondered how he would react when the time came to undo the wish.

"And what do I call you?" Ron asked.

"Oh, me?" The Wish Doctor did not like to give out his real name, especially to creatures of wish, since the power of names was a key element of magic. Instead, he said, in order to create a bit of a mean and serious presence, "You can call me Edison."

"Is that right?" Ron said skeptically. "How is your father, Ed?"

"Pardon," said the Doctor, noting he was not being taken seriously despite his attempt at a mean and serious presence.

"I don't think this is just right," said the bear named Ron. "The last time I came to life, some smart Alec insisted I be turned back into stuffing. I could well understand, if I were not a talking, thinking, feeling, doctor-fooling, hockey-playing bear, that it would be safest to take that action. But I am a very nice and personable bear. I do not hurt humans. Even the ones who stand on the side of the road and insist they take my picture, when I'm clearly just trying to get to the restaurant for lunch."

The Wish Doctor did not have much sympathy. Perhaps he should. But he could not do his job if he didn't have some insensitivity in these matters. If he let too many wish creations continue, even the ones that seemed benign, soon there would be a storm of wish magic across the globe and even into space, causing unmitigatable damage.

No one wanted that to happen again.

"I understand your position," he said. "But understand mine. You are a creation of wish, not a real hockey-playing bear. All that you say comes not from you but from the heart of the boy behind me. Isn't that right, Syd?"

"Hey, how do you know my name?" said the boy, finally turning his attention from the bear.

"Of all things related to wish, I have been made to know. You are very powerful in the magic of wishes. How long has your teddy bear been playing hockey?"

"Well, just the last couple days, since none of my friends could come and my brother is home with my aunt."

"Is this the only time you have brought the teddy bear to life?"

Syd turned away, muttering.

"Syd?" Edison, but not Edison, said more assertively.

"Once before. Maybe a couple times before that."

"I see," said the Doctor.

As they arrived at the campfire, he turned to the parents. "You don't think a marshmallow-eating, talking bear is a little unusual?"

"Well," the father said as he tried to blow out a flaming marshmallow, "It doesn't seem that strange to us. Syd's had lots of unusual friends over the years."

The mother just shook her head, mouth gummed up with bear-sized marshmallows.

"Now, just wait a minute," Ron said. "I'm not that unusual. And don't talk about me like I'm not here. I'd like to plead my case. I could have run into the woods where you wouldn't catch me."

"You'll get your turn to speak, Ron. These folks need to know what's going on. Syd, tell your parents why they didn't think Ron unusual. Tell them, or I will."

Syd kicked a pebble accidentally toward Ron, who reflexively stopped it with his thick-bladed goalie stick.

"Because I wished that they wouldn't make a fuss," he muttered.

"Louder please," the father said, before Edison, also known as the Wish Doctor, could speak.

"Because I wished you wouldn't make a fuss."

The father's eyes came alive with realization. The mother swallowing the marshmallow, felt her mouth open.

"That kind of wish is called compulsion," the Wish Doctor said. "It's dangerous magic. Going against someone else's will using magic is considered unethical even by the shadiest practitioner. When you cross the lines of ethics, there are things that will seize upon the power of wishes and twist them. You are on an island once joined to Ireland and Scotland. The fairies, the Tuatha de Danaan, and other tricksters inhabit this land, same as there, with one difference. They are here in greater numbers. This is not a place to play with wishes."

After letting the boy think about that for a moment, the Wish Doctor continued, "Syd, you are unusually strong in the magic of wishes. You don't know how strong. If you are not taught properly, you will cause problems that will hurt many people."

The father walked to his son and put a hand on his shoulder, all the time looking at Ron, who no longer was Ron, his son's friend, but a bear. A potentially hungry and mean bear. "So, what kind of quicksand are we in?" Syd's father said. "How do we get out of it?"

"Ah, I'd like to point out that I'm still here and still cognitive and can understand what you are saying," Ron said. "I believe you are talking about my situation in a roundabout way. I would prefer to be part of the conversation."

"You will be, I promise," the Wish Doctor said. He was glad the bear was not already going wild with anger. The boy's wish had some control, some detailed imagination behind it, but he also knew the bear's goalie persona and his goalie stick were based on a real-life goalie who had a temper. If the bear's natural instincts for protection didn't lead to trouble, the angry temper of a Canadian goalie, with a stick to grind, surely would.

He continued, "The quicksand here is much broader than you. Syd, you need to learn properly the dangers of wishes. You need to be taught how to protect wishes so they don't go wrong, so that you aren't hurt, others you care about aren't hurt and innocent bystanders aren't hurt. I won't prohibit you from making wishes, but I can teach you how to be cautious in their use and the dangers that may happen."

He said to the parents, "I run a school not far from here. For a student of your son's talent, there will be no charge. He will be granted a scholarship of room and he won't be bored. Besides wishes, he can have his choice of other courses from science and arts, just as in private high school."

The Doctor looked to Ron, who he realized, oddly, was the calmest of the beings in the clearing. "What do you think, Ron? Is it a good idea for Syd to come to my school, and learn to control and manage wishes, so that he may, when needed, wish into being very fine bears? Can I have your support?"

Ron growled and threw his stick to the ground, finally showing some of that Ron Hextall spirit. "What does my opinion matter? Why would they believe you hadn't just wished me to support you?"

"Because if you are truly a bear of good intentions, you will know my intentions are the same."

"Fine. Yes, Syd should join the school. It's probably the only way to stop you from interfering in my existence. Syd needs to learn to control his power. Some of his other stuffed creatures aren't as cute and cuddly as me."

The Doctor smiled, then frowned a little. He hadn't seen those other less cuddly creatures.

"It sounds all very exciting," Syd said, "but what about hockey? Will I have time?"

"You will have time to play recreationally. Unfortunately, you won't be able to train full time to be a competitive player. Syd, though you may be talented, do you think hockey is your best talent? Are you likely to make the NHL on your own talent, or will you need to wish yourself into the NHL? Would you be satisfied if you wished yourself there?"

Syd opened his mouth and closed it again.

"Your best gift is this talent for wishes. In my school we will have 19 other students like you. You made a bear come alive to have a friend. There you can have many friends. They will not think you strange for what you do. They will not stay away from you. Some might even have their own stuffed bears. I will teach you how to make wishes wisely and avoid unforeseen circumstances. You won't have to worry about someone like me coming to reverse your wishes."

Syd looked to his parents. "I wasn't fitting in at school," he said. "You know I wasn't. This would save the costs of my private school. Maybe I should do this. You won't have to worry about me getting in trouble anymore and you can have more time for my brother. He may get to be more trouble in a year or two. It could be that somebody made a wish about him."

The mother, finally over her shock, said, "I think we knew this day would come. I think we knew it had to. He is special, but things do go on strangely in our house. It would be nice to know he was in control."

The father was holding the boy around the shoulders and nodding. It was all settled except for one thing.

Ron was slowly backing nonchalantly into the woods. Or at least as nonchalantly as a large black bear in an orange hockey jersey could.

"Syd, you can bring Ron to the school with you, but you must turn him back into his original form."

To the bear the Wish Doctor said, "Ron, I'm sorry. But Syd has to do this. Don't back away. It won't help: the reverse wish will happen no matter how far away you are."

"Please, Edison, let me be a real bear," Ron said. "I really am. This is more my true form than that stuffed suit. This world could use a magical bear who is a good role model for other magical creatures."

"You know we have to do this. You feel this way because of the wish magic. And if any of it loses control, you can become very angry, and you would hurt many people and maybe many other bears. You might even have to be shot or captured, and you would not like that."

"Do I really have to?" Syd said.

"Yes. If you don't, I will have to. It's always better that the original wisher makes the reverse. There is less chance of an error, less chance of Ron being hurt. Something bad could happen like a game warden coming to shoot him."

"I wish game wardens to quicksand," the boy said, though he was all out of wishes and game wardens generally were protected against quicksand. Except for that one in the Nile delta, and he had deserved it for being cruel to a hippopotamus.

"You're going to have to be careful with that expression," said the Wish Doctor. "You could really make quicksand happen if you have a wish available."

"Oh," Syd said. "I'm not trying to create quicksand. I just say that because my grandfather likes to say it."

Edison looked at the father and then the boy more closely. He wondered. There had been a lot of quicksand over the last forty years.

Not as many occurrences as teddy bears coming alive. Still...

"Okay, Ron," Syd said, looking sorrowful. "It's time to go back to sleep."

"All right," Ron replied wistfully. "This was a nice time to be alive. Thank you, Mr. and Mrs. Syd, for the marshmallows and allowing Syd to play with me. Thank you for bringing me into your home and on this fine camping trip. Thank you for helping Syd, Son of Ed. Take good care of him, and someday maybe we can talk again, when you have had lunch and a good supper, and care to carry on a positive conversation with a harmless and most polite bear."

To Syd, the bear said in a low voice, "Can you put me back like you did last Tuesday? You know, into hibernation?" He then winked as only a magical bear could.

The boy winked in return. The greater magic surrounding the boy blocked the Wish Doctor from noticing the mutual exchange of winks. Thus, the Doctor did not realize that, even as Ron returned to his small, less cuddly, form, he would be back in all their lives again very soon.

And that the Wish Doctor would be very glad he was.

3: The young doctor

The Wish Doctor was not always young. Sure, he had been young in the beginning. At least he thought he had, though it was hard to remember any days of innocence. For sure he had been a boisterous man in his twenties and thirties and had grown sombre in the Middle Ages. He had had a long run of wisdom in his elder years, and then, forced by necessity, he had become young again.

He had been stuck so longer than he dared think. Not that he intended to defy the natural laws, but he had duty and skill and, like all great doctors, was dedicated to his practice and to the care he could provide.

How old was he? It was impossible to tell. He had given up celebrating birthdays as he had used up all his birthday wishes to stave off a potential crisis that most likely would have destroyed all life on the planet. Caused of course by poorly thought-out wishes (with a little help from an evil prankster spirit, tired of its own existence).

Someday he might be able to become old again, in the modern way of aging gracefully, but only if he could find a successor. That was proving harder than he had ever expected.

He wondered what the chances were that this class would produce the candidate who would not only be capable of replacing him but would *want* to.

He knew some of the things that kept students from wanting to stay on. Many wanted to go where the emphasis on progression in knowledge was based on technology, which in many areas was causing more magic than magic. Many did not like the immense effort of study and concentration required, the deep need to understand the classics. He would have thought that after the Greek and Latin texts (especially the Latin texts that translated the earlier classic Greek texts) had been so carefully recovered in his hometown, they would never go out of style again.

Honestly, he knew the biggest reason. The time commitment. It was not just a job nor even a career, nor even a lifetime. It was many lifetimes.

Did it have to be that way? It all depended on how many Wish Doctors were available. Today, there was only one. Him.

He had to admit it was not an easy route, though he had found satisfaction where he could, and most certainly when he started getting enough experience to be confident. There were not too many jobs where people could work for a century and still be considered a rookie.

He took a breath as he entered the classroom, which had been the broad study that the estate's creator had spent so many hours in, dreaming ideas and holding discussions with brilliant minds from the world over. Although he was just a guest at the Lodge of Wonders, it was the one place in the world where the Wish Doctor felt the most comfortable.

Especially when Alex was visiting. And when the caretakers were not. No matter who was there, the beautiful solitude of the estate and the waters of the Bras d'Or were calming. The estate was quiet anyway, but Selva had installed harmonic dampeners across the property to protect against the noise of rogue wish magic.

The Doctor had needed to adjust to the growing clamour over the last few days, as Selva got the new students settled and acclimatized to their new school and home. Although some of them might be shy, Selva's enthusiasm, and the qualities that led them here, had them all chatting. If you could not have your imagination triggered here in the Lodge of Wonders, it was very unlikely any other place would do so.

It was a place of optimism. If there was ever a place where you could feel the future was getting better, where all problems could be solved, it was here. The mix of future tech and the items of historical power tied together the waves of human progress as no other place the Wish Doctor had known.

And he had lived in many places.

Then there was the guest who had moved in and renewed his spirits. He was always most welcome, though the Wish Doctor hoped he wouldn't interfere with the students. His old friend could sometimes be unpredictable, even if he mostly meant well.

He surveyed the class of students. Selva had briefed him on certain aspects, but on others he had stayed silent so the Wish Doctor could form his own impressions.

Selva's choices, like everything he did, were spot on. The class had a balanced, diverse mix. It had students tinged with experience, and students who did not know yet the power they could manage.

Well, there was no point in delaying. There was a lot of learning to do.

And discoveries to make. The students might get something out of it, as well.

"Hoy, hoy, everyone," he said, his feet bouncing as he made his way to the far end of the room.

To most of them, who had been taught by rather ordinary teachers, his frothing energy made them sit upright. He looked like a young, bright, country doctor, except for the missing stethoscope. If he dressed as if from another century, it barely changed that impression. Although most of his clothing was just a step from being fashionable, it was certainly functional, made from techniques engineered by Selva and using the most advanced nanotech.

He stood in front of the large cabinet which contained many of the original maps of the National Geographic Society. "My dear students, we are going to have fun today and in the days ahead." He smiled a most mischievous, Machiavellian smile. "I trust you have settled in nicely, and that Selva has told you the rules of the estate.

"There are dangers here, but as long as you follow the rules, the dangers can be mitigated. There are almost no restricted areas, as long as you follow the protocols. I know from too much fiction and movies that if we stop you from going somewhere, you will only find a way to go exactly there, so it is better that we equip you with knowledge so you don't unwittingly release a griffin, or turn into a snake."

There was a slight snickering, but the Wish Doctor showed no sign of being even the least bit silly. "For the areas marked danger, it is best you do not go there, but I will not punish you if you do. Those areas have their own punishments. I will have tried my best by the end of the year to give you the skills to avoid those punishments, but I cannot promise."

The snickering disappeared. There was something ominous beneath the Doctor's cheerful appearance. Some in the class already knew the dangers of bad wishes, if not dangerous places, but all could take heed of a veiled threat that was not so much a threat but a fact.

"There are only three really restricted places. I am not going to even tell you where they are, as that will entice you to go there."

A brave girl at the front of the class raised her hand.

"Alfalfa, please ask the obvious."

"If you don't tell us where these places are, isn't there a risk we go in them by mistake?"

"Well done. This is a place where assuming the obvious is never a good thing. The places are hidden, but not in a way you think. Not with invisibility, not by magic, not by nanotech. The harder you would try to find them, the harder they will be to find. Yet, if you stumble upon them, you will know. There will be no doubt. Each place will give a unique warning. Two of the three places you might even survive, if you heed the warning.

"The third, well, even I don't go into the third place. And I have had to go into the most dangerous places of humankind. So, I would highly suggest that if you stumble on the third place, you don't go in there."

He looked over at Selva. He was the only student to have ever experienced the third place. And lived.

Most of the class got it. They had all seen the movies where, as soon as someone mentioned a place they should not go, someone foolish would go there and get in trouble or hurt; or, if it had "the 13th" in the title, killed.

Most readied themselves not to go to any of the three places, but all looked around to try and figure out who would be the one or ones who would try to enter the third place, so they could run and join another clique.

"Just to be clear. Safety is our most important mission. I may not always remind you to think of it. You must learn to take responsibility for this yourself. We are also in the risk management business. After all, learning wish magic is about managing dangerous magic."

He paused. He knew some of them knew how dangerous wish magic was, and yet they still came to the school. Fear wasn't necessarily something you came to naturally. He would just have to introduce them to the risks one by one, until they understood that, like a glowing stove, you must touch wish magic very carefully.

And fear it.

"While most of the forces that trigger wish magic are benign, there are powers you will encounter that are dark and angry. You must take these things seriously."

The students quieted, but one raised her hand.

The Wish Doctor squinted at her. She seemed familiar. "Loretta, yes?"

"Selva said there are bears nearby. Is this real? I'm scared of bears."

"Yes, very real. In fact, I talked to one just three days ago." He winked at Syd, who was still holding his hockey stick, when attention turned to Loretta.

He looked at her more closely. Had she been the one he had saved from the stuffed Smokey come alive? She had been so young then. Even he had been afraid of the fire-breathing bear.

The class wasn't sure what to say. Some of them knew first-hand the power and danger of wishes or bears. One or two had actually benefited from a good wish. Others were just a little skeptical, whether because their minds had yet to accept the turns their lives were about to take or because they did not yet comprehend the seriousness. Was this just an eccentric school for bright and imaginative individuals, or was there really such a thing as the magic of wishes?

"All I ask is that you follow my instructions carefully, no matter how silly or tedious they may seem. My only intent is to keep you all alive. Does everyone understand and agree?"

There were nods across the class, but the Doctor had already identified those most likely to hurt themselves.

"Hoy, hoy, let's get on with the learning."

~

Alma felt a chill down her back. She was wondering if she had made the right decision joining the School of Wish. She wasn't sure the school was going to be any safer than if she had gone home with the angry half-witch with the magic crystal.

4: The Wish Doctor's first lesson

"This is no ordinary school," said the Doctor, continuing his introductory remarks. "We will learn amazing things in odd and unpredictable ways. We will get to know more about each other than you know about anyone else.

"Let's start with learning about brave Loretta, who asked about bears. Loretta, where are you from?"

"I was born and raised in Manhattan."

"Why are you here?"

She pointed at Selva. "He asked me to come."

"Is that all?"

"No." She shook her head lightly. "Wishes never seem to happen when anyone is around me. My friends started telling me I was bad luck. I didn't know that could be a good thing, until Selva told me. I want to learn how to use this talent to help people, to stop bad wishes from happening. And maybe learn how to reverse a wish that went bad."

"Hoy, hoy. What a splendid answer." The Wish Doctor could feel her willingness to make a sacrifice for others if required.

"Wishus interruptus, so rare a talent." Selva really had outdone himself recruiting.

"Welcome, Loretta. So glad you are here. Would you like to take my job someday? I'm not kidding that much. Think about it. I hope you will learn all you ask for.

"Ladies and gentlemen, we can learn while having a lot of fun while we study and practice hard. It will not be all wish work, as you know. We have tried to choose practical subjects that will be useful on their own. Some of you will cringe that we focus on algebra, but it has proven extremely useful in figuring how much we can afford for a mortgage, and you will learn shortly how important algebra is in fighting wishes. If I had paid more attention earlier in my life, I might have been able to afford a mortgage and my own place to live."

Not a single student was smiling. Dangerous bears didn't frighten most of them, but mortgages did. Even those that didn't know what a mortgage exactly was had heard the ominous word used to scare adults. He would have to remember that.

"Selva's too modest to tell you, but his ancestor created the concept of zero, so he loves algebra. If you need extra help, see him. By the way, Selva is one of the best wish teachers in the world."

Selva smiled. He was always on the lookout for the Wish Doctor's flattery. The old young man would trick Selva to take his place if he could. "Well, I'm in the top three. Considering there's only three in the world, I don't get too excited."

"This is a special school." the Wish Doctor said. "There is no other like it. We only put on this training every twenty years, so it is truly a privilege for you to be here, and a privilege for Selva and myself to host you."

There were startled looks on several of the students, especially whose algebra abilities had helped them gain admission. *If the Doctor puts this training on every twenty years, why does he look so young?*

"Each of you who graduate will be sought after for your talent by every nation that understands the deepness of the world, and truths beyond the superficial.

"Not all of you will make it through, though. Some of you might take too great a risk in putting your skills into action and be harmed or dismissed. Some of you may find the curriculum too hard. Some of you will fail to grasp what we do here. Some will not heed the warning signs when you reach the three restricted zones and be disintegrated...or worse.

"Others of you, though, will find this the most rewarding experience of your life and may even come back to teach, like Selva."

The Doctor found his eyes wandering to Alma Faye, one of the two he had recruited. Her face was ashen. He didn't want to scare her away, but she must hear the same speech as the others.

"We will start mostly in the classroom, but as time goes on, we will go into the world to use what you learn. The faster you learn, the more you will be allowed to do. We may seem isolated, here on this island, but we have many surprising ways of transportation."

He broadened his look from Alma out across his class. Twenty-two students from all over the world; two more than normal because Selva had convinced him to count the triplets as one. One recruit had dropped out, so there was no difficulty with Alma taking his place. He certainly wasn't going to fight with the powers of numerology. Ages ranging from

14 to 38, the oldest not showing her talents until she was a little older, so she had missed the last training session twenty years ago.

He took a deep breath. "Enough preamble. It's time now for your first lecture."

The Wish Doctor's first lesson was always the same. He was an average speaker, yet his first words always captivated his students. At least the few who would make it through the first gruelling semester.

"All magic is wishes," he said. "Magic is simply the desire to accomplish things without making the natural effort. In other words, wishing for something to happen instead of doing it. It is a truism that all things that can be wished can be made to happen, even the impossible."

He paused. In the first moments, he could usually tell who was listening intently, who was understanding the best. Sometimes the slackest surprised him. He dismissed Syd's lazy, wandering eyes. He knew already what Syd could do.

"Magic, or wish power, is not to be confused with stage magic, people who play card tricks or who appear to make you disappear. Most magic shows are based on sleight of hand or engineered tricks, easy once you understand them. Others are managed by distraction, or the power of suggestion. The closest any come to magic are those that use hypnosis, which in itself can be very powerful.

"In your electives, you may choose to study this type of magic, which is really showmanship. It has its place. Sleight of hand is particularly useful, but all types of stage magic that can fool audiences have a purpose.

"Wishes are both a part of our world and separate from it. Some are natural, others require sources to aid them—like a fountain.

"Wishes are complex and not meant to be used by everyone. They are powerful magic. In fact, it is the power of wishes that created the world. You must remember that a strong-enough wish can do or undo reality. It is not our role in the universe to do this.

"We use wishes at a more elementary level. They can be a very powerful tool, but only if you use them carefully and with good intent. Without training, most wishes simply go wrong, and some go terribly wrong.

"A simple wish, such as you wanting to go on a date with a pretty girl or boy, can turn bad. Because when you wish the date into being, the person you desire often turns out to be the most awful person in the world, no matter how handsome or pretty they are.

"Some wishes, like wishing a stuffed lion to life, can kill." He did his best to avoid looking at Syd. "The range of wishes and issues made by wishers is infinite. We will teach you some standard ways to reverse wishes. But we will also teach you how to adapt, how to find your own way to reverse a wish. There is no way to teach every possible way to overturn a wish. You must be able to think on your feet. It is why some of our field trips will place you in some tense, real-world situations."

He paused again, looked at the students, assessing how many took him seriously, how many thought this was a lark. The latter needed to be corrected quickly. The danger was too great.

"We will start with wish reversal. This may seem backwards, but in learning what can go wrong with a wish and how to correct it, you will learn about wish mistakes, and how to make a better wish. You will often hear the expression wishtake. That is when someone makes a mistake making a wish. Common wishtakes are using language which can be mis-interpreted, or not thinking through the secondary effects of a wish. When you have some mastery of wish reversal, we will introduce how to *make* wishes. You will not get to make wishes in the field this first year, except as a counter in a wish reversal. Let's be clear, though: our primary purpose here is not to learn to make wishes for our own benefit, or really anyone's benefit. When we use a wish, it will mostly be for wish reversal, and only in cases where the potential damage of a new wish is less than the damage of the wishtake."

~

Alma, despite feeling overwhelmed, felt a sense of growing purpose. She glanced across the room to the boy in the sport sweater, who was always fidgeting. He didn't seem to be taking it seriously.

Nothing could be further from the truth. Syd had not given up his wish to be a hockey player without remorse. He was afraid of his own power and, the more he thought about using it, the more uncomfortable he was becoming.

~

"There are many types of wishes you will learn to reverse. Today, I will start with the hardest wish to make: the pure wish. Let's learn first how this type of wish can go wrong and later we will learn how to reverse it."

The Wish Doctor took a breath. It was a long lecture yet the class was attentive. They would not have been chosen otherwise. Even Syd had listened despite his fidgeting. At least he had set his hockey stick flat on the floor.

"You make a pure wish without assistance, like a wishing well or a shooting star. It is not dependent on time or place. It is solely based on the will of an individual—on your will. Pure wishes are hard to make; few have the skill or the power. They can drain the wisher and leave them weak for a long time, unable to enjoy or see the wish take action.

"A pure wish takes a certain amount of natural talent, but many people can learn to make them. We expect everyone here to be able to make a pure wish if they hope to graduate. A pure wish made for yourself is most susceptible to problems. A pure wish made selflessly, in silence, is the least likely to go wrong; though if you speak of it later, it may tarnish."

Alma looked around the room. None of her wishes ever came true. (She had forgotten the wish she had made over the crystal about her brother, but had she remembered she would not have known if the wish had been a pure wish or aided by the crystal.) She wondered how many of the students could make pure wishes.

"Not all wishes have to employ magic," the Doctor was saying. "Some of the strongest wishes are of pure will. These are wishes where you work hard and focus on your outcome. You will learn to do this as well.

"Glenda, will you assist me please?" he said, motioning. From the other side of the room, a lady with dark hair and a broad, pretty face walked bravely to the front of the class.

"Where are you from, Glenda?"

"I'm from Catalonia." Her accent was barely noticeable.

"Why are you here?

"I'm here to learn to control my wishes. I have a habit of predicting the future, and then making it happen. My papa says it's because I am unconsciously making my predictions come true. But it always seems it's the bad predictions that come true."

"Ah. That is a hard habit to break. The first thing to learn is to control the time and scope of your wishes, to think of something immediate, rather than in the future. I want you to think of something that could happen right now, that would not hurt anybody. Don't wish it; tell me what you want to wish."

Glenda thought for a moment. "What if I wanted everyone to have ice cream?"

The Wish Doctor shook his head internally, then pulled an unused birthday wish from Glenda's mind to protect her. "Go ahead."

Glenda closed her eyes and thought of ice cream. She'd only been in the province for a short while but had found a flavour called grapenut. It was so delicious and the grapenuts (not made from grapes but made from what she wasn't sure) gave the texture a nice little crunch.

"I wish for ice cream for the class," she said. It was barely noticeable, her Catalan accent, but just enough that the phrase 'ice cream' sounded slightly different to a trained set of ears.

For a moment nothing happened. Then Glenda began wailing uncontrollably at the top of her lungs. Almost everyone in the class slammed their hands against their ears. Even Erin who was deaf could feel the scream.

No-one realized the Wish Doctor had dampened the power of the banshee's scream. For though there was no spirit to pull the students to the afterlife, the scream of the banshee, now in Glenda's scream, was enough to harm their ear drums forever, if it had roared out of her mouth with full power.

In the world of wish, even an ice cream scream could be deadly.

The Doctor scanned the class for reactions. He had to be alert lest this demonstration went too far. Even dampened, the banshee scream coming from Glenda could harm them.

A few students were near immune to the screams, yet fascinated by the power they could feel. Others were shaking in fear, though fighting through it, trying to understand. They would be likely the most successful students.

A few, though, were in pain. He had suspected a few would be. He could train them for many things, but to survive as a Wish Doctor, you had to be able to resist the banshee's wail of death.

Two or three of those in pain found a way to fight through it, but there was one who seemed to be absorbing most of the sound. A small drop of blood oozed from her ear.

The Wish Doctor felt a little shock of disappointment. It was not whom he would have expected, but that of course was the point of this test. He might still be able to train her properly, but it was unlikely. At least her overconfidence would be subdued.

At the second drop of blood, it was time for action.

The Wish Doctor snapped his fingers, and Glenda was able to gain control. It was the residual power of a wish he had used to counter screams of banshees before, and thus he did not have to waste another rare wish. He didn't have time to demonstrate the more complicated wish reversal technique they would spend much of the semester mastering.

Slowly, the volume faded away as the spirit left Glenda's body.

The class looked petrified, even those who were intimately aware of the danger of wishes gone wrong.

"Thank you, Glenda. Return to your seat."

He rang a little bell he suddenly had in his hand. A man on a large pedal bike with a large container on the back rolled into the study, just squeezing through the doors. Alma was sure the man was from a commercial she had seen on TV.

"Everyone, this is Dickie Dee, the ice cream man. Raise your hand if you want an I scream treat. Dickie, make sure Glenda has two. I know you don't have grapenut, but she also likes Häagen-Dazs chocolate covered almonds."

Half the class looked at Glenda and half at the ice cream man. Glenda seemed rattled, but at the thought of ice cream truly fulfilling her wish, she seemed to relax, and a smile appeared on her face.

Alma wasn't sure she should take the ice cream. It seemed like this could be part of a bad wish.

"It's safe," said the Wish Doctor, looking straight at her. "You could even eat it in one of the three restricted places."

Had he winked at her or was she imagining things?

"I told you this class would not be normal. We will have danger, and we will have fun. Now enjoy this ice cream, but beware of how wishes of ice cream can go bad. Any wish associated with a birthday can be dangerous.

"Just as an aside, ice cream is one of the worst tricks of the world. It seems like the best treat you can have, but, in the long run, it is full of sugar and saturated fats that can clog your arteries and cause other diseases. Never wish for ice cream. Take it only when it is offered freely or at a fair price. Pretentious ice cream eaters most of all will learn the badness of it. I am only half-teasing. There is so much in this world that is not as it seems. Now, what does this lesson tell us?"

Nola raised her hand. "Pronunciation must be exact when making a wish. You must make sure you are carefully concentrating so there is no confusion."

"Good. You were listening well."

The triplets together said, "Glenda is very strong in the power of wishes."

"Perceptive," replied the Wish Doctor. "And you should know, right?"

Loretta spoke next. "Anything associated with a birthday wish has a possibility of trouble."

"Yes. Someone who can make a power of a pure wish can even avoid the powers of a Wishus Interruptus, although, to be fair, your powers are dampened on these estate grounds."

"Wishes are not to be taken lightly," the older, curly-haired lady said most seriously.

"Yes, I think you have all learned what I meant to say. Now, I know this may have spoiled your lunch, but it is time to eat. In the kitchen you will find sandwishes.

"Oh, say goodbye to Dickie Dee. By the way, Dickie Dee is here by accident. I rescued him from a little girl's wish gone bad. Now that he's discharged his duty, he can go back to the safety of the TV."

Some of the class waved, and Dickie Dee disappeared from the room, only to reappear in the television monitor near the map cabinet.

Alma nearly choked on a caramel swirl. What exactly had she got herself into? She almost wished she could scream. She would have, but for fear of having her wish twisted and being drowned in hot fudge sauce.

5: The meaning of algebra

Alma normally found math exciting. She liked knowing there was a right answer, and she didn't have to rely on anyone's opinion, like when writing an essay, to know she was good at it.

But it was hard to concentrate on math, even the simple problem they were working on now, when her head was filled with ideas of magic, and wishes and illusions. And ice cream so good it almost didn't seem real.

Lunch time had been a blur. She was usually pretty boring with her meals, so eating ice cream first had disoriented her. The sandwishes were delicious, but she wasn't sure what to believe when Selva declared they'd been made that morning from wishes on the beach. She couldn't tell if she was imagining the gritty feeling in her mouth, or if the sand had appeared when she started doubting.

There had been a ruckus at lunch, as the students laughed, and asked questions as they got to know each other. Alma was feeling overwhelmed, having sat most of the time at the corner, but she had a moment of warmth when Syd, wearing what apparently was a hockey jersey, asked her if she wanted the last sandwish, before he slyly wrapped it in a handkerchief for later.

He wasn't the most talkative, but clearly one of the most popular, as several of her female classmates and Brad tried to sit next to him. Nola and Loretta had sat near her, and talked politely, both interested that she was from the United States, Nola, wanting to move there and Loretta being from New York.

Alma liked them both and felt they could be friends. She wanted to make sure she made friends with whomever would have her. She realized this was a great opportunity to meet people from all over the world.

Everything had been so astonishing and scary since the moment the Wish Doctor had asked about Morse code. Now, being asked to work on an algebra problem that once she would have found interesting, seemed so mundane she couldn't focus.

She looked around the classroom, and realized she wasn't the only one unable to concentrate. Except for that one older lady. Curled hair, furrowed brow, she had easily the most serious face in the class. Old enough to be Alma's mother, she was working hard, focused on her problem.

Alma had to catch herself. She had almost wished she was close enough to read off her paper.

Alma forced herself to look at the problem. She started moving elements of the equation around, but the maze of parentheses confused her. She found her knuckles tapping the table, her feet tapping the floor.

Selva stood up in front of the class. His skin was darker than Alma's and he was so much more serious than the Wish Doctor and much thinner. "Everyone put your pencils down for a second," he said.

When he had everyone's attention, he said, "Has anyone noticed something odd happening?"

Alma looked around. Had someone made a wish? Was she making too much noise drumming her pencil on her wooden desk, unconsciously tapping out Morse code for 'Help Me'?

"It's too noisy in here," said the guy from Scotland in an accent she could barely make out. *Is he talking about me?* Alma wondered.

Selva smiled. "It's always noisy somewhere. That is part of life. Does anyone find it hard to concentrate? I need you to be honest. This school isn't about grades. It is about helping you learn."

Several of the students, including Alma, raised their hands.

"As I said, you needed to be honest. If we are out in the field encountering a wish gone bad, we need to trust each other. Our lives will depend on it. We need to know when we can count on each other and when we need to help each other."

The majority of the class raised their hands. Only the curly-haired lady made no move to do so.

"You may have wondered why we presented an algebra lesson after the introduction to true magic. It would be hard for most people to concentrate in such a situation. That is why we did it. Distractions, emotions, excitement; all of these things help wishes to go bad. It's critical for us to be able to concentrate when we are fixing wishes, because if we do not, we can make things worse. A lot worse. When you are strong enough, we will tell you some of the methods, but we do not want you to unintentionally misuse an idea we talk about here.

"Stand up, stretch, step outside on the lawn if you need to. Clear you head and then concentrate on the math problem. You must be able to do this without distracting thoughts of magic. This skill will be critical in moments when you have to reverse a wish and have little time."

Alma stood up, wondering again why she was there. She felt panic. She needed to step outside, but was afraid to until she saw a few others heading for the door.

She walked out, made her way to the lawn and a spot where she could see the ocean. She felt the calmness and beauty of the landscape force her panic down.

And there was Syd ahead of her, turned slightly to a small clump of trees. He seemed to be talking to someone, and then, after looking right, then left, he tossed something among the trees. She couldn't be sure, but it looked like the last sandwish he had taken at lunch. It seemed to disappear into thin air.

She didn't know what to say, wasn't sure if she should bother him, when the triplets burst through the front of the house and surrounded him.

Alma turned as Loretta pulled alongside of her. Loretta was maybe a little older, but not by much. "The triplets won't leave Syd alone," she said. "Been all over him since they got into town. We were all staying at the Bell Motel with family before we moved into the school."

"He must like them, then."

Loretta laughed. "Watch closer. My brother once wished for triplets and, trust me, he got into a lot of trouble."

Alma did look closer. She wasn't sure why, but she was relieved to find Syd annoyed.

"I'm not sure this is the kind of school to find a relationship," Loretta said. "I've seen some crazy wishes in my time, but this place is wild. Hard not to have a relationship without making some sort of wish, and this place would just magnify it. I'm just glad my talent protects me."

Alma nodded absently. She wasn't sure if she was going to like the triplets.

"A couple of us are going to walk down to the beach after class," Loretta said. "You want to join us? Won't be too many more days when it will be warm enough."

Alma almost asked if Syd was coming, but refrained. "Will I have time to go change my shoes?"

"Sure. See you after class. By the way, the answer to the problem is zero."

Loretta smiled and headed back into the Lodge of Wonders.

Alma watched the triplets surrounding Syd for a while, then shook herself. They surrounded him so tightly she couldn't even see his face. As handsome as he was, he was also mysterious; but not as mysterious as the curly haired lady, though Alma sensed secrets within him.

It then struck her he was becoming almost as much of a distraction as the thought of magical ice cream. She'd never master wish magic if she let Syd or triplets distract her from even algebra.

When she returned to her desk, she tried to ignore Loretta's hint. It was no use. When she thought of the answer, she could see the whole problem fall out for her. She hoped this didn't mean she wasn't going to learn how to concentrate when dealing with wishes.

She'd already determined she wasn't going to end up screaming like a banshee, or with one inside her. To avoid that, she would need to learn how to master algebra and the art of concentration.

And she better do it quickly.

6: Beach Night

Alma stood on the edge of the steep embankment. Two classmates sat below on the gravel shore, talking excitedly. She was having second thoughts about joining them.

The day had been overwhelming. She was feeling exhausted, not to mention shy. She realized this was not going to be like any other school. Hard not to realize, when the instructors and other students keep saying it. You might think they were going out of their way to make it unusual.

It wasn't hyperbole or even boil. It *was* unlike anything she'd ever known. Although she found long lectures boring, she preferred those to classes when there was too much discussion, or, worse yet, group work. She preferred not to voice her opinion if she didn't have to.

Growing up, she was an understudy to her brother, there only in case something happened to him. In the last two years she had felt like an assistant as her parents helped him prepare for some unknown special school. Her mother showered attention on him, but rarely cared for Alma's opinion. Jean spent his attention on their son, too, although that was mostly because her mother kept dragging his attention to Peter.

They only ever consulted Alma when they needed pure practical knowledge. Which was why she read so much, and learned things like Morse code, because you never knew what would bring yourself to the centre of attention. Increasingly, she wanted to be anything other than the centre of attention, because it led to chores like holding a heavy crystal steady for 24 hours straight.

Not being the centre of attention carried over to her school days. She knew things from books, not the cool internet stuff like what happened when you ate a Tide pod from a dish of cinnamon.

She missed her friend Liza. She felt bad she'd never had a chance to tell her she was going to a new school. Other than Liza, she didn't miss her old school.

Still, she just wasn't sure she was cut out for this School of Wish. Her original excitement had turned quickly to lack of confidence. Obviously, you would need to talk, you would need to answer questions, you would need to tell people about yourself. Maybe it would have been better if her brother had come instead of her.

She would need to keep her wits about her. Maybe she was slightly better at that than her brother. Not so that she looked cool, not that she avoided saying something stupid, but so she didn't do something that could flip her innards inside out or turn her skin purple. Or end up with a sausage on her nose. (The only book she'd been able to find on the internet about wishes was a book that told eight different stories of how people making accidental wishes ended up with sausages on their noses.)

She wasn't worried about her current looks. Okay, she was somewhat worried about her looks, but if they never improved, she could live with that. She wasn't risking any hope, let alone wish, to make herself look better and have that wish go bad, maybe changing her nose into an edible elephant's trunk.

She felt sorry for Glenda, who had disappeared during lunch, then been quiet during Algebra, though she remembered her being quite chatty, well, whispery, to several other students at the start of the day. If Glenda's screaming had happened to Alma, she'd be mortified.

She looked over the water. The day was still nice and she was glad she was dressed in short sleeves and shorts. The light breeze caressed her skin. Slowly, she felt less like a need for a nap.

The internet, having being on and off since she had arrived, seemed to be permanently off. Hard for her to nap without the internet playing music. How many times had she fallen asleep with YouTube drowning out her mother and brother shouting at each other?

Maybe she should try and make friends. She wasn't sure she should be making too many friends in case she had to leave.

The blue water, reflecting pinpoints of light, was pretty, but the landscape and seascape felt mysterious. As if a bear or shark could appear at any moment, or maybe something more subtle, like a leprechaun.

Though she felt nature surrounding her, which she never experienced in the intercity suburb of New Orleans, she had another feeling she couldn't quite place. It was neither the sense of civilization, nor the debris of a city going to ruins. She *could* feel the magic of nature. This might indeed be one of the most beautiful spots in the world. But there was something else, a sense of...mischievousness? Or trickery?

It didn't feel quite evil; it felt like it was laughing at her.

Maybe it was just the atmosphere of the school; that whole thing with Iscream. It was maybe a little fun since it hadn't been happening to her, yet a little disturbing. She wasn't quite sure she wasn't still in the car, holding the crystal orb and dreaming a crazy nightmare.

Alma might have turned back to the lodge to be by herself, but she heard laughing behind her.

Two classmates, Brad and Naomi, charged down the embankment. Syd followed leading the triplets. He turned slightly to her and said, "Come on, Alma, time for the beach!"

He smiled and winked, and she couldn't have refused even if she had tried. If he wanted her to come along, she had to.

One of the triplets, the shortest one, gave her an ill look, but Alma didn't care. She scrambled behind them, as close to Syd as they would allow. The triplets guarded him like they had once played together on the same offensive line.

On the gravel beach, Nola and Loretta were chatting nicely on a log, as Brad, Syd, Naomi, and the triplets, followed by Alma Mae, tumbled down the embankment. Or at least she thought those were their names. It was so hard to concentrate on that small stuff when you were afraid almost anything could turn into a monster and eat you.

She hoped she wouldn't make a mistake pronouncing one of their names, or even say the wrong name. She felt a bit angry that they weren't wearing name tags. Students always did on their first day back in New Orleans. Unconsciously, she wished everyone was wearing a name tag.

Suddenly everyone was, though she was unaware that she'd made the wish, or that they'd been without name tags before. Nor did she know how dangerous a wish could be when one was surrounded by untrained and significant wish talent. The wish power might have come from any one of them, or might have been borrowed in pieces from all of them.

Or maybe there was a mysterious sprite hiding in the woods, waiting for the moral of the story to make everyone wiser, but unhappier. Maybe it was releasing magic to use for its own self, like buying caseloads of Seven Up (it was one of the oddities of the spirit world, that sprites could not get enough Seven-Up).

Fortunately, all these thoughts were deep in her unconscious, or her fear would have gotten the better of her.

Oddly, the only wish she was aware of was for a cold, crisp drink of an uncola.

Loretta, her large name tag underlined by a rainbow, looked up with a smile as the screaming classmates made it to the beach unscathed, though Nola seemed upset as if she was about to say something profound.

The triplets continued to push each other around Syd. One looked embarrassed when she tripped and bumped into Brad, who had to grab her to keep them both from falling.

Alfalfa, (*could that be her real name?*), seemed annoyed, until she steadied herself by grabbing Brad's bicep. All of a sudden her smile was back again, as bright as the sparkles on her name tag.

The other two triplets were named Wheatgrass, and Dahlia. Alma guessed the triplet's parents were either hippies or obnoxious, pretentious celebrities. Thank heavens for the name tags; she wouldn't have believed their names without them.

Even though she knew Syd's name, she was surprised he didn't have a name tag, and that everyone seemed to know his name anyhow. He wasn't that talkative, but with his bright smile and goofy winks, he was already one of the most popular. The girls surely liked him. And Brad, too. Although Alfalfa was sticking to Brad like wheatgrass.

Name tags seemed to make everything funnier.

"Who's going swimming?" Syd shouted.

Most everybody looked stunned at the suggestion. It wasn't that warm this far north, and most of them were from warmer climates.

Daniella, whom Alma hadn't noticed coming to the beach but was pretty sure was from northern Estonia, didn't quite say yes but doffed her shoes.

Syd pulled up his shirt to reveal a lean set of muscles that could only have been formed by shooting hockey pucks at 125 miles an hour. His skin was dark red and starting to peel. He dropped his shirt then started toward the water.

Alma couldn't tell if her eyes were true, but his name tag seemed to be on the skin of his back! The letters spelling 'Syd Cowsby' were clearly outlined in his skin. At least she thought so.

She tried to get closer for a look, but he was already diving into the cool water of Bras-D'or, the great saltwater lake of Cape Breton Island. He gave out a low yell, and not quite convincingly said, "The water's great. Come on in!"

Daniella put her feet in the water and shrank bank. "I thought the Baltic Sea was cold, but not compared to this."

Brad too put his foot in bravely, though his face showed no expression as he waded into the water. Alma had the feeling he was trying to keep up with Syd, trying to impress him or the girls, or both.

Alma backed up a few strides as a small wave crashed against the shore. Out in the bay, a motorized sea raft on pontoons was moving very fast, certainly faster than the top speed of the car that had brought her to Baddeck.

"Hey, look: it's a hydrofoil!" Syd pointed and yelled as he bobbed in the water. "A lot of the technology that make them fast was invented right here!"

The group on the shore could barely hear him, though most continued to look at him, and nodded dutifully as if they did.

The triplets were definitely staring. Standing together in a row on the shore, they looked exactly alike, though if you saw them apart they looked quite different. From behind, it would be hard to tell they were sisters. The one in the middle was considerably taller, and the one on the right the shortest.

Were they playing some trick on everybody? Or was the terrain of the beach enough to cause the illusion? Alma's family had driven past a place in the town of Moncton, New Brunswick called Magnetic Hill, where illusions existed. Maybe in this part of the world there were lots of illusions.

Alma felt bad for Syd being in the water alone and took a tentative step toward the shoreline. Close enough to the smallest triplet, she could have reached out and touched her. She summoned her courage and stuck her foot in the water.

And instantly jumped back. This was definitely not the Gulf of Mexico. The only way to get in would be to jump right in.

"I wonder how deep it is here," she said to no one in particular. Syd, the only one to know for sure, was now further from shore than she thought safe.

"Let's find out," said the shortest triplet. Before Alma Mae could say anything, Alfalfa stepped up behind her and gave her a sharp, hard shove.

Alma went diving, in no way like a swan, into the cold lake waters. On the way down she feared her face was going to hit rocks under the water, but the only sensation was the hard splash of water on her face. She had fallen forward enough that the small lake tide and rapidly descending shore created a drop-off so that all she touched was water, as she struggled for air and to gain control.

Once fully underwater, only slightly hindered by her waterlogged clothes, she was able to start swimming, though only slightly more gracefully than when she had fallen in. She pointed her nose upward and swam to the surface. At least she was in control.

For twelve seconds.

The hydrofoil had reversed direction, sending tall waves that pushed her into a powerful rip current that gripped her like a vice. Alma felt herself being pulled sideways, as water cascaded down her throat. She tried to touch bottom, but couldn't, as she moved faster than she'd ever moved in water.

She flailed her way to the surface again and, before the coughing took her, was able to call, "Help!"

If felt like forever as she battled the water until a strong arm encircled her waist. She could barely hear the voice as she bobbed up and down awkwardly. "Don't fight the current. Swim with it. Swim with me, and we'll break out of it."

Alma had no choice but to let Syd guide her. It was like she was feeling the strength of her father when he was younger, before his bad back, when he had taught her to swim. Oddly, she could vividly remember the time they had gone to swim with some dolphins. She kept herself from panicking, hoping Syd knew what he was doing.

Slowly the firm grip of the current relented. Syd touched bottom, pulling her along. She couldn't think to try to stand on her own. Oddly, despite her misery and embarrassment, she enjoyed the feeling of strength and security in Syd's arms.

She was so cold her knees buckled as he set her upright. Without hesitation, he cradled her in his arms and carried her up the beach.

It would have been a lovely moment, but she could feel the rest of the students looking at her, the triplets smirking. One of them seemed oddly jealous. Was it the one who had pushed her? They suddenly seemed to look too much alike again.

If Alma hadn't heard the Doctor and Selva's stories and warnings, she would have wished the triplet's harm.

Loretta and Nola surrounded her, while Syd retrieved his jacket and put it around her shoulders. Her teeth were still chattering.

"You alright?" asked Nola.

Alma could barely speak. "That girl pushed me."

"We saw. She said she didn't mean to. It was an accident."

"What? Didn't you hear what she said?"

Alma had been pushed around enough by her brother. She had come to this school to not be pushed around, and quite frankly she wasn't going to take it anymore. "I said, 'I wonder how deep the water is,' and she said, 'let's find out.' Then pushed me. That was a deliberate shove on my back. I've been shoved around enough to know a deliberate shove. That was not an accident."

"She doesn't look remorseful," said Loretta. "I didn't like the look of those triplets the moment I saw them. Selva said everyone chosen to come here was carefully screened. I'm not sure of those ones."

"You may be right," said Nola. "Let's get Alma up to the lodge. Thanks, Syd, for helping her."

"I feel bad this was my fault," he said. "If I hadn't gone in the water—"

"No," said Alma, "This is not your fault." Though for a moment she felt it kinda was, even though he had rescued her.

"Well, let me make it up to you. Let's meet here after supper. I'll build a bonfire. Just us and maybe Brad. We won't tell the triplets."

"Okay, sounds like fun," said Loretta, helping Alma put on her shoes as Nola gathered their clothes.

Alma turned to Syd, and through chattering lips, mouthed 'thank you'. She was too cold now to form words. He winked at her, and she was soon glad to be heading away from the beach and the triplets, glad for the comfort of the girls.

She felt a hatred for the triplets she hadn't felt, since, well, since when her brother had called her a piggy.

7: Alma loses her temper

Alma made her way along a convoluted route through the lodge to her room, dripping sea water. The quirky layout of the residence-turned-school, with its many corridors, made for a long trudge, even if you didn't want to avoid any classmates. The drippy seawater seemed to make the floorboards squeak. She had left Loretta in the back kitchen, and twice had to double back to avoid a classmate so as not to have to describe her embarrassment.

Her room was about as far from any of the entrances as any room in the deceptively-large lodge. Not for the first time, she felt like the least important person there.

She had two more corridors to navigate when she heard a sudden jolt, then a wailing: *ma ba arrrr uuuu nrrrrrr*. It wasn't as frightening as Glenda's scream though it set her nerves alight. Alma stopped, couldn't sense her direction, then resumed, choosing a way to go at random.

There. Another bump, then a rustling of wind or maybe the rattling of paper.

It sounded like it was coming from behind her. She twisted around, saw nothing. Then, as her eyes came around, the woman in the painting above her seemed to move.

Alma started running and it was like the painting was laughing.

She kept on going, not caring if anyone saw her, and finally plunged into her room. Her roommate Christine was there, still asleep on the upper bunk. She thought about waking her up, wondering if she heard the noises, then decided to leave her alone. Christine had been constantly sleeping since she'd arrived, except while at breakfast and in class. Having just arrived on a long flight from Taiwan, she was so jet-legged, she could barely talk.

Alma closed the blinds, peeled off her wet clothes, dried herself and changed, then lay down on the lower bunk and just held herself. She couldn't sleep, her brain thinking too hard. It was almost too much.

There were no facts she could grasp to give her confidence. It was if the school was built on whimsy. Whimsy with a dangerous side. She clung to the bed even as supper came and went.

Even when Christine started to snore, Alma decided she was going to stay in the room and forget about the fire Syd had promised.

Until the barking and moaning started, finishing with a distinct knock on the door.

Alma didn't want to open it, but feared not doing so would be a kind of wish. When she did, Loretta and Nola were there, their faces telling her they would not take no for an answer, and before she knew it she was down on the beach.

Syd had already stacked the firewood. He grinned when he saw her in the twilight. He was as cuddly as a teddy bear, and she was glad she had come.

Brad and Emma were there, as well as Erin, her name written in a Scottish clan's tartan colours. Alma wondered which one.

It was something she had noticed once they had crossed the provincial border between New Brunswick and Nova Scotia: there were symbols of Scotland everywhere, especially tartans, and even more so as they had come to Cape Breton.

It wasn't surprising, since Nova Scotia was Latin for New Scotland. Alma always thought that was cooler than if it had been named just New Scotland. Whenever a town was named New, it seemed boring to her, New York being the exception, though she wondered how the people of poor York felt.

Her brother had not known Nova Scotia meant New Scotland, and from the look of her mother's face, Alma didn't think she had known either.

Odd...Lavinia couldn't have read that in the crystal. It seemed important, an odd feeling that there was no coincidence to the School of Wish being located here.

Alma yearned to go to Syd to tell him how much she appreciated his pulling her from the water, but he was working seriously on building a tower of wood that augured a large bonfire. She wasn't sure if he normally built such large fires, or if he was trying to impress his new classmates. Not that he needed to.

Instead, Erin came up to her. "Hi," she said, "I'm Erin. You must be Alma."

"Yes," Alma, said suddenly realizing she was the only one not wearing a name tag. "Glad to meet you. Sorry I wasn't at supper. I had an accident."

"I heard one of the triplets pushed you. So sorry to hear that."

Alma looked around, wondering who had told her. She could not have expected anyone to hold it secret and there seemed no malice in any of them there, only sympathy. Alma nodded.

"I have never liked triplets," said Erin, "not in sheep, not in people. And I can't say I even thought of liking this group from the start."

Alma smiled, feeling the sympathy. "It was the short one who pushed me, I think, but they were all laughing at me."

"They think everything is a big joke. One of them grabbed the last dessert right from my hand. That's why I brought stuff to make s'mores."

She handed a package of Graham crackers to Alma. "Have a few of these while you wait. You must be hungry if you missed supper."

"Thanks," Alma said, realizing how hungry she was.

Syd was now working to set kindling under the tower of wood, and trying to find matches, but she couldn't wait, and started chomping.

"So, are you from here?" Alma said through the crumbs. "Are you a native Nova Scotian?"

Erin laughed. "No. You could tell if I wasn't trying so hard to keep my Scottish accent safe. I'm from the old, boring Scotland."

"Oh, and which tartan colour is on your name tag?"

"I'm from clan Ogilvie. It's a smaller clan, but we are pretty tough. Our motto is 'To the end!' I was here to learn Gaelic. One of the best schools for Gaelic in the world is near here. I was there trying to learn, but strange things kept happening. Apparently, I'm the cause, so Selva recruited me for here."

Alma wanted to ask what kind of strange things, but Erin felt it was her turn to ask a question. "And where are you from?"

Loretta and Nola crowded around as Syd finally had the fire crackling. They were reaching for Graham crackers and Alma felt it rude not to answer, especially when Erin continued, "You sound like you are from the United States, but I can't tell what part. Your skin colour is so pretty, not like my freaky burning mess."

"Oh, I think you are pretty with the orange hair," Alma said, thinking how she might describe herself. When observers tried to place her race, they were often mistaken. She considered herself human, nothing more, fairly fluent in three languages and working on Mandarin.

She was a mix of races, which she thought gave her character, but certainly not as much as her brother, who she had to admit took after her grandfather.

"I'm from the southern U.S., born and raised in the same house in New Orleans. My mom likes to think of herself as a Roma, but her mother, my grandmother, was Filipino, and her father was a Roma, or called himself a Roma, living in Spain when they met."

"Is it true the Roma are originally from India?" asked Loretta. "I heard that recently and was totally surprised."

"Yes," said Alma. "My mother always wanted to go to India to learn more about their history, but she mostly thought of that part of the family as European. My grandfather, who was born in Europe, certainly felt he was European."

It always seemed easier to talk about her mother's side of the family. Mostly because her mother did most of the talking in their house, she supposed. Certainly, when it came to family, her mother was the most talkative. She often used the crystal to find things out about the family.

Alma used to think it was all stuff her mother made up, but now she was believing there was some power to her mother's crystal. Except, like wish magic, it never worked exactly like you expected, like sending her to this school instead of her brother.

She knew her mother would be still angry Alma had been accepted into the school instead of Pierre, but she wondered what her father would be thinking.

When she thought of him, she felt a sudden tug. It was as if a force was grabbing her and pulling her out into the water. No not quite: a force wanting to pull her the shortest route that just happened to go over water.

"My father," she said, "Is from New Orleans, grew up in the Cajun quarter."

"Oh," said Syd. "You know the roots of the Cajuns are here in Nova Scotia."

"Yes," said Alma. Though she hadn't learned it from her father and certainly not her mother. She'd learned it from reading a book on the history of Nova Scotia. Whenever she travelled, and that wasn't often, she always tried to read about the history of the place before she got there.

"Oh, that's interesting," said Loretta. "My uncle lives in New Orleans. He's not Cajun, obviously, but he has a girlfriend who is. What is the connection between New Orleans and here?"

"Well, it's quite sad," said Syd, joining them directly now that the fire had rushed from the kindling to the tower of leaning wood. If it hadn't been obvious before, he was very proud of the province and its history.

"The first Europeans that we know for sure settled here were the

French. They came in an expedition under Champlain. Later the English started to settle here and fight the French. The English won and asked the French settlers to take an oath of allegiance to the English crown. Those who didn't were forcibly deported. Many of them were deported to Louisiana, which the French owned at the time."

Alma stood feeling the pull from the north east. She hadn't really thought about it before, but her father descended from people who had settled in this place. She suddenly felt a little more at home, as if the land was welcoming her. It was as if there was an old tie to the land beckoning her.

"Wow, that is sad," said Erin, who knew something about sadness. The rest nodded their heads in agreement. It wasn't unusual for people who had characteristics that would make them good wish managers to be sensitive to others.

"Well, if you really want to read something sad, you need to read the poem about Evangeline."

"What's that about?"

"It's about a girl whose fiancé was deported, and she spent her life searching for him."

Alma suddenly felt angry. The force of tugging was even stronger. She almost staggered into the fire.

"Did you feel that?" she asked.

The others shook their heads.

"Something was pulling me in that direction." She pointed north east.

Syd looked thoughtful and said, "You're pointing toward Louisbourg. That's the fort the French built to control the gateway to the St. Lawrence River which goes all the way to the Great Lakes. It's also the scene of two battles. The great deportation happened after the second English victory. There is a great fort restoration there. When we get a weekend free, we can visit."

Alma felt the tugging stop as the thought of her making a visit became real in her head. For some reason, she needed to go there. "Yes, I would like that very much. Are you old enough to drive?"

Syd tossed back his head and laughed. Neither Alma nor anyone else saw what was funny, but Syd's laugh was contagious.

"Yes, I'm old enough to drive. I might have to hot-wire a car to take us there, but no problem with my age."

Alma wasn't sure whether he was kidding, but maybe it wasn't time for another question.

It's too bad the name tags didn't have ages on them. For some strange reason, she suddenly envisioned the number 87 on his back, below the Syd Cowsby name. Alma looked at him closely, trying to ascertain his age. She didn't want to ask.

"You don't believe I'm old enough to drive?" he said. "I wear 87 on my back cause that's the year I was born."

Alma watched as he frowned. "No, that can't be right. I'm definitely not in my mid-thirties. Trust me. Here look at my driver's license."

He flicked out a tattered cardboard card. No picture, just his name. She tried to check his birth date, but before she could get a close look, from nowhere there was a large growling.

Alma looked around, but couldn't see anything now that twilight had darkened, even though the bonfire was roaring.

The growling sounded again.

"Wow," said Syd, almost nervously. "Somebody's stomach is hungry. Somebody here must really want the marshmallows."

Alma wasn't sure the growl was from a stomach, certainly not a human stomach. Maybe her imagination was too fired up from the day. Grunts and groans in the lodge, ice cream men appearing and disappearing, Banshee screams.

"Okay, grab a stick," said Loretta. "Start toasting the marshmallows. If you want s'mores we have Graham crackers and chocolate over here."

The group scurried to prepare their s'mores.

Again, Alma wondered about age. At her own school, whenever there was a bonfire, there were people drinking and often doing more than that. She was no prude, but she certainly was too young and wanted her wits about her. But here, no one seemed to smell of alcohol.

Syd had moved to the edge of the lighted area and she thought she had seen him throw a marshmallow to the woods. He looked back at her suddenly, conscious of her gaze. She couldn't ignore him and so crossed over to him.

"Thanks again for saving me," she said. "I was kinda scared."

"Don't worry about it. We're going to have to look after each other. I was supposed to go play hockey at a private school. In hockey you have to really look after your teammates, so that's how I look at classmates. There is always one player or two on the team who think they are better than everyone and trying to get drafted ahead of you, but mostly the team looks after you. I think it's going to be the same here. Look at this little group. I bet we are going to be great friends. But there will be some, like the triplets, who just won't know how to be team players."

She nodded. She never had a chance to play team sports, but her father had talked about playing football and fighting as part of a platoon, and it seemed the same. She felt a little more comfortable than she had earlier in the evening.

"Why did you leave hockey school to come here? You wear that jersey all the time. It must be important to you."

Syd looked too serious for a moment. Alma could tell he was churning over a hundred thoughts. "It was tough, though I don't really think I had a choice. Not when it was explained to me. I'm not sure any of us here have a choice."

"What did they explain to you? I'm here by accident. My parents wanted my brother to come here but the Wish Doctor wanted me. I'm still not sure why, except he asked some quirky questions, and I could answer better than Pierre could."

There was another slight growling. Syd threw another marshmallow into the woods, pulling it from his stick as if it was too hot.

"You might as well know," he said. "I can make some wishes come true. Nothing big, nothing major, but the Wish Doctor convinced me I have to be able to control my ability or I could cause unintended trouble."

"Oh," she said. "What kind of wishes?"

"Little things. I have to be careful. Like If I wished to give you a dozen roses, I could make them appear. But they might be covered in thorns that would cut you, or maybe have a beetle that would burrow into your brain."

"OMG," she said. She was still struggling to believe that his idea of wish magic was real, despite what she'd seen. The Wish Doctor had such an odd sense of humour, part of her wondered if this was all just a big theatrical joke. "Have you hurt yourself?"

"A couple times. But someone always sews me up and puts me back to normal. It could be worse. You have to help me. If I sound like I'm making a wish, you have to stop me, okay? Sometimes I just do it by instinct. I don't want to hurt anybody."

"Oh my gosh, of course, of course. I'll let you know any time I hear you even starting to make a wish, unless it's part of our training."

Alma had a terrible feeling. She would find it just awful if Syd made a wish and hurt himself. She owed him and she would do what she could to protect him.

She took a bite of her cracker and asked, "Before you went swimming, I noticed you had letters on your back. Was that some kind of tattoo?"

"Are you afraid of tattoos?"

"No."

"Well, you should be. I saw a spider come alive from a tattoo on the internet."

"You're kidding."

"No, no. My friend who showed me thought it was a prank, but I know it wasn't. A lot of people wish for tattoos and things go wrong. Then a lot of people wish they didn't have tattoos and that can cause even more troubles, like them losing a limb."

Alma wrinkled her face. Her mother had said she'd rip off Alma's arm if she ever got a tattoo. Syd might be telling the truth.

"I don't know if I could get one," she said. "So many of them are ugly. I'm not against them in principle, just ugly ones. It would have to be really something perfect. Like my children's names or a picture of my dog. My brother has one that he thinks is secret, but my parents know about it. They had a big fight about who caused him to get it."

She stopped. She didn't like it when her parents fought. When they fought about Pierre it was always heated and angry. She wasn't sure if she was glad or not that they rarely fought about her, and that when they did there was little passion or anger.

There was something about the fight regarding Pierre's tattoo that seemed important. She had always tried to block out all conversations about her brother, though, whether tied to the crystal's portents of his magic powers, or just about how important he was going to be, or how annoying he was.

Had they been really talking about a magical tattoo? Had her brother got one? Where was it? She hated to look at Pierre, so maybe it was right in plain sight. It seemed like the kind of thing the Wish Doctor would ask about, but he hadn't.

Those sagging marks on her father. Did he have magical tattoos as well, or had he tried to get them reversed?

How naive she had been, thinking all her mother's talk of magic was foolishness. She wondered now how much power the crystal had. Where did her mother get it? The history of her parents' families suddenly seemed important. She needed to know more.

There was something else. Alma knew she was different from them all, maybe not in a way destined for magic like her brother, but because of all the different bloodlines in her. She was something new. Someday she wanted a symbol. Someday, maybe, she would have that symbol as a tattoo.

"Are you okay?" said Syd, mouth full of cracker and marshmallow and chocolate. He was making so much noise eating, it was like listening to a bear eat dessert when it hadn't had the main course. "I didn't mean to get you upset about tattoos."

"No, sorry. I was just thinking that maybe someday I should get a tattoo. My parents would never have let me, but now that I'm away...."

"Well, don't get a spider tattoo, that's all I can say."

Alma, laughed. "I don't think I will. I don't know what it will be yet. You still didn't tell me if that was a tattoo on your back. Are you trying to hide something?"

"Yes, but it's not a tattoo." He laughed, and she couldn't tell if he was joking or not. "You won't be able to see it out here in the dark. It's a sunburn. I had this t-shirt that said 'Syd Cowsby' on the back in big letters, and I fell asleep on the beach over in Prince Edward Island, and the letters melted in the sun. It was some cheap dye. Anyway, it didn't sting, but the sun burnt through the letter holes on the shirt."

Alma looked intently at Syd. Initially, he seemed like such a pleasant, average guy, but there was a mystery about him. It made him even more attractive, but she wasn't sure that story sounded perfectly true. For a guy who could bring wishes to life, who knew what could happen to him?

"What does Syd Cowsby Mean?"

Syd laughed again. "Did you like that ice cream we had today?"

"It was pretty good, until I started choking on it."

"What?"

"Never mind. It wasn't the ice cream, it was all the craziness going on."

"I hope, you get used to it," Syd muttered, then more clearly said, "Well, the best ice cream in the world is made at a place called COWS over in Prince Edward Island. Do you know where that is?"

"Yeah, I have never been there, but we saw signs on the way here."

"It was once part of Acadia, which is what the French called the maritime province area, before the English came. Anyway, one of my favourite places to go. Great beaches, lobster, amusement parks—small ones, probably, to you, but lots of fun. And the best ice cream, really, anywhere. Google did a survey to prove it. And if Google did a survey, it must be right, right?

"There's an outlet in Halifax, too. Alma, I'm not kidding. It is the best ice cream ever. Whoever started the company must have made a wish to make the best ice cream in the world. It's the only explanation."

Alma's mouth was dry and she suddenly craved ice cream. That morning, she would never think that someone could wish to make the best ice cream in the world, but now she couldn't wait to try her first Cow's.

"What does this have to do with Syd Cowsby?" she asked.

Syd grinned. "At Cows they make all these silly t-shirts based on a cow image and bad puns. The Wish Doctor loves the place. They have stuff like Cow Story for Toy Story, and Dr. Moo for Dr. Who."

He turned to her. "How much do you know about famous Canadian hockey players?"

"Not much, I just know the famous ones like Wayne Gretzky, and oh... So your t-shirt was a pun on that other hockey player?"

Syd grinned. "My favourite hockey player. Well, my father's favourite hockey player cause he named me after him. And a lot of my friends call me Cowsby."

"Oh, that's fun," said Alma.

"Sometimes," said Syd. He turned sombre for a moment.

"Syd, why are puns and word play associated with wishes? When we brought my brother here, the Doctor asked a bunch of questions. The reason he chose me instead of Pierre was that I knew what a palindrome is and what a pun is."

"I heard someone say the whole magic thing is a joke. Maybe that's why." Syd thought for a moment. "I don't know really. Sometimes my wishes aren't funny at all. I don't think it's because any of this is supposed to be funny. It's just you have to be so precise with what you say, it's like I'd like to give you some roses like I said, but I wouldn't want you to have any thorns."

Alma blushed. "The Doctor seems to have a sense of humour, when he isn't so busy."

"Yeah, he cracks the odd joke. Pretty dry sense of humour. I guess no one can take themselves too seriously. My mum use to say only people who make fun of themselves can be happy."

"Wow, that's a pretty smart thing to say."

Alma pondered a moment. Maybe she should stop making fun of Pierre and start making fun of herself. Maybe her mother needed to make fun of herself, too.

"Hey, look, a shooting star!" someone called out and Alma could feel Syd freeze next to him.

"What's the matter?"

"I hope nobody tries to wish on that star. I'm having too much fun here and don't want any trouble."

"Oh," said Alma, "Right." *How many bloody types of wishes are there?*

"Wishes on stars are maybe the most powerful. If you really need a wish to come true, wish on a star. Just be careful. They can also cause the most problems if they go wrong."

"How do you know this?"

Syd's brow furrowed as he tried to remember. "I heard the Wish Doctor tell it in one of his lectures."

"When?" said Alma, "I thought this was the first class." *And the last class was twenty years ago.*

"I...maybe it wasn't a lecture, maybe he told me when he recruited me. He always seems to be lecturing, especially when he's telling people how silly they are when they make a wish that goes bad. Or telling them how to correct it."

~

Syd tried to think when he had heard the Wish Doctor talk about shooting stars. Maybe when the Doctor had brought him in his kite machine, but he didn't think so. They had talked about how he could control his pure power.

He had gone with the Doctor when he fixed a couple of wishes, but that had been in the daytime.

It had felt like he had been in a classroom, but he couldn't remember when. Had the Wish Doctor done something to him, or were his memories mixed up from one of his own wishes gone crazy?

He didn't have time to un-mix his thoughts because he felt a hand on his back, touching in a way he wasn't looking for. It certainly wasn't Alma, because he would have welcomed that.

He turned, and there was Alfalfa, the shortest triplet.

"Hi, Syd," she said sweetly. Sickeningly sweetly.

~

Alma saw Alfalfa at the same time as Syd. Maybe she'd come to apologize, but no, she only had eyes for him. The other two triplets were not to be seen.

Alfalfa turned to look at Alma, not so sweetly. There was a hidden menace in her features that was frightening. Suddenly, Alma felt wet, and angry, and out of control.

She barely noticed that the shooting star was still tracking brightly across the night sky, when she wished the triplet was not on the beach with them.

And then Alfalfa was not there on the beach.

But neither was Alma.

8: The Island of Misfit Toys

Alma had always loved the Christmas special *Rudolph the Red-nosed Reindeer*, despite the fact her father was always mimicking the snowman singing 'Holly Jolly Christmas' even on warm evenings like this one. He said the special was made in the year he was born, and he would keep living as long as the show kept airing.

She could hear him irritatingly singing the lyrics now, even as she felt herself disappearing into a dream and reappearing in a nightmare. When she had wished the triplet was not on the beach, she had unconsciously wished Alfalfa was far away on the Island of Misfit Toys.

She now grasped fully and completely the first lesson of the Wish Doctor. She had wished the triplet onto the Island of Misfit Toys, but nothing in her wish had prevented her from going, too. Yes, she had always loved that TV special, but as she came awake on the island, she knew she would never love it again.

She was not dressed for an island near the North Pole. The closest she had ever come was the town of Stewiacke, which she had driven though on the way to Baddeck. There a sign proudly proclaimed, "halfway between the equator and the north pole."

She was shivering already.

Something else. When she had pictured an island of misfit toys, she had not pictured the ultimately happy ending of the toys, nor an abominable snowman that proved friendly in the end.

No, she had pictured the Island of Misfit Toys as a kind of punishment for kids who deserved it.

Kids like Alfalfa.

And now herself. For making such an awful wish.

The wind was blowing cold snow, making her teeth chatter.

How could this be real? How could a wish, even if wishes were true, make an unreal place seem this real? What damage might that do to the world? She realized there was more mathematics she had to learn. The power of wishes had an effect on the very physics of the world, and one needed math to understand that.

She also knew she had to get back to the Baddeck beach. She didn't know how. She could try to make a new wish but she was sure the only way this one had worked was that she had been looking at a shooting star. And been near Syd, whose power of wishes seemed to influence her.

There was one other person she knew who had the power of wishes: the triplet. Alfalfa. She had to find her.

She took six steps and banged into something solid.

A sharp yelp, and there she was.

Alma brushed away the snow from her eyes. Even with the wind blowing the snowflakes, Alfalfa looked far different than when she was with her sisters. Her face was broader. She was definitely shorter, legs stockier, arms full of muscles, not as dainty as she looked dressed in frills. No wonder she'd been able to push Alma so hard.

"You. What did you do? Did you bring me here, you little—?"

"You pushed me in the ocean! I almost drowned. This is an accident. We need to figure a way out of here, or we're going to die."

"Where are we? Where'd you take us?"

"It's an imaginary place. It's called the Island of Misfit Toys."

The triplet understood. In a world of wishes, an island of misfit anything brought to life could be extremely dangerous.

Alma clenched her teeth. The island on the show had been bleak but not necessarily dangerous. Its citizens, while morbid and, well, misfits, were not exactly menacing. She had added that detail as she made the wish, picturing a land of menacing creatures. "There's a talking, flying lion, who is king. There's an abominable snowman."

"You have got to be joking me."

"I wish I were. Can you make a wish, take us back?"

"No. I'm not one of the ones who can make a pure wish. It's why I'm at the school, you dumb ass."

Alma felt like swearing herself. If she could figure a way out, it would be tempting to leave Alfalfa, but she wasn't tempting the forces of wish anymore. If only they'd been at school longer, maybe she'd know what to do.

"Wish, reverse!" she called.

Nothing happened.

"Wish undo!" Again, nothing happened.

"Arrgh!" said Alfalfa.

Behind them, a grating, high-pitched voice sounded through the foggy, snowy mist. "Halt where you are!" it commanded.

Alma swivelled around. There was a giant purple box with two diamond shapes on each side. The voice had either come from within or there was a ventriloquist nearby.

"Who are you?" said the triplet before Alma could stop her.

"Why, I'm Charlie in the box," the thing said.

The tune of 'Pop Goes the Weasel' started grinding somewhere inside the box. Charlie's head, with razor-sharp teeth, leapt out toward her.

Alma reacted quickly and pushed Alfalfa out of the way.

The triplet looked up at her in anger, thinking Alma was getting revenge for her earlier shove, but then saw the teeth and neck reaching for her. She let Alma pull her from the ground.

"You have to reverse this," said Alfalfa.

"I'm trying. Give me a moment!" Alma tried to think how to undo a wish. What had she learned today? It was hard to concentrate, as images of the misfit toys started to appear around her.

A soft voice spoke to Alfalfa. "Come nearer. I could be your friend."

Alfalfa intrigued by a doll half-protruding from a snowbank, leaned forward and picked her up. She did not know the reason the doll was on the island was that, as the TV producers said, she had psychological damage.

Alma kept spotting other creatures of her imagination gone sinister. She had no hint of what to do. *Wait. What is Alfalfa holding?*

A doll named Sue. Then she realized the doll was a boy. A boy named Sue. An angry, father-hating, gun-toting, cash-hungry doll.

"Alfalfa!" she screamed as the doll began to pull a gun. "Throw the doll away."

Alfalfa panicked and threw the doll to the side just as the gun went off loudly. It was no toy!

Alma grabbed Alfalfa's hand, an awful, slimy-feeling hand, and dragged her away.

Where was the elf that wanted to be a dentist? He'd been friendly on the show, but she had no doubt he'd be less friendly here.

There would be no pleasant reindeer, either. Her brother had made up a song to the tune of 'Rudolph' that went 'Bruno the antimatter cornflake' instead of 'Rudolph the red-nosed reindeer'.

She did not want to encounter him.

Toys were converging from all directions. Alma sought a path between them, leading Alfalfa. She needed time to think. She tried to make a pure wish but couldn't. She needed something like a shooting star to help her.

She felt a moment of despair. She had always felt like a misfit, even within her own immediate family. Maybe she belonged here. What made her think she belonged in a special school? A school of wish. How arrogant.

Yet she was to blame for Alfalfa's presence. She had to figure a way out.

She needed to talk to the Wish Doctor.

She thought of devices she could use to communicate. But the TV show was too old and the island reflected 1962 technology, the landline phone age. She would find no broken toy cellphone.

If there was no cellphone, could there be a broken Fisher Price toy phone, like the one her father had saved from when he was a kid? Or some other way to communicate? She couldn't remember any of those things from the Island of Misfit Toys. A pistol that shot jelly or a cowboy who rode an ostrich would be no help now.

As she ran, leading Alfalfa, the snow was blinding. She felt the first tinges of hypothermia. "Doctor, I need to talk to you," she said to the dark white sky.

Then she saw the telegraph station.

She almost smiled, remembering how the Wish Doctor had picked her over her brother. It had to be a sign.

She went into the shop. No one was there, but there was a bright and shiny telegraph. She knew the sounds of Morse code to make a message but wasn't sure how to work the machine.

"There's creatures coming," screamed Alfalfa. "We can't stay here."

"Yes. Hold, please. I'm going to send a message to the Wish Doctor."

Alma fumbled with the machine. She vaguely remembered seeing one used on a movie clip on YouTube. The person more or less clicked the device.

She tried but could hear no sound.

"Hurry." said Alfalfa.

Alma continued fiddling, trying to find a way to bolster her efforts with a wish. She was sure she didn't have much time. She looked at her watch. It was 11:10.

She stopped in shock for a second. That first night when the internet was working, she had researched all she could about wishes. One thing she'd learned was you had a better chance of making a wish at 11:11. Dandelions and ladybugs were good, too, but not in the winter.

"Alfalfa, hurry. Come here and hold my hand. At exactly 11:11, we need to wish that the telegraph machine works."

Alfalfa looked at Alma as if she were crazy.

"Are we not in a blizzard on the Island of Misfits Toys, in the middle of summer? You are enrolled in a school to teach you how to control wishes. Help me."

Alfalfa took her hand, her expression a mix of contempt and desperation.

"Together, when I say 'go', say, 'I wish the telegraph machine is working'."

Alma looked at her watch, wondering when the last time was she had made sure her watch was accurate. There was no time to change it now.

"Go," she said as her watch turned to 11:11.

"I wish the telegraph machine is working," The two girls said as if they were twins, with a similar cadence of speech.

Suddenly there was a hum and Alma knew how to work the machine.

```
dear wish doctor stop
alfalfa and alma are trapped on island of mis-
fit toys stop
Came here by inadvertent wish while looking at
a shooting star stop
```

There was a thirty second wait, then the machine began to clack out a reply. "What's it say?" asked Alfalfa.

```
I was waiting for your message stop
be there shortly stop
stay away from the a******* snowman stop
```

The adjective for the snowman was garbled, some kind of static interfering with the machine.

```
If he shows up, ring me stop
```

After the final clack, the telegraph machine went dead, as if it would never function again.

The silence didn't last long. There was a sudden crash as a creature burst through the door. It was a large, white, furry creature.

Yeti was not cuddly like a bear. He had teeth like stalactites and large hands as if made for basketball. He moved jerkily, as if one frame at a time. He carried a large, shiny, brass object in his hand that appeared like an inverted church bell. And sticking from the bell were what could only be the fuses of sticks of dynamite. A bomb.

In that moment, Alma, and maybe Alfalfa, realized just how dangerous puns could be if used inappropriately.

A bomb in a bell.

Wearing a Yankee baseball jersey and no doubt speaking with a Bronx accent. A bomb in da bell snowman.

An abominable snowman.

But if one bad pun was dangerous, could two be salvation?

On the bell was a logo of a bell. Alma had learned when she had researched Baddeck, that it had been the summer home of the inventor of the telephone. His name was Alexander Graham Bell. That was his and his wife's company's logo on the bell.

'If he shows up, ring me.' Alma couldn't believe the Wish Doctor had made the pun in a telegraph message, but she smiled.

The telegraph had gone dead, because like in real life it, had been replaced by the telephone. By the Bell telephone. She had to take the risk. And quickly, before the cellphone made the Bell phone obsolete.

She dropped Alfalfa's hand, as she saw misfit toys entering the telegraph shop, most of them more like the demented toys from the first *Toy Story* movie than those in the Baskin Robbins Rudolph special. It was still 11:11.

Alma ran to the snowman and slapped the bell so it rung. even upside down. It made a crackling, explosive sound. An annoying ringtone if ever there was one.

The dynamite fuses began to flare.

"Wish Doctor, we need help!"

"Be right there," said the Doctor.

Then he was.

His eyes sparkled with the excitement of danger, and the knowledge of how to deal with it, and the thrill that he might not.

"There is magic in words," he said. "A bomb in a bell snowman melts in the summer."

And just as he said it, there was a torrent of melting snowman that easily put out the fuses to the dynamite.

As if there had never been an island of misfit toys, Alma, Alfalfa, and the Wish Doctor were suddenly on the beach in Baddeck. The fire was not as bright as when Alma had left, but there was Syd to give her a hug like a teddy bear until the Wish Doctor's frown made her pull away.

The Wish Doctor lightly scolded her for the poor, uncontrolled wish she had made, but she didn't care. He seemed oddly satisfied despite his scolding. "Come sit by the fire," he said, "my little shooting star."

She couldn't quite understand the look on this face. *Is he mocking me?*

She might have thought this whole adventure would put her off staying at the school, but it hadn't. She had felt danger and loved it. She had seen how her qualifications had helped. How she had found a way out, even if she had caused the trouble herself.

She no longer felt quite so out of place. In fact, she felt she had more right to be at the school than the triplets. She did not have the gift to make pure wishes, at least not naturally. But she could make wishes with aids, like a shooting star. And powerful ones.

She could extricate herself from trouble. Deep, snowman trouble. With little training. She had kept her wits about her, but she could do better. She could do a lot better once trained.

For a moment she felt a hesitation. Had her wish in the car changed her destiny, made her a more acceptable candidate for the school than her brother? Or had her talents really impressed the Wish Doctor?

It didn't matter, did it? Either she had pure power, or she had skills to be trained.

She remembered the look on the Wish Doctor's face. The Doctor had never for a moment considered her brother. No wish had made the Doctor choose her over her brother. She did not think one could have, anyway.

The fire had thawed her out, and she was surprised how deeply the Wish Doctor was smiling at her.

She realized she wanted to be just like him.

9: Wish reversal

Though the lodge was big for a house, it was not big enough to avoid a single person, let alone triplets. Alma was so glad everyone was wearing name tags, except for Syd, who still wore his nickname on his sunburned back. She was able to recognize the triplets when they were separated only by their name tags. They looked so alike when they were together, but maybe that obscured their actual looks, so they were harder to recognize when separated. When you saw them together, all you saw was their sameness, not what they actually looked like.

The triplets were cool to her, but Alfalfa blushed beet red in anger when they were near. Alma tried apologizing but Alfalfa would have none of it.

Maybe it was because Alma could not be completely sincere. She would never have wished her to be on the Island of Misfit Toys if Alfalfa hadn't pushed her into the cold ocean.

Alma had not slept well, too excited from her adventure. Her stomach was still too upset in the morning for her to eat. In the kitchen, it was even more difficult to avoid the triplets, so she hid behind Syd when she could.

He found her attempts to hide amusing. "You have to get famous first before you get a bodyguard," he said.

Alma wasn't so sure. The triplets, one or all three, would try to get back at her, and she had to be ready.

In the classroom, the triplets sat in the front of the room on a long-backed seat, right in the middle, so Alma sat in the back left, as far away as possible. She sat at an angle behind Alfalfa, so Alfalfa was in a line between Alma and where the Wish Doctor stood lecturing. Alma could look over her head and see the Wish Doctor's face, although as soon as her sisters sat next to her, Alfalfa seemed taller.

Loretta and Nola wanted to sit near the front, but in solidarity sat next to Alma. Syd was in the row ahead.

"We were scared," said Nola, "when you guys disappeared."

"I was, too. I think I finally figured out that this is all real. I mean, the school and wishes and everything. I don't know if I thought it was before yesterday."

"You lived in New Orleans, known for magic, you're the daughter of a witch, and you didn't think this was real?" Nola looked confused.

Alma shrugged. "What can I say? Even if I believed, I never would have thought what happened yesterday could happen."

"We need details," said Nola.

"I have plenty of details. It—"

The Wish Doctor walked into the room with Selva. He smiled politely but seemed tired.

Selva had told Syd, who had told Alma, that not only had the Wish Doctor taught the class yesterday and saved her, but late in the day he had to make rounds to correct seven wishes gone bad. She didn't feel good that she had added to his fatigue. She would have to make it up to him somehow.

"Today, we start with a little warning," the Wish Doctor said. "Maybe every day we will start with a warning." His tone was less playful than the day before. Alma found herself inadvertently looking away. She had no doubt she was the cause of the warning.

"We had a little incident last night. I won't give details, but most of you either already know or gossip will fill in the information. Doesn't really matter if you hear them or not, as the facts will never be precise. Truth is, someone made a wish last night without controlling it, and it came true. If I didn't stress it enough yesterday, this land is powerful in the magic of wishes. Our gathering only makes it more powerful. That's part of the reason why we are here, because we need to harness the power here for those few times when we need to make wishes, but mostly we need the power to undo wishes that go wrong. Let me make it clear, the wish that was made last night went very wrong indeed. It is lucky that no one was hurt."

Alma slid down in her chair, though Loretta kicked her to sit up straight or it would be too obvious.

"Last night there was a shooting star. Wishes on shooting stars are some of the most powerful wishes. I don't put any blame out. It is inevitable we will make some wishes we shouldn't. It means, though, we need to be especially careful to make sure we minimize this and that any wish gone wrong is not too powerful. I think most of you by now will know not to make a conscious wish. If you don't know how to now, we will teach you how to detect any wish starting to materialize even before you voice it. You should and must be able to quell that wish, unless you are controlling it under supervision."

Alma wondered, *Had I felt a little sensation of the wish against Alfalfa coming on? Had it been there but buried by my anger?*

"More importantly," continued the Wish Doctor, "we need to be careful about subconscious wishes. Because we will be talking about wishes, you will be naturally thinking about them, and there is a tendency to make wishes without thinking. Wishes and hopes and dreams are so much a part of our nature we naturally think of these things constantly. You are going to have to be aware of wishes forming in your mind.

"If you have any talent for a pure wish, this is absolutely necessary. Do you understand the importance of this?"

Selva looked at each student, until he could see the nod of realization from each.

After a long, sombre pause, the Wish Doctor continued, "Before we get to our main topic of the day, I want to go through the major categories of assisted wishes, those wishes that need an aid to happen like a shooting star. Can you give me some examples?"

Alma raised her hand, feeling she needed to improve her impression. "Wishes at the time of 11:11 or using the number 11."

"That, too," the Wish Doctor said with a smile. "We surely know that is true, don't we?"

Alma found herself wanting to wish that she was not blushing but caught the instinct in time to stop it.

"Wishing on a coin thrown into a foundation," one of the triplets said. Alma couldn't tell which one.

"I think you mean a fountain," the second triplet said, the third nodding agreement.

"Yes," the Wish Doctor said, trying to hide a saddened frown. "This can extend beyond fountains, to wishing wells or many bodies of water."

Erin raised her hand. "Leprechauns, fairies, genies, other mythical creatures."

"Yes. Except they really aren't mythical. You must be especially wary of any of these. In many cases the creature is deliberately trying to trick you. If you are ever enticed to use their wishes, try not to. These should be your last resort. What else?"

"Wishkey." said Brad tentatively."

Half the class laughed, some thinking he was joking.

"Are you old enough to drink whiskey?"

"Yes. Just this month. But only if I'm in Montreal."

"Brad you are right. Some day we will go to where it is made. Wishkey is also very powerful. And often hard to control, as it blurs your senses and unleashes your imagination.

"Sometimes in order to make the most powerful wish, you might need to combine several things, like wishkey and an eyelash, and a shooting start at 11:11. Beware. If a small wish like 'I scream' can go wrong, you do not want to have a wish go wrong with all those items put together. Let me be clear, anybody who attempts to abuse their power here to make selfish wishes will be expelled."

Nola put her hand up. "I've heard of other things that can help make wishes come true. Dandelions. Wishbones. Wish stones. The first star at night, not just a shooting star."

"Very good. I'm surprised, though, that no one has noted the most popular, most troublesome of all the wishes. I will give you a clue: it uses candles."

"Birthday wishes," someone said.

"Yes,"the Wish Doctor said. "We will devote a good deal of time to birthday wishes. Throughout history, they have caused some of the worst trouble."

He let the thought sink in before continuing. "In addition, we need to worry about warm wishes, holiday wishes, wishes for good time, wishes for good luck, unicorns, four leaf clovers, ladybugs, dragonflies and many others. All these things may come to be tools for us to use at some time. But for now, until we have learned how to reverse wishes with other means, we shall not use wishes. Can we all agree to this?"

Most of the class raised their hands.

But there was something odd with the triplets. They would put up their left hand, then take it down, then put up their right. There was just enough pause in their movements that it made Alma wonder.

"Today we are going to talk some basic strategies for wish reversal. When using examples for purposes of discussion, we will never use the phrase, 'I wish'. We will substitute it with other words that don't conjure the same power. For example, we might say I *hope* for a feather bed. Or I *would like* to have a feather bed. This phrasing will generally avoid diffi-culty. On some days, we might discuss magic derived from wish magic, when *hopes* and *would likes* have special powers. On those days, even that safe phrasing may be difficult, but I or Selva will give you some ad-vance warning.

"Now, let's get onto the main topic. This is the foundation of all we shall learn, so please give me your full attention.

"Any suggestions on how you might reverse a wish?"

"Say 'wish undo' or 'wish reverse'." said Loretta.

"Yes, and for someone of your power, you will find that this works just fine in many situations."

Loretta could not help but smile.

"This will not work for everyone or for every situation, even for you, Loretta. You have to know when to use it and how to control it.

"The simplest wish reversal is to say a wish in reverse. Say it backwards. Now when I say 'simplest', I mean simplest in intention, but not necessarily simplest in execution. The first thing you need to determine is what sequence to say things in reverse.

"For example, do you say, 'Bed feather a for hope I'? Or do you say, 'I epoh rof a rehtaef deb'? Or, 'Deb rehtaef a rof epoh I'?

"There are other combinations, using the syllables or the phonetics or the punctuation in reverse. Sometimes, if you are looking in a mirror and saying things backwards, then that will turn them forwards again, defeating your purpose. In that case, saying the phrase frontwards might even be backwards. I know this is confusing, so we will go over it several times.

"All these reversal approaches might seem appropriate and sound well. Getting them wrong, though, could be disastrous. You could turn yourself into a bed, you could trap yourself in a bed. You could end up in a prison, where a huge inmate uses you for a bed. Or just sits on you from time to time. You could turn yourself into a feather, or you could turn your bed into the world's biggest feather. Don't laugh. It has happened, and it's not as funny as it seems if it happens to you."

Not for the first time did Alma's doubts about staying in the school surface. Even after her exhilaration of the night before, she felt acid fear rising in her gullet. She almost felt a dry heave coming on. She sometimes stumbled over her words, as opposed to her brother who was always so glib. What if she made a mistake and the Wish Doctor wasn't there to help her? She wasn't sure the Island of Misfit Toys was the worst thing that could happen. In fact, she suspected there were much worse things.

Even the triplets looked at each other on that one, as if a combine harvester was bearing down on them. Not even their cheery name tags could avoid it. They were all playing with danger.

Despite the Wish Doctor's often light demeanour, there was no doubt. It was like the gallows humour Alma remembered from endless cop movies and TV shows.

The Doctor continued, not giving too much time for fear to set in. "If you can identify the pattern needed for the reversal, *and* if you enunciate in reverse, this is the simplest of tools. We will discover together that not everyone here will have the same strength, or the same inclination to undo a wish in the same way. There are many types of wishes, but at least as many types of reversals. For most wishes, there are multiple types of reversals.

"The one way I will expect everyone to learn is how to repeat a wish backwards, how to identity the best pattern, and how to use several patterns. This will be on your final examination. I tell you that freely now.

"In fact, I will ultimately tell you *all* that will be on your final exam. The only thing that will prevent you from knowing is if you *wish* to know what's on the exam." He smiled. "In a later lesson, we will learn how to make a wish booby trap."

He said it as if there was a wish booby trap already in place. Which of course there was.

"In case you haven't guessed it, most of the illustrations we use here are based on real-life examples."

Alma had a terrible feeling that someday he would be talking about an ignorant daughter of a half-witch with a crystal, who saw a shooting star and ended up on the Island of Misfit Toys with a snowman from the Bronx.

"Another thing you need to know is that, in the same way you can reverse wishes that go wrong, you can often reverse bad luck items. Bad luck is just really a bad wish, so it is often easy for us to fix bad luck by reversing it, like reversing a wish.

"For example, getting a black cat to go backwards or lie upside down might give good luck. Going under a ladder with an umbrella sometimes works, if you walk backwards.

"Once we complete the lesson, you should always have the number 31 on a flash card in your wallet. If I have to explain why, you are not going to do very well at this school.

"I also have to warn you do not use the number 20. Not by itself and not in conjunction with itself. Time has proven there is no cure to this.

"Breaking a mirror can sometimes work, but we usually can't wait seven years."

Alma's head spun, as the thoughts and ideas kept flowing from the Wish Doctor, some joltingly different from the one before. She wondered if this was a part of the lesson, like algebra the previous day. In real-life situations, maybe facts, and clues would come at you in a mad rush, and you would need to be able to handle them quickly.

"All right, for the rest of the morning, we are going to work on wish reversals. I am going to start by telling you a wish and I want you to simply repeat the words in the exact tone. I want you to repeat in the format of my first example, that is 'bed feather a for hope I'. When everyone is comfortable in doing that, we will try the next example. "Let's start with this one, 'I would like if I was a real boy.'

For the rest of the morning, they practised. Alma was feeling fatigue in her tongue before lunch. She could not believe the range of wishes they practised their linguistic reversals on. The Doctor insisted they were all real.

Halfway through the exercises, as she was feeling her tongue literally twisted, a thought caught her and she raised her hand. "What if our saying a wish reversal now, reverses a real wish that turned out well?"

The Wish Doctor smiled. Alma was a quiet one, but every time she spoke there was meaning behind what she said. Maybe she really did have real intuwishin.

"Where were you the first time we put on this class?" he asked. "You are very right in thinking about that kind of risk, because that's exactly what happened in one of our earlier classes. We had to reverse the reversal of wishes, and twice we even screwed that up, so we had to reverse the reversal of the reversal.

"We have since implemented a procedure here, with some physical elements that block wish reversals. Unfortunately, it doesn't block all wishes, but stops most practice wishes. Later we will have you practice on real wishes and we will turn the blocking power off."

"Can you tell us more about this blocking power?" asked one of the triplets.

"I can. And if you make it to third year, I'll even let you ask again."

All three triplets glared at him, and then glared at Alma. She couldn't figure out why, other than that she had asked a question that had received a smile, and they had asked a question that received a frown.

10: The beauty of painting

Alma awoke hungry, to more moaning and groaning. Lunch had followed the morning lesson with more sandwishes, and then an afternoon focused on trigonometry. The Wish Doctor had given for homework several phrases he expected the students to be able to say backwards. She was too tired after her late-night adventure to join her classmates afterwards and went back to her room to enjoy a well-earned nap.

She decided she better join the group for supper, ate quickly, excused herself, then went back to practice in front of her mirror. The internet again was not working, despite there being more bars than in Ireland. *Does whatever dampens the chances of wishes, also dampen the internet?*

Christine, finally showing some alertness, had stayed on after supper, with enough energy to at least listen to other teammates if not openly share herself, so Alma was alone.

It's nice to have some time to myself, Alma thought. The Wish Doctor didn't want a report out for a few weeks, but after last night, the need to be ready and as skilled as possible spurred her on.

She looked into the mirror and watched her lips move as she spoke. The Doctor had said reversals were best silent; there was power in the motion of the lips, not just the sound. You also had to be careful that your lips did not convey extra meaning. Just the way that you could have a slip of the tongue to make the wrong sound or word, you could also have a slip of the lip.

She started with the word wish. She could not contemplate any other four-letter word that could be more difficult to try. If she could, she would wish that there was a simpler word to use than wish. She knew that the code words that they used in class like 'I hope' would not be sufficient.

She pursed her lips tighter and tried. *hish*. It was almost as if she was saying wish. She tried again: *shiiii*... She stopped herself quickly. Since she didn't like to use cuss words, she didn't like where that was going.

The next attempt was more like *siss*. She was missing the h sound altogether. She wondered where the h it had gone.

Another attempt and it was like she was saying *whizz*, and that made her think of her brother standing at the side of the road with his fly open.

She was getting giddy. She looked into the mirror. Although this seemed silly, she knew it was important.

She tried several more times, but it all sounded so weird. She concentrated on her mouth, and thought she had found the problem.

She was starting her mouth in the whistling position, as if she was going to make the *wh* sound, but that's where she needed to end up. She watched as she mouthed 'wish' front to back. She noted her lips spread wide rather than pursed together.

So, she carefully made a forced smile and worked back to pursed lips. *Hiswa*. She was getting closer.

She leaned nearer to the mirror, watching her lips closely.

Something was making a sound but not her. It was almost in sync with her.

She looked around, couldn't see the source and tried once more.

The voice was there again, though this time it wasn't exactly in sync with her. It started with her, then deviated as if pushing her in a new direction.

She lagged the voice but adapted quickly, following its pattern. She concentrated on her mouth and realized there was no voice at all. There was a subtle pressure from somewhere, almost if light invisible fingers were gently pushing her.

Hsiw. She was close but not quite there.

She continued, getting closer and closer better and better, until she realized the fingers and voice, if there had been any, were gone. Her room was suddenly cold.

The walls were moaning. She hadn't minded the invisible fingers. They had felt helpful, gentle; but the moaning like the night before, not so much.

Christine had not returned. Alma was scared.

She opened her door to her room and almost jumped, anticipating something from the Island of Misfit Toys would be waiting for her.

She ran past the painting that looked at her. She headed toward Syd's room, and the moaning seeming to be exactly the same distance behind her, neither closer nor further.

Syd was one of only two students to get their own room, mainly, he had told her, because it was so small. So, when she knocked on the door, and he motioned her in, she was surprised at the amount of space. It was certainly bigger than the room she shared with Christine, though there was a faint animal smell like a wet dog.

Before she commented, she blushed dark purple as she saw Nola sitting on a chair. "Oh, I'm sorry."

"We're just talking," Nola said with a laugh. "Trust me, this is all safe."

"How was your homework practice?" Syd asked. "You were pretty serious about it when you left supper."

"It was good until someone starting moaning, and then followed me here."

"What? Someone? Who?" It was hard to tell what Nola said and what Syd said; they were speaking over each other.

"I don't know. Will you guys come out with me, and at least tell me if you hear it? I want to know if I'm going crazy, or if there is more craziness to come."

Alma followed behind Syd, Nola behind them as they left Syd's room. Alma felt a chill in her shoulders, but not the creepy chill she had felt earlier. This was a slightly pleasant chill.

"Syd, hold up," she said, "Don t you fill that chill?"

Syd whose hockey jersey provided an extra layer, nodded and stopped. "That's not cold," he said.

"Then what is it?" asked Nola.

"Look, did you see that painting move!" Alma exclaimed.

"No, where?"

"Look, there it goes again." Alma said, pointing to a striking portrait of a young woman.

The three crowded around the painting.

"I don't see anything moving," Syd said.

Then the painting winked at him. Or at least the beautiful girl did.

The three looked at each other.

"Did either of you cause that?" Alma asked.

"No," the other two chorused.

They all stepped back at once, unsure if there was danger.

"This looks like a Botticelli painting," Nola said. "It's not as big as the 'Birth of Venus.'"

"Bottlewho?" Syd said.

"Botticelli. He was an Italian Renaissance artist from Florence. A lot of his paintings were lost, but the 'Birth of Venus' is one of his most famous. She was naked in the painting," she said, looking for Syd's reaction.

"I think this lady is even more beautiful," Alma said. "What do you think, Syd?"

Syd obviously had to struggle to keep from drooling, almost using a wish to do so.

Unbeckoned, a feeling of jealousy swelled within Alma. It didn't help that the beautiful woman in the pretty green dress clearly turned and blew what could only be called a passionate kiss at Syd.

His white hockey jersey suddenly blushed red.

Alma wasn't the only one who was jealous. Nola clenched her fingers on Alma's shoulders.

"I think we should get out of here," Alma said.

She started pushing Syd, but a voice behind them said, "She's no danger."

The three looked to see Professor Selva behind them.

He smiled. "Some of you have seen amazing and strange things before you came here. Some of you may have caused them. The range of things that have happened because of wishes will astonish you. They astonish me. And I have worked with the Wish Doctor a long time."

"What is this?" Alma said.

"Nola, tell her."

Nola sighed. Alma wasn't sure why. "She wished to be beautiful," Nola explained, "and she ended up taking the place of the figure in the painting."

"What?" Alma said. "And she's happy?"

"Yes," Selva said. "Look at her. We don't know how she looked or what she was like before she entered the painting, but she wanted to be beautiful forever. This picture has been in a flood, been burnt in a fire, but nothing harms it. She got her wish. She will be beautiful forever."

"But, but—"

"Look at her smile. She is happy."

"I don't understand. I thought our job was to fix wishes that go bad."

"That's a big part of it. What makes you happy may not be what makes everyone happy. Her family called us to get her out of this painting. We could have. This was a relatively reversible wish. By the end of this semester, you all should be able to reverse it. But she doesn't want the wish reversed. She has given up a certain sense of freedom in exchange for eternal beauty. Every twenty years we ask her if she would like the wish reversed and to be free from the painting. Her answer is always the same: she wants to stay."

The lady waved at them, and then, seeming to tire, settled back into a still pose. Unless you knew better, she was just globs of paint on canvas.

Globs of paint masterly put together.

Alma wondered if the lady became the figure that had been painted, or if she had entered as the subject of the masterpiece, inspiring the artist.

"Is she safe?"

"Oh my, yes. She has lived in there for 300 years. One thing you will have to learn is that what we may think of as a bad wish may not be what someone else thinks is bad. If, like this one, there is no further damage from the wish magic, we leave it, because there is always danger of infuriating a hostile force if we undo their wish, even if they were playing a trick."

"I heard some dreadful moaning in my room, and then in the hallway. If she is happy, she's not the one who was moaning?" asked Alma.

Selva shook his head, a wry smile on his face.

"Then if she's not the cause of moaning, who is?"

Selva's wry smile only widened. "What you think is moaning may be a very different sound. There are many mysteries to the House of Wonders. You have learned one tonight. You will learn more in due time...if you are brave enough to finish the school year."

11: A musical assignment

The rest of the first week seemed to fly by. There was more instruction on how to reverse wishes, more mathematics, and a history lesson that didn't seem to tie in to anything else. The lecture was about the history of Antarctica, with many strange details, and Alma wondered if some of them were made up.

There was no mention of wish magic, but she didn't dare not pay attention. It seemed everything at the school served a topsy turvy purpose.

Selva had ordered a rest night for Friday with no studying. They all went into Baddeck for a meal. Alma didn't dare ask yet about the town's name. It seemed obvious there was an intentional pun. Maybe one that had to do with wish magic.

She got to know more of her classmates, and continued to avoid the triplets, even when they pestered Syd. Christine, now alert, was still quite shy. It wasn't because she didn't speak clear English. She did, and several other languages.

There was a short lecture on Saturday morning by Selva, mostly on the relationship with math and music.

The Wish Doctor made a brief appearance at the end. "Fourteen wishes to deal with this morning," he said to Selva, looking tired.

He then proceeded to give a strange homework assignment. "Besides practising linguistic wish reversals, I would like you to listen to some music. Some specific music. I want you to listen to classical music, Strauss, (any Strauss will do) and Chopin. I want you to listen to Hank Williams Jr. I want you to listen to Fado music, which is a particular style of Portuguese folk music. I want you to listen to Drake and Lady Gaga. And any musician who died at 27. There will be a detailed list in your rooms.

"Anybody want to hazard a question as to why I want you to do this assignment?"

Several students raised their hands, including Alma. She slowly dropped hers as the three triplets had all six, or was it seven, hands in the air? Not sure what had them so excited. Either they were right and Alma would let them have this one, or they would be wrong, and someone else would have a chance to answer.

She shouldn't feel so cocky on this. The answer seemed so obvious, maybe too obvious.

"Anyone here so confident they know what I want you to do on this assignment that they would be willing to risk a wish on this? In this program you will be given three wishes to use for your own benefit. If you are right, I will grant you a fourth wish. If you are wrong, I will take away one."

Most of the hands went down. Only the triplets, all three of them, and Christine had their hands up.

Alma second-guessed herself. There had to be a trick, but she couldn't see what it was. She never expected that she would ever get three wishes, so gambling for a fourth seemed risky.

"Okay, Alfalfa, what is it I want you to figure out?"

"One of the musicians made their music because of a wish. You want us to figure out which one."

"Oh, is that so? Wheatgrass, what do you say?"

Wheatgrass looked at her sister, a slight hesitancy in her movement. "I say the same."

"And Dahlia?"

Dahlia pursed her lips like the petals of a flower, considering. "I would not call my sisters wrong. I think there are other possibilities, however, I think at least one of these musicians used a wish to achieve their career."

Three sisters. Three answers the same.

"Christine. What do you say?"

"I thought at first that one of the pieces of music was the way to make a wish, or if played could reverse a wish. But now I think the triplets are correct."

"I can only have one answer. Which one?"

Christine closed her eyes. Alma wondered if she was dreaming. There seemed a small glow under her closed eye lids. Her eyes flickered, and she said, "I am going to stay with my first answer. It was my first instinct."

"It's good you did. You are correct. When the time comes you will be granted a fourth wish. Assuming you pass all curriculum."

Alma breathed a sigh of relief. She didn't know why, but it sure didn't seem a good thing that the triplets would get an extra wish.

She looked at them, could barely see their expressions from where she was. She noted not just disappointment in their faces, but fear, clear, trembling fear. It was hard to believe she had any sympathy, yet the fear made her uncomfortable.

The Wish Doctor surprised her, smiling. "The triplets are also right."

The faces of the triplets lit up like three letters of a neon sign. All shaking was gone. There was a sigh of relief from Wheatgrass, the tallest, and then high-fiving, and a sneer from Alfalfa directed at Alma.

"I'm sure many of you, maybe all of you, had one of these answers. Maybe some of you were afraid there was a trick or couldn't decide which was which. I am glad you were careful. You must be in the beginning. As you become experienced, you will need to be confident in your actions, confident enough to know if you choose wrongly, so you can overcome it. Alright. That's it for the week. Enjoy the weekend. Smaetag, stay behind if you will. You are going to come with me and Selva on a field trip. We have a few wishes to fix, and you are going to watch."

There was a rumble through the student body. They hadn't expected a field trip so early.

To see wishes fixed up close seemed exciting. Some were glad Smaetag, clearly the oldest amongst them, got the change to go first; for others it was a struggle to contain their sulkiness. The triplets and their extra wish, for once, seemed content.

"Oh, and also, for the rest of you," the Wish Doctor said slyly, "mandatory volleyball game this afternoon. It helps hand and eye coordination, which is important in wish magic. Also a great way to work as teams. The most powerful wishes can only be made by well-functioning teams.

"Syd and Alma, you will be team captains. You'll pick the teams as they say on *Survivor*: in a school yard pick."

Alma shuddered. Wish magic was one thing, but volleyball was really frightening for someone awkward in any sport but running. Having to pick classmates for a team. That was just plain torture.

12: Smaetag

Smaetag waited patiently, standing next to the desk she always chose at the front of the room, near the map drawers, while her classmates filed out for lunch. Several wanted to wish her good luck, but caught their breath and said something along the lines of "Have a good experience," which certainly did not have the ring of a wish of good luck but was surely much less dangerous.

Selva and the Wish Doctor were deep in conversation. She was not sure if they remembered they had told her to stay behind, and felt awkward by herself. She wasn't sure if she should try to listen, but given her age, she had no time to waste. She might learn something listening as opposed to standing awkwardly.

"This is a health and safety issue. We'll need to take the device," the Wish Doctor said to Selva, who looked uncomfortable.

"Are you sure we don't have enough time to go by kite?" Selva asked.

"No. Not with the number of wissues we have to deal with today."

Selva sighed. Despite his aversion to heights, he never minded the kite. The device, on the other hand, always set his nerves a flutter.

"What are you so worried about? You installed the new harmonic dampeners. You don't think they will work?"

"Yes, they'll work, of course. The device needs other attunements, though. It's bending the bloody laws of physics. It's still very dangerous."

"You should have crossed the ocean during the days of scurvy on one of those awful ships. You would think the device is like the Orient Express compared to that. Our kite is comfortable, no doubt about it, but not fast enough. If our benefactor wasn't so bored, he could probably make the kite go faster, but he's working on lots of other things to help us."

"Okay, got it. I have the tool kit ready to take. Make sure you introduce the device to the rest of the class. I know Smaetag is our most mature, most trusted student, but the device does things to people. I think it wants to convince people to tell others about its existence."

"You think it's lonely?"

"Yep. Zero chance it isn't."

The Wish Doctor twirled his whiskers absently. It was a realization that seemed overly familiar.

"Alright. Easy enough. We'll change the order of the lectures. We'll introduce the device to everyone by the end of the week."

And Smaetag suddenly realized he was looking at her.

"Smaetag, sorry to keep you waiting. We were just discussing how we are going to reveal a secret to you that you will feel compelled to reveal ahead of when we want you to. Follow me. We are going to travel in a most unusual manner."

He led Smaetag and Selva to a small closet door, and opened it with a key in the shape of St. Augustine. She saw the shape of the key and smiled, remembering St. Augustine had been a monk.

She'd done a lot of things in her life before she had discovered what she thought of as a curse, this ability to cause trouble with wishes. Because of her curly orange hair, she was often compared to the Las Vegas prop comedian Carrot Top, especially during the two years she had spent in Las Vegas working to help set house odds in a gambling casino. She wondered if the Wish Doctor was a fan of stand-up comedy. She didn't take him for a Mark Twain fan.

She had often wondered if her liberal arts degree had been a waste of time, but the arcana she had collected in her mind seemed to be randomly useful in this school.

She felt out of place, being so much older than the other students, but she was not here to make friends. She was not here to make enemies, either. Too much time had passed in her life without knowing how to use her talent. She had to take advantage of the opportunity to learn to use her dangerous gift of wish magic.

She was pleased that she was the first student to go on a field trip, and didn't intend to displease her teachers. She watched the Wish Doctor's every move and also kept Selva in her peripheral vision at all times.

There was more than one mystery to the Wish Doctor, who she sensed was flawed in more than one way. Selva, although his assistant, in some ways seemed his superior. As if he really had his act together.

Cautiously, but without hesitation, she followed the Wish Doctor into the small closet, feeling Selva at her back. In close quarters, she could smell the breath of one of them. It was a sweet mint tea scent.

At the back of the closest was a panel, which the Doctor opened to show another keypad. He punched in a code, said six words in a language she didn't recognize, and gazed into what she believed was a retinal reader.

Another door opened, and there was a short hallway. At the end of the hallway, another door.

The Doctor turned to her. "If all three of us are to pass, you have to command the door in your native language."

"Deschide," Smaetag said, a hint of a Romanian accent in her voice, and the door opened, revealing a ladder leading down.

"Please follow," said the Doctor, as he started backwards down the steel ladder.

At the bottom there was a chain-link fence, with a sign that read DANGER HIGH VOLTAGE.

"Here: put these on," the Wish Doctor said, handing her thick rubber boots that had appeared from nowhere as if he was using slight of hand.

As she put them on, she noted he and Selva were already wearing tall black rubber boots. "Newfoundland sneakers," said the Wish Doctor but she didn't get the reference. She'd not been to Atlantic Canada before.

She realized they were all wearing rubber gloves, though she couldn't remember putting hers on. The right glove kept sliding off as if she was performing sleight of hand until she noted the strong Velcro strap at the bottom of the glove. She quickly did up the strap.

"In a moment," said the Wish Doctor, "I'm going to open the fence. There is what appears to be a glass wall beyond the fence. It's not glass. It's a crystal that changes its configuration. Right now, it's dark, but it will light up when we go in. I'm going to open it with the monk key.

"Once I do, I will need you to silence every thought in your mind and make no noise. There are harmonic dampeners in your gloves and boots that will muffle your heart and breathing, so don't worry about that. Focus on keeping your mind blank. Until I give the signal."

Smaetag tried not to look uncertain. She failed.

"Don't worry. If we follow our precautions, there is hardly any risk. Inside is a device that will transport us to where we need to be. The device is kind of like the transporters you see on *Star Trek*. I'm going to employ wish magic to make the device work. If anything disturbs it while I make the wish, we could end up in the wrong place or the wrong time. Or any terrible place or time you could imagine. Like I said little risk. Big consequences."

Smaetag's heart raced. She wondered if the dampeners were strong enough to control the sound of her heart.

"When we get to our destination, you are just to observe. If I snap my finger or touch my nose twice, you can think where I'm going wrong, or think about solutions, but otherwise just watch. What I'm doing may not make sense at first, but if you try to interfere, it could make things worse. Unless I ask you for a suggestion or a question, don't do anything, okay? It will be a balance, but you'll need to separate the teaching moment from the moment of action. Is that clear?"

"Uh. You want me to speak only when spoken to?"

"Precisely. You understand me completely."

Smaetag nodded. Though 38 years of age, she'd learned about wish magic late in life, and knew she had a lot of catching up to do. Although her power was supposedly strong, she did not come to it easily.

The doctor used his key on the large padlock, twisting it this way and that, all the time a lightshow, the envy of many firework displays, coruscated behind him, the dark glass becoming a living kaleidoscope.

The lock sprung open, and quickly, almost in a panic, he pulled the lock with the heavy casing from the gate so he could open the door.

"Follow me," he said, and she did, Selva behind. The glass door, looking like an oversized shower, continue to glow.

"Choose a colour," he said.

"Pink."

The glass was suddenly vibrating a bright pink.

The Wish Doctor opened the door, manoeuvring it with slight nudges of his glove.

The inside of the shower was not shower-like at all. It was a steampunk's paradise: gears and levers and tracks everywhere. Antique lamps within the pink shed additional white light.

Smaetag noted thin wire. Her brother had been an engineer working on fibre optics, and the wires and switch boxes looked out of place with the steampunk equipment. It was as if the technology of many different eras had been used on the device. Yet everything looked well engineered.

Except the giant seat in the middle, a huge red shell of metal, with a clown's face on the top. It was like the seat of an amusement ride, a tilt-a-whirl.

She realized that's exactly what it was, raised slightly on corrugated metal planking, and attached by wheels to the track.

"We're using the three-seater today, I see," Selva said.

"Yep, I don't plan on bringing anyone back, and no time for us to take separate trips."

Selva raised a metal bar, motioning Smaetag to sit down in the centre of the seat, while the Wish Doctor walked behind the device. He came back into view, a streak of grease on his face. He tried to rub it away with his rubber glove but it only smeared worse, so it looked like he had a sideburn on one side. The pink shadows seemed to create a second sideburn on the opposite side, so the Wish Doctor looked like a man from a bygone era and not the healthy young hunk he was.

Smaetag remembered she was not supposed to be thinking.

"It's okay," said the Doctor as if reading her thought. "I haven't powered up the wish yet. Now is the time for you to close your thoughts."

Smaetag concentrated, trying to ignore Selva, who sat up beside her. He was definitely more modern than the Wish Doctor, and handsome. She bit her tongue. Time to quell all thoughts.

"New wish or stored?" Selva asked.

"Stored," the Wish Doctor said. "The device is packed tight with wishes. I don't dare try to squeeze any new ones in."

"Ready?" The Wish Doctor blinked and the room was plunged into darkness. The tilt-a-whirl started to move.

No not move, tilt. Smaetag bit her lip as the Doctor jumped onto the seat, pulling the bar down as he did.

The sky became a swirling palette of colours as the device began to twirl faster and faster.

Smaetag closed her eyes without conscious thought, her stomach whirling. She was glad she hadn't had time for lunch.

Just like that, the device was in a field on a festival ground, a true-life tilt-a-whirl with other rides within walking distance. The sky was pure blue.

The Doctor brought up the bar, and said, "Come on, we have to hustle. The girl's condition has become worse while we were travelling. We don't have much time."

Smaetag could barely keep up as the Doctor sprinted along the fence and through an opening to a series of picnic tables, with several food trucks nearby. There were people at the tables and on blankets on the ground. A few were pulling away from one of the tables as if disgusted by something.

There was a fairly sturdy and tall girl sitting at the table, a thin blanket draped over her shoulders.

Smaetag barely had time to register a sign in the background that said 'Leamington, Tomato capital of Canada'. The sign seemed to have significance, but she didn't know why.

Two men leaned over the girl, one likely her father since they looked alike, the other an older, sterner gentleman with grey hair, holding a large Gatorade bottle, demanding the girl drink.

"Stop, don't give her anymore," the Doctor said. "You're only making it worse."

"Who are you," said the old man, seemingly accustomed to getting his own way.

"He's a specialist," the father said. "I called Karen and she called him. Family friend."

"Give me room," the Doctor said. Father and old man inched away.

The Wish Doctor's stethoscope dangled from his neck. He was after all not just a Wish Doctor.

He touched the girl's forehead with his bare palm, having discarded the rubber gloves in the tilt-a-whirl seat. "106," he said. Having been friends with both Celsius and Fahrenheit, he would always use Fahrenheit scales. Celsius had been such a beeyotch.

He checked her pulse. "It's not just racing, it's sprinting."

He held her hand gently. "It's going to be okay," he said. "We got here in time. Can you talk? I need to ask a couple of questions."

The girl nodded slightly. Despite the heat, there was no sweat on her forehead. No makeup, either, which meant one less complication.

"When did you start feeling like this?"

"L-last night. Started feeling sick at 10. Headache. Felt like throwing up; couldn't. Was better this morning, but had to join my team here."

He looked at her with the skills he'd borrowed from Sherlock. *A leader by natural skill, not cocky. Hard worker. Willing to get dirty, indicated by the dirt under her nails that aren't covered in ketchup.*

He smiled. *A college quarterback. Back up. Trying to make first string. And this is the least of her talents.*

He put his stethoscope on her chest. The coolness of the metal helped, but her lungs were full.

He stepped back and noted what everyone else was seeing.

Her arms were covered with large red hives. And now her face.

He sidestepped just as she quivered and shook, then vomited a fierce quantity of thick red sauce, almost like spaghetti.

Selva spoke before the Doctor could. "Did she have pasta last night?"

"No, chicken wings and steak and a hamburger," her father said. "Bacon and eggs and pancakes this morning."

The Doctor shook in anger. *Don't people know when their body is a cauldron for cholesterol? Why feed it under such conditions?*

He said, "I will solve this affliction. But unless you fix her diet, she's going to have a heart attack in 18 years, this same day."

Neither the father nor the old man, who Smaetag realized, was a sports coach, said anything.

"No doubt," the Doctor commented, as if he had read their minds. *Wish in error,* he said into Smaetag's head.

Smaetag nodded, watching the girl sit upright as the Doctor tenderly checked the hives. "When was your birthday?"

The girl half choked back nausea as she said, "Yesterday."

The Doctor's touch triggered a reaction, and more red mass, like what she'd vomited, erupted from the hive he had touched, and then another.

"Stop the bleeding!" Her father said in panic.

"She's not bleeding. That's a toxin. It's ketchup gone bad."

The father looked incredulous.

"How old in age is she?" Smaetag said, feeling the need to ask the question swelling within her.

"Twenty," the father said.

The Doctor grimaced. *The evil number.* After 2020, nothing related to 20 was going to be safe again.

The girl began choking, then coughed, a thick, green, chunky sputum falling everywhere.

"I don't relish that. Did you make a wish yesterday?" the Doctor said.

"What?"

"Did you make a wish yesterday?"

Her nose started to run, and a thick yellow liquid poured from heir nostrils.

"This is important. Your life is in danger. Did you make a wish yester-day?"

"No. I didn't have cake."

"Are you sure you didn't make a wish? It didn't have to be on a cake."

The girl tried to think and hold her stomach together at the same time. "I-I may have written in my journal, would that count?" she said, ending in a coughing fit.

"Yes," Selva and the Doctor chorused.

"What did you write?" the Doctor asked.

"I wish to be more confident."

The father and coach looked at each other. How could anyone like her need to feel more confident?

The girl recoiled, then threw up again. Salsa or ketchup, with grains of corn.

"Written or electronic journal?"

"What? Why does it matter?"

"It could mean your life. Written or electronic, please."

"Electronic. On my iPad."

"On notes? Do you have an iPhone? Is it stored on the cloud?"

She pulled out her phone and handed it to the Doctor.

No passcode, fortunately. The Wish Doctor flicked through the notes. There were too many. "Quick," he said to Selva, "Use spell check. What could 'confident' end up as?"

Selva was already looking though his thesaurus of corrupted words on his own iPhone when Smaetag said, "Condiment!"

The Wish Doctor finally found the note labelled 'journal' and there, sure enough, amongst other private comments and birthday thoughts, was the notation he suspected: 'I wish I was more condiment.'

On a new note, he keyed in the word 'confident' as 'condifent', switching the letters f and d. Spell check worked its 'magic', correcting the word to read 'condiment.'

He sighed as he deleted both versions, leaving the three letters 'con', in place. The Apple spell check function was perhaps the single biggest source of wish corruption he'd ever seen. No need for evil spirits to trick individuals if the coder who programmed the spell check did their work for them. Left the evil spirits with more time to cause other problems.

It reminded him why, in this modern age, his replacement should be someone like Selva, not just able to derive calculated formulas with no prior knowledge but knowing how to keep ahead of technology. And most especially to stay ahead of hackers, evil or not, intentional or not.

One might think they needed solely a natural phenomenon like a shooting star or a four-leaf clover to make a wish or make it go badly, but it was so much easier if technology was making it happen.

The mere ability to replicate written wishes within technology many, many times allowed the power of wishes to grow. Although a hundred handwritten wishes would always be more powerful than 10,000 electronically-replicated ones.

The Doctor glanced quickly through the journal for context, confirming what he had already deduced through touch and observation. The girl was special. Despite her inward thoughts and doubts, she appeared confident to others. The team of boys wanted her to be quarterback, couldn't wait, in fact, to have her replace the jerk who was leading them to a .500 season.

As with many who had suffered bad wish attacks, she was destined to be a person of importance and influence. If she survived.

The Wish Doctor passed the phone to Smaetag, thinking through his options of helping her as if his mind was a computer (although a faster one than humans could currently think of building). Many times, he had to cause a little damage to fix a risk, but he dared not with this girl. He felt some sympathy, remembering when he had been in a similar position with his own daughter, and how he had failed.

For this one, he needed to more than fix the bad wish. He needed to make the wish come true.

"Smaetag, do you know how to change the date and time on an Apple device?"

"Yes." She nodded.

"Okay, change it to yesterday, with one minute to go to midnight. Do not activate it until I say so. When I do, activate the new time, then flip over to the journal. Finish the word 'confident'. You must not miss a key and allow any chance for spell check to corrupt the word.

"Once 'confident' is spelled correctly, save the file, then flip back to the system, count to 15, and turn back the time to today and now. Selva will give you the time adjusted to Greenwich Mean Time, to the second. You have to have that keyed in and activated before the time on the phone shows midnight yesterday. You got all that?"

Amazingly, Smaetag did as if it had been drilled into her.

"Selva, can you set a counter cloak? Though this was a spellcheck accident, I think there may have been some deliberate act of wish sabotage here."

Selva nodded and pulled a cape seemingly from nowhere.

The girl vomited again, this time no doubt all ketchup; coming fast, not slow. *Good.*

The Doctor touched her shoulder gently. "Hold still. You will be better soon."

He put his fingers to his chin, felt for the right hair, then plucked a long grey wishker. "Go," he said to Smaetag and counted the time in his head.

As she activated the time change on the phone, he touched the girl's eyelash with the whisker. "Say your wish you wrote in your journal before it was spell corrected. Say it now."

"I wish I was more confident."

Smaetag finished typing as the girl said the word 'confident'. The Doctor closed his eyes and channelled the wish captured in his hair through the eyelid into the last second of her birthday, inside the cloak Selva had set.

"Let your wish live!" he said.

Smaetag raised her head from the phone, and it was over.

The hives on the girl shrivelled. She stopped coughing. The dark red under her skin dissipated. Her posture shifted; she grew taller. Lines of worry fled as if in fear from her face.

"I need to see if this worked inside you," the Doctor said.

From his black doctor's bag, he took a needle and pricked her finger. A blood-red substance oozed, but this time not ketchup, or catsup, or Heinz or a generic brand, but blood.

The girl stood, flinging the cloak from her body, confidence oozing. "Thank you," she said. "You will not regret this. I will pay this forward for all my life."

The Doctor smiled. He was not usually sentimental. Unless he was spending too much time thinking of his daughter.

Several of the girl's teammates, all guys, now surrounded her. She was so clearly their leader even as a backup quarterback, even sick. It was odd she wished for confidence, given all her talent, all her potential he sensed. It took, pardon the pun, a lot of balls to do what she was doing.

Maybe he was too tired, maybe he needed something positive to be happening because he had missed a detail. Not able to look beyond the positive, he thus didn't realize the mistake he was making. There were a hundred ways he could have solved the problem, most with minor or no consequences. If he had been thinking clearly, with that great brain of his, no spellcheck would have been needed and he could have avoided the damage he had just caused. Confidence in someone already too confident could only lead to one thing. Overconfidence. Granting such a wish was the one thing sure to catch up to him.

After fixing the wish of condiments, Smaetag might have thought they would have taken a break or rested a bit. Instead, they moved rapidly.

Selva looked at his iPad as if it was a crystal ball. "There are several more wishtakes here, but more dangerous ones globally. I suggest, since we are out in the device, we keep at the more dangerous ones."

The Doctor concurred. He hadn't felt this tired the last time they had taken in students and still managed his wish load. This year the wishtakes were more than double, so he was glad for Selva to take the lead.

Back in the tilt-a-whirl, they were off to Paris, and Brazil, and New Orleans.

"Down this alley," said the Wish Doctor, as they narrowly avoided Alma's mother.

"Whew," he said to Selva, "That's a complication I'm glad we did without. We'll have to deal with it in its own time."

He realized Smaetag was listening and said, "Smaetag that's a wishper. An innuendo about wish magic that must be kept private."

Smaetag had no idea what he was talking about, so had no intention of repeating the comment she didn't understand.

There was little time for talking as they proceeded to correct wish-takes. At every location, the Doctor and Selva rushed to solve a problem that was either threatening immediate death or would in the future. Smaetag followed, observed, listened and felt the ambient wish magic, soaking in more knowledge in a day than she had in a lifetime.

There was the person who had wished they were famous and were about to topple off the top of the Eiffel Tower, creating their fame. There was the child who wished he was a famous football player on TV and was turned into a tiny action figure that stood on an old-fashioned TV. There was a person who wished she had more Brazil nuts, and soon was transported to a tourist getaway in Sao Paulo, where people were dressed in carnival gear but drunken out of their minds, and had almost capsized a boat.

For some darned reason there were three different cases of people who had turned their noses into sausages.

Smaetag saw tricks and wishes and reversals and mirrors and sleight of hand, and learned more than any single day in her life. In fact, she could not have wished to learn any more, for fear her brain would not work. And that was before supper.

After supper there was Bangladesh, then Austin, Senegal, Samoa and Madagascar.

As the day went on, she noticed the Doctor tiring quicker, sometimes resting and Selva giving him a push, then Selva taking charge directly, or saying, 'Let me handle this one.' Their methods were different. The Doctor seemed to use more words. Selva seemed to use more math. Often, they combined the two.

No matter how ridiculous the situation, they seemed to know how to solve the problem. They worked together, complementing each other though their styles varied immensely. She had never realized there were so many wish problems in the world, not even when her wish awareness first came to her.

As darkness set on the Western Hemisphere, they concentrated there, with no time to stop for food; though when she had feared she would become hypoglycemic, the Doctor provided the ever-present sandwish. Which of course was delicious and filling.

At the end of the day, on their last trip in the device, the tilt-a-whirl now swinging only slightly, the Doctor turned to Smaetag and said, "You did well. You helped reverse the worst wish of the day. I could tell you studied and learned. So now I have something for you."

He fumbled in his pocket and handed her a metal object shaped like the castle or rook of a chess set. She took it and he said, "I know you are the oldest student here, maybe one of the oldest students ever, but you are still young at heart. You may live the longest of everyone here. In my view, you are a veteran, but I never want you to forget the lessons that brought you here."

"Thank you," she said. The object was beautiful, and she did love chess, but she knew there was more to it.

"There probably will be a time when I will need your help. It may be when you are a student, or it may be when you have graduated. If I call you, if you can, I hope you will heed my request. I will not call often, but when I do, you can use that to find me. Touch the crown."

She did, and a piece of metal with serrated edges popped up.

"You saw me enter the passwords. Your eyes and fingerprints will now work on the device. The last thing you need to control the device is this."

He smiled and winked.

She understood after the day that his work was often dark and dangerous, but there was time for fun too.

And after today, unlike her new key, she was no rook key.

They arrived back in Baddeck in the sub, sub-cellar of the lodge. As they stepped from the device, all passwords and keys locked, she noted on Selva's iPad the time of 10:59:59.

Both Selva and the Doctor looked relieved.

She could not know they had just made it home before the wishing hour.

13: Volleyball as metaphor

Alma had no doubt the volleyball game wasn't just about recreation. There would be a lesson whether she wanted it or not. Perhaps it was a simple learning of teamwork, something certainly needed, as she could feel the swirling energy of cliques starting to make its way through the class. She already knew whom she was most uncomfortable with and whom she was comfortable with. It was a cruel joke that not only would she and Syd be on different teams, but that they would be opposing captains.

She knew little about volleyball, let alone how to judge athletic talent. She felt almost as inept as a Toronto Maple Leaf scout.

She sat outside by herself, trying to think who she would pick for the volleyball team. She was happy for Smaetag, but a little jealous. She wanted a field trip. Maybe she had had a small taste of one, unintended, already with her trip to the Island of Misfit Toys.

Alma watched as her classmates came outside. Team-picking required all her concentration. She knew she risked making enemies and alienating friends. She also worried about losing to Syd.

She didn't know whether or not it was good that she had the first pick. It would be a lot of pressure. With Smaetag on a field trip, and Erin feeling under the weather, the teams would be even in number.

Even if Syd wasn't wearing a sports jersey and carrying a sports stick, he would still exude from his right arm more knowledge of sports and picking people then Alma could ever imagine.

She wanted to delay the game, but Syd was calling everybody into a circle, a big smile on his face. Of all the students, he was the most obviously athletic, while she was the most obviously unathletic. If you didn't count running. Let's just say that her hand to eye coordination was not in the running for archery school and she would never be a cat, niss or otherwise.

"Okay, Alma," he said. "It's your first pick. let me know if you need help."

She eyed him carefully. He seemed to be enjoying this too much. Was he toying with her or was he teasing her? She knew from her brother's antics they were often closely related.

She closed her eyes. She had a feeling the tallest of the identical triplets was a good volleyball player and was maybe a good choice. It was hard for Alma to bring herself to select her, given her other dealings with the triplet triumvirate. (Alma was impressed with herself she could think of such an impressive word, given all the stress she was feeling.)

She wi,,.no, she *would like* to choose Loretta, but was that because of her friendship and comfort as opposed to volleyball skill? She wondered what to do. Then it struck her.

For Syd, tired of waiting and wanting to actually play volleyball rather than fret about playing, had tossed the volleyball so it hit her on the side of the head.

Most of the students laughed. Though it only stung a tiny bit, she felt her face flush with anger.

"Loretta," she said. The ball had struck some sense in her. Not only was she a good choice because she was a friend, but she would nullify any wishes the other team might use to win. Suddenly, it was important that Syd not get the better of her team.

Loretta ran to her and patted her back. The strength in Loretta's fingers as they touched her back told Alma that Loretta might have more than a little talent.

Alma watched feverishly as Syd indicated his first pick. She nearly fell off the chair she wasn't sitting on when he said, 'Dahlia'.

She was glad he picked one of the triplets; it meant she didn't have to have her on the team. But why did he pick the nicest of the three? Alma was now more likely to have to pick one or both of the other two. She groaned.

She really wanted to pick Nola for her friendships, but she noted the sand under the net, and saw Christian's buff beach body. From California, he likely was a pro at both volleyball and surfing. He winked as she chose him. She liked the jealous look on Syd's face though not so much Nola's disappointed face. She shrugged. There was no easy way with volleyball.

Syd chose Brad. Alma couldn't argue with choosing the tallest students. She noted, though, that the tallest remaining triplet, and tallest remaining student, was looking irritated that she hadn't already been picked.

Instinctively, Alma knew she needed a talent to counter Brad. Staying ahead of Syd was more important now than her fear of mingling with the triplets. Without much thinking, she said, "Wheatgrass."

She nearly grimaced as she realized what she had said. But the logic was incontrovertible. She broke up the triplets, with whatever collective power they held, and she kept her team tall.

The rest of the picks went back and forth. Syd took Nola as if to spite Alma, knowing they were friends, as well as Magnus. Alma took Aaron, but moments later forgot she had taken him, as did Syd. For some reason she always seemed to forget about him, and he always seemed out of view.

She took Daniella, Venn and Juanita, all of whom looked athletic, although Venn was walking with a crutch as he had torn a ligament playing rugby. Syd took Eugene and Tahiti, both relatively tall.

As they went through the group, Alma had a nauseating feeling in her stomach. She knew what it was like to be picked last.

Her eyes were drawn to Christine and to Alfalfa, which made her stomach spin even more. Christine, with all her sleeping, seemed too weak. She wondered if picking Alfalfa would bring disaster, or if *not* picking her could do more damage.

She was staring at Glenda, but she couldn't get the image of her screaming out of her head, so she chose Naomi, while Syd took Joyna from Nigeria.

Alma looked again at Glenda, as if trying to stare away from Alfalfa. She couldn't get the feeling out of her head that this was a test. Glenda had already been made an example of by the Doctor, but she still seemed too smug, so Alma could not pick her. If someone needed to be tested it was Alfalfa; but still, she couldn't pick her. She felt guilty she wasn't thinking of her roommate, but she would have enough opportunity to bond with Christine.

She picked Ian from Peru, Easter Island. There was a mysterious factor about him and it gave her a good chance to learn about him. He smiled, but she saw he was disappointed in being picked so late.

She crossed her fingers, then uncrossed them, hoping she hadn't activated some wish magic. She wanted Syd to pick Alfalfa, but he smiled directly at her as he picked Glenda.

Alma felt her face tightening. Where was the guy that had saved her from the current? It was as if the competitiveness of sport was turning him into a jerk.

It was down to her last pick, Christine or Alfalfa, and whoever she didn't choose was going to be the last chosen. She should have worked through the logic sooner.

Alfalfa would be bitter no matter what, but to be chosen last...

It had to be a test. She had contact with the two of them, but only one of them had been through adversity together. With her.

"Alfalfa," she said at last, knowing she was painted into a corner. If Alfalfa was picked last, it would be her fault. Whatever resentment Alfalfa held toward her would only increase if Alma picked her last.

Alfalfa nodded, tension clear in her face, but she said nothing and walked to join her taller sister as Christine walked to Syd. Was it Alma's imagination or did Christine stick her tongue out as she walked past?

Alma had no doubt know there was a lesson in the picking for the volleyball game, even if had nothing to do with wish magic. No matter what happened at the lodge, she had to be thinking. Everything here was going to be a test or lesson. She might not agree with the methods, there would be no straight logic, but she was determined to learn, and when she next saw her brother, she would be a success.

"Huddle up, team," Syd said, a broad smile on his face, as he gathered the folks in a huddle and slapped backs.

Alma's team quietly gathered around her, but they didn't look to her for leadership in the same way, or in any way.

"Anybody here know how to play volleyball?" she asked and realized that might have been a good question to ask, out of Syd's earshot, prior to the game. She thought she'd been overthinking things, but maybe she hadn't thought enough.

Everyone on Alma's team raised a hand. "You mean you don't?" Ian asked.

Alma shook her head, but felt a smile emerge on her face. There was no way that everyone in the class knew how to play volleyball. Surely someone on Syd's team couldn't play. Unless there was some uncanny connection between volleyball and wishes. If that were the case, why was she there? So maybe she had an advantage.

"Six players go out on the court at a time," Loretta said.

"Six players," Alma echoed, "so some of us will have to sit out, right? Well, since I'm the only one who's never played, I'll sit out."

"Hold," Ian said. "This is for fun. Everyone should play. We are allowed substitutions. We should change a player every time we have rotated around the court."

"Rotated around the court?" Alma said, as if she wasn't the team captain.

"Okay," Ian said, smiling nicely. "Sounds like you need to learn the rules."

He picked up the ball and tossed it to Loretta. "You guys go practice, while I explain."

Loretta grabbed the ball and jogged to the nearest of the two courts set up on the lawn. Alma had thought they were set up for badminton which she hadn't played before either.

She took a moment to look at Ian, his swarthy features. She realized he should have been team captain. *Would* have been, maybe, if it was purely about winning a volleyball game. She was becoming concerned the lesson was for her. Had she drawn too much attention to herself with the trip to the misfit toy island?

Ian, growing more handsome by the minute, quickly explained the rules so she easily understood. She nodded gratefully.

"We should have first serve. You want me to tell him?"

"I'm team captain. I will."

She jogged over to Syd. "Hate to interrupt," she said, finding herself using a smarmier attitude than she intended. "We're going to practice for ten minutes to get warmed up. I assume we are going to play standard rules."

"Yes'm."

If she was ever going to slug the guy that had saved her life in the current, this was it.

"Just one change to the rules," Syd said. "We've always done this at schools I've been at. We will rotate servers after every point, okay? It keeps the game moving faster."

"Absolutely," said Alma as if she knew what she was talking about, "who wants a slow volleyball game? We'll play best of three sets, okay?" she added. "Or do you want to have fun and play all three sets no matter the score."

"We have a lot of people on our team who like volleyball, so we will play to have fun. Three sets no matter how far we are ahead."

Alma wondered if *a lot* meant fewer than *all*, then said, "We will have first serve."

Syd's smile, until today so comforting, was infuriating. "Whatever you wi—uh, want," he said. "Won't make any difference."

"Hmpph," she grunted, not like a magic hog she had read about that morning, and turned away.

Alma watched her team practice. They all had good hand-eye coordination, which she did not. Was that part of the secret of wish magic? The Wish Doctor had alluded to sleight of hand illusions. Maybe there was a connection with volleyball. *At least it wasn't golf.*

She tried not to look at Alfalfa. The girl knew what she was doing, bouncing the ball so it sprung in the air, jumping, hitting it over the net or putting it into position for someone else to hit.

Alma could see the teamwork needed for the game and that her group was working well. She took a quick look over at Syd's side. Christine was not doing so well. Syd seemed confident anyway. Maybe Alma cancelled Christine out.

His grin irritated her more than Alfalfa's presence.

Alma wasn't able to watch for long, as someone, Ian it turned out, lobbed the ball to her. She grabbed at it awkwardly but managed to catch it.

"Do you know how to serve?" he asked.

If it had been Syd asking, she would have made a smart remark about how he was going to be served. "No," she said, wondering what a serve was.

"Come, let me show you. We don't have time for you to watch YouTube videos."

He set his posture, lofted the ball with his left hand and struck it open-palm with his right. The ball went cleanly over the net with moderate force. The opposite side rallied the ball and sent it back. Ian grabbed it. "Sorry guys, just practising the serve to show Alma. That was an easy one. Now I'll ace it."

Ian leapt, stretching his frame, using his full leverage. Alma wasn't sure if her eyes were deceiving her, but a vision appeared around Ian as he leapt, a giant stone face of power.

The ball smashed across the net and dropped cleanly on the ground. Several of the players looked at each other, then hooted. Ian knew how and who to play.

Alma should have agreed with that emotion, but the image of the figure of power had her wondering. It was just like the stones she had seen from Easter Island, where he said he had been born. Had she imagined the image because she had been thinking about how nice he was to her and where he was from?

He tossed the ball to Alma. "Here, you try."

Alma took her place. Alfalfa was on the other side of the net. For a second Alma imagined smashing the ball at her face, but calmed herself. She knew from trying golf that if you hit too hard, the ball would either go the wrong way or not go very far.

She couldn't believe how nervous she was. Although this was a practice attempt, all her team's eyes were on her. She could feel Syd staring at her. She lined up the ball carefully, tossed it, and with her open palm smacked it.

The ball went flying not just over the net, but over all her team picks and the back of the field.

She smiled. "That's good, right?"

Ian shook his head laughing. "You are a lot stronger than I would have thought. That's a great first attempt, but a little too hard. Actually, a lot too hard. Remember what we said about out of bounds?"

"Oh, yeah," she said, as the ball finally stopping rolling when it hit Syd's shin.

She shrugged her shoulders. It was just like golf. She'd rather hit the darn thing 200 yards way off in the bushes or pond, then have it dribble near her feet.

She was ready to try again when Syd yelled it was time to get started.

There was nothing she could do to delay the inevitable. She looked up at the sky. Clear blue in all directions and no wind. The mosquitoes were done for the year and she couldn't come up with another excuse, so there was no escaping her afternoon's fate.

Except maybe... "Since some of us need to sit off, I'll—"

Before she could finish her sentence, Loretta, Christian, and Wheatgrass moved to the side to stand with her. Her three top picks were sitting off to start. She didn't know if that were good or bad.

"Let's get a look at what they got," Loretta said. When she saw Alma's worried face, she added, "We're all going to get a turn. This is for fun, right?"

Alma didn't say anything, but Loretta laughed. "It's okay, we'll beat Syd for you."

That comment didn't help her any. She wondered who else had realized she was developing feelings for Syd, who up until this point had seemed perfect, other than being a little bearish when he ate.

Syd was on the court already in short sleeves. Unlike Alma's team, his four bottom picks stayed off the court. She wondered if he saw this as a test as well. She wanted to talk to Loretta about it, but not with Wheatgrass so close.

Ian took the first serve for her team and, with no mercy, jumped, driving the ball right in front of Syd, who scrambled awkwardly to try to hit it, but couldn't.

Syd showed no sign of frustration, but his eyes were suddenly more deeply focused.

Ian winked at Alma.

They rotated positions as per Syd's rule request and Naomi took the serve. Alma had to hold herself from jumping as Naomi hit the ball at least as hard as Ian had, and with seemingly less effort. How did she and Syd let her go so low in the draft?

Venn took the third serve and was not as clean. Brad managed to knock the ball up, so Nola had a clean shot, and volleyed back. This time Venn hit it past Nola. Score 3-0.

Alma could tell Venn was hampered by his bad leg. If he was healthy, she thought her team might just have a chance, even with her as captain. She was beginning to think she liked volleyball. (Especially if she didn't have to play.)

Syd was now chanting. "Let's get 'em, team." Which she thought was a bit of a bad sport chant. He was not a guy who liked to be down 3-0, apparently. Even in the early going of a friendly match.

Alma couldn't believe she was rooting for Alfalfa as she took her turn to serve. "You can do it, Alfalfa!" she yelled.

The triplet, appearing taller than her short status, looked at Alma quizzically and started a rally that Ian ended. 4-0.

"Wha hoo!" Alma found herself yelling as Syd's face turned redder.

Juanita now had her turn to serve. Alma glanced over at Syd and he was puckering his lips, as if kissing someone or blowing air.

Juanita looked to be making a fine hit, but sneezed as she hit the ball, so what would have been a professional strike floundered. The ball cleared the net but was easy to return. Brad did, which started a sustained volley.

Alma sweated in worry and anticipation. She looked at the sun. It was warming steadily.

She turned back and wasn't sure if it was the sun in her eyes, or her own sweat but her vision seemed blurred. Syd looked indistinct, as if a second more blurred image was surrounding him. It also seemed to make him taller.

"Let's go." he said. "4 to 0, easy to get back from; 5-0 never." He'd seen several hockey teams, even the Leafs, come back from 4 to 0, but rarely 5-0.

The ball volleyed once more, then landed near Syd, right inside the line. He'd not a made a move, judging it would hit outside the line.

Alma couldn't help herself and waved to him.

His look immediately froze her face. There was no sense of the gentle teddy bear she had come to know. This was definitely not a side of him she had seen before.

Daniella took her position. She looked athletic, but more like a gymnast than a volleyball player. Her serve was smooth but easily returned, though Ian smoked it back like a bullet at Syd.

Alma saw the blur around Syd again. She glanced at the other players, they were all distinct shapes, no blur. The blur made him taller, his hands bigger, wider, like giant paws, almost if there were claws at the end.

Syd had to jump to his left, hand up, stretching his height. Alma's eyesight was not the best but she was sure it was the tip of the blur that hit the ball, and returned it in front of a startled Ian.

5-1.

The ball was now turned to Syd's team. The same blur surrounded Syd as he served, and suddenly the score was 5-2. He looked relieved and the blur seemed to fade.

Was Alma imagining it, or was he using some kind of magic? Was this some part of a wish that stayed with him, or that he had made now?

She needed Loretta on the court. If Syd was using wish magic, Loretta could neutralize it. She looked helplessly as the score now went 5-2, 5-3, 5-4, and then tied. Her team looked at her as if suggesting, she suggest a change.

"Time out," she said as if she knew what she was talking about and called the team over to the side.

"Would you mind if we substituted Loretta in? I want to test something."

"What's that?" Alfalfa asked almost conversationally, as if she didn't have a burning hatred for Alma.

"I have a feeling Syd is using wish magic. The Doctor said there are wish dampeners, but not everywhere. I think the volleyball courts are areas where you can make wishes. I think if we put Loretta on the court, she neutralizes Syd's wish."

Venn said, "I'll come off. I probably shouldn't be out there."

"What happened to your leg?" Alma asked.

"I made a wish about playing rugby and it didn't go so well. It's a long story. Ask me later."

Alma nodded, hoping that wish was over and wouldn't affect their game.

The team went back on the field with Loretta in place, Syd having made two substitutions in his team. He took himself off for a while, and the game played out like maybe it should have, Alma's team leading with a slightly better performance.

It was 13-12 when Syd substituted himself back on.

Alma watched for the sign of his blur. He was clearly refreshed, jumping like a maniac, diving, cheering. She saw a small haziness around him, but no paws, no height, and the score stayed balanced. There was no way to tell for sure, but she thought Loretta was making a difference.

The score went to 24-23, and Alma's team served to win, but Syd's team volleyed.

Loretta dived, landing awkwardly on her hand. She writhed on the ground, then had to be pulled off to the side.

Selva came out the front door of the lodge at her yell. "Come inside, I'll look at it," he said, touching her other arm gently.

Alma's eyes bulged as Loretta was escorted into the lodge and Syd's blur returned.

Alma's team couldn't win the point, so the service returned to Syd. 24-24.

The serve went to Syd and his decided paw spiked the ball, 25-24. he grinned at her with a toothy smile.

Cheater, she thought, then watched as Nola scored, winning the game.

Alma felt her whole-body grimace in tension.

Syd jogged by to grab a water bottle. "Noticed you sat out the whole game," he said nonchalantly to Alma. "Maybe with Loretta hurt, you should help your team."

Alma gritted her teeth. *Why is he being so unbearable*, she muttered to herself, starting to feel like a mother bear whose chair had been sat in, and her porridge eaten.

As the second game started, Alma marched defiantly to the court. She was doing everything she could to hold herself back from making a wish. She was even angrier than when she had made the wish toward Alfalfa. Or the wish toward her brother.

The Wish Doctor's words echoed in her head. "Do not make a wish with ill intent. All wishes of ill intent will sooner or later hurt the wisher. It is the one absolute rule of wish magic." It was what had taken her to the Isle of Misfit Toys.

She dared not wish to turn into a great volleyball player, fearing some deformity or disease, or being turned into a volleyball. She had to play well without a wish. She positioned herself in the sixth position to delay the scrutiny of serving.

Syd took the first serve of the second game. Right at her. She got her hand on the ball, but it fluttered out of bounds. He waved at her. She couldn't tell if his blur was back, she was so angry.

Ian returned the next shot, keeping the ball as far from Syd as possible.

As the game went on, it became clear that, unless he was in one of the corner positions, Syd could reach the ball no matter where it was on the court. *How is he using a wish that doesn't backfire?* Alma wondered. Was it a wish that was operating before he came into the game?

Syd dominated the game, the score climbing to 6-2 when he stepped out as most of his team changed for rotation.

Another thought struck her. *Is Syd's wish backfiring in fact, in that he is angering me so much I may never speak to him again?*

Alma made to step off the court, wanting solitude to think, but Ian held her in place.

"You didn't play any of the first game. Hang in there."

The play was a little more even with Syd off the court. Alma's team narrowed the gap. Unfortunately, it was her serve as the score settled to 7-5.

She took a step toward the sideline, ready to motion someone to take her place. Alfalfa had whispered to her that it was a good strategy in volleyball to make substitutions so that you had your strongest server in place. Ian shook his head. He patted her on the back.

She readied for the service, knowing she had to control how hard she hit. She bore down on the thought of being relaxed. Which of course made her hit the ball even harder. Right over Syd's head on a trajectory out of bounds.

Syd, clearly eager to defend against her, didn't even try to judge if the ball might be heading out of bounds and leapt, arms stretching, the blur definitely back. He struck the ball, returning it, but the leap had taken so much force, his hit was too light, though directly at Alma.

She nearly froze but got her arm under it enough so that she was able to lift it up just high enough for Ian to smash it back right through Syd's legs.

Alma jumped up and down clapping, and moved to the next position, Ian winking at her.

Venn yelled, "Way to go Alma."

In fact, the whole team was clapping. Even the two triplets, the twiplets.

The clapping didn't last long, though. As if the embarrassment of the last point had given him wings, Syd dominated the next several rallies, with Alma's team scoring only one point. It was now Naomi's serve and Alma swore she saw her flipping a coin just before she served.

The score crawled upward to 13-7. Alma needed to do something desperate. Emotion was ruling her, but it wasn't fair Syd was using a wish to win.

"Can I take a second time out?" she said to Ian, who nodded.

"Can any of you make a wish and control it without having bad side effects?" she said without any preamble.

Her teammates looked at each other.

"Kinda why we are here," Ian said. "To learn how to do that. I can make a wish, but it will go off in an unplanned direction."

Alma looked at her team. She had two of the triplets. *What kind of power do they have?* "Can you synchronize a wish?" she said to them.

Ian looked worried. He knew the harm that could be done by wishes. "What does that mean?"

Wheatgrass answered. "Synchronizing wishes makes us reinforce each other's wish. But it has to be perfectly repeated or said exactly at the same time. The simpler the better."

Hmm, Alma thought. "So, does that mean there's a larger risk of the wish going wrong?"

Neither twiplet said anything, but she could see it in their faces. It made what she was thinking more difficult.

"Is there anything around here that could aid us in a wish? Like a shooting star or wishing well?"

It was a good reminder she needed to get that tattoo.

The group looked around but no one said anything until Juanita pointed to the ground, and there was a rather large four leaf clover.

Without thinking, Alma picked it up. Maybe she could just wish her team good luck.

Juanita said, "Didn't the Doctor say that good luck was often associated with good wishes?"

"I don't know," Ian said. "Good luck can go bad just like bad wishes. Sometimes it works in reverse. I have had my best luck when I had a black cat walk in front of me on Friday the 13th. The day I had a lucky rabbit's foot when I was travelling in Australia, a kangaroo punched me in the face."

For a second volleyball seemed unimportant, as the group didn't know whether to laugh or run to their rooms and get rid of anything resembling a lucky rabbit's foot.

Wheatgrass looked at him. "Sorry about the kangaroo, but does everything work for you in opposites?"

"The only time I had a wish go right was when I wished for exactly the opposite for what I wanted."

"Interesting," Wheatgrass said. "Works for us sometimes that way, but not always. We have had problems with wishing the opposite, like having the wish taken literally."

"Alma," Ian said, "you are not seriously thinking about making a wish here and causing trouble. I really would like to have a pleasant afternoon."

Venn pointed to his leg. "We'd be ahead in this game if I was at full capacity."

Alma smiled, trying not to look at Alfalfa. "Yes, I know wishes can go wrong, but look at Syd when the action gets going. He's using some kind of magic and nothing's going wrong."

"Okay, granted," Ian said. "But let's try just a little wish and not take too much risk."

Alma held up the clover. "Let's use this to reinforce a wish. Let's say, 'We wish no wish made today has unintended consequences.'"

"Tried that once," Ian said. "Not so good."

"Did you have a four-leaf clover?"

He took a long moment sucking air, Alma's bright eyes, making him want to agree. "Okay, tell us the wish first. I reserve the right to veto any wish that's too crazy."

"Everybody else with me?"

There were uneasy nods. Everyone was tired of Syd's unbearable behaviour.

"Okay, let's all synchronize."

"No," Wheatgrass said. "We have trouble synchronizing and we are used to it. Let just the two of us do it."

She and her sister were already holding hands and reaching out for the clover. As the twiplets touched hands, whatever differences between them disappeared. They seemed to be of exactly the same grain. There was no telling them apart.

Alma handed the clover to Wheatgrass, but Alfalfa grabbed it.

"We wish that no wish made today in this volleyball game has unintended consequences," they said in perfect unison. Their words were slow and careful.

There was a slight tingling in the air and the clover turned brown and fragile. The team looked at each other.

"I don't like this," Ian said. "We could win the game as someone broke a leg, or inherit all the problems of an Olympic volleyball star."

Alma felt a chill in Ian's words, but hardened herself. The Island of

Misfit Toys had been scary at first, but she had found it a challenge. She hadn't realized how boring her life had been previously, despite the presence of a magic orb. She knew she had to be careful, but she wasn't about to hide. They were there to learn to manage wishes. Especially when someone else started trouble by casting the first wish.

She turned to Naomi. "Do you have a lucky coin?" she said, knowing full well she did.

Naomi would have tried to avoid the question, but the conversation was making her nervous and she had been flipping her coin in her hand as a coping mechanism.

"Yes, but—"

"He's using magic against us," Alma said. "Can you help?"

"I can only use the coin three times a day. I already used it on my serve, and I always keep one in reserve."

"So you have one use left? Can you make another wish, that anything we wish for does not backfire within the course of the game? Our other wish should protect us outside the game, but this should make the game safe."

"Okay," Naomi said.

She flipped her coin, sun glinting off it, then caught it gracefully. As the coin was in the air she said, "For any wishes our team makes today, I wish that they do not backfire."

Alma thought the wording could be improved. There was maybe room for error with the use of backfire, but she wasn't about to stop now.

"So," she said, looking at Ian, "do you feel okay? Any wish shouldn't cause damage right now."

"Still nervous, but, okay, how do you propose to make a wish? I definitely am too much trouble to try a pure wish, and I bet Venn doesn't want to, either."

Alma looked around the group. "Anyone here comfortable in making a pure wish?"

Everyone was shaking their heads, some more vigorously than others.

Alma looked for something to wish upon. She saw blue winged insects that had seemed blurred with the not-so-distant water.

Dragonflies.

"Look, quickly," she said, "two dragonflies. We can make a wish on them. Is anyone here of Japanese descent? For them the dragonfly is good luck. For Germans and some European cultures, they are bad luck."

Venn shook his head. "I have some distant Japanese blood, but not much. I'm not taking chances 'til my leg heals."

Alma felt someone or someones staring at the back of her head. She turned to look at the twiplets. Neither of them looked the least Japanese from far away.

"We are one eighth Japanese," Wheatgrass said. "We can make a wish. What do you want us to say?"

Ian and Venn waved their hands wildly. "Make it simple," Ian said. "We don't know what we are doing. Even though you set out some wishes that might protect us, they might not."

"Then what do you suggest?"

"Why don't you just wish that our team plays well in the game?"

"Don't say well," Venn said, "and have us fall into a well. Say that you wish we play excellent volleyball."

Alma was a little disappointed. *These big strong guys are scaredy-cats.*

Then she saw the third dragonfly. She was an amalgam of so many races. Maybe there was Japanese blood in her background. Did Romas wish on dragonflies? Did Filipinos? Did Acadians? Maybe they would all cancel each other out.

"Sounds alright," Ian said. Naomi and several others nodded.

The two sisters held hands, stepped on the volleyball court and said as if in one voice, "We wish we play excellent volleyball for the rest of the match."

At the same time, Alma standing behind everyone said silently, mouthing the words, "I wish to win the game."

Everyone held their breath, but nothing immediately went wrong, so they resumed positions on the court.

Syd was sitting out as they resumed, but Brad blistered one across the net. The twiplets, responded, volleying. Naomi drilled the ball, taking back the serve.

Naomi set a spike and Wheatgrass followed.

13-9.

Alma felt her muscles loosen. She was less tense than, well, before she had ever held a crystal. Even though the ball didn't come to her, she could track it better.

Alfalfa served next. Brad returned and this time the ball came like a fastball at Alma. She could see it as clear as day, as if it was moving in slow motion.

She set and levered the ball so Naomi could smoke it past her competitors.

13-10.

The stroke felt so good, Alma turned to look at Syd, and suddenly felt sad. She couldn't take her eyes from him. He was hurt. She didn't know why.

And then she realized a ball was coming right at her. Too late.

As the ball struck her nose, she realized playing well didn't mean you won every point. She inhaled, holding the blood from oozing out of her nose.

Loretta, now coming back out of the lodge, her arm bandaged, said, "Are you alright?"

Alma nodded. It was time to get her head in the game. Or at least out of the way of the ball.

From then on, her team played, well, excellently, if not perfectly. The only time they were scored against was when Syd's team placed a perfect ball that no human could handle. But anything humanly playable, they played, and made their own perfect scores.

Alma took some time out to soothe her nose. She watched in marvel as if it was an Olympic match. There was too much skill on the court for wish magic not to be in effect.

She held her breath as her team tied the game. When they did, Syd returned, and so did she.

The two teams traded points and volleyed until the game stood at 24 apiece. And Alma's serve.

Her instinct was to sit out, but her wishing confident self felt she could not leave the game in anyone else's hands.

She felt adrenaline pumping, watched as Syd motioned his teammates back to the deepest position each could play. They knew she could not control her temper.

She felt the strength well in her. She could pound the ball, but could she control it from going too far?

She looked at Syd and thought of her brother. How many times had she had to hold her tongue in frustration to avoid upsetting the whole family? How she had turned her frustration into control, holding the crystal.

She tossed the ball, wound her right arm backward, looking to pound as no volleyball had ever been pounded, and then hit it as gently as a breeze, in the slightest of arcs, so it dropped on the other side of the net harmlessly.

Her team whooped and roared. 25-24. They needed one more point.

It was Ian's turn to hit, and Alma couldn't be happier. He had been magnificent to watch before the wish to play well; but afterwards, it was like watching Apollo, especially as he stripped to a singlet.

He winked at her and hit the ball with such force her ears almost exploded.

But if he hit it with force, Syd moved so fast, it seemed he was on ice skates. His hand reached so far it was as if he had a hockey stick. The blade of the invisible stick scooped the ball and lofted it so that Nola could set it nicely. Brad dropped it just inside the line.

The game was tied.

She had almost had him. Yet she had a wish in action. Would the dragonfly wish be as powerful as a shooting star wish?

Dahlia took the set position. She had been relatively quiet though the game, the weakest of the three sisters at volleyball, despite her place in the picking. Alma felt her team could take back the game.

Except she had never seen such confidence in a face before. Alma glanced at Dahlia's two siblings and noted concern in their faces.

She wondered why Syd had picked Dahlia. *Does he know something I don't?*

Dahlia hit a rather mediocre shot right at her sister, Wheatgrass. It was the kind of shot that was easy to return, but one that came awkwardly, so that Wheatgrass's reflexes took control, returning it awkwardly.

Brad returned it easily toward Wheatgrass, who was twisted out of position from her awkward return. She danced toward the ball, leaving awkwardness behind. Yet she misjudged her shot, which dropped harmlessly out of bounds.

26-25 for Syd's team.

Alma felt her confidence failing. Syd's team was up by a point and had the serve.

She gathered all her will. She was excellent at volleyball. The team wish made it so. Her wish made it that they would win. She glanced at Alfalfa next to her and saw her, too, gather confidence.

"We are excellent at volleyball," they both thought in unison.

It was Joyna's serve. She'd been an average player, better than Alma before the wish for sure, but mediocre against some of the talent.

Alma gulped, because if they didn't win this serve, they would lose the game. She suddenly realized that, if they didn't win, there was a wish she had made despite the others' request she take caution, still open, still hanging. Ready to go wrong. The twiplets' wish had come true. The team had played excellently, but if they did not win....

If the ball came anywhere near her, she would have to make an extraordinary effort. She could feel the power of the twiplets' wish. She was an excellent volleyball player.

Syd held up his hand, just as she felt ready. "Time out."

What could she say? She had taken two.

Syd didn't leave the court, but showed Joyna a motion, then grabbed her by the hips, gently positioning her, then pulling her back.

Surely, he was doing it to improve her motion, but the touching bothered Alma, she wasn't sure why.

It couldn't be Joyna's gleeful grin, could it?

He whispered something in her ear. She laughed, no, giggled. They were flirting! Alma's determination became that much stronger.

"Let's go," Ian said.

Joyna lifted the ball and hit a line drive perfectly placed between Alma and Alfalfa.

Alma felt the power within her, the confidence from it. She had never dived toward a ball in her life, not in any sport. She dived now.

The ground jolted her, her angle and muscles and movement absorbing the shock. Her arm reached and stretched into the distance. Her eyes could see the ball clearly, her angle toward it perfectly, her hand and wrist held power, and slid under the ball just before it hit the ground. She lifted it upward with just the right amount of force, so that it was in a perfect position for Alfalfa to volley.

Except under the wish of being an excellent volleyball player, Alfalfa had dived as an excellent volleyball player might dive. She felt the same extraordinary wish-powered skill of volleyball as Alma, her hand reaching under the ball also pushing upward.

But Alma's momentum was maybe just a second too fast and the two girls collided, heads smashing against each other. Alma felt her skull quake.

Miraculously the ball lofted from the touch of the two hands, just before the heads collided. Wheatgrass from out of nowhere, in an impossible reach, was able to put it across the net.

Toward Syd, who promptly punched it directly toward where Alma and Alfalfa were lying, clutching their respective heads. He hit it with such force, only the two of them could reach it.

Had they not collided, surely one would have returned it with the magic power of volleyball on their side.

Both tried to stand, Alma up quicker, her determination so strong. Yet even the power of the wish couldn't stop her head pounding enough to stop the triplicate vision. So, when she swung and connected with the ball, in a beautiful stroke, it was the ball in the middle and not to the one to the left as it should have been.

Syd let out a great cheer and was hugging Joyna, while Alma could only put her hand to her head, the pain rollicking.

Next to her, she heard great laughter, as her team rushed together, clapping, cheering, maybe even jumping, the residual excellent volleyball wish lifting high in the air.

Alma turned to them, not understanding why they were so happy. Even Alfalfa was excited and smiling at her.

"Why are you so happy?" Alma asked.

"Because it was a terrific match and we played such excellent volley-ball. All of us knew that we played better than we should. We all learned how good we could be if we trained. Two of us made unbelievably spec-tacular dives at the end. If your boyfriend wasn't cheating, we would have won."

Alfalfa turned away to continue the jumping and cheering.

Alma thought about it. Given what the Wish Doctor had said about bad wishes, she figured a bad headache was a small price to pay for how well they had played. The score could have been a lot worse. She didn't feel embarrassed, like she had in almost every other sporting contest she had ever participated in. She didn't even feel embarrassed by her collid-ing noggins with Alfalfa.

Still, she worried what it meant that her wish hadn't come true.

14: The Shupershark

Sunday was a day of rest. "Except if we are really needed," said the Doctor.

The Province of Nova Scotia was very late in changing laws that allowed Sunday shopping. He would have preferred to keep things as they were, of course. While one might think having a day of rest enforced every week would create more wishes, it was untrue. People with more rest, and time to enjoy life, were more satisfied and less likely to make wishes (especially those prone to manipulation).

If the Lord could rest from making the world, he could rest one day a week from making wishes or solving problems of wishes.

Plus, he was feeling all of his 29 years, and was quite tired.

Since many of the fairy folk had come to the highlands of Nova Scotia in the last three centuries, the relative rest of Sunday had grown on them. As they set the tone for their family and friends in European locales, the total number of wishes that went bad, certainly those driven by fairies, were minimized.

The Wish Doctor began his day with oatmeal, which he had started eating long before his years in Scotland. Even he wasn't immune to cholesterols and things that clogged his arteries, things so hard to explain to his students. Few people realized that heart disease was still the number-one killer. It was an evil, old wish by a very embittered warlock who had resented everyone. It had happened before the Wish Doctor's time, but the wishtory logs outlined his predecessors' attempts to stop it.

They weren't able to completely reverse the evil wish, it was so powerful, but they had stopped the warlock from worse things, and had kept the evil wish limited to causing heart and artery damage. It would be a cruel world indeed if the warlock's wish as intended had come to fruition in full intent, stopping medicines from working, stopping bypass operations from happening.

It was still warm enough to be outside, so he donned his cloak, greeting the students who were up. He had heard about the volleyball game and was content that emotions that needed to be brought out had been. One had to be aware of one's prejudices when dealing with the magic they dealt with.

Nova Scotia was a friendly place, and welcoming to most strangers, but it, too, had some prejudices.

Of course, most of his students were from other places, but like anywhere, people soaked up prejudices from their new place. He was glad Nova Scotia, or most of Nova Scotia was working hard to deal with its old prejudices, though it sometimes felt like new ones were being discovered more quickly now that the growing population was hooked on social media. Still he'd been to a lot of places, and you could do a lot worse than the province shaped like a lobster.

As nice as the Bluenosers were, he had to admit the Newfoundlanders were funnier. He wished he had a student from that province this time round. Well, Mrs. Higgins was still willing to assist him from time to time, and a moment of her time was delivered pleasure by the bushel.

He walked along the shore. If he hadn't been travelling by kite so much lately, it would be a nice day to let out a line and set one of the kites flying. It was nice not to think about air currents on his day off.

Tired, even though it was early, he sat down on a rock that had warmed nicely. He looked off into the view. His friend had certainly picked a beautiful place for the lodge. It was a setting where one could truly recharge.

He brought up the predictor calendar on his watch. It looked like another busy week, with frontal highs conflicting with backward lows. By Thursday, he figured he'd need a full day of weversing. He was too tired to even think of the full phrase, wish reversing.

He touched another button. Gears clashed and collided. He hit the buttons in sequence and, in the language of the crow, sent a message of Morse code. He hoped her Splendiferousness wouldn't mind switching days and giving her lecture on Wednesday.

He wasn't sure why, but he was feeling a bit lonely. Seemed it usually happened when a new class was settling in. Maybe he was thinking too much of his own past, and education that once felt promising but had turned sour.

It was nice to have Selva staying on for the course, but he could not keep him forever. He was fascinated by his energy. He was out running, training for a marathon, he said. The Wish Doctor shook his head. Even in the days with his peak energy, he'd never imagined wanting to run 26 miles. Why Selva would want to be in the middle of a crowd of people, so full of wish therapy, he couldn't tell.

He noticed a slight movement in the water, when his watch dotted and dashed. Her Splendiferousness was more than happy to come on Wednesday, if he wouldn't mind having two servings of fresh blueberry grunt ready for her.

He sighed. Blueberries grew aplenty in Nova Scotia, caused by an ancient wish that had dire implications at the time, but over the centuries had proved a blessing. They formed the basis of the grunt dessert, one of the best desserts he had never not wished for. It was a fair exchange, though he'd have to travel four miles to the magic hog who gave the grunt its special flavour. (From his actual grunt, which was magical, not from bacon or ham. The magical hog was after all protected by a true and irreversible wish from ever being butchered. There was no rule that hogs, if clever enough not to be tricked into making a bad wish, could not make such a wish to protect themselves.)

In deference to the hog, who did indeed ensure that blueberry grunt, or any type of grunt for that matter, was the tastiest one could imagine, the Doctor had never even tried to think how the wish might be reversed. Not even if the Doctor's neighbour, on whose farm the hog lived in wallowed pleasure, begged.

Unlike Selva, he would not run the four miles to the hog. He was definitely taking a Sunday drive for that visit.

He looked back out in the blue of the Bras d'Or lakes. There was the fin again, a very peculiar shade of orange. Which could only mean one thing. The Shupershark was back in its home waters.

The Wish Doctor went near the shore, wondering if his old friend might want to chat.

The soundtrack of *Jaws* began to emanate from all directions, as if there were a million sonic speakers (the best kind). 'Din na, din na, din na.'

The Doctor smiled as he heard the Shupershark replay his favourite practical joke. To the sound of *Jaws* he would say, 'Din na, Din na, Din, na,' as if he was truly chasing his next meal.

The fin rose higher above the dark-blue and slightly-choppy water. The Shupershark's head and eyes crested above a wave.

The Doctor walked briskly along the dock, and the great shark came cruising alongside. "Hoy, Hoy! Good to see you Shupershark, how've you been?"

"Been well," said the shark with a gangster's smile. His entire demeanour seeming menacing, if you didn't know how he had metamorphosed into one of the greatest ambassadors of the sea. "Heard you been busy the last little while."

"Yes. The work goes through phases like that. Sometimes busy, sometimes not so. This has been one of the longest busy phases I can remember. Maybe the busiest ever."

"Well, you humans keep multiplying. That's got to make a difference."

"It does, though many are turning from the old ways, so a lot of wishes aren't heartfelt. And you? You still happy to be a shark?"

"Are my teeth sharp?" The Shupershark's grin widened. The story of his sharp teeth could fill a whole book and the Wish Doctor also smiled, knowing the story.

"I'm just getting the hang of it," the Shupershark said. "More and more sharks are accepting me. The dolphins and porpoises aren't scared anymore, so we have boundless discussions on philosophy. They have a great sense of humour too, without the angst most of your human comedians have."

"I can still help you turn back, you know."

"I appreciate the offer. I'll keep it in mind. Ask me again in about twenty years. Still a lot of ocean to explore and many creatures to meet. There's some crazy stuff going on here under the sea; you humans surely wouldn't understand."

The Wish Doctor nodded. He had spent a lot of time under the water. After all, there were a lot of wish in the sea.

"I do appreciate all the help you've given me, so I didn't stay a mindless predator. Transition wasn't easy. But once I got used to being a shark, it's been great. I don't even miss the cards anymore."

"I'm glad we could help your ill-timed wish become a positive."

"If I'd stayed a normal shark, I don't know how I'd feel. Since I got over my initial panic of being turned into a Shupershark, it's been fantastic."

The Wish Doctor smiled. It was good to see an old friend at ease with himself. He truly was unique in all the worlds. "So, what's been keeping you busy?"

"Had a lot of visitors, mostly sharks, coming to ask me advice."

"Oh, so you're like a counsellor now."

"Exactly. Now that I've turned vegan, I got to use my wisdom teeth for something."

The Wish Doctor shook his head with a gentle laugh. The Shupershark was his kind of personality.

"Lot of them asking about my diet and about wishes, of course, but a lot of them hearing all these conversations about the environment. They have long oral traditions, so remember many warmings and predictions of crisis. They are wondering if this is truly different."

"That's probably a better question for Selva. I don't know the answer, but it's probably a good idea that we all work together to have solutions to keep pollutants out of the air."

"And the sea."

"Yes, and especially the sea."

"Way I been hearing it, both sides of the argument are pretty entrenched. One side just says stop everything, without good alternatives, and not remembering what pitiful conditions you humans lived in, and many still do, before energy. And the other side, heads stuck in the sand, not thinking about the future, not wanting to try any solutions. Can't figure out why they just don't get together and consider that everybody's interest is special."

"You sure you don't want me to turn you back human? Sounds like we could use someone like you up here."

"Too much stress for me. I need the feel of cool water around me at all times to keep me relaxed. If you want someone to do that, I'd suggest one of the Pacific dolphins that can speak English and French as well as Polynesian. They are much better at politics than me and don't get so stressed about it."

"Maybe. Haven't had a bottlenose up here since someone confused a French dauphin."

"Ha, that's a good one. Did that happen?"

The Doctor smiled. "Of course, how could you even doubt it? I hate to interrupt this chat, but I have to go see a hog. URME is visiting on Wednesday, and she wants a grunt."

"Oh," the Shupershark said, not exactly excited. "Wednesday you say. I'd drop by tomorrow to see if you can chat, otherwise, I'll be swimming out early."

"She's still mad at you?"

"Holds a grudge, she does. You'd think she'd be the most appreciative of a practical joke make by Shupersharks, but not so much. I'll try and swim by tomorrow. Otherwise, you can look me down when you're out in the kite."

The Doctor laughed as the Shupershark submerged. Oh, what whimsy and fun the world could be, if we could all just get along even when making practical jokes. If only all wishes were pure, and there were no value judgments placed on them. Why, if sharks, even shupersharks, could learn to live without eating other animals and have a philosophy of reason, and a hog's grunt could form the tastiest treats, how great would the world be?

The Shupershark's visit had not just brought a smile to his face but a renewed energy. His mind was a-pop again.

He wondered if Selva had yet grasped the project the Wish Doctor hoped for him: the Unified Wish Theory.

~

Alma was worried about the consequences of the wish to win the volley-ball game. Her mood continued to sour as the skies darkened ominously, and sheets of rain descended on Baddeck late Sunday afternoon. She could not see how her volleyball wish would come true now even with bad effects, but still she worried. Was the sky trying to tell her something?

Syd ignored her all Sunday, which was just as well, since she had planned to ignore him. Plus Venn and Ian now felt more comfortable sitting with her. Even Alfalfa had joined the group for meals and was at least tolerable company.

Alma didn't have any great insight into the music riddle, and so spent her time working on wish reversals, saying words backward. For no particular reason, she practised on the phrase 'I want to win the game'.

15: Musical wishes

The rain from Sunday continued into Monday morning. Despite all the lively discourse of music, the class was a little bit surly under the dark, sombre clouds. The glow of volleyball triumph and recognition of excellent mastery of the game had dissipated under the dark skies.

The rain had helped the Doctor sleep, and he awoke refreshed and in a good mood, certainly more so than his students. A visit from the Shupershark always lifted his spirits. He was also much looking forward to Wednesday and her Splendiferousness and the taste of heavenly grunt.

He walked into the class, proclaiming "Da da da da!"

There was barely a smile. He had planned to put Beethoven's Fifth on the list, but decided not to. That one was too easy to guess, and with too many bad pronunciations, too easy to cause additional wish ripples.

"Are we feeling musical today?" he asked.

The response was as varied as the students. Some felt the homework was a useless waste of time, some that it was a useful waste of time, and a very few found it a useful use of time.

The latter few, of course, would likely become his favourites, but not necessarily. There were many ways to gain wish knowledge, which was why there were so many approaches in his class.

"Hoy, Hoy! Let's get right to it. If you understood the assignment, I'm sure you have your thoughts ready and collected."

"I'm guessing Drake," Syd said without hesitation, as if his thoughts were ready and collected. "He is too good, too talented. Canadians don't usually get that much success."

Syd's favourite song was one by Elvis Presley, of course. Of modern performers, though, he did indeed prefer the male duck. A prize to the reader who first posts the correct name of Syd's favourite Elvis song to the Facebook group fan page 'Tales of the Wish Doctor'. No jumping ahead in the book to find a clue to the answer. The clue's already been given.

The Doctor laughed, both at the fourth wall breaking and at the suggestion of Drake, whom he was quite fond of. Though he never called him on the telephone or cellphone or photophone or wish phone.

"That's a good guess, and good rationale, but we have never detected Drake having needed to make a wish. Not since his *Degrassi* days for sure. Where he was cleared of ever smoking weed. Degrassified. Okay, made that one up. No idea if Drake ever took weed, though it's none of my business."

"He never needed to make a wish. But he does give wishes to others. NBA championship. Need I say more? Let's try again. I want the person whose success in music is due to making a successful wish."

"I'm guessing Chopin," Brad said. "His name is open to misinterpretation."

"You are correct on that. In fact, he is often associated with death wishes, but he did not gain his talent through his wish. His talent was quite natural."

"Hank Williams," Christine said.

Alma gave her a look. Was that what she had been humming all night? Could that word she kept repeating like a snore really have been 'Jambalaya'? Christine had clearly not wished herself to have musical talent, or, if so, the wish had gone wrong.

"What is your reasoning?"

"He was successful in a short period of time; his success brought him pain and anguish like bad wishes do. It was probably a strong wish, since residual power carried over for generations. The power of his music resonates like a wish harmonic."

The Wish Doctor pondered. He'd only speculated that Hank had received his talent from a wish. He'd only met him the one time, and Hank had been drunk on something other than wishkey.

He wasn't at all surprised at Christine's knowledge that wishes were part of physics and were indeed a part of the scientific laws that had created the universe. Just because she slept a lot didn't mean she wasn't thinking when she slept.

"You make a good case, and I don't know for sure. I can say he is not on the official record of having made such a wish."

"What about Tay—?" Christian was in the midst of saying when the Doctor interrupted.

"Do not say her name! Use the code or her power will reach us even here."

"What about the fast clothes maker?" Christian said. "Very good looking, very talented, records everywhere. Apparent unhappiness underneath."

"Insightful, but we are going to leave this matter. This person is an amazing talent but incredibly powerful. If they were to be accused of gaining their talent from having made a wish, they might decide to enact a terrible revenge. Not themself, of course, but the terrible influence that sours them."

"But, but the fast clothes maker makes her own decisions."

"No, no, no," the Wish Doctor said. "Be careful not to think some things. Wish or no wish, some power is not to be tampered with."

Every single female in the class nodded, and some of the males. Christian thought he was being insightful, but suddenly there was a gag on his mouth, so he could not speak.

The Doctor was almost showing fear. Reputation might be overstated, and he was confident he could extricate himself from any single wissue. But these were troubled wish times and he needed all his energy. Some damage could be permanent.

The triplets were about to say something when Brad, wearing a tight white t-shirt, said, "This discussion has been critically bogus. Of course there is more than one musician who has earned their way through wishes. How could so many live such devilish lifestyles, be so famous and be so ugly? If we are going to have sympathy for the devil, then let's just say the truth of it. At least one group of musicians that received their talent through the wishes was the Rolling Stones."

"Who?" asked some of the younger members of the class, who hadn't done as much of their homework as they should have.

"Exactly," Eugene said. "I am satisfied."

The Wish Doctor smiled. "I believe we have a winner."

As always, it was important to attune his students to popular culture, for there, at least in appearance, the most successful wishes existed. Of course, in some, the most danger existed.

He had no time to tell them the true story of Strauss. The Stones were obvious, but at least someone had made the deduction. Who knew if anyone in the class even knew of Strauss? In his last class there had been few who knew, in the class before that more; but mostly because of the soundtrack of *2001: a Space Odyssey*.

Was there a more beautiful piece of music than 'The Blue Danube'? Had there been a better wielding of cinema and music? Well except for the same movie's opening sequence.

Strauss had not been the most despicable man in the history of the planet, not even in his life in Vienna; but still, he did not deserve the credit for arguably the most beautiful piece of music. The Austrian mountain fairies did, of course. Strauss did not know his tune, which he thought derived from a wish, was actually one played by the fairies for centuries before. There had always been such magic in waltzes.

Oh, for one more night to be at a ball in Vienna! Corrupted wish magic or not, was there not a more magical time to be had?

For a moment, the Doctor was melancholy, thinking of lost loves. Then he righted himself. He had adopted duty as his love, and as he had for the longest time, he loved duty with a passion few could.

It was good he did, for if he didn't, there would be no human alive today, at least on Planet Earth.

16: A short chapter of a day

Tuesday was a short chapter of a day. With her Splendiferousness coming on Wednesday, with a presence and a lecture few could match, there was hardly any bother trying to provide anything exciting. The Doctor thus spent the morning outlining some dull but important facts of historical wish magic. He outlined key tales, and the truth or fiction of each. He summarized some thoughts on how to use tales and stories. He also spent some time on the science of riddles: how to defend against, how to answer, how to identify word play and word work. He debated whether to get into a discussion of fairies, but decided against it. It was too complicated and too important at this stage.

And he wanted to avoid infantile giggles. Principles of diversity had not advanced enough for that (although the LGBTQIA2s+ community wasn't doing too badly in Nova Scotia, the actual acceptance of the ancient fairy people was not where it should be), but later in the semester his students would be more appreciative, as they learned each other's secrets and quirks.

It was interesting how those who felt the most odd and different were usually the most susceptible to wish magic, even those who didn't know why they felt that way.

He supposed everyone was odd in their own way. It was what had made his job so interesting back in the days when there was enough time in a day to fix a few bad wishes, or help good wishes, then relax and enjoy the world.

He had a salad for lunch then did a quick check to see if he could spot the Shupershark. He waved at a fin in the distance. No doubt headed for warmer waters.

Then the Doctor was off to Southeast Asia, using the device to travel quickly amongst many wish needs. He had thought about Selva's advice and would introduce the device on Friday, after her Splendiferousness' lecture. It always took a few days after her appearance before anything else could seem as magical. He doubted even mature Smaetag would be able to keep her stories of their adventures completely silent much later than the weekend. There would be much interest in field trips, even if she only leaked a little of what had happened.

It was a busy afternoon and a busy evening. He was challenged more by the number of wishtakes, than by the danger of any single one. That was what was likely to trip him up, a more moderate wish problem in the midst of many minor ones. When he had few, even when they were more dangerous, he was best able to handle them.

He arrived late back at the lodge and took a sniff of ordinary alcohol to help him sleep. He needed to be refreshed for her Splendiferousness' appearance.

~

Alma sat with her teammates from the volleyball team at supper time and, for no particular reason, in the midst of a boring conversation, she realized she missed Syd. They had not spoken, not even exchanged glances, since the volleyball game. Monday and Tuesday had been long hours of avoiding him, trying to forget he even existed.

He was not necessarily a better conversationalist than Ian or Loretta, but there was something about him that gave her comfort. Having saved her life was certainly a big part of it.

She found herself sighing. He had been so nice and then turned out to be a jerk in the volleyball game. She wondered what percentage of the time he was a jerk.

She'd read in an article that Canadians were nice except when you put a hockey stick in their hands. Syd often had his hockey stick with him and hadn't been a jerk. What was he like when he played hockey? He still had all his teeth. Or at least she thought he did.

Is volleyball the only thing that makes him a jerk?

Alma hadn't realized it, but as she sat musing, she was staring right at him. She must have done it for a long time, because her table was now half empty, and he was staring back.

Maybe pretending to not be staring back, but definitely staring back. She wondered how you nonchalantly turned your eyes away from someone who was pretending to not stare at you, while you were staring at them.

She didn't have a chance to solve the problem because he was on his feet now, walking toward her. As if by magic, all of the other members of her team, Ian included, stood up and excused themselves.

Syd seemed nervous as he came up to her, and she had to admit she had a flutter inside.

"Hi," he said shyly, as if he was in class.

"Hi," she answered, not quite looking at him, not quite looking away.

He looked around to make sure no one was nearby. "Why are you so mad at me?"

"How do you know I'm mad at you?"

"Just 'cause you won't talk to me, doesn't mean no one from your team will talk to me."

"Oh."

"You know I was just trying to have fun, right?"

She looked at him, a bit bewildered. "Your fun might be different than my fun."

"I wasn't trying to hurt anybody. We were on opposite teams, and captains."

She shrugged.

"Sports are important to me. I take them seriously. Sometimes I get a little carried away."

"A little?"

"Think of the things that are important in your life. When you are playing the flute, don't you want to be the best you can be? I noticed you weren't very vocal in Monday's musical discussion. I think you were afraid to focus on music, because you didn't want anyone to know about your flute playing."

Alma felt herself getting angrier, then realized he was probably right. She would have played any other instrument if she could, but she was good at playing the flute. Then she got angry again, as he distracted her.

"It's like that for me with sports, only I get really intense. I'd do anything, have done anything, to be good at sports. Including making bad wishes."

"No doubt," she said. "Why were you using wish magic in the game?"

He sighed. "I can't control myself sometimes. It's hard here. Some spots block you from making wishes, so you don't have to think about not making them. When you get to a place that's not blocking you, it's harder to resist. I don't know why, but I can make wishes come true really easily. And, yes, they cause bad things to happen unintentionally sometimes, but not always. It's taken me a long time to learn what trouble I can cause. The first time they asked me to join this school I refused, but so much has happened, I couldn't refuse this time. I'm really trying hard to control my wishes.

"Look, I know I can be a bit of a bear sometimes, but I didn't mean for you to get hurt. I didn't know you hurt your head, or I would have seen to you right away."

He suddenly dropped to one knee as she started to soften. If Ian had really liked her, he wouldn't have left her alone with Syd, but she was kinda glad he did.

"There's something I would like to make a wish for," he said, "but I do not want to screw it up with any kind of bad intentions, so I'm using all my control for making this wish. I really wi—, *hope* you can forgive me. I am a jerk when it comes to sports, no doubt about it. But the thing is, I really like you, and someday I will ask you to be my girlfriend, someday, when we have gotten to know each other a lot better, and no one is making a decision hastily or because of the wish."

Alma found herself shocked. Very pleasantly shocked, but shocked nonetheless.

She didn't know what to say, but he didn't give her a chance. He pulled a small object from his pocket and unfolded it. It was a small, pure-white toy bear.

"This is a Beanie Baby bear," he said. "You are too young to remember, probably, but these were real collectors' items when they first came out. This one was really valuable at one time. You could trade it for a fair bit of money still, but I hope you won't."

He held it out to her, and she took it gently, looking into his eyes. They were deep and dark, and unblinking.

She took the bear carefully, knowing she would treasure it. It was a cute little polar bear, as cute as a west highland terrier puppy when it was calm. Around its neck was a collar in the colours of the Nova Scotia Tartan, royal blue with lines of green and yellow.

She touched Syd lightly with her left hand. "Thank you. This may be the nicest gift anyone ever gave me."

"I-I'm glad you like it," he said nervously. "I have also placed a wish in it."

Her eyes lit up in terror at that thought.

"No don't worry about it. There is one type of wish I'm expert in and can control the consequences of. It's how the Wish Doctor found me. I can bring teddy bears alive. If you should ever need help, just ask the bear to help. It will either get me to come to help or will help by itself."

She looked at him, more marvelling than frightened, and kissed him lightly on the cheek. It was fuzzier than it looked, but very pleasant none the less.

He blushed.

"Okay, I forgive you," She laughed, hugging the beanie to her chest. "I love this bear."

He laughed back and for a long while they held hands, the bear keeping an eye on both of them so nothing got out of hand.

"I mean it," he said. "Someday I will ask you to be my girlfriend. But now I'm sorry I have got to go to bed. All this emotional stuff tires me out."

Alma laughed and gave him a quick, tight hug. Her mood had changed as much as a mood could change. "Good night. I'm so glad we came to the school together!"

Syd stood, bowed, smiled, then walked away, tired but with a skip in his stride.

Alma's eyes lit up in realization. Her wish had come true. She *had* won the game, only not the one that she had thought she'd been playing.

17: The Mother of All Guests

"Our guest lecturer today is one of my best and oldest friends," the Wish Doctor said, almost as if it was true. "She is also a little mischievous, so you better all be on your best behaviour. Let's not have any of you transformed into a newt, please."

Alma tried to look at Syd, on the other side of the triplets. He was nearest the guest lecturer and she wanted to gauge his reaction.

"I will not tell you her full name in its original language because we don't have time for all the syllables, but we will call her by a lesser known first name. For today, you can call her URME. Please give her your capital attention at all times.

"She is going to give you a broader view of magic, and the powers that underlie wish magic. This is one of the most important lectures of our program. We are very privileged to have her. It is fortunate that this is one of the many places she calls home. We are lucky she happened to be available for the day. Now, please welcome URME!"

URME smiled at the genuinely-polite clapping as she took to the middle of the room. Her soft brown skin and dark hair positively glistened with health. Her eyes and eyelashes looked as if they could be sprouts of growth on a tree. She was as alive as any being on the planet. Even her nails and hair were alive within her. To say nothing of the infectiousness of her smile, which spread from luscious moist lips without makeup to her cheeks, and past to the corner of her eyes. Her body was relaxed, yet exuded power and femininity. She was not skinny, but curvy in all the right places.

Her clothes were casual earth colours, but patches of red, yellow, orange, and blue, meticulously placed as if by an artist like Van Gogh, made vibrant her entire being. It was if she was channelling power the way a tree channels energy from the earth into leaves and buds and fruit.

"Good morning, everyone. It's another perfect day here on the island. Don't you all agree?" Her voice was silky like honey.

Alma Faye found herself smiling broadly in return. URME projected caring and comfort, like a warm but vibrant mother. The question was so simple and so mundane that if it had come from anyone else, it would be easily ignored. From her, it seemed to take on broader meaning, like she was proud of the day, like she had something to do with it.

Alma's eyes bulged. Was her imagination running away with her?

She could spend her life in the presence of URME and never be uncomfortable and never be bored. But she had the terrible sensation you should never mess with her.

Alma nodded her head vigorously and called out, "Yes, yes." She had a feeling this was going to be an extraordinary day indeed.

URME took a long drink of water, placed her recyclable cup on the podium and walked to the first row, still smiling. "I suppose the Doctor has told you a bunch of crap about wishes being the only type of magic."

The class laughed as she radiated mirth. Alma would normally find the word crap annoying, but somehow it reflected URME's earthiness.

"He is not entirely wrong. If you think of the typical kind of magic, where you want things to disappear, or know something you can't possibly know, or get a girl to like you when she probably shouldn't, or a boy if you are inexplicably into that kind of thing, or just want to be invisible, it really is a wish, no matter what you call it. It doesn't matter whether you use a wand or wish on a shooting star. So, yes, for all intents and purposes, magic is wishes."

Alma took a sneak look at Syd. He was staring intently at URME but she knew he was also trying to look at her, his future girlfriend, out of the corner of his eye.

"Is the fullness of reality just a series of wishes, or is there something that interlocks them? Is there a deeper meaning that unites all the things we see and feel?"

The Doctor, as he always did at this point of the lecture every twenty years, looked toward Selva. Could he not convince him that the unified wish theory was their most important undertaking?

"I believe there is. When you wish to be invisible, you are creating actions and reactions that impact things far beyond you. The world is integrated more than any of us know. We are interdependent on all the things around us. Is absolutely everything in the world necessary? No, but we have to protect as much of everything that exists, because we do not know all the impacts. We have lost so many species in the world of living things, and we continue to exist, but what we don't know is, has the fullness of the world been lost? I believe it has. I believe the fullness of life has been diminished because impacts our forefathers could never have predicted caused things to disappear. There is no mystery as to why the dinosaurs are so fascinating to us.

"That doesn't mean that things can't be improved, not just by protection but by selective removal. Let us take the subject of mosquitoes, all 4000 varieties. We have yet to find value in mosquitoes. They are, in fact, nature's mistake."

For some reason URME seemed contrite.

"Nature might have supplied the power, but it was an ill-fated use of magic pulling on nature that created mosquitoes. We can assume, in the lingo of your headmaster, that these creatures can only be the product of a bad wish."

The Doctor nodded his head vigorously. Not only did he believe mosquitoes were the result of a fundamentally bad and malicious wish before his time; he was particularly attractive to their bites.

"There is always a different perspective, though," URME continued. "If you really like dragonflies you might like the mosquitoes. Dragonflies are their one constant predator. Or maybe you think it is a good thing that some of the world's surplus population is taken by disease. I might give you the dragonfly argument, but I have to disagree with you about the virtues of disease.

"The only other argument of any merit is that mosquitoes force people to stay away from nature, keeping themselves locked in their buildings, leaving nature to its own resources. Over time, nature has a way of protecting itself with more useful guardians, so I rebuff this argument, too."

URME paused, then smiled again, opening her arms as if hugging all in the room. "Do not mistake my anger about those itchy biting, moronic insects for anger at all the creatures of the ecosystem. Save those, I love all the things lovingly created in the world, and their purposes. I mourn for creatures lost and hope for new creatures yet to be. Now let me return to the true fabric of my talk."

The Wish Doctor let out a voluntary sigh. He didn't mind her mentioning the mosquitoes, but sometimes she did go on too long on the topic. Someday, maybe, he could look into curing the world of mosquitoes. It was definitely an itch that needed scratching.

"Let's say that, being polite to the Doctor here, his theory is correct, that all magic is wishes. Is it the wish by itself that creates the magic, or does the wish merely pull on forces that already exist? Could it be that there are many types of wishes, some of which contain their own power, others that merely create a path for other power, or some perhaps that create power? Understanding the power behind wishes will help you control them and will also help you undo them.

"It is argued that there is only one true source of all power in the world, even if that power takes on many forms. First you must look to the power to see if it is alive and sentient and wilful. Did it, or does it, have a motivation in the way that it grants a wish? Is it malevolent, seeking to trick, or is it literal?

"Is the power passive, to be shaped and used, but by a skilled hand? Is the power represented by a symbol or an entity? If so, is the entity a gateway to the power, or are you using their power?

"Is there a difference between borrowing and taking?

"There are among you some who already can conjure magic, but you don't yet know the power underneath. To avoid the unforeseen consequences of magic, you must begin to understand this power.

"Now, let us ask, what powers there are that we can draw upon?"

Christine, who now had an appetite to collect wishes, raised her hand. "Where I come from, there are stories of many powers, but I believe the most important is the power of our ancestors."

URME smiled. "Yes, and too often these days we ignore the potency of that power. There are many aspects to the power you allude to, some dangerous, some not. I believe in the third year at this school you will explore this power."

The Doctor nodded.

Scottish Erin raised her hand. "There is the power controlled or spawned or gate-kept by the invisible ones, the fairies, the genies," she signed.

URME nodded. "The tales are well-recorded. The truth behind these powers is more complicated than any tale can tell. These are very active, as you will learn in detail soon."

Alma raised her hand, bursting to answer, but URME shook her head. A voice like honey seemed to say in Alma's head, 'Let's leave that to last, shall we, so that my lecture may be more effective?'

Syd, who was typically quiet in class, certainly quieter than he was on the volleyball court, raised his hand. "I do not know if this is a power of itself, but the power of imagination?"

"Say more."

"It seems to me that some things happen by accident and we can't have control over them, but there are other things that happen because we imagine them. If no one had imagined that we could talk through a device for hundreds of miles, then I doubt that would ever have happened. Nor would there be mechanical devices in the shape of a car that can turn into a robot."

URME looked pleased, then troubled. It was a thought that she had meant to say. Had in fact said on every other visit to the School of Wish. She turned to the Doctor, sensing the varied power of the youth in the hockey jersey.

The Wish Doctor shrugged. Her Splendiferousness enjoyed knowing all things, and the mystery of all things, and was always thrown off her stride, when something didn't quite make sense right in front of her. "Very good," she managed, "You have set upon a critical principle, no matter the source of power.

"What else, my lovelies?" she said, recovering. Her confidence assured her she would know more of the young man before the day was done.

One of the triplets was resisting her hand, as it tried to raise by itself, as if by instinct drawn in by URME'S natural charisma, while the other two tried to thwart her raising it.

URME turned to look at them with a knowing look and said nothing, waiting for them to respond to her look. Few, if any, could resist her for long.

Their secret was more obvious than Syd's, yet the final impact and form it would take was still unknown. When she had the chance, she needed to warn the Doctor.

At last, the shortest one said, "We have been talking mostly of wishes going bad. Does that mean that one of the powers is from the dark world?"

URME shook slightly, noting the Doctor's reaction. Were Selva present, his logic might have demanded immediate action. Better to draw out possibilities than leave them hidden, he would say.

"Is there another word you mean when you say 'the dark world'?"

The girl swallowed. For a second, she looked nothing like the other two twiplets.

URME couldn't always command the truth, but she could often influence it to appear. After a struggle with herself, the girl said, "Evil. The devil. Goblins. Witches."

URME stepped back. That was a little more than she was looking for. Though she could interact with many powers, she preferred those of the light that helped make crops grow. "Powers are not always as straightforward as they may seem. To label anything evil or the equivalent without knowing the pure motivation may be to risk the very thing you state. Let this be said, though: poor motivation can lead to wrongness. Whether it is by the need for survival or indignation or pain or anger, forces can be corrupted. Our focus must be to understand the motivation and try and stay away from labels.

"My advice is to be assured of the rightness of the mission of this school, which is ultimately to help people, and maybe, as just rewards, have the odd desire come true for ourselves. Let us say no more, for to give a positivity to this negative form is to give it more credence than it deserves."

There was a silence in the room, a dangerous silence that lasted a moment longer than the Wish Doctor cared for.

URME broke it at last with a grin. "Now let us speak more truly of the powers that are most in vogue and of one that I best represent.

"Let's begin with the magic of mathematics. I am told that it is built into your curriculum. That is good. Much of the world can already be described by mathematics, and much more will be, even some of those things that appear to us as imagination." She looked toward Syd.

"There is magic in certain types of mathematics that can be used to power wishes. The combination of math and imagination can create power itself. When this is welded to logic and creativity, we can create power where none existed before. It will take you a long time to learn all this, but all I can say for sure is this is true.

"There is the power of story, of human mind, of emotion, of objects: familiar things like shooting stars. There is the power of indignation. But it is too close to the dark world, so please resist it.

"There is one power I prefer overall. Alma, I think you had a suggestion."

Alma stood up a little nervously. "The power of nature."

URME stretched out her hands, reaching to the outside. "Yes, it is all around us, already there for the using. There will be many times you will need to call on it. Be gentle and polite. Nature has its own will and purposes. When you ask her to do things, she must do so willingly and not be coerced. Coerced she can be, but it's like damming a river. Coerce a river with a dam and sooner or later the river will find a way to go around and through and over the dam.

"It is good it is so, for even the tricksters who abuse nature for their trickery and selfish purposes must be careful. The root of their undoing is already present, and mucking around with nature will get you hurt pretty quick."

Every eye of every student was focused on URME. None could avoid her gaze or her words as she talked of the power of nature.

"There are forces beyond nature. Life and death are serious forces that touch nature and they can be utilized in making wishes, but they are beyond nature itself, and even more dangerous to tamper with, and even less predictable.

"You students must understand all these powers. You will not learn them all at once. You must learn which ones you can use, and what prices must be paid to use them, and which ones you must never use.

"Some of you may have guessed my other names, that my name URME is an acronym. If you have done so, I ask you to keep it to yourself. There is the power in the unravelling of a name, even if that isn't my true one. If you someday need to call on me, and some of you will, I will be able to come more easily if you guess on your own."

Alma looked up. She was sure she had guessed URME's identity, if not the exact words of the acronym. But she was sure with time she would figure that out, too.

She watched in fascination as URME made one last gesture and, as if by magic, a small container appeared before each student.

URME spread her arms wide and smiled with her whole body. She chanted:

> One little gift to leave you drinking;
> With some magic to keep you thinking.
> Consider the beverage that stands before you,
> born of magic or a wish that's true?
>
> Solve that and increase you knowledge of magic.
> Else your end will be quite tragic.
> If you need energy to help revive,
> Drink this and feel again alive.
>
> This elixir, once drunk, shall quickly refill,
> But only for those with true strength of will

In the biodegradable container before Alma was a red beverage.

"Take one taste, then save the rest for later." URME commanded.

The class did as they were told. There were gasps, and whirls of glee. For not one, not even the one who was child of the chef whose skill was made of a wish, had ever tasted anything so sweet.

URME ended her lecture to grins and applause. "Now let us go outside, and, as is the custom of my nature, I will ask that you all accept my hug."

It had been raining earlier, but as they stepped out of the lodge, the clouds were parting, and a huge rainbow hung over the Bras d'Or. The fragrant perfume of the last blooms of the year bedazzled everyone's sense of smell.

Syd was the first to receive URME's hug. Her natural perfume put the blooms to shame. Her hug was warm and cozy, like a snuggly bed with a puppy. *One could live forever in such an embrace,* Syd thought. *Motherly, not romantic.*

As URME hugged Syd, her confidence in understanding bore fruit and now she knew the secret he himself did not know. She whispered sweetly in his ear, "Do not repeat yourself."

He heard but did not understand. At least not yet. URME knew she could hint no more than that. He would need to solve the riddle on his own.

As she hugged Smaetag, she repeated the Wish Doctor's quip, knowing it would get a smile. "Good luck, my rookie." She wondered if Smaetag would become the mother she was originally destined to be, or would the coming distractions, well, distract her?

URME had a rare moment of uncertainty as she saw the row of similar-looking girls. Did she hug all the triplets at once, or one by one, or did she let them choose? She had to hug both ways, for it seemed that two of the three wanted everything together, while one was willing to be independent. The togetherness was more for protection than sameness. First, she needed to hug each alone.

So, with ease of distraction, there was suddenly old Sarge, a border collie, pulling gently on Alfalfa's dress, and Brad tripping over Dahlia.

With URME moving quickly to greet her, Wheatgrass came reluctantly alone to hug.

URME hugged her warmly, but her tone was somewhat stern. "Choose thy path and thy sisters' path carefully. There are several ways for you yet to go. Remember, I fear no path, and will block thy way, if you choose yours poorly."

The other triplets came soon in succession, missing the opportunity of a group hug.

URME's words to each were similar but different, and not for mortal ears.

Then she took the hug of all three together, to get a sense of them together and what difference that wrought from being alone. She gave them the warmest hug she could, wanting them to understand there was a place for them. Even though she feared at least one would choose a path she would one day need to block.

Alma let the triplets move away before she proceeded with hesitation. She did not know how to hug. Not in any meaningful, unawkward way. Her family had not been huggers, at least not to her. They had certainly not left any desire for a hug.

So, when URME's welcoming arms swung around her and the great warmth of URME's body and personality enveloped her, she felt as if she had discovered heaven. The hug was so comfortable, despite her own arms and thin body providing little comfort to URME, that she didn't want to leave. It was as if she had found her true mother, or her mother as she could only dream of, or as if Alma had been the crystal hugged close to her mother's bosom.

It could have only been seconds, but the hug seemed to last a wonderful eternity.

Unlike the warmth of a most comfortable bed that made you want to sleep, the hug seemed to give her energy as if electricity, pure energy, was travelling into her body.

Alma felt URME's sweet breath as URME whispered into her ear. "You are but a caterpillar, my love, and yet to blossom. When you do it will be as a beautiful butterfly and as independent as a shooting star. Inside you is a will and spunkiness that will challenge the status quo. Do not be afraid to be yourself. Your time is coming."

Alma nodded, trying to hold back tears. She could feel herself changing already and knew more was to come. She had never felt such pure love from any other human being. She did not want to pull away.

As they separated, URME winked at her, and turned to the next.

Alma paid no heed. All of the students were there on their own journey. For this moment, she needed to reflect on her own.

As each student hugged the great Splendiferousness, the Wish Doctor watched her whisper an insight into each student's ear. It was not for him to hear. Some insights he would guess and learn on his own if he already hadn't, for others it was none of his business. Even if on occasion these insights were at cross-purposes to his own. It didn't matter much; this was all a matter of tactics, in which they might differ. For all their differences, they sought the same purpose.

As URME hugged the last, the winds of the Bras d'Or began to swirl, but not of her doing and not of her blessing. They were not in and of themselves a problem, but they foretold of a much bigger problem.

"It has been a great time," she said, her hands outstretched. "Thank you for such wonderful attention, and such great hugs. We will meet again as needed, but as there are things that require my attention, I must go. Be good to yourselves and the world around you."

The Doctor came to say farewell. "Can't you stay for your blueberry grunt? I used up a considerable amount of good will in its making. It is of the finest quality."

"No doubt," she said abruptly. "I would not turn it down after I earned it, but the winds are serious. I need to go."

And in a swirl of dust and storm she was.

The Doctor stared as she left. For once, he could not even think of a pun. He certainly didn't want to say anything to offend her.

She was one person in the whole world, you did not want to anger.

It was unfortunate though, that she did not have time to give her warning regarding the triplets.

18: The danger of birthdays

The pleasure of URME's hug was still with Alma but was fraying a little as she began to fret about the triplets. There was something odder about them than normal.

For the day and a half after URME's lesson, Selva commanded the class, delving more into the power of math as magic. He also began to outline in more detail the types of wishes that could be made and that needed to be reversed. All leading to one of the most crucial lessons of the semester, and the one Selva clearly remembered receiving himself those years ago.

The Wish Doctor's ninth lesson:

"A birthday wish is almost always useless. Unless you want to invite trouble. It is the single type of wish most likely to go wrong."

"Why?" Christian asked. "I make birthday wishes all the time."

The Wish Doctor felt like shaking his head. "I'm well aware of that. It's why the true colour of your face is purple and why you always have termites in your pants."

The other students laughed. They thought he was joking.

"To get a birthday wish right, to make it so that the language is airtight, that nothing can go wrong, to overcome a granter's desire to make the wish go wrong, is almost impossible.

"Since a birthday wish is yoked to the turn of time, it can rarely be used or boosted in conjunction with a pure wish, making it even more difficult to use, or use without something going wrong. Yet even so, a birthday wish sometimes may be your only way to solve a problem.

"Everyone has a set of birthday wishes, and though you may give them away, no one may take them. In an emergency, if you know how, you may borrow a birthday wish from the future, as long as it is from a year in which you will still be alive.

"To make a birthday wish work takes great effort. If you can do that, you can make almost any wish work. You must use the principles I will discuss with you now in making most wishes, but most certainly for birthday wishes. But first I have to make you promise one thing."

He looked around the class with the most serious expression the students had yet seen upon his face. "You must promise me you will not make a birthday wish until you have entered the fourth year of this course, and then only with my blessing. We cannot continue until you promise me this. Raise both hands if you agree."

Syd was the first to raise his hands, and most followed quickly. Alma could not help looking at the triplets. Not for the first time did they raise their hands last, but they did.

The Doctor took a deep breath and called for all eyes to look upon him, and all ears to hear. If ever anyone of them were to learn enough to be his replacement, they must learn this lesson.

"To make a wish happen, you must never have just one wish to use. At minimum you need nine wishes. Nine wishes, so maybe, maybe, you can make one come true. Without disastrous circumstances.

"Use the first three wishes as protection wishes, to protect the actual wish you make. Use them to guard against misinterpretation, whether wilful or unwilful.

"The last three wishes are mitigation wishes, wishes to make sure that another wish doesn't come along and undo the wish you made. The power of magic is always in flux and seeks to find balance. An unprotected wish may seem okay today, but other wishes will seek to undo what you have done. Unless you mitigate your wish, it will be undone.

"The fifth wish is usually the best wish to be your actual wish, but you must know the nature of the granter, if there is a granter. There are some who just detest the fifth wish. If it is a wish using natural forces, then five is the best because nature favours the number five." The Doctor held up his left hand spreading out his five fingers.

"Use the fourth wish to protect that the wish does not later become unbearable. We call this the Midas protection.

"The sixth wish is a wish that allows you to reverse the wish you just made in case something went wrong. We call this the escape wish.

"Your studies over the next year will be difficult, let me warn you. You need to learn how to harness the power of nine wishes to make a wish to help undo a wish that has gone wrong. And, rarely, for the pure benefit of the wish itself. Most of you won't be able to do it. Most of you will be sent home. But maybe one of you or two of you will learn to do it and be granted tuition for a second year.

"I wish you well," the Wish Doctor said.

For the rest of the morning, the Doctor outlined the types of wishes to use around the main wish. "We must master these first. Only then can we talk about how to construct the language of the actual wish."

Any student who thought wish magic would get them out of the study of language or math, now realized they were mistaken. Some of them even realized that it was a fitting trick, that those who hoped to avoid study and hard work by making wishes would have to do the most studying and hard work, if they were to use wish magic. They would not be able to use a wish to make their work lighter.

After lunch, knowing he would have a busy afternoon, and freeing Selva to handle wishes born of math, the Wish Doctor decided it was time to introduce the device. Rather than take everyone through all the codes and locks, he had the device transport itself to the front lawn.

As the students gathered there, almost all eyes opened wide as the device appeared. For some who had watched an episode of *Doctor Who*, it looked familiar.

The difference was that the device looked unique to each beholder. For just as all wishes are different, so was the appreciation of the great device born of wish.

Alma saw a device of shimmering crystal that almost blinded her. Smaetag had said it looked like the seat of a tilt-a-whirl. Alma looked to her, and there was a little awe but not surprise that the device looked differently.

Syd saw a device that looked like a hive with concave circles, and a curved door. The triplets saw three different things, but would not admit to what they saw. To Daniella, it looked like another carnival ride, the spider, while to Brad it appeared as a hot air balloon.

Every student saw the device in a form much different than it was, as a thing not of magic. Which was true enough, since it was powered more on science than magic. But without the little dollop of wish magic, it could not work. For the students to see it in its actual form might be too harrying, so a little underused wish allowed them to see it in a way meaningful to them. It also protected itself from misuse.

Although there had been several accidental attempts to use the device, there had been only one purposed unauthorized attempt, and that the Wish Doctor would not allow again.

He began, "Some of you have already heard stories from Smaetag. They are all true. Sometimes we can undo wishes from far away, but often the only way to fix them, is to travel to them. We have more than one way to travel in our work, but behind us is the cleverest, most powerful, but most dangerous way.

"We sometimes call it, affectionately, a device, but what it really is, is a wishmethere."

~

Alma looked at her classmates, to see if they were as impressed as her. Somehow, she understood the device could receive telegraph signals no matter where it was. Was the thing itself a wish or was it inside a wish, or was a wish inside it?

The triplets grinned greedily. Alma wondered what that meant. Was she interpreting them wrong, or did they think they were going to go Bonnie and Clyde (and another Clyde) and steal the device? She figured the Wish Doctor would have some trick built into the device to protect it. They were a mystery to be solved for sure. She hadn't decided if all three were evil, but even if they were just mean, they surely weren't her kind of people.

Syd seemed particularly excited. When he took a step toward the device, he began shaking gently, then his arms suddenly spasmed.

Alma seemed to be the only one to notice and moved to hold him steady. "You okay?"

"I think so," he whispered. "I just had a strange feeling like I'd travelled on this thing before, and it wasn't a good experience. I haven't though; they brought me here on a kite. Maybe I somehow dreamed about this."

Alma wondered. Her mother sometimes talked that way about premonitions. If all magic was wish magic—was the crystal somehow powered by a wish, or were the crystal and maybe Syd's premonition managed more by science? Just science she didn't know.

She had not time to conjecture further. The Wish Doctor was speaking again.

"The wishmethere combines forces of technology and wishes. It can track wishes and travel to them, taking the most glorious shortcuts. The ride can be bumpy at times, as Smaetag has learned, but the views, well the views, are nearly perfection.

"Each of you will get a turn to travel in the wishmethere, usually when we go on your first field trip. As needed, we will take it more frequently. It can be configured to take as many as seven passengers at once. If you learn sufficiently on your field trip, you will be given a key that will allow you to ride the wishmethere again. Be warned, earning the key requires more than just going on the trip. You have to be ready, and hold yourself with composure no matter what you see. You must put to use what you have learned to help, and put to use the knowledge of when to do nothing, perhaps the most important truth of all. As you should have learned by now, sometimes the greatest strength is to refrain from making an unnecessary wish.

"Assuming each of you will succeed, you will each receive a key that is unique to you. You cannot share it. The device will not allow you to. If appropriate, and necessary, sometime in the future, some of you may travel in the wishmethere on your own."

He snapped his fingers, and the wishmethere sputtered, sighed, and then was no longer there, leaving a group of amazed faces.

"Okay," said the Wish Doctor. "That's it for the week. Hard practising on your assignments. Loretta, Nola, you will come on field trips with me tomorrow. Have a good weekend, everyone."

The class broke into small, chattering groups. For everyone it had been an exhausting and exciting week.

Alma's mind was almost overwhelmed. There was something here she hadn't understood before. Wish magic was potentially more than just magic. There was science to it. It could be understood, manipulated, explained. Perhaps. At least there was more to it than memorizing spells, or knowing which wish to say when, or yelling louder at a crystal, or knowing when not to wish. Although it was clear now how important that was.

The studying of math was no coincidence, and Selva's presence was critical. While the Wish Doctor was clearly more of a social arts kind of guy, Selva was a man of science and logic. And the wishmethere, a combination of science and wishes. It was almost too incredible to be true.

Alma had been concentrating on studying the wish side of their courses, looking at math as just a learning exercise to control her excitement, but now she understood she had to focus on the math and science, too.

She'd have to if she someday wanted to build her own device.

She looked at Nola and Loretta; gazed at Smaetag. She was jealous and anxious. *When will it be my time to ride the wishmethere?*

19: The plot thickens

After a late supper on Saturday, and no word from Nola about her field trip, Alma wasn't going to sleep easily, so she grabbed Syd by the hand and took him down to the beach.

They sat on a thick, bleached driftwood log, at first talking then just looking at the sky as it turned dark. The air was growing cooler. There was no thinking of going into the water as there had been the first day she met Syd.

He volunteered to build a fire, but she just wanted to look at the stars and sky without any other light source. You could see so much more of the sky here than in New Orleans, so many more lights, stars and planets. It was beautiful with the frogs croaking, and a few last crickets of the year chirping.

She snuggled against Syd, her arm around him, his arm around her, and they mostly stared at the sky, so comfortable with each other's presence they didn't need to talk.

Who knew volleyball wishes could have so much power? Alma could not have known that when they left New Orleans, stuck holding the crystal, she would be this happy.

Her mother had studied astrology, sometimes used it to supplement her readings of the crystal. It was always more accurate, she said, if she got correlation between the two.

Astrology, Alma had always thought, was pure fiction. In her weakest moments, she might have agreed that the crystal had powers, but not astrology. She wondered, though, if there was something behind it. If wishing on a star or a shooting star had power, could there not be something to astrology?

She sighed. She certainly didn't miss her mother, but if she could make a wish, it might be that her mother would teach her what she knew. She wondered how her brother was doing.

And then Syd distracted her, pointing to the sky. A shooting star.

She held her breath and made a roaring noise in her mind. She'd almost made a wish that would have had her talking to her mother for hours, maybe taking her away from the school.

She let her breath go and he looked at her oddly, and then both looked up. Another shooting star and then three more in succession, each brighter than the one before.

They looked at each other, and instantly kissed, delicately, lightly.

Alma pulled away feeling giddy, Syd grinning. "Do you think good wishes can come true?" she asked.

"Yes, and we are going to learn how to do it. My bear wishes are usually good."

"So why, then, are there so many bad wishes?"

"Because wish magic is an easy way to get things. And nothing is easy in this world. At least nothing is supposed to be easy. That's not nature's way."

"Maybe. Don't you get the sense there are more bad wishes now than ever from the way the Doctor talks? Smaetag told me how many they dealt with when they went on their field trip. Loretta was exhausted today, couldn't even talk about *her* field trip. The Doctor keeps changing classes because he's so busy."

There is something to this, Alma thought. Before Syd could say anything, she felt a thought forming in her head, a possible explanation.

But before it could fully come to her consciousness, the sky went absolutely dark. Some cloud had obscured almost the entire sky, except for a rim of starlight near the horizon.

"What is that?" Alma asked, her thought completely forgotten.

"Don't know," Syd replied. "Sometimes clouds can come in very quickly. Maybe you had us kissing so long, a storm blew in."

She punched him lightly on the arm. "Stop that. I'm scared. We should get back to the lodge."

"Okay."

They took a few steps. In the darkness, it was near impossible to see. "Alma, you trust me, right?"

"Yes."

"Can I trust you to keep a secret?"

"Of course."

"When I told you about wishing teddy bears to life, it's real. The Doctor knows this, but sometimes I bring them to life here. That he doesn't know. There is something dangerous about this darkness. I need to bring a bear to life."

He pulled from his jacket pocket a small action figure he had picked up in a museum in Michigan. "This one really annoys the Doctor, so I'd appreciate it if you didn't mention it."

She nodded. What her boyfriend did with his toy bears was his business. For her, the only thing left to worry about was, what could go wrong with falling in love with someone who could turn stuffed animals into killing machines at will?

Alma heard Syd murmuring, then more murmuring in the night, then an odd-shaped bear in a frumpy grey shirt, holding two very bright lightbulbs, appeared from nowhere. He looked almost human, but had an inhuman intensity.

"This is Ed, I's boy," Syd said casually, as if introducing a bear carrying lightbulbs was the most everyday circumstance. "I would like to meet you, but he sent his son instead."

Alma looked at them both unbelievingly, as much for the hackneyed play on word names as the fact that he had made a bear come alive. She was not swift enough to say, 'I have already met you,' but that probably would have only created more confusion.

"Pleased to meet me you," the bear said pleasantly, its voice a bit rough, like a man who had stayed up too late, but not like a bear.

"Please to meet you, Ed," she said in return and the bear bowed. "It is Ed and not I, right? I'm a little confused."

"Yeah, it's Ed. I often get confused for I, him being my father and all. Syd, was that doctor guy using my name?"

"Yeah, but he meant no harm."

"You sure?"

"Yeah. Mostly. There's a little rivalry between his benefactor and your benefactor, but nothing malicious other than long-ago lawsuits. There was a joke in using the name if we can all agree that jokes don't always have to be funny. No worry. You are safe here. Unless you try to steal secrets."

"I won't unless I ask first."

"Please do." Syd said. "The Doctor's benefactor has passed on from any lingering rivalry with your benefactor, but the caretakers here are quite vigilant."

"Should I know anything about this rivalry?" Alma asked.

"You will know more about one side of it, maybe as early as tomorrow, but I'm no longer allowed to tell the future." The bear looked somewhat chastened, even in the dark.

Syd and Alma raised an eyebrow each, but Ed would say no more.

"Would you mind doing us a favour," Syd said, "and guide us back to the lodge? For some reason, the night sky has gone completely dark."

Ed looked up and grunted. "No problem."

He held his arms out wide, and the bulbs' light grew in intensity, until they were like two spotlights. Alma had to shield her eyes until they adjusted, then held Syd's hand as they followed Ed to the lodge.

Whatever danger they had felt lurking in the dark ran before the power of Ed's light. The light seemed to reveal all before it, and anything that didn't want its identity revealed had no choice but to disappear. They could still feel a menace close by, but the light kept it far enough away that they felt safe.

"Thanks very much, Ed," Syd said when they got to the doorstop, all sense of menace now in the distance. "I supposed you will expect the usual."

"If it would be satisfactory."

"Well, I can't ask you to do favours for nothing. You can remain here until Monday morning. Is that sufficient? We can't have too many bears in the woods and the Doctor does get sensitive."

"Monday morning will be fine. Do I need to come back to you here?"

"No" Syd said, finally letting out a breath that Alma realized he'd been keeping in. He stretched out his hand then closed it. "You'll return to form at dawn Monday, wherever you are, and I'll come get you at lunchtime."

"Excellent. Well, say hi to Ron for me. Nice to meet you, Alma."

"Nice to meet you, too. Thanks for helping us out, Edison. I hope you don't mind me calling you by your full name."

Ed, son of I, winked. He'd originally been a bear in the gift shop in the museum honouring the inventor of the light bulb, holding two lightbulbs. Syd had taken a shine to him on his parents' visit on the way to Kalamazoo for an uncle's wedding.

Ed then turned and walked into the woods, the bulbs in his hands slowly dimming.

Alma looked at Syd. "I'm frightened."

"Of Ed? You shouldn't be. He's a friend. Don't make his father mad, though. I can be a real bear."

"No! The sky turning dark. I think it means something. My mother would say it's a portend."

"Hmm, I can't pretend to know what that means. Let's not worry about it. This is the safest place we could be."

"If you hadn't been here, I think the darkness might have swallowed me. I think we still have to be careful. Will Ed be safe?"

"Ed will be fine, unless I is angry. I, Syd, have to turn in for the night. Sometimes turning toys into live bears takes a lot of energy from me."

He leaned over to give Alma a goodnight kiss. As their lips touched, lighting sizzled all around them.

Alma looked up and the night sky was back. *That's a pretty good kiss,* she thought and went contentedly to bed.

~

Syd's reaction was somewhat different, despite his reassurances. He was worried. And not like the worry he had when he was down 5-0 in a sports competition. This was real deep worry.

The sky had interrupted someone coming to an important conclusion. It hadn't been him, so it must have been Alma. Or Ron. He wondered what they were thinking about and what force had decided to interrupt them. He vaguely remembered this happening before.

He didn't want to spoil Alma's happiness, so it was time he had a chat with Ron.

20: How to say 'wish' in reverse

Loretta had a smile on her face at breakfast but was still absolutely exhausted, saying she had had no sleep. Nola was sleeping in, having come back late in the evening, later than when the bears were put to bed. Alma felt jealous again that she hadn't been selected to go on a field trip.

It didn't help when the girls showed her their keys to the wishmethere. Loretta had one in the shape of a shamrock. It had taken her a while to understand it was a luck key.

Nola had been disappointed at hers at first, as it was shaped like a small horse. She felt it was an insult to have a don key, but then the Wish Doctor explained it was also a dawn key, and that it would help her make wishes at dawn.

Alma wondered what her key would be like if she ever got one. She found herself drifting as she thought about it and had to force herself back to her studies. If she was going to be ready for her field trip, she had to pay attention. The Doctor had urged everyone to work and study over the weekend, as there would be a special event if everyone could pass the test that was to come next week.

Alma tackled math first, and then spent two hours on physics, before getting back to the core work of wish magics. She read 100 pages on mythology, and, when the internet was running, searched for stories of wishes gone bad. There were not many documented from real life. The only ones recorded seemed to be in fictional stories.

The Doctor had provided a small book, like a field guide, with objects they had talked about that could help make wishes work. She began to understand how difficult it was to make a pure wish if you didn't have Syd's gift, though she was feeling there was something more to his gift than she understood yet.

For a break, she stepped into the hallway to stretch her legs, and ended up visiting the painting of the beautiful lady. The lady waved at her and she waved back. No doubt she was happy.

Alma found that looking at the lady made her head spin with ideas. *Maybe no wish could be perfect, but if you could take advantage of a wish gone differently, or see how the alternative was what you really wanted, maybe that was success. Could you construct a wish in such a way that the alternative outcome could be good? If you could, would the wish work out that way?*

Could whatever caused wishes to go wrong, pick up your intent to have the wish go wrong, knowing that's really what you wanted?

Suppose the woman in the painting had known her wish would go wrong but anticipated her outcome. Suppose she was happy with the wrong outcome, knowing that eternal life and beauty more than made up for her limited range of movement. Would whatever controlled wishes anticipate this approach and turn the outcome into something else?

What about the Island of Misfit Toys? Was there a way that could be turned into a positive? She had wished she and Alfalfa were somewhere else. Probably couldn't change that, but if she had been prepared to go to the Island of Misfit Toys, could the visit have worked out well?

She would need to think about that.

Even if Alma could do all that, there was so much unknown and so many risks. She was overthinking things, she knew. She could see how the Wish Doctor's thinking was always far ahead of everyone else's. She would have to gather enough knowledge to be ahead of everyone else if her dreams were to come to fruition.

For now, she had to master the basics of wish reversal.

Alma was relieved that Christine had left for the evening to study with someone else. Christine had been drinking too much coffee, and where before she had always seemed tired, now she was always frenetic.

Alma pulled the full-length mirror in its wooden frame close to the end of her bed and sat on her knees, looking at her face. The Doctor had given them a number of common wish phrases to reverse. He had said unless they stated the wish frontways they would cause little damage, and if they got it right, they just might fix a wishtake.

The first phrase read, "I wish I was a cowboy." She'd been to Texas a few times, so she knew there were many people who still wished for that kind of thing.

"Cowboy a was I wish I," she said practising the simplest reversal. She only needed to practice it a few times to get the tone close to being in reverse, and the words were easy to say.

She then tried reversing it like a pure palindrome. "Yobwoc a saw I hsiw I."

It was all pretty simple, except she could not find the way to pronounce the word wish. For some reason, she had forgotten her earlier revelation. How could one pronounce hsiw?

She tried the phrase without the word 'hsiw', then concentrated on just the word itself.

It was no doubt that this word was the problem. The iw was almost like ew, or more like oe as in 'shoe'.

Wait a minute, she thought, and tried 'shoe'. Then 'hsiw' like 'shoe', carefully moving her mouth and lips.

And then she could see in the mirror a face behind her face—an oldish man, with wild thick grey hair.

Not an old man, a ghost.

A ghost who was mouthing words. The ghost's face was friendly, immediately comforting.

She did not feel afraid, even in the face of the face of the supernatural. Alma studied carefully, trying to read his lips.

He was saying 'yobwoc a saw i shupe I'.

'I wish I was a cowboy' in reverse! He was showing her how to mouth it. His movements were exact, precise, but slightly exaggerated for her benefit.

He repeated three times and she answered, "Yobwac a suw i shoesh I."

Then "yobwoc a saw i shoesh I."

She could feel herself getting closer. On the third time, she moved her mouth exactly in sync with his, saying the sounds exactly as he did.

"yobwoc a saw i shupe i."

For whatever reason, the word 'wish' backward sounded exactly like 'shupe'. It made no sense. She didn't know where the p came from. But it was true.

She would confirm it later when she was finally able to download an app that let you read in words then have the app read them backwards. If anyone were to argue with her on this, she would tell them to go try it. She'd even be prepared to bet money on the outcome.

The ghost in the mirror winked at her and held up his hand as if he was high fiving.

"Uoy knaht," she said, and they smiled in unison.

She was not sure why she was so comfortable in the presence of a ghost, but he did not in any way seem threatening.

She knew it was not a polite question, but she had to ask. "Are you dead?" she said, exaggerating her voice movements so he could read her lips.

"In a manner of speaking," he mouthed. "But I don't really like to be classified that way."

"Can you make sounds when you talk?

"I can when I am fully in your physical space, but I am in the corridor of mirrors, just giving a look see what is going on in the lodge. I often prefer to communicate by non-standard ways. Lip reading is a good way to talk, when sound cannot be made or when you need to keep a secret."

Alma now felt her original comfort with the ghost slipping away. There was more to the ghost than being a language instructor. She could feel it. Was the ghost's presence some outcome of a wish gone bad, or a trick someone was playing on her? He was keeping a secret from her.

"Do you need to have a secret?" she asked.

"Good heavens, I need to keep a lot of secrets. I think I have eight right now."

The ghost laughed uproariously. Alma didn't know why. Was it an in-joke or something more sinister?

Alma grew more nervous. "Why do you need to see what is going on in the lodge?"

The ghost laughed again, then mouthed several words she could not understand.

"Pardon?" Alma said. She was having trouble reading his lips now, as her fear began to take over.

He repeated again and she shook her head. He repeated the third time. The ghost was extremely patient.

"I am here to invent things," he said again and smiled, lifting what appeared to be the weight of his beard.

"Who *are* you?" she asked.

This time she could read his words on the second try. She said out loud the words the ghost formed with the motion of his lips.

"Why, I'm Alexander Graham Bell, of course."

21: A Bell rings

Alma's mouth dropped open in shock. *Alexander Graham Bell.* The inventor of the telephone. Teacher to the deaf and mute, friend of Helen Keller. If she had to reverse a wish right now, she would need a shooting star. No way she could use her mouth to say a wish forward, let alone in reverse.

After a while, she realized she was being impolite, and that he was nowhere near as frightening as the creatures on the Island of Misfit Toys. "It's a very great pleasure to meet you sir," she mouthed carefully, but used air to voice her sounds.

"It's a great pleasure to meet you, too, and glad you could visit my house."

Alma unconsciously raised an eyebrow.

"Hoy, hoy, yes, I know it's not my house any longer, but since I paid for it, I doubt they will mind me visiting. I should correct that. It was really my wife who paid for this."

Alma caught something in his phrasing. Hoy, Hoy. *What an odd expression.* And then she realized where she had heard it before. The Wish Doctor said it every morning.

"Do you know the Wish Doctor?" she said.

"Of course, of course, but by a very different name. In my time he was a very popular fellow. I let him use this place. Maybe I don't have the right to do so, but I'm kind of that old generation that believes in hospitality for those who need it. I'm not going to ask my great-grandchildren for permission. And the Wish Doctor keeps you out of the way of everybody."

"I don't mean to be rude, but there are a lot of strange things about the Wish Doctor. Are you part of a wish of some kind?"

"Oh, my. I'm sure I was tied up in a bunch of wishes when I was alive, but I'm not here now because of a wish. At least I'm not here *due* to a wish. I may come and help out with stopping wishes or giving the Doctor new toys to help with wish work, but I certainly am not a manifestation of a wish."

"Are you a...I can't ask you that. It's too rude."

"Yes, sometimes I am. But I am other things."

"So, you died?"

"Yes. And I stayed that way for quite a while. But people kept asking me questions, especially the Wish Doctor. To tell you the truth, I was getting quite bored. A lot of unanswered questions in this world. A lot of new toys to make. Too many ideas in my head to just give up the ghost. Oh, wait, that doesn't make any sense. Hoy, Hoy, you know what I mean. I can't Rest In Peace, no matter how great the company or how peaceful, with so many things to discover. So once in a while I come back. Probably too often, if you ask Mabel. I do have a habit of getting caught up in new projects, especially late at night."

"And does your wife, Mabel, come here, too?"

"Not as much as I do. She usually comes just to make me go to our new home."

"Did you by chance help the Wish Doctor build the wishmethere?"

"Yes. Have you received your key yet?"

Alma shook her head.

"I am sure you will soon. I also help him with the box kites, and the photo phones, and several other things. He's not quite as perfect at language as he thinks, so I help him there. It's one of my passions. I also help with geography and culture. I do try to keep up with things when I can." He laughed, a jolly but silent, reflective laugh.

"What is a photophone?"

"It's a phone that uses light for signals. I was working on it in 1910, and it could have had the same features as a smartphone you use today. Except I didn't think it would take a hundred years to get the 'zoom' to just two times magnification.

"I'm toying with it, to see if I can create a device that helps you out with wish magic. Hologram projection. Space and time bending, that kind of thing. Being resident in another dimension has me thinking of these things quite a bit.

"By the way, are you the girl whose mother has the powerful crystal?"

"Yes, how did you know?"

"Your family wasn't exactly quiet when they showed up here. Made enough noise to wake the dead."

Alma looked extremely embarrassed.

"Don't be extremely embarrassed, at least not more than normal. That crystal of your mother's is very powerful. She does not know how to use it. It's a fine instrument that blends both the energy of physics and the energy of magic. It could be used to power many devices or help understand things, like the building blocks of the universe. Maybe someday you will let me examine it. I promise to give it back."

Alma didn't reply.

"I understand your mother is very possessive. I'm sure there is something I could offer that would make the loan worth her while."

"Why did you visit me in the mirror? Are you interested in me just because of the crystal?"

"Oh, my gosh, no, dear child. I came to help you with your elocution. We need more strong people to help with all the problems with wish magic. We had a wish recently that even affected my new realm, and that was disconcerting, and interruptive of another work I'm trying to do.

"Do a little research on me if you would feel more comfortable. I was never about the money, just helping people. Why, Helen Keller slept in the very bed you are in."

Alma's eyes opened wide. She felt terrible that she had impugned the great inventor.

Bell laughed. "You know that there are many people who have wished to talk to me since my passing. If I weren't so humble, I might tell you it is quite a privilege I'm talking to you."

"I'm sorry if I offended you."

"No offence taken if you are sorry. I try not to hold a grudge. Well, I must be off to see to other things."

"Will you come and see me again?"

"Would you like that?"

"Of course. I would like to know more about what you are working on, and if I can help."

"I have a feeling your teacher will soon need a couple of the things I'm working on, so I will be around a little more. I will try to make time to visit, when I think of it."

"If I can, I will let you look at the crystal."

"That would be terrific. If you talk to your mother, ask her what favour an old ghost might do for her. Well, time to go. Mabel will be annoyed I've been gone so long. Keep working on your backwards elocution. You will get it, you know."

With that, Bell faded away.

For some time, Alma continued looking into the mirror, but only seeing herself. She was beginning to see how much she still had to learn.

And how amazing were the things she was learning.

One of the things Bell had said intrigued her. The Wish Doctor had been a good friend of his in his day. But the Wish Doctor only looked about 27 or 29? *Could he have wished for a longer life?* Another mystery.

For whatever reason, she couldn't bring herself to ask such questions of the Wish Doctor. It seemed so much easier talking to ghosts.

Alma checked her watch and realized it was past midnight. She couldn't sleep. Not because she was scared, but because she had talked to one of the greatest minds of all time. She was now very glad she had had to change that tire all those weeks ago.

22: The Case Study

Selva took Monday's class as the Doctor was nowhere to be seen. Selva had seemed distracted at breakfast and as he entered the class, as if he had other things he felt he should be doing.

The whole class sensed this mood and was more sober than normal, except for Alfalfa, who seemed to be bothering her sisters with spitballs. Alma kept herself low in her seat, not wanting to be part of that.

She found herself daydreaming more than once about the presence of ghosts. She wondered if any of the other students had seen any. The only one she felt comfortable asking was Syd. He was spending a lot of time talking to the bears in the woods, so didn't have much attention to give to her.

She thought about Bell sitting in the study that was their classroom, meeting with great minds, discussing great ideas. She thought about the planning of aircraft, and hovercraft, and helping the deaf talk. She thought about Bell's family living in this estate. It was too amazing to be true that she was living here.

There was some mystery as to how they were able to use the house undetected by the caretakers, but that was a topic for a different time.

After the afternoon class, Alma grabbed Syd. and took him into one of the hallways.

"Have you seen the ghost? The ghost of Alexander Graham Bell?"

He was surprised at the question, actually knew who Bell was, though, and was impressed she had talked to a ghost.

He asked an odd question. "Did Bell ask you about the photophone?"

She was beginning to wonder if Syd had wished he had psychic powers.

Then he said something really odd. "You know we are like ghosts to the caretakers."

"What?"

"Bell and his wife used to own this estate, but it has passed down to his descendants, and they rarely allow visitors here."

"Then who are we?"

"We are students, but there is some kind of wish magic that hides us like ghosts from the caretakers. They know we are here, but as long as we don't make too much noise, and keep the place clean, they don't cause us trouble. It's partly *why* they don't allow many visitors."

"What do the caretakers look like? I haven't seen any of them."

"The moaning you sometimes hear is them. There are pictures on some of the walls, and in an album in the parlour. I will show you. They are really quite lovely people."

Alma didn't disbelieve Syd, even though it all seemed incredible. Was there some kind of weird quantum alternate universe effect, where they were coinciding in the same space?

"How do you know all this? Didn't you arrive here after I did?"

"I'm not sure. I just remember things when you ask me questions. Look for the caretakers. You will know I'm right."

They spent the rest of the afternoon and evening re-touring every part of the lodge that was open. Alma saw things with different eyes. She kept imagining the Bell family and their guests living in the building. How many great minds had stayed at the lodge?

As she retired to her room for the night, it was one of the odd times when the internet waves were working. She immediately set to researching A. G. Bell.

What struck her more than anything was his vast knowledge of different types of communication, of how to talk to the deaf, and of course the invention of the phone and knowledge of Morse code.

Alma wondered how the Wish Doctor had discovered the ghost who lived in the lodge.

She looked in the mirror. The ghost was not there. She wished she'd been more alert the day before. She had a lot of questions. Not the least of which was, what was so important about her mother's crystal?

And why Syd knew things he shouldn't.

The Wish Doctor was in class first thing Tuesday. Selva was out, apparently taking a turn looking after more bad wishes.

Syd whispered to Alma that the number of bad wishes kept increasing. Selva and the Wish Doctor didn't feel they could both be in the classroom at the same time. They were even thinking they needed to build a second wishmethere.

Alma looked at Syd to see if his ears had grown bigger. Maybe he was overhearing all these facts.

She never got a chance to discuss it with him, as the Wish Doctor went directly into his lesson without any preamble.

"Today, class, I am going to give you a case study. You must read it, discuss it in your groups, and then chose a speaker to report out your discoveries."

Wish Gone Wrong: a case study

There was a young boy who was jealous of two of his classmates. He had been the smartest boy in his local school, so he was accepted into a private school for bright individuals. In the private school, there was one girl and one boy who were just maybe a little bit smarter than him. It didn't help that he liked the girl and hated the boy or that the two of them liked each other.

He tried to study harder to beat them on tests so he could impress the girl and embarrass the boy, but that never worked. He got closer to their marks, but they always seemed to beat him.

He asked if they could study with him and they laughed and said, "Sorry, we don't study that much."

He begged his parents to help. They found smart people to tutor him.

He worked hard. Yet he never could beat the two classmates.

One day, he saw a shooting star. He made a wish that he would get the highest mark on the next test. Later that week his test came back for history and he had the highest mark in the school. He had scored higher than the girl and boy.

He didn't know, of course, that they both had serious cases of the A-flat strain of influenza. The boy had sneezed on the last page of his test, so the teacher never marked the last page, knowing the boy was getting an A+ in the class anyway. Nor could he know the girl was so sick, she had had a momentary fit of dyslexia and was writing dates backward, which she would never do if she was not sick.

The Magna Carta signed in 1512, Preposterous. (By the way if you don't know what the Magna Carta, is I really would like you to find out, but please don't wish that you knew!)

The boy thought his high score was due to his wish, and that he was smarter than the boy and the girl for the day of the test.

That night he went out again looking for a shooting star. And again the next night. His birthday was too far away, and he didn't want to wait, so he took the coins he had in his pocket and rented a horse.

He rode the horse from the estate where his school was to the core of the city where there was an old fountain with water splashing from the lips of ugly but self-satisfied fish. (Or that's at least what they looked like then. He could not know they were once young boys like himself who had all made a wish they became fishermen, only to be turned into stone fish that had the eyes of men.)

If you were going to make a wish it was a good place to do so if you wanted the wish to come true. Not so much if you wanted to have the wish come out just as you had wanted, though.

The boy threw a florin (an old coin) in the fountain and said, "I wish I was the smartest person in the world."

The boy didn't feel anything different at first, certainly not as he rode back to the estate. What he felt was very sheepish. He felt as if he had taken the wish too seriously and that nothing had changed.

But over time, the boy's wish came true. Only it wasn't exactly as he intended. The girl was not impressed, the other boy became his bitter enemy, and he was never happy for the rest of his life.

Discuss what may have gone wrong, what else could go wrong, and what could have been done to fix this. For your suggestions of what could have gone wrong, what might the boy have done to prevent those wrong things from happening?

There was lots of interesting case discussion. Alma was impressed with how smart the people in her group were. However, when it came time to report out to the group, she couldn't wait and was the first to stand to speak.

"He wished he 'was' the smartest person. If he used the past tense 'was', he could have been turned into the smartest person sometime in the past, maybe for a second or a moment or even for a week, but not now."

"Yes, good, could have happened, has happened. What else?"

"Well, he didn't issue mitigation wishes against anything else going wrong, so he might have become the smartest person in the world, but was sick, or didn't live very long."

"Very good. What else? Alma, give others a chance to respond."

"He didn't make a protective wish first, or a clarifying wish afterwards so he was asking for trouble," Alfalfa said.

"Good. Was the fountain a good place to make a wish?"

"No!!!" screamed most of the class.

"If the fountain was made by a wish that went wrong, it was a dangerous place for magic," Glenda said.

"He could have been so smart that he became so arrogant, he lost all his friends," Syd said.

Alma wondered if he was thinking about the volleyball game.

"He could have terrible headaches because he was thinking too much or feeling too much pressure to solve problems." Christian, who had earlier complained about headaches, said.

"He could be so smart that he found everything else around him boring, so he became unhappy." Was Christine finding the class boring, Alma wondered.

"These answers are all good. You are actually learning. It's as if my wish was coming true. Now here is what happened. The boy indeed got his wish. He became the smartest person in the world and stayed so for a long time. Now, What about fixing this wish if it was later causing problems?"

Alma felt it was her time to speak again. "You could do a simple wish reversal, by pulling the coin from the fountain, and reciting the wish backwards."

"Good, might work. But this fountain was protected from any of its wishes being reversed."

"Could set up a wish matrix, with protection and preventative wishes and use a new wish to revoke the old one," Ian suggested

"You could have somebody else wish they were the smartest person in the world, and that contradiction might disrupt the wish," Glenda added.

"If he was really smart and using his smartness for evil, you could kill him," Smaetag said, shocking everyone.

"Maybe have a new wish that makes the boy happy, so he can be happy and smart," Syd said, seeming hopeful.

"Maybe turn him into something other than a person, so that the wish would fall apart, then turn him back again." Christian was definitely doing a lot of thinking.

The Wish Doctor nodded at all the good ideas. Maybe all of them, or even just one, would have worked.

"What if this man was needed; what if he had to be smart so he could help others or stop bad things from happening? What if he was unhappy because he had to work so hard with his smartness?"

"So, you are saying a bad wish can be a good wish," Alfalfa said. Alma thought her tone was especially thoughtful.

"Perhaps. Or a bad wish can be bad for one person but good for others. Everything is not as clear and simple as it seems. That goes back to our first lesson. A wish almost never turns out exactly the way the wisher wants. Usually, the wish is a terrible mistake, but sometimes a bad wish can have good purposes even if the wisher gets hurt in the process.

"I must caution you," the Wish Doctor continued. "This is the first of our advanced lessons. Do not get too hopeful that a wish turned wrong can be a good thing. It can lead you to making a rash decision when you start to understand how to make a wish that will work. We *will* make wishes that will go bad. They will be minor wishes, where the hurt will pass. But these can be magnified."

The class looked a little stunned. It was the first time he'd ever said they would actually make a wish.

"Okay, class, enough for today. Go do some homework."

"Wow, good lesson," Alma said to Loretta as they walked past the Wish Doctor on their way out of the class, "I feel sorry for the smartest man in the world."

The Wish Doctor nodded. He wasn't sure he really *was* the smartest man in the world any longer.

It had seemed so innocent the day he had thrown the florin in the fountain. He had not known the path it would put him on. Had he the choice, he would not have walked this way.

Still, he had learned what he did was needed, and he had learned to accept his fate. Maybe the unseen forces behind wishes had wanted him to take this course. Or maybe there was some other force he had yet to identify that had selected him to offset the forces of wish magic.

Even now, when he knew how to undo that one wish that had changed his life for the worse, he wouldn't. He had to carry the pain of his life, he had to do the things he did, or the world would be in trouble.

In fairness, he could not wish the awfulness of his life on another.

23: The bus

Alma had a hard time sleeping Friday night. She kept staring at the mirror in the room, but the only thing she could see was reflections of Christine's feet on the top bunk and her own tousled clothes.

She wasn't afraid of seeing a ghost in the mirror again; she was afraid of *not* seeing one.

She was feeling overwhelmed. Could all of this be real? Was she not at home dreaming, so tired from chores Lavinia had given her that her mind was creating a fantasy world? Had the crystal taken over her mind?

She bit her lip harder than she intended and squealed. If she was dreaming, she was a pretty realistic dreamer.

Why do wishes have to go bad? she wondered. *Is it the universe's way of poking fun? Does it have a grudge against laziness? Or is it a way of making things happen that need to happen, just not in the way people want them to happen? Or do wishes need to be selfless, for others?*

In what the Wish Doctor was teaching, there was a kind of rationality of understanding how wishes work, but his own sense of humour, if not mischievousness, hinted that there was also a pure creative force behind the magic.

There seemed to be a connection to pure science, too. She remembered that the famous science-fiction writer Arthur C. Clarke had said, "A sufficiently advanced technology would be indistinguishable from magic."

A second after this thought, an image of a very old telegraph machine appeared in the mirror, then a phone, then a kite, then an elaborate box kite, then a heavy cell phone, then a biplane, then a space shuttle, then a ring that she knew was some kind of technology, then the wishmethere.

It all disappeared, to be replaced by a bagpiper blowing hard into a set of bagpipes, yet making no sound.

Until she realized she had been asleep and a sound was blaring in her ears. Bagpipes. She had overslept and was about to be late for the

Thanksgiving field trip.

She looked in the mirror, saw nothing but herself, then scrambled to grab her bag, comb her hair and ran like a maniac down the corridors of the lodge, and out the back entrance.

A yellow school bus was parked in the driveway. Selva stood next to the door, motioning her to hurry up. She jogged, carrying her overnight bag, not carefully packed, then stopped, realizing she had to go back and close the door of the lodge.

She reached inside the lodge to grab the knob on the door and there was the ghost of A. Bell, not in a mirror, but standing at the foot of the stairs to his study. He winked at her, waved, then headed up the stairs.

She shook her head and closed the door. He was probably glad he had the place to himself for the weekend.

Alma scrambled up into the bus, passing the Wish Doctor, who was standing looking at a map as Selva took the driver's seat. All the other students were packed in together, the back seats all covered with empty water containers. She saw Syd against a window seat, one of the triplets, she couldn't tell which, next to him. He shrugged his shoulders as she passed by, the triplet flashing a smug look on her face.

Alma took one of the empty seats, surrounded by the water containers.

Somebody made a comment about being on the magic school bus, and most people laughed. Alma didn't see the humour.

"It's about a ninety-minute drive," said the Wish Doctor. "We will stop a couple times along the way. This part of New Scotland is very much like the highlands of Scotland, with several similarities. Our first stop will be the Gaelic college, where they teach the ancient Celtic language the Scots spoke. It's so well known as a school even Scots and Irish come here to learn the language. And of course, there will be bagpipes."

The Doctor then proceeded down the aisle and sat in the only open seat. Next to Alma. As he sat by her, his shoulder accidentally brushed hers.

It was the closest she had ever been to the Doctor. She felt slightly nervous, sliding to the window, hoping she hadn't offended him. Her nerves began to settle as she took in the scent of lavender.

Whatever aftershave he was using, she had to find it out and get six bottles for Syd. His worst fault, other than being mean at volleyball games and sitting with triplets, was that he often smelled, well, like a hockey player's duffle bag.

The Wish Doctor, as often he did, wore a dark tweed jacket and a button shirt, but no tie. He took off the pork pie hat that crowned his head as he sat down. His hair stood up and he had to brush it down with his hand.

"Sorry, you are stuck sitting with me," he said. "I'll probably fall asleep if Selva is steady with the driving today. Just push me out of the way if I get too far over into your space. Make sure you stay awake and appreciate the landscape here. It's truly magical. What you see on this journey may help you in your lessons."

Alma understood. That meant there *was* something to learn. She still felt awkward with everyone else talking, yet asked him what she thought was an innocent enough question. "Are you from Scotland originally?"

"No, but I spent twenty years there one summer."

She looked at him, thinking he was making a joke. "Is Scotland that bad a place to be?"

The Wish Doctor laughed. "No, of course not. Rain there isn't any worse than here, and it doesn't get any colder. One of the reasons I like it so much here is that it is very similar to Scotland. I did have a good twenty years there, though I was working hard for most of it."

She looked at him oddly.

"It's a long story," he said. "I'm sure there's a lesson I could share, but I've much better lessons with much shorter stories."

"Where are you from originally, if I can ask. Sometimes you have an accent, and sometimes you don't."

"To tell you the truth, I don't know where exactly I was born. My parents moved around a lot while I was young. Then they had me stay with uncles and cousins when they had things to do. I went to school in Europe and ultimately settled here because a good friend had me visit and I fell in love with the place."

Alma nodded. She had a feeling he was being evasive on purpose.

She wanted to ask him how long he had lived at the lodge but wasn't sure she would get a straight answer. Instead, she said, "Thank you very much for asking me to come to your school. I am learning a lot."

The Wish Doctor turned to her with a serious look on his face.

"Never stop learning," he said. "Every piece of knowledge can help you. Whether it's science or history or art, or language, it will help you. This world can be a tough place. Two things can help you more than others. Knowledge and humour. That is why we are going to stop here and hear more about the bagpipes."

The yellow bus, running much more smoothly than any school bus she had ever been on, the wheels making a shoe, shoe sound, turned off the road leading out of Baddeck at a sign that said Cabot Trail and Saint Ann's. Shortly, it pulled into the parking lot of the Gaelic college.

The Wish Doctor hustled the group to follow him out of the bus and into a large back courtyard.

Alma felt a sense of excitement. She knew she likely had Acadian descent in her blood, and thus some origins in Nova Scotia, but she didn't think she had Irish or Scottish roots. Nonetheless, since they had entered Nova Scotia, she had found all the Scottish links very interesting.

She could not have imagined any place as Scottish as the Gaelic college. There were pretty highland dancers in period costumes. There were men in kilts, and lots of souvenirs of a Scottish nature. She studied everything, knowing every piece of knowledge could be someday of aid.

And then of course she studied the bagpipes.

Who had ever wished for those things?

24: Well to do

After the break at St. Ann's, Alma wasn't sure whether to try to get the seat next to Syd. The Wish Doctor might be insulted, so she took the seat she had been in and waved Syd off when he tried to join her.

The Doctor chatted amiably with her, asking about New Orleans, and her favourite foods. He asked her about her ambitions, but Alma didn't dare say she wanted to be just like him, or that she would like to have the skills to run a school like him. She said instead, "Once I wanted to be a flutist."

"And not now?"

"Well, it's somewhat out of style."

The Doctor laughed. "Yes, for some time. A version of the flute was very popular in Hamelin when I visited there."

"I'm not quite sure yet what my ambition is. I have always wanted to acquire knowledge, but I'm not sure what to do with that knowledge."

"Any particular kind?"

"History, science, art, architecture, computers, and wish magic."

"You could be a teacher. Or a professor or a doctor. Or lead a nation."

"Maybe. I have thought about being a teacher."

"My graduates have gone on to do many things. The things you learn with us will help in many pursuits. Do not set your limits low. Let's talk again on this sometime."

With that, the Wish Doctor lay back his head and quickly fell asleep. She was thankful that he didn't, as warned, fall over and end up with his head on her shoulder. Not like the triplet who was drooping onto Syd's arm.

Alma settled into watching the scenery which made her reflect. She'd been so wound up in the crystal and her brother that her thoughts for ambition had been rather limited. Her time at the Lodge of Wonders had been brief, but she realized there was a life beyond her family.

She was not sure that she could ever go back. She loved New Orleans, and once had thought she'd spend her life there, but the cooler temperatures in Canada seemed to agree with her. She loved the scenery. It was so relaxing.

She wondered what it would be like if she moved to Canada and stayed, maybe with Syd. It did not seem a bad life. It would be difficult when she told her parents.

She shook her head as they passed an amazing view of the ocean. She was getting ahead of herself.

The scenery all the way along the drive was beautiful: glimpses of Lake Ainslie, a beautiful blue amidst a spectacle of fall coloured leaves, reds, and golds, and yellows, with a beautiful shade of orange she'd never seen before.

Alma felt herself relaxing into the scenery, but not enough to sleep. There was too much excitement. She had an inkling there would be another adventure at their destination.

She marvelled at the beauty of the town of Inverness, overlooking the beaches into the Gulf of St. Lawrence. There was a tranquility through the Margaree Valley, the soft rolling mountains, the forests, the scent of wildlife even in the van.

The final leg of the journey seemed a little off the beaten track, but again, so amazingly beautiful. She remembered a quote from Mr. Bell she had read on a place mat: "I have travelled the world and seen the Alps and the Andes but for simple beauty nothing compares to Cape Breton." She had not travelled that much, but had seen so many pictures of beautiful places on the internet while daydreaming of travelling, that she had a feeling that he may well be right.

It was thus a little surprising, when the bus slowed down, that it was approaching a long, white, two-story building with the word 'Distillery' on the side.

She was turning to the Wish Doctor who was still asleep, when someone called out, "They make Scotch here."

Alma was not a drinker, but she knew enough from her father that Scotch was a type of whiskey. She smiled. She had no doubt now this was going to be an adventure.

The Wish Doctor, now awake, had a broad grin on his face.

Selva ushered everyone off the bus and the Doctor stood in front of them.

"Some of you, maybe most of you, have realized this is our home for Thanksgiving. Some or maybe most of you will know this is a place that makes whiskey.

"The really clever ones among you will know this place also makes *wish*key. We will all learn about wishkey as part of our lesson. There is also a lesson to be learned about distillation that may serve you well. Those of you who are over 19, the legal drinking age in the province, can accompany Selva for a tour of the distillery and may, if you desire take a sample taste of whiskey. For those younger than 19, you will also get a lesson, but, alas, you will have to come with me.

Selva motioned to a pathway leading into the distillery. "All those over 19 wanting to come with me, stand here."

The majority of the students congregated around Selva.

Alma suddenly realized what she should have known all along, that she was one of the youngest, being only 16, well, almost 17. Her birthday was but two days away, on the tenth of October. She didn't know why, but she was surprised at how quickly Syd joined the group. She had once wondered if he was even 16.

There were five who stood with the Wish Doctor. Alma already knew Eugene and Tahiti were not of legal drinking age, but she was surprised Brad wasn't. He was already bigger than Syd. If he grew even more, he'd be the size of a Grizzly. And Aaron, well, she didn't know anything about them.

Smaetag clearly was older, but Alma heard her say to the Wish Doctor, "I'd prefer to join you, if that's okay. You may recall I had a little trouble with alcohol when I was younger. I don't touch the stuff now."

"Of course you may join us, rookie," he said with a wink. "I think you've already guessed the nature of this lesson."

She nodded.

As Smaetag started to trundle away with the group moving in the direction the Doctor pointed, he called to Alfalfa. "Dear Alfalfa, hoy, hoy, please come here."

Alfalfa stutter-stepped, and tried to act as if she hadn't heard him, but the stutter-step gave her away.

"Alfalfa, Is there something you are forgetting?"

"Ah, don't think so."

"Hmm. Is it possible I know something about your age you don't?" the Doctor said.

Alfalfa stuttered. It was easy to see she was trying to avoid Alma's eyes. "I'm not too young. My sisters are old enough to drink and we're triplets."

The Doctor smiled. "Look at your driver license."

"I don't have one."

"Exactly. Oh, and happy day before your birthday. I already wished your sisters well and told them not to drink too much on their first legal day."

Alfalfa fumed. "There is just an hour that separates us."

"Yes, but if I have taught you anything, in the things we deal with, technicalities are very important. In no time system and time zone, especially this one, are you old enough."

Alfalfa's lips pouted.

The Doctor came to her and whispered, "Did you think Selva would have the only important thing to teach? Grant that I may have a lesson planned that might be the most important. Your sisters might be jealous."

As much as the Wish Doctor could grin, he grinned at Alfalfa, who found herself grinning back.

"Before the day is done you will have a drink that will be fancier than a tickle."

He turned back to his small group and said, "Follow me."

They walked along a path near a bubbling stream amidst a beautiful field with delightful cottages, with a mountain in the background. They came to an old stone well. For a moment, Alma wondered whether she was overusing the word 'beautiful' to describe her surroundings but then decided it was the only word appropriate.

"This is a wishing well." The Wish Doctor smiled. "And not an ordinary wishing well. It is old and powerful. It was originally dug by some Chinese sailors who were blown off course 3000 years ago."

Alma's eyes widened in incredulity. *Can that be true?*

She was beginning to think almost anything could be true. To think that she had ever doubted magic, just because of a dull crystal. Even what she had learned from a ghost was not so dull!

She had to concentrate. Whatever lesson was coming was important.

"Do you know why a well of this type was originally called a wishing well?"

"Because you make wishes in it to be better," Brad said.

"Yes, exactly: well done. I see my stressing of word play has not completely fallen on deaf ears. A wish to be better is still the best most effective wish that can be made in a well, whether to enhance something about yourself, make yourself nicer for instance, or to wish that someone who is ill or injured gets better. That's where it has its best power."

"You can't make any other type of wish in a wishing well?" Eugene asked.

"Oh, yes, water of any kind has power of wishes, as it's so fundamental to life. Wells were first invented to help corral wishes and the first wishes were mostly about betterment, or revenge. Wishing wells never were really good for revenge wishes, though. Over the years, the wells have adapted to let people make wishes for more than just betterment. It is never easy to make a wish, as we know, but betterment is one of the harder ones to make. Wishing wells are the best places to do so. Still not good for revenge wishes, unless you really want a wish to go wrong.

"Let's demonstrate. I'll need some help for this. We need to make sure the light is reflecting as best we can on the water."

"Should we use some mirrors?" Brad said.

"No, we need to reflect the light naturally with our bodies. Alma, and Alfalfa, your light-coloured clothes will reflect the best, so I'll get you to stand on the other side of the well. Brad and Eugene, you stand to each side of them. Great, I'll stand to the west, here, and Smaetag and Aaron, you stand on the opposite side....Okay, good positions, but bend over slightly to reflect the light at the water. I need you to raise one eye toward the sun and have the other looking at the water. That will channel the light perfectly."

"That's better," he said as they adjusted their positions, mimicking his posture.

"I'm going to speak a few words to get the well's attention."

He put his hands together and cracked his knuckles. "Well, Well, Well, how are you? Can you see with this light? Can you tell us what wishes have wrought?"

The water in the well began to swirl, then splash, then take on colour. For a minute it spun around the well, climbing higher as if filling to the top. It was like a whirlpool, but also like a kaleidoscope of bright, changing colours. Pink, then chartreuse, then orange, then yellow, then finally red as bright as a lobster sunset.

"Freeze, if you will, well," the Wish Doctor said, and the colours and water froze, forming a picture as if Rembrandt had painted on ice.

There was a tall lady, slightly hunched, a look of both humility and pride on her face, a wide-brimmed hat on her head. She was clutching her side as if in pain.

As the students looked, the lady's clothes slowly changed colour from a generally brown and earth-tone palette to a distinct yellow, perhaps the colour of margarine.

"What do you see?" the Doctor said.

Alfalfa described the lady in the vision.

"Good, that means you can see what the well is telling us. What is important about this lady?"

"She's just made a wish?" Alfalfa said, as tentative as her older sisters when they were by themselves.

"Very good. It was probably two days ago, based on how long it took for the colours to change. She made a wish, all right. Do you think the wish came true the way she wanted?"

Not a one of them was not shaking their head.

"Correct. This is an unfortunate wish gone bad. Fortunately, I fixed one just like it—well, worse, really. Well, Smaetag did. You let the others guess this, okay?"

Smaetag nodded. She had already figured it out.

"How do you know what's wrong with her?" the Wish Doctor asked, directing his voice to everyone not named Smaetag. When he directed his voice at you, it was almost as if you heard it in your head. Or if you were hearing it from top-of-the-line Bose noise reduction headphones (or apple ear pods if you were under thirty).

"Can you tell what she wished for? Read the clues in her looks. One of the keys is the changing of her clothes' colours. The other is knowing the kinds of wishes people attempt to make. This lady wants her friends to think she is quite the activist, and out helping people. She hasn't always had the time. So, she wished to make herself better."

"Oh, she didn't make herself better."

"No. Because more and more people are using keyboards to type in their wishes. So when she typed her wish, she didn't type better at all. Let's just say that if you have klutzy fingers, or are apt to drop things, it's not a good idea for you to be typing up your wish."

"OMG,", Brad said. "You mean...?"

"She got her wish to be a butter person," Alfalfa stated. "And the yellow is her turning more into butter?"

"Isn't that dangerous?" Brad asked.

"Fatal," the Doctor said. "Too much butter, no matter how tasty, will clog your arteries. That's why she's in pain."

"Can we help her?" Alma asked.

"That's why I talked to the well. Sometimes I don't have time to travel, and use the well to help reverse spells. Now, if Smaetag told you of her adventure, you know we need to retype the wish."

The Wish Doctor gestured, and within the image of the water, there was a giant touch screen, displaying the wish written: "I wish to be butter."

"Alma, if you would do the honours, just reach with your fingers, point at the screen and correct the offending letter."

Alma, did and her hand turned cold, as if she was touching ice, but it was easy to point and change the letter u to e.

"Will that work?" Alfalfa asked, "or will there be some trick to the wish 'I wish to be better'?"

"In many circumstances that does get a person in trouble. Since we are focusing the wish correction through a wishing well, and we've established that the primary purpose of a wishing well is to make you better, it's unlikely. The 'better' wish will now only correct the 'butter' wish and put her back where she started. She will only be better relative to how she is now, not better relative to how she was when she served up her butter wish.

"This is the key to fixing many wishes. We try to get the wisher back where they started, not to get their wish to work. If we just try to get the wisher back to the state they were in before they made the wish, it's less likely we will have a further problem. Note I say *less* likely.

"You have to pay particular care to three wish circumstances. If someone has a wish go wrong, corrects it, then makes the third wish, it will almost certainly be an even more virulent wishtake. If the third wish has to be used to correct the first two wishes, because the second wish just made the first wish worse, then it's not too bad and may even work.

"Watch. She will throw up for a little bit, then her skin will lose its yellowness. She will need a good rest, but essentially she's fixed, and, we hope, has learned her lesson."

The young students looked at each other. This was a pretty cool lesson. Even Alfalfa had to admit she had seen a better vision than if she'd drunk too much whiskey.

"Well, well, well, anything else?" the Doctor said.

The water swirled and settled down.

"That means there is nothing urgent, nothing we need to make well. That does not mean there are no other wishes happening, or in progress. I'll show you that in a minute.

"If you are ever caught needing to fix a wish, and Selva and I are not around and someone is sick, the wishing well is the most effective way to identify and fix the wish. You might need to make a wish yourself to be able to understand the well and know what to do, but most wells will adapt to your wish, if your intent is pure and you are wishing someone else well.

"Now, congratulations all of you, you've all earned the title of well-wishers."

He smiled genuinely as if he wasn't making a pun. Regardless, this was serious. One or more of them would shortly have need of this knowledge.

"Follow me now," he said as he walked twelve steps to a perky stream that rolled by in a nearly straight channel. It was so close to the well that any right-minded individual might well ask why the well was nearby and necessary. Alas, the question was rarely asked.

Alma looked at the water. It appeared as crystal and pure as any water she had seen. The little stream bed was mostly polished rounded stones. The water moved at a steady, unhurried pace. She licked her lips without knowing it. The water looked so tasty, you wanted to drink whether thirsty or not.

"Please stand in a line. We just need to wait a few more seconds and the sun will be at the perfect angle," the Doctor said.

"The source of this water is the mountain you see in the distance. It's more like a hill now, but was once a much more rugged peak. There has been very little human activity here for some centuries, so it's some of the purest water to be found anywhere in the world. Its primary purpose is used in the production of the whiskey your colleagues are learning about. This distillery makes whiskey in the Scottish style, using distilling equipment made in Scotland. This brook, in fact this entire landscape, is very much like Scotland. And it's not surprising, since, as I believe I told you before, the land here was once attached to Scotland.

"The water is not just used for whiskey. It is used in another beverage that we will talk about over supper.

"Okay, sun's almost at the right point. Please close your eyes. When I count to three, open them and look straight at the water ahead of you. When I say so, you may look up and down the stream. Follow my instruction and there may be a message for you."

The students closed their eyes.

"Three, two, one. Open your eyes."

Alma lifted her eyelids. The stream was full of colour, just as the well had been. She studied a rectangle of water in front of her, but she had the sense the entire stream was alive with images.

She gasped. The image in front of her was Lavinia, staring into the crystal, a strange smoke all around her.

Her mother, startled, almost as if she could sense Alma looking at her, lost her hold on the crystal. It went spinning, whirling with the pace of the water but now faster, until it wobbled off the side of the table and to the floor.

It fell, and there was a crashing sound.

Her mother reached for it frantically, then lifted it upward, tears in her eyes. The crystal was no longer purely oval in shape. One of the ends had broken off.

Lavinia held the two pieces. Despite the break, she was about to make a wish...

The image wavered, and there was a picture of a New York baseball jersey with the number four. A Met four. A metaphor.

Alma tensed. *What does the breaking crystal portend?*

She had no time to figure it out.

The Doctor called, "Look along the stream."

Despite her worry, she knew more could go wrong if she didn't follow the instructions. She looked left along the stream, then right.

The images were endless. People standing by wells, or looking up at shooting stars, or blowing on candles. People everywhere making wishes.

"Look and see the folly of the human race," the Wish Doctor said.

"Everyone is hoping for easy answers, rather than working hard, and practising and training and learning how to use language. Still, they are but a reflection of ourselves, and we must all have understanding and compassion, for who amongst us has not wished for what we might not have?

"These are the people currently making wishes. Most will fall away harmlessly, but a very few will come to be pictured in the well. The image you saw is someone making a wish that you might have to deal with as part of your training."

He tried to keep his eyes away, but he too saw images. He could see a flurry of animal and creature images that might come soon to the well. He would need to pay attention.

"Okay, now, everyone, blink three times, then turn away. This is critical or you may be contaminated with others' wishes, and that is one thing we must avoid."

Everyone did as they were told. Suddenly the stream was just a babbling brook again, spilling secrets amongst the splashing words of gibberish, if you but listened carefully.

"Good," the Wish Doctor said. "You have all cleared your mind of wishes, but they are still there reflected in the stream. Again, should the need arise, if you need to understand the wish activity going on, you can come here, or find another stream. Just remember to clear your mind of wishes afterwards. Most streams can do this, but some you will need to train, and that may be difficult until you are old enough to drink whiskey."

He smiled. "Come on, now. Let's get settled in our rooms and then it will be time for dinner. And a taste of a beverage you will never forget."

25: Wishkey

The Wish Doctor treasured Thanksgiving dinner. It was a time to be thankful for those wishes that had gone right, for the help he had received in curing wishes gone bad and for the knowledge he had been given to do this work.

Today, the image in the river had him glancing continuously at his wish watch. Something was happening and he might need to leave at a moment's notice. Unconsciously, he drew his key, and summoned the wishmethere to park behind the school bus.

Still, he needed to focus on his duties. Things taught here in a land as Scottish as Scotland had magical meaning.

He grinned as the whiskey tasters finally joined them. He gazed across to see who had held the tasting and not gotten too inebriated. He was especially pleased to see that no one was wobbling as they walked

The triplets, or more accurately duplets, were hardly phased. He was sure he could keep at least two of the three triplets from following their baser instincts. And if not the third, well, there had been a wish brewing for at least a century to deal with such a contingency.

He stood from his chair and shook hands with everyone as they came in. The group was split into two long tables, with him at the middle of one and Selva in the same place at the other, so they could look across to each other.

Before the conversation among the students could get too lively, the Doctor said, "I hope everyone has had a good afternoon. Tomorrow will, I hope, be pure fun, but I have a couple more serious things to say tonight, and then we will have some fun with a little meaning.

"First, thanks, everyone, for being such great and attentive students. Selva deserves immense credit for being such a great recruiter. It is always wonderful to have talented students, and you are talented like few others. There is nothing more important for a teacher than to have students who want to learn, and for that I am very thankful.

"I now ask you to take a moment to think about what you are thankful for. A proper thank you, given freely, and meaningfully, and at the right time and place, can often be more powerful than a wish, and quite less likely to be misconstrued. Unlike a wish, a thank you never has to be kept quiet. In fact, the more it is shared, the better.

"How much better would the world be if we thanked more and wished less? In some ways, wishes and thanks are opposites. Thanks are a happy thing allowing you to appreciate what you have, while wishes are in some way unhappy, lamenting what you do not already possess. Do not undervalue the power of thanks.

"When we return to class on Monday, we will again be talking about wishes, and how to make them. I ask you not to forget this night and the power of thanks. There may be a moment, or more when your acceptance and gratitude will serve you much better than a wish."

He made a sweeping gesture of welcome. "Selva?"

Selva stood up, smiling. "I would like to say thank you for the wishmethere, and that the new harmonic dampeners are working. I would also like to say I am thankful that I am good at driving a school bus."

The Wish Doctor smiled. Selva knew he had summoned the wishmethere.

"Okay, everyone, please close your eyes and think about something you are thankful for. You can share it later."

The Doctor watched to ensure all closed their eyes. In some, he could see the thanks on their lips; in others it was buried deeper. It was important they all had something to be thankful for, to keep human desires from running unchecked, from keeping wishes from running unchecked. To keep them from being tempted to use wishes for their selfish gains.

He looked at the triplets with uncertainty and, unfortunately, missed the strain on Smaetag's face as she struggled to find something to be thankful for.

"Very well," he said, "Now open your eyes, and I will give you something else to be thankful for. Notice in front of you the drinking crystal."

Alma did, noting her glass was large but empty of liquid. Syd, who was sitting next to her had a glass about 20 per cent smaller than hers, and Smaetag's glass on her other side was very tiny, almost the size of a thimble. In fact, almost everyone's glass was a different size, and some were of different shapes.

"I told you before all magic is wishes," the Doctor said. He raised his arms in a flourish.

A golden, bubbling liquid began to fill the glasses, from the bottom up, appearing from nowhere, with no one pouring, with no spout or spigot attached.

The students felt their tastebuds light up uncontrollably.

"How come everybody has a different-size glass?" Alfalfa asked, as if trying to take satisfaction that, if hers was not quite as large as Alma's, it was bigger than most others', and certainly bigger than her sisters'.

"That is quite simple, my precocious sprout. You have before you what I promised, maybe the most delicious drink in the whole world. This is wishkey."

Some of the students felt like groaning, except their tastebuds were telling them this was a potent drink.

"This is a potent drink," the Doctor said "It affects people very differently from whiskey. This drink has no alcohol in it, but it has the power of innocence, a blank slate, on which any drawing can be made. For those of you who abstain from alcohol, not only do I congratulate you, I tell you wishkey is allowed under all religions, so do not fret about drinking it. Just drink carefully according to your age.

"While the older you are, generally the more whiskey your body can handle, the exact opposite is true for wishkey. With wishkey, the younger you are, the more you can imbibe."

He smiled. He was one of the world's most knowledgeable wishkey experts, having spent several decades in Scotland learning how to make the perfect blend and how to use it to complement any wish.

"The reason is simple. As you grow older, some dreams are set aside never to be recalled again. Without dreams you can't absorb the power of wishes. They will simply overrun you. The younger you are, the safer it is to wish, for all wishes are possible when you are very young. Only as you grow older do wishes for certain things become unnatural and then dangerous and unlikely. These are most susceptible of becoming wishtakes. This does not mean you cannot make a wish when you are older. It simply means you must be wiser in the type of wish you make.

"As you can see, the glasses fill themselves, according to your age and need. They will stop filling when you have had enough, so don't feel the need to stop, until the fill stops the need.

"Now, ladies and gentlemen, I would like to make a toast. Before I do, note that a toast is in fact a kind of wish. It is a formal wish of staid and ancient power. It is the most conservative type of wish, and while not as powerful as many wishes, it is more likely to come true. A toast made with whiskey, especially for those of you taking the first sip, may have an extra kick. So, let's see if we can do this right. Everyone, raise your glass with me. 'To all you students. May someday your wish come true.'"

The students raised their glasses as Selva said, "Hear, hear." Then they took the first swallow.

To Alma, it was like tasting bliss. It was sweet like pineapples, and cherry punch, but the bubbles frothed in her mouth with the energy of life. She could feel a cozy warmth spreading. She felt her body relax with confidence.

She knew she had become paranoid about making wishes, having seen how badly they could go wrong. It was almost as if the wishkey gave confidence she could make any wish come true if it was of good intent and to help others.

She wanted to take another drink, but she also wanted to savour the taste in her mouth. It was like a first kiss, with all the promise of the future. She did not want that first taste to end, but she knew the sensation would stay with her forever in memory. That taste was a taste to be thankful for. If she'd known about it, that's what she would have said her thanks for.

There was a temptation to wish the taste would never leave her mouth. Instinctively, though she knew that was the one wish she dare not make with the wishkey. A wishkey gone sour could create great damage.

She licked her lips and turned slightly toward Syd. He too was savouring the drink. As her eyes turned to him, he turned to her. She had to hold her breath, as he did.

There were wishes beneath the surface, wishes attracting, aligning.

She had to turn away. The power was too great, and they'd not known each other long enough. Another moment and their unborn wishes would join, and then they'd come to life. For while there was a selflessness in those wishes, there was also a great, personal, selfish desire that they could lock themselves together away from the world.

She knew that their dreams must not come together in such a way.

And she must first solve the mystery that surrounded Syd.

Alma glanced across the tables, at her classmates, all in their own contemplation, savouring, feeling, dreaming, wondering, and all growing confident.

The glass before her was already full again, and the bubbles had become so lively, it seemed her glass itself was tipsy, tipping. She took it again, and the crystal of the glass felt as if wish magic was dancing through it.

She lifted it, took another taste.

If it could be possible, the second taste was even better than the first. She swirled it in her mouth, feeling it caress her tongue, her teeth, enlivening tastebuds she didn't even know she had.

As sweet as the first taste, there was another level of complexity in the second. It was like the descriptions her father would give about wine, when he had been training to be a sommelier.

Except instead of the hint of pepper, there was the wind of a warm summer breeze. Instead of the aroma of vanilla, there was the first smile of a new baby. Instead of the flavour of cherries, there was the sensation of hope and pleasure, and at last an aftertaste of satisfaction.

Her third taste was completely different, as it went straight to her mind.

She could see the moon as if she sailed in a solar sailboat only kilometres away, and yet distant as well so that she could see the craters, and grains of dust, but also the image that looked like a man. She could feel its influence on the tides, could feel how its strength was enough at times to touch the fluid of her brain. She understood its influence on the earth in a distant way, but also knew it could be called upon. Its influence on people and landscapes could not be understated.

She could feel the energy the moon had absorbed from all those who had looked upon it, who dreamed upon it and wished upon it. No one had ever said that a wish upon the moon was powerful, but she understood now how powerful it was. And not just for wishes, but dreams, and hopes, aspirations. The moon had been for humankind a guide, and those who knew it well found it a beacon to better times, to fulfillment.

She looked to her glass again, and realized the colour was not amber at all, but the colour of the moon at harvest, like now. She had a moment's urge to run outside to look to the sky, but then she didn't need to. She could see the moon more clearly than ever before.

The moon beckoned.

It was something to strive for.

She looked up. The realization had satiated her thirst. The bubbles in her glass for a moment lay dormant after their vigour.

A quiet moment settled across the room. There was a confidence in that silence. No one felt insecure, or the need to speak to fill the silence. All could feel the pleasure of their companionship. While joy was often noisy and arrived with laughing and shouting, there was a collective, quiet joy here and now.

The quiet confidence lingered pleasantly and contemplatively until someone said, "Pass the rolls please."

The voice was unmistakably Brad's, and his tone set the room once more to laughing and talking. Alma was not as addicted to bread and rolls as her brother, influenced by her father's efforts to stay healthy, but now the light, fluffy dinner rolls were all she could imagine.

She took one as Smaetag held a basket in front of her, not seeing the consternation in Smaetag's face, and tore a piece off to chew while waiting for the butter to be passed.

It was fluffy and moist and chewed as easily as if a cloud. It had the flavour of a dream. She shook her head as the butter came. There was no need to alter the taste of the roll, already sweetened by the wishkey.

"I used to work in a bakery," Smaetag said. She seemed to be thinking of the past.

"What did you do there?"

"I'm trying to remember. I haven't thought about it in a long time. I worked hard there and didn't have much time to sample the wares. I remember the smells when the foods were baking, and the burning odours when they stayed in the oven too long. Those were the times when you could sample, even when you couldn't afford a roll yourself, when you could pull away the ash, and burnt pieces, and still savour the inside where the fire hadn't reached."

There was something in the way Smaetag spoke, something in the melancholy that was different than the rest of the emotions in the room, that worried Alma. It was as if the burnt rolls were an allegory for Smaetag's own life. What must it be like to be so much older than the rest of the class? Alma could not imagine being in a class with her own father, let alone her mother.

"I remember the ovens being hot," Smaetag said as she carelessly chewed her roll as if not tasting it. "Sometimes, like in winter it was good. In the summer it could be terrible, even though we started early, before the worst heat of the day."

Alma felt a slight chill, then a roaring heat that seemed to have nothing to do with this cozy little corner of Cape Breton. Was Smaetag causing it?

Alma glanced at Smaetag's thimble, which was still half full. "You haven't drunk all your wishkey."

"Oh, no. It's quite powerful isn't it? I think I'll save some for later," she said and took a drink of sparkling water.

Then she said, "I think there was a boy there. He seemed very nice at first but the way he kneaded the dough made me uncomfortable."

Alma glanced to her other side at Syd who was laughing with one of the triplets. Except for Smaetag, everyone seemed to be laughing. Alma felt the sensation of the wishkey, the nearness of the moon, but something told her she might need more. She took another drink.

The bubbles popped in her mouth, like pop rocks her father had bought for her in the Peak Frean candy store when they had stopped in Halifax.

She heard clapping across the room and looked up as a troop of waiters brought salad plates with a rainbow of colours, red beets, cranberries, oranges and orange peppers, blueberries, pineapple, and yellow beans, kale and slivers of broccoli and purple cabbage. The sauce was a strawberry vinaigrette that tasted divine.

Smaetag took a bite and groaned in delight. "That tastes so good for a salad."

Alma felt relieved that the melancholy had stalled for a moment.

But across the room, the Doctor grew agitated. He looked at his watch again and again, growing more uncomfortable by the minute. While others took their time with the salad, he ate it as if he might never eat again.

"These berries are so tasty," Smaetag said. "I don't remember eating berries when I was young."

Alma took time with her own salad, knowing fresh salad would come less likely in the colder months. The taste went so well with the wishkey, she just wanted to concentrate on that, to enjoy the pairing. She did so as much as possible, as Smaetag interrupted periodically, to tell her about something she wished she could remember.

Alma wondered if this was what at it was like to get older, to forget so many things, or was this more advanced in Smaetag?

The Wish Doctor looked up from his watch, with a loud "Hoy, Hoy" as one set of waiters took away salad plates, and another brought in plates of vegetables and cruise ships full of gravy, more rolls, and cranberry sauce, and fluffy mashed potatoes the look of which made the rolls look stale.

And four turkeys so large, they looked as if they had been birthed in prehistoric days.

The Doctor and Selva carved the turkeys and passed the meat along to the students.

Alma was surprised at the taste. Unlike the dry turkey she remembered her parents serving, this was succulent satisfaction, and complemented the wishkey grandly.

Even melancholy Smaetag sighed with pleasure at first bite.

There was no more talking at either table, as students and instructors enjoyed the meal as if it was doused in magic sauce.

~

The Wish Doctor, whose nerves had been growing more and more shaky over the last few weeks due to the growing activity of bad wishes, seemed to forget everything except the taste of the food. Mixing cranberry sauce made fresh with stuffing, he had a hard time controlling his otherwise delicate appetite, so much so, he did not feel the vibration of his wish watch.

Only when he raised his wishkey glass to take a satisfying swig, when the watch's alarm blazing the sound of bagpipes that could not be ignored, did the taste seem secondary to other feelings.

He put down his glass and fiddled with the dial of the watch. The watch vibrated as if springs were to blast out of it. The sensations he had been feeling all day were reaching a crescendo. It was as if a tsunami of wishes had broken all at once.

Now that he knew where they were originating, he had to act. He stood up, pushing his chair back, hurriedly. He wiped his mouth with his tweed jacket sleeve; no time for better manners.

"Dear students, I am afraid an urgent matter requires my attention. As per usual, the people in the United States are so unaware that Canada has a different date for Thanksgiving that they can't take a day off from bad wishes. Darn inconvenient that they put themselves first, considering that the first thanksgiving started in 1528 with the Franklin expedition to the Arctic and the pilgrims' thanksgiving started in 1604. I'm sorry, this one appears to be one of the worst wishtakes I have seen in some time. I need to travel posthaste. Selva, I'll have to use the wishmethere."

"Thought as much," Selva said. "Do you need me to come?"

"Later maybe, but first priority is the students. I'll call if I do. This one is still brewing. I won't need you until at least tomorrow.

"The rest of you enjoy the weekend. Heed my words on the wishkey, and no one use any of the turkey wish bones. Save them. We might need them later."

With that, he was hurrying out the door, the wishmethere already generating heat as it prepared to travel.

~

Alma felt sorry for the Wish Doctor. He always seemed so frantic. No wonder he had fallen asleep on the bus. She felt bad he had to miss the rest of dinner.

There was a clatter beside her and she turned to see that Smaetag had let her cutlery fall from her hands to rattle on her plate. The pleasure that had been on her face as she enjoyed the meal only moments ago was suddenly distorted into despair.

She must have felt Alma's eyes on her. She said, "Gone in the middle of dinner, just like my father." Smaetag continued looking straight ahead, her eyes blank as glass.

Alma felt her throat tighten. Poor Smaetag, old enough to be her mother.

"Do you want to talk about it?" she asked calmly, genuinely. Maybe a crowded dining room wasn't the right place to have such a discussion, but there was also a desperation in Smaetag's face that Alma feared.

"Talk about what?"

"Talk about your father."

"My father. Why would I want to do that? I haven't thought about him in years."

Alma's face crinkled. She said quietly, "You just said he left in the middle of dinner."

Smaetag's eyes swivelled, a dark glint within her glass eyes. "He did, didn't he? He did and never came back. Except that time he came to try and change me. Why, did he do that, Alma, why?"

Alma didn't see or hear the waiter come up from behind. She was distracted when he came from the opposite side to place the desert in front of her, thus she did not notice one of the triplets switching the Doctor's wishkey glass with Smaetag's water glass. The Doctor's wishkey glass was full.

Alma shook her head and Smaetag coughed. She was choking back tears. As if to cover her emotions, she lifted the large water/wishkey glass in front of her face and slowly drained it.

"When was the last time you saw your father?" Alma asked cautiously.

Smaetag, didn't say anything for the longest moment, staring through Alma as if she were a pane of glass.

"I—I'm trying to think. There's a whole bunch of thoughts in my head, but I can't reach them. It's as if my childhood wasn't real, or if I had two childhoods."

Alma was growing worried. She didn't notice the glass refilling on its own, as she tried to get Syd's or Loretta's attention. Both were so involved in conversation they did not see her motioning at them.

Smaetag took another long drink, slouching, as the wish liquor seemed to loosen her limbs, but then suddenly jerked upright. "I—I. Alma, I feel all kinds of memories, but they won't show themselves. There is too much pain involved with them."

"Maybe it's better if you didn't think about them."

"No! No! I wish I could remember!"

~

And of course, suddenly she did.

It wasn't that she had come to her wish power late. Smaetag had developed very early, very powerfully; too powerfully, with too little control. Things had happened. She had hurt people, hurt herself. Her power had had to be suppressed.

She screamed as she remembered her power unchecked, new wishes coming to help solve the old, but backfiring, creating more chaos, and then a group of people coming to stop her.

Gently, at first, and then more violently. They hadn't meant to hurt her. Her father hadn't meant to hurt her, but his wishes backfired. And she had felt pain.

Which she had shared.

She stood up suddenly, pushing herself away from the table.

~

Syd finally took notice, stood up quickly, came to help.

Smaetag backed away a step from Syd as he approached, then screamed. "You. You hurt me! You stopped my power but you hurt me! You grabbed me in a bear hug, and you squeezed until my power was gone."

Syd stood stunned, as did Alma. He could feel the amount of whiskey and wishkey he had taken enhancing his powers. He didn't need to make a wish to understand this could not be possible, that Smaetag was troubled.

And that she had taken too much wishkey. The odour on her breath was overpowering, and now it seeped from her pores, the liquid turned sour.

But how? She had only a thimble full to drink.

He looked at Alma, who, looking perplexed, pointed at Smaetag's drinking glass, the one that held that refreshing sparkling strawberry Perrier. It was refilling of its own accord! With a bumbling amber colour!

Somebody had spiked her water glass! How much wishkey had she drunk? She veritably smelled of the power of wishes.

"I'm trying to be thankful," Smaetag said, "but it hurts, and now the pain is back again."

"Make a wish," Alma said.

"What are you crazy?" Syd said.

"No, she's taken too much wishkey. She needs to make a wish now, or she's going to deconstruct."

To Smaetag, Alma said, "Make a wish. It will help you."

"What if something goes wrong?"

"Then we are here. If we need to, we will go to the well, but all of us have drunk wishkey. We may not be Wish Doctors, but we are all so powerful right now, we can stop it."

Smaetag's face was in torment. "I feel like I'm going to hurt someone," she said. Her eyes watered. "I was never happy. I always wanted to be someone else, anyone else. I can't really find the way to make thanks. Alma, it hurts so much, I think I'm going to hurt someone."

"Release some power," Alma said. "Make a wish."

Syd held his breath a second, and said, "Smaetag, do as Alma says, make a wish!"

Smaetag's eyes rolled back in her head. She said through tears, her words slurred, immense layers of pain obvious, "I wish I was d-dead."

26: The death wish

The last word hung in the air as if suspended by time.

Alma's eyes went wide with fear, and with horror at her own guilt. She grabbed Syd's hands, and Loretta's. "We have to negate her wish!"

"We can't," Loretta said. "Not even my negation power works on this type of wish. Everyone dies. It's a rule of nature. You cannot undue that."

"But we can change the *time* of it. Syd can help. We can stop the dying of today. We have only seconds, while something's stalling her wish. We must make the stalling permanent, or at least push the wish to her natural date."

In a panic, Alma grabbed the Doctor's wishkey glass and tried to drain it. She couldn't. The whiskey kept refilling as quickly as she drank.

She took as much as she dared until she felt her whole body about to explode. She turned back to her friends who were looking at her in horror.

The wishkey was bubbling through her, giving her confidence, so much so that she could even face down her mother. A hundred new ways to make a wish were in her head. Two hundred better ideas were there to reverse them.

"We don't change her wish!" she exclaimed. "We just give it timing. We have to grab it and clarify it."

She reached toward the wish in her mind, seeing the forces behind the world that shaped not just all wishes but all of reality. She was in the Matrix, in a video game, in the hand of science, behind the veil of nature.

She pulled Syd and Loretta to her. Smaetag was shaking, foam flicking at the corners of her mouth.

"Say with me on the count of three, 'She wishes she was dead when her true time has come.'"

"One, two, three…"

They synchronized their words as if a ghost spoke with their lips.

Alma felt the wish budge as a boulder might budge, or if a stuck car may budge, rocking, giving a sign it could be free.

"Again," she said. "This time, Syd, you speak louder and concentrate on the phrase her true time has come. You must reinforce the state of time."

Syd squeezed her hand. "I will. I can help."

"One, two, three...."

"She wishes she was dead when her true time has come."

Alma felt Loretta's hand as they surrounded the wish, stretching it, feeding it power, while Syd spoke louder as if commanding time itself.

Smaetag's shaking stopped; her tears stopped. "I wish to live as long as I can before I die," she said.

Wish magic exploded as it rarely does. Wishes that had gone barren for miles around now came alive.

Lovers found their unrequited love calling, boils and laceration and cleft lips were healed. Red hair became green. A beloved dog that had disappeared and feared dead returned, bringing back a family from the verge of divorce. A young hockey player who had lost confidence because of a body check into the boards regained his nerve and scored the first of four goals, setting a path that would take him to the National Hockey League. A young writer discovered an email accepting their novel manuscript just as they was about to take an overdose. A girl finally laughed at her boyfriend's joke, staving off an impending breakup that would have halted 60 years of marriage and 32 grandchildren.

And that was the fraction of the power, for most of the power that could fuel wishes to go wrong did not have a chance to reach toward a wish, but instead was grabbed, siphoned, stored for a future day.

Energy radiated from Smaetag. Wish magic by nature was subtle, calm, and cagey, but the magic in Smaetag now was fuelled by the mystery of an internal furnace. Like any furnace, it needed fuel, and the brighter it burned, the more fuel it consumed.

The influence of Smaetag's eruption of wish power would be felt for eons, not even accounting for that part of her energy that had been harvested and stored.

She began to wobble as the torrent of power faltered and became a trickle. Her arms wove in desperation as if trying to swim to safety, but then at last she collapsed, as Syd stepped forward to catch her, the image of the bear surrounding him, strengthening his arms. Gently, he lowered her to the ground, the other students staring.

"Is she okay?" someone asked nervously.

Loretta lowered her ear to her chest. "She's breathing," she said, and Alma felt her stress release just a little.

"What's wrong?" said Selva, who had suddenly appeared. Alma didn't know where he had been during all the commotion. "Is she okay?"

Alma explained quickly as Selva slowly touched Smaetag's arms and stroked her orange hair.

When she awoke, she took a glass of water. And opened her eyes. In that order. Selva whispered something to her and she seemed to relax.

"I will take her to her room," he said. "This wish you can't reverse, but you did the right thing to clarify it. I have reinforced it. She might in fact live longer now, but this was a close call. The rest of you can go to your own rooms. There's been enough excitement for one day."

Once Selva had settled Smaetag, he walked to three points surrounding the student's cabins.

All was not right in the world of wish and he could not take any chances. He set up three portable dampeners and activated the circuits. In hindsight, it should not have been a surprise that this year's vintage of wishkey was particularly powerful. And that someone or something not very pleasant had tried to take advantage of the students' first tasting.

27: Cats, rats, and elephants

As the Wish Doctor crossed the border into the United States in the wishmethere, he felt a wave of energy behind him. The wishmethere's batteries kicked into overdrive, absorbing the wave. He had to hold tight as the energy rocked the device.

At any other time, he would stop to investigate, but the wish watch was overheating. Whatever had happened behind him could wait. What waited ahead of him could not.

One stuffed animal coming to life could cause a lot of damage, but not to the degree the wishwatch was frantically signalling. There was something unusual going on. Unusual even for New York City.

He could see the lights twinkling, a harvest moon behind the Empire State Building, the bright neon of Times Scare, the shadow of Central Park as he neared Trump Tower and Tiffany's on Fifth Avenue.

The wishmethere dropped precipitously, sensing the urgency. The Wish Doctor undid his seat belt, stepped through the door and arrived in the middle of chaos.

It was not a single stuffed animal come to life, but thousands, the entire stock of FAO Schwarz, the famous landmark toy store, including the storeroom holdings. Not a single one left that he could use to neutralize some of the wishes.

This was not one wish that had created the chaos, but almost as many wishes as there were animals.

Was there some channelling of forces that brought all these bad wishes to the fore at once? Was it a mass psychosis, or had the power that turned these wishes alive been able to collect all the wishes at once? Had some sprite or fairy behind the wishes wanted to make their presence felt? Was some creature of the wish world trying to get his attention? Some of them just liked to play.

The Wish Doctor didn't think this was the case. His watch confirmed it: this was no single wish.

Had there been a concert, perhaps, where the musicians had implored the audience to make a collective wish? The last time he had seen anything remotely like this, that had been the cause. There was that other time where a hypnotist's performance at a corporate retreat resulted in innumerable people using practical joke props from 1960s comic books, ultimately all harmless, (although even he had fallen prey to the itching powders).

This did not have the feel of practical jokes, where no more than slight offence was meant to produce a laugh. Even if practical jokes went wrong more often than wishes.

It was the Wish Doctor's worst dream come true. Unlike the last encounter with a stuffed animal come live, Syd's bear, there appeared to be real menace in the crowd. The gorillas' teeth were sharp and their faces decidedly not friendly. The bears looked like they were protecting their young. The alligators had lost all inhibitions.

He was surprised FAO Schwarz had enough demand that there were two hundred buffalo and bison, forming a bisontennial.

You might think that a stuffed 'Where's Waldo?' doll come to life would not be menacing.

But you would be wrong.

Fortunately, it was easy to neutralize Waldo because it was obvious where he was: coming to attack the Wish Doctor.

The Wish Doctor said, "There's Waldo," and immediately the doll was a doll again, although something was clearly wrong with it, since it lay on the pavement and did not return to the store.

Around the Doctor, people were getting hurt as animals attacked or trampled innocent bystanders. He connected eyes with an ostrich with full plumage. It had been a birthday wish that brought it to life, but the wisher was nowhere near; no way to understand the exact wording that had brought it to life. If they were all like this it would be an effort to counter all.

He held its gaze as the bird ran at him. "Wish, fish, ostrish, go, go, kapish."

The ostrich kept coming so he repeated the phrase, holding his will firmly and then the ostrish did indeed kapish.

The Wish Doctor knew then there was something strong here—many things strong here. He could not manage the entire group.

He summoned the power of his wish phone, and Selva appeared in the tiny screen. "Selva, it's me. Can you see what's happening?"

"Yes. It's not one wish, it's hundreds."

"That's what I thought. Even I can't manage it all. The wishmethere should be charged shortly. Wish a chauffeur's license for Venn. He can drive the rest of the students back to the lodge. When you've got that done, come, but bring help. Bring Loretta and Syd, and if you have time, contact any of the graduates to come. See if you can contact her Splendiferousness. I can't make a connection. Oh, and tell Syd to bring Ron."

Selva hung up and made arrangements. Then he woke up Alma and Nola. "Watch Smaetag," he said.

As the Wish Doctor broke connection with Selva, he leapt into action. Something was wrong in the world of wishes. There were cats, and rats, elephants, and sure as you were born there were unicorns. It was if Noah's ark and been commandeered for evil.

He could detect no specific class of wishes dominating. There were birthday wishes as there always were. There were wishes on the moon. There had been a minor infestation of dragon flies chasing mosquitoes. There had been a new fountain opened, and it was a major source but barely ten percent of the total. It was some sort of wish alignment, no doubt.

The Doctor could detect no pure wish; all wishes seeming abetted. There was a conference of people who liked denims, low level jeanies who were creating three wishes each.

"In a while, crocodile," he said, and a giant lizard about to bite him was on top of the Trump Tower, helpless.

For once, common sense was occurring in New York and people were fleeing.

Unfortunately, stuffed animals that come alive can be just as fast as animals of nature. Fortunately, it was still early in the wish day, and they had not all come to their full power.

By now there were dozens of police, firemen, dog catchers, and game wardens helping to corral the animals. The Doctor would usually prefer to wish them out of the way, but today, all assistance was appreciated.

Since the popularity of the show "Tiger King", the ability to wrangle big cats was second nature to some. Those trapped in the back of trucks or tranquilized, he could deal with later.

It was not enough.

There was no way he could undo the damage one wish at a time. He had to find a way to use a reversal to cut across many wishes.

The Doctor reached into the pocket of his tweed jacket and removed a gold case, too big for business cards but just right to contain tarot cards. He fanned the deck and found the card he wanted.

Another of Selva's genius inventions, with a little help from Bell, trapped the essence of the most powerful wishes in cards. He had no wish so powerful on his person to counter all this at once, not without great risk of things going wrong. He didn't really like Tarot cards, but they were a good way to turn what would have been evil wishes into beneficial wishes. He needed a collective wish, a wish made jointly by many, to knock out as many aspects of the wish as possible.

The current card had the picture of a comet, and a powerful ghost mask. The Doctor had captured it before the witches' coven had used it in 1896, several evil minds wishing on Halley's Comet all at once. They'd been pretty angry, but he'd managed with some difficulty to take it from them, and was glad now that he had taken the trouble.

He'd already built a protective spell into the card, so he merely had to ignite it for the wish to take effect. "Wish of card," he said, "take tooth and claw and now discard."

The card disappeared in flame. The powerful sabretooth about to attack him looked very ineffectual, with suddenly flapping gums and declawed paws. The creature lunged, but it was like being attacked by, well, by a stuffed animal. Although it was heavy enough. It almost knocked the Doctor over, as he managed to throw it over his shoulder.

"Time to stop rattling," he said. "Back to your cages." The command had the effect of disarming not just the tigers and biting animals, but also the snakes.

"That was quite mean of you," said an amusing looking creature of pale purple in front of him, the monocle giving away his identify even without his vampire fangs. "I'd been counting on escaping that infernal store and having some free time."

The Wish Doctor shrugged. He didn't need a wish to put a defanged vampire puppet, who had only one joke, in its place. Sometimes, just the power of dismissal was needed.

The Doctor took only a second to glance backward as the vampire returned to its puppet incarnation. "Besides," he said, "I always found cookies funnier."

As creatures scurried everywhere, blocking the areas around 5th Avenue and 61st Street, the Wish Doctor had little time to think. Many of the creatures who relied on teeth and fangs either lost their courage and went back to the toy store with their tails between their legs or were able to be corralled by the municipal workers.

There was no end to other menacing animals, though: boxing kangaroos, elephants, hippos, pecking birds, who kept their razor-sharp beaks if not their talons. The Wish Doctor made a note to ensure he included beaks in any future defanging wishes.

Moose blindly stood in the road, in no way menacing but blocking the efforts of the municipal workers. At least the giraffes, pleasant animals that they were, were merely standing, chomping on leaves.

It made him a little worried what the monkeys might be up to. They could be friendly, protective, angry or mischievous, or just hiding in barrels for some strange reason.

Many of the dinosaurs, even the vegetarians, held menace: powerful tails, causing damage to buildings and cars. There was a griffin or two, but no dragons. He'd had enough of them recently. Selva had placed a bug in computer ordering systems, so no new stuffed dragons could reach retail sites for some time.

There were other imaginary things, such as the unicorns, but most of them were harmless, frozen looking at their own images.

And of course, there were bears. Literally thousands of bears. They did not need teeth or claws to swat you with a paw, sit on you, or, worst of all, hug you to death. That their nature made them want to hug, whether malicious or not, did not soften the Doctor's view of them. In fact, that their danger could emanate from such an innocent and pure place made them all the more dangerous, since you could not sense malice coming.

He checked his wishwatch. Selva was taking longer than he expected. He dealt with one, two, three bears, the latter nearly catching him in a hug. He needed help, because the bisontennial were starting to get organized. If they stampeded, lives were sure to be lost.

Except for the most immediate dangers, the Doctor focused on the creatures that could travel the fastest and escape his ability to handle them by sight. He started with the birds, pecking the crows and ravens from the sky. Somewhere there were stuffed dragonflies come alive. He summoned them, so he could generate new wishes.

He reached into the canyons of Manhattan, into the audition halls for dance and theatre, into the publishing houses for the dreams of writers, into the finance section for the dreams of financiers. He sought out entrepreneurs, and waiters who wished to be something other than waiters, and gathered the unfilled wishes of millions to him. It was a strain to hold so many wishes at once, but he was running thin on wishes he had with him, with so many threats still to counter.

He felt the wish power within and knew there'd be a price to pay.

He set a barrier that contained the birds, and the fast animals on land.

He then cleared an area so the wishmethere could finally land.

His annoyance at Selva's late arrival was on his face. He said nothing as Syd, Ron and Loretta stepped from the wishmethere. He didn't have to ask the question, but Selva replied, "Couldn't get any other help. There's magic trouble across the globe. Everyone is busy."

The Doctor nodded, turned to Loretta. "I need you to extend your power. Stretch your hands and create as wide an aura as you can."

Loretta was more powerful, more confident in her power of wish neutrality than when she'd last been home. She'd forgotten how many broken and active wishes lived in Manhattan. She felt many of them residing in the Doctor.

"Carefully," he said, stepping back. "I need wishes for reversals, so don't neutralize every wish. I just need you to neutralize the animals. Put in practice what we've been working on. Decide which wishes to neutralize, and only those. We need to keep your energy focused on this problem."

"I'm holding my power. I'm in control, but just. I need to let it go."

"Follow me. I've cleared this area, but there are many more wishes to contain. Syd, for now just bear with us. You will have your turn with some heavy lifting soon."

"And me?" Selva asked.

"Need you to go to some of the strongest sources. There's some sort of wish alignment. Start with the fountains, stop the denim convention, see what other multiple sources you can get to. There's a lot."

Selva set off toward the first fountain while the Doctor led Loretta and Syd up 5th Avenue toward Central Park. "Let me get ahead of you a bit," he said, "so you don't accidentally turn off the wishes I've collected."

When he'd gotten twenty yards in front of Loretta he said, "We'll walk straight up Fifth. I want you to negate every stuffed animal wish we contact within your reach, save bears."

Loretta nodded. She could feel the fear in the air. Fear of her. She didn't disappoint.

As she walked, creatures of all types fell to the ground, turning back to stuff before their heads could touch pavement. Parrots and eagles fell from the sky. A sloth dropped from a tree. Tarantulas fell *en masse*. The giraffes lay down as if to nap and shrank in size.

Still no monkeys, but there was a badger, a family of brontosauri, and now napping turtles.

In almost any other city, the animals that lay down would have filled all the toy stores. Here they seemed limitless.

The Doctor saw Loretta starting to strain. "Okay, now just the big animals," he said. "You need to conserve your powers."

By now they were at the 64th Street entrance to Central Park. There they saw the largest menagerie of bears ever collected.

Panda, grizzly, brown, black, teddy, polar. Bears from fiction, from bedtime stories, from cartoons, from children's dreams. A Paddington lookalike looked quite uncomfortable and quite awkward. Despite his reputation, as a cute bear, he did not really liked to be hugged.

There were three bears off to the side, one a baby, but still huge, hugging a blonde girl, who was none too happy about it.

Someone called to her, "Are you alright, Karen?"

The Wish Doctor suddenly realized that this was not part of the current phenomena, but an older wish bringing justice.

He glanced sideways at Syd. Syd gulped, and turned to Ron.

"I've got your back," Ron said, and suddenly the goalie stick was in his hand, as he stood tall on his hind legs, his back against Syd's, ready to defend against any intrusion.

Syd looked at the gathering of bears and intoned a pure wish. It was not that he couldn't turn them all back, though that would have been difficult, it was that it would pain him to do so. He knew more than any how such creatures brought joy into the world; brought necessary warmth when there had been none.

Had a bear ever hurt anyone, when not provoked (other than the odd honeybee)?

He wasn't as good at other wishes, but he could control bears. In fact, he could control them so well, the Doctor called him a bearometer for measuring the strength of wish control.

The bear eyes looking at him were as a group sympathetic, pleading, but not meek. They gave strength, not generally taking it. But there was something sinister in the air, something malicious that had brought them to life. Although they now resisted that sinister power, better than the other animals had, they would succumb.

Syd snarled, angry that anything could do this to very fine bears. He felt a rumbling in his belly, and as he did, he felt his wish power, his pure wish power, surge.

He spoke loudly, his voice a bearitone. "Your time of life will come again. Fear not sleep, for it will be but fleeting, and you will hunger for life again. For now, though it is time to hibernate."

He crossed his arms and hugged himself tightly. "Good night," he whispered, and across the lawn some thousand bears lay down asleep, all except the three chasing after the blonde Karen.

A polar bear held on the longest, trying to resist Syd with the same effort it was trying to resist climate change. It too fell asleep, helpless in the face of powers beyond its control.

Syd felt a tear in his eye. Ron's paw was upon his shoulder, and it steadied him.

There was no time to be remorseful. It had to be done.

The municipal workers gathered up the bears, now toys of fleece and cotton.

There was no time to rest, though both Syd and Ron had joined Loretta in fatigue.

"We can't rest now," the Wish Doctor said. "Whatever brought the bison alive, made them come alive in anger. They've gathered in the park, but are coming our way soon. There will be a stampede."

"I don't have enough strength to stop bison," Syd said.

"I can try," Ron said.

The Wish Doctor studied him. "Of course you can, but I have an idea. The absence of all these animals from the toy store is going to create enough of a vacuum that there will be repercussions. We need to lead them back to the store."

"Will they follow us?" Ron asked.

"Maybe if you put a red flag on that hockey stick and wave it hard enough. We've been playing defence too long. It's time to take control. Knock the stuffing out of this problem. Fight fire with fire."

"Follow me," he said and soon they were at the Central Park Zoo. With all the chaos, they were able to get past the turnstiles without trouble. The animals there were far calmer than any of the stuffed animals come to life.

"Schwarz is not the only place in Manhattan with stuffed animals," the Doctor said. "Look there."

Through the gift shop window, they could spot a series of shelves with stuffed animals, and a display of animals from the *Madagascar* movies.

'You want me to bring all those toys alive?"

"Could you?"

"Don't know, don't usually do this kind of trick."

"It's no trick," Syd said.

"Sorry," Ron said. "Not trying to offend anyone."

"I just want the penguins," the Doctor said, "the *Madagascar* penguins." He was grinning. "Promise them you'll bring them alive for 24 hours if they will do us a favour."

"Done."

Ron waved his hockey stick like a wand, and suddenly there were three sets of penguins saluting, the three captains saying, "At our service, your bear ness."

Ron pointed to the Doctor. "He'll tell you what to do."

The penguins saluted the Doctor. "Ah, the man. What do you want us to do?"

"Simple, I want you to shuffle off the buffalo."

"Good one," said the Skipper. "To the toy store I take it."

"Yes, I do not want Buffalo going over Niagara Falls."

"We could make it happen."

"I would not want you to eat into your 24 hours of freedom."

"Toy store on Fifth Avenue it is. Corporal, you know what to do."

It took what seemed only moments for the penguins to organize in ruthless efficiency.

Had Babe Ruth been there, it would been quite inefficient.

In a day of chaos in New York, it was still a sight to see a group of twelve penguins roller-skating, leading a herd of snorting bison down Fifth Avenue. The bison were amazingly calm, which only goes to show that, when necessary, it isn't so hard to roller-skate in a buffalo herd after all.

Loretta, Ron, and Syd followed behind, as the buffalo filled Fifth Avenue, growing smaller as they made their way back to the toy store, toy-sized by the time they crossed the entrance, then nothing but stuffing as they lay quietly on the store floor.

"Thank you, penguins," Ron said.

"No, thank *you*," the skipper said. "Please just don't confuse us with any mopping up you have to do."

With that the penguins were off for 23 hours of well-deserved partying.

The Wish Doctor looked relived. "I can handle the rest. Why don't you three wander down to Times Square? I'll join you there when I'm done."

The three headed off, Ron looking for all the world as if he belonged among the Elmos and Mickeys.

The Doctor took his time as he undid the rest of the wishes. With time to think, he knew there was something bigger at play, but he couldn't fathom what.

The air had crackled with wish energy, and now there were no remnants of it at all. He pitied any new dreamer coming into the city. There would be no power for a wish for a long time.

As he turned toward Broadway and the stroll toward Times Square, he did not notice the boxing kangaroos jumping the other way. It was as if the world was upside down.

28: The revelation

The Wish Doctor limped into the classroom Tuesday morning after the Thanksgiving weekend eyes tinged with red, his hair unkempt. Alma had thought she'd seen fatigue in her teacher's face before, but now there was no denying it. He looked haggard.

More haggard than Syd had looked, and he had looked twice, maybe three times, his age when he had returned, so tired he hadn't come to class.

Alma slowly put up her hand and held it there for long minutes. She was still feeling distraught over Smaetag's wish, even though Selva had assured her she was going to be okay. Despite his comment that her quick thinking had saved Smaetag, she couldn't help but feel she had triggered Smaetag's terrible wish.

Her stomach was tied in knots; she didn't think she could concentrate on the morning's lesson and what she needed to ask seemed to be important to her understanding. While the adventure to the Island of Misfit Toys had been just that, an adventure, for all its danger, what she saw happening now—the danger to Smaetag, the craziness in New York—made her fear a disaster was coming.

For a moment, the stress of the moment seemed to overwhelm her. Alma felt if the lights were going out all around her. The question she was going to ask disappeared from her tongue.

But the wishkey she had drunk was still with her, overwhelming any small doubts. She pictured Ed the bear holding his bright bulbs, and the moment passed. It was as if clouds trying to obscure her mind were pushed away. Her head was clear again.

And the question was back on her tongue. "If so many wishes are going wrong now, more than ever, could it be that someone is making them go wrong?"

The Wish Doctor stopped in his tracks, a deep frown, an old man's frown, on his young face.

"I'm sorry," she said, I didn't mean to be a pain. It's just that every time I tried to make a birthday wish, my brother would say, 'I hope your wish goes wrong.'"

"No, no, It's okay. It's a good question. It's a very good question."

~

The Wish Doctor stopped to think. *Why haven't I thought of this before?*

Now that he heard it, it seemed familiar. His young self did not remember the thought, but his older self did. Could it be that someone had wished he not know this? He was at times as susceptible to wishes gone awry as anyone else. Sometimes more so.

He looked at his young student. He had been right to invite Alma Faye into his school instead of her brother. What had given the brother the idea? He almost wished he knew, but he knew what trouble that would bring.

He said slowly, "We have an adversary. There's a person who makes wishes go wrong. We must find out how the person does it. And why."

29: Green hair and an orange Mustang

All his life, which admittedly wasn't that long, Syd had wanted to drive a Mustang. When the Wish Doctor tossed him the keys to the Wishtang, he was not just gassed, he was flabbergassed.

Alma was surprised the Wish Doctor let Syd drive. Despite all the chores her parents gave her, they would not let her drive for fear their great jalopy might get damaged. Even Pierre, who was long overdue for his license, was not allowed to drive.

Yet here they were in a car unlike any other. It was a custom-built car, a Shelby of some sort, but no ordinary Mustang. It was sleeker and more powerful, with so much electronic gadgetry she would not *want* to drive it.

"How did you get such a car?" Syd asked, after he had spent fifteen minutes geeking out about what a great ride it was.

"Purchased it at a great discount at auction. Someone wished for the coolest car in the world, but turns out, they had wished for the coolest car in the world without wishing for good financing. They bankrupted themselves and the family, and they died impoverished. I would prefer not to have this car and that they had lived. However, I think it would soothe them to know we are using it to combat other wishes gone bad. The wishmethere needs some repairs after the damage from the elephant tusks in New York."

The Wish Doctor sighed. He hated using the device to combat wishes gone wrong. That was his job.

"Are you sure you are okay for me to drive?" Syd said. "I'd hate to hurt this beautiful machine."

"Trust me, I couldn't afford the insurance for a collision, so I've put in some protections. We'll be safe, as long as you don't go too much past the speed limit and don't fall asleep. That's my job."

The Doctor smiled slightly. Once in a while the confluence of personal benefit and the needs of his profession came together, allowing him the enjoyment of fine things such as this car. He definitely needed it in his line of work. It had allowed him to stop more damages than the pleasures he earned from it, so he did not feel guilty about having it. "The drive is pretty easy, mostly flat, not much traffic. If I fall asleep, wake me up before we hit the bridge to the island."

The Doctor climbed into the back seat, which was much too small for him, and Alma road shotgun. He didn't seem to mind as he examined his wish watch, often gesturing. There was some kind of video panel on the seat behind Alma that she felt him tapping, sometimes furiously. Clearly, he was solving wish problems as they drove.

The tapping slowed down by the time they were off Cape Breton Island and onto the mainland of Nova Scotia.

The Wish Doctor yawned a little. He had not gotten enough rest lately. This thought of an adversary bothered him, the worry making what little sleep he could get restless.

Despite the rough braking and acceleration as Syd became used to the most powerful car in creation, the vibrations of the tires eventually lulled the Doctor to sleep.

Looking at him in the rearview mirror, Alma found it hard to believe that one so knowledgeable about, well, everything could look so innocent.

The last two weeks had been frantic at the school. Lessons were clearly rushed so the Wish Doctor and Selva could spend more time at wish reversals but also trying to solve the problem of the adversary. The homework assignments were longer and more complex, and there was disappointment if any student failed to master the material. There was a growing sense of seriousness. The number of puns made by the Doctor had almost reduced to zero.

The Doctor had come to Syd and Alma three days earlier and said he was taking them on a field trip to a place where he could relax and, he hoped, gain insight into what and where the adversary was. Alma would get her first chance to help do a wish reversal.

The Doctor didn't say it, but he was more worried than ever, and was trying to get his students ready faster than originally planned to help against whatever threat the adversary represented.

Smaetag seemed recovered, but everyone wondered if there were some connection between the adversary and her incident.

As they drove west, Alma glanced at Syd, wanting to know more about the weekend in New York, where so many wishes had gone wrong at once, but he was all concentration, learning the workings of the car. She settled in to enjoy the scenery.

The fall colours were at the peak of perfection. "They have held their colour longer than any year I remember," Syd said. "Must be they know the prettiest girl is studying them this year."

Alma rolled her eyes but was secretly thrilled.

Crimson maple leaves, golden oak leaves, yellow birch, and pink leaves she did not recognize decorated the roads and the waterways. Her mouth hung open as mile after mile of beauty engulfed her as they made their way over the New Brunswick border and the Tantramar salt marshes. The marshes straddled the narrow isthmus that joins Nova Scotia to New Brunswick, though they both had once been part of Acadia.

When Syd turned to look at her and noticed her open mouth, he asked if she was hungry. She was about to say no when the Wish Doctor spoke from behind. "I am. Syd. Do you know where the Big Stop is?"

"Of course."

"Head in there. It's time for a hot turkey sandwich."

Syd had a quick look at Alma, grinning. Neither had met anyone so fond of turkey as the Doctor.

After lunch, the Doctor was full of energy, telling stories as they drove, mostly of wishes gone wrong. But then he began to talk about imagination and dreaming.

The road from the Big Stop to the Confederation Bridge, though still scenic, was not quite as spectacular as the landscape near the Cabot Trail, yet the Doctor's tale telling made it seem so.

His energy continued to increase the closer they got to the island, seeming to peak as they embarked on the bridge, the twelve-mile link between the provinces of New Brunswick and Prince Edward Island. "I much prefer the ferry crossing," he said, "but the bridge is more dependable. It was a very dependable and sensible wish that allowed it to be built. If all wishes were so made, with proper precautions, I would have much less to do and much more leisure time.

"The crossing is also much quicker this way. The one thing I don't like about this car, is that it is not high enough to let us see over the side of the bridge. It's quite a sight out there, looking out over the waters of the Northumberland Strait and toward Prince Edward Island."

The only thing that quieted the Doctor was the beautiful rainbow stretching as a gateway over the island at the far end of the bridge.

After a moment, he said, "Can't tell if it's natural. So many rainbows wished for here, it's easy to get confused."

"Which way do we go?" Syd asked when they arrived under the rainbow.

"Straight to Cavendish. No use in wasting time. Might as well go to where dreams are made."

Alma was amazed by the brilliant green of the fields this late in October. She felt a thrill thirty minutes later as they pulled past a sign announcing 'Green Gables.'

"Up that road," the Doctor said, pointing right as they reached the intersection of highways 6 and 13.

On the left, a bus of Japanese tourists hustled into a graveyard.

"That's where Lucy Maud Montgomery is buried," Syd said. "Many fans of her books visit here."

Alma tried to keep her sudden excitement hidden. She was in Anne's land. Lucy Maud was the creator of Anne of Green Gables. Her few friends at home would be so jealous. She was also impressed by Syd's knowledge.

As they turned up Highway 6, she got her first glimpse of the Cavendish shore beyond the cottages and hay fields. It was beautiful. The green grass, the yellow hay, the blue water created a canvas of calm and belonging.

"To the right," Syd said, "Is Montgomery's grandparents' homestead, and a post office where you can get 'Anne' stamps."

Alma found it hard to concentrate on wishes. It was like one had come true. She had to fight the instinct to wish she would never have to leave this place. The gentleness of the land was so welcoming.

"Take the next right up past these cottages. We're looking for number 16."

Syd geared down smoothly and drove up the rust-red road past the delightfully quaint cottages. Alma thought she could live there the rest of her life.

They pulled to a stop in front of Number 16.

"This is it. Alma, this is your wish reversal. There are a father and a young girl from New York. He brought her here to celebrate her birthday and she made an uncontrolled wish. You'll see the problem right away. It's more significant than it appears, so be careful."

It was the kind of wish the Doctor didn't like to bother with, but it was the perfect teaching tool as the wish was hardly malicious. The risk of making things worse was small. Relatively small. He wanted to observe, to see if the adversary had any influence.

He led the way to the door and knocked.

An attractive man with slightly graying sideburns answered, and waved them all in. "Thank you for coming," he said. "My ex-wife is already upset for me having custody on Ann's birthday. She'll be furious if she sees what happened."

The man pointed to the dining room table, where his young daughter sat. She was pretty, slight of build, freckled, but instead of dark red hair as might be expected, her hair was the deepest shade of emerald green.

Alma wasn't sure what was wrong. In this age, it wasn't unusual for someone to have a dark shade of emerald hair even if it did clash with her freckles.

She looked at the Wish Doctor for guidance. His face was stoic. It was up to her.

"Hi," said Alma, "We're here to help. This is the Wish Doctor. Syd and I are apprentices. Are you feeling okay, Ann?"

Ann nodded slowly, but her face was unhappy. "I'm okay, but I feel like I drank too much raspberry cordial. My mom is going to be so angry with me."

"I understand. We will try and help you so there will be no anger. Tell me, did you make a wish recently?"

The girl nodded.

"Can you tell me what the wish was?" Alma asked.

"I wished to be like Anne of Green Gables."

Alma didn't understand at first. She had been young when she read the books about Anne.

Then she remembered. In the first book, Anne had tried to rid herself of red hair with dye and ended up with green hair.

The girl was like Anne, but only the Anne in that one scene from the book.

Alma looked at the Wish Doctor. There was so many ways for wishes to be misinterpreted.

"Can you tell me the exact wording you used?"

"I wish I was like Anne of Green Gables," Ann without an e said.

Alma concentrated on how she could help. If she conjured a wish to let Ann's hair grow out, would the dye diminish? Her intuwishin warned this was not temporary dye. Something more powerful was at work. She looked at the Doctor, who was frowning in concern.

"There is no stigma in having green hair these days. You could keep it."

"I could. If I lived with my father. Trust me, my mother will be angry. She will take it out on Dad. I may not be able to see him again."

Alma understood. She missed her own father and wasn't sure when she would seem him again. The poor girl was frightened of more than green hair.

Alma considered the problem. The first approach had been to see if the wisher could live with the wish, maybe even appreciate the side effects. Ann couldn't. Alma had to find a way to reverse it.

She'd practised saying wishes backwards so often, she was an expert. She tried saying the wish backwards, with each word reversed, but nothing happened.

She tried it in several combination—letters reversed, the whole sentence inverted. Nothing took effect.

She had Ann repeat each word in reverse, but there was not even a peep of reversal.

"Syd, you mentioned there was a costume shop nearby," Alma said. "Can you go get some Anne clothes that would fit Ann?"

Syd raised his eyebrow for a second, then understood. "Will do."

"Ann, how did you make the wish? Was it a birthday wish as you blew out the candles?"

"Yes. I also threw a coin in a well at the Green Gables house and made the same wish."

"Oh," said Alma. The Doctor hadn't discussed the impacts when the same wish was made more than once.

"What was the exact wording of that wish?"

"Close to the first. I've made the same wish over a hundred times in my life."

The Wish Doctor had a startled look on his face that he tried to hide, but Alma saw it. He was right. This case was not as simple as it first appeared.

"We're going to try to reverse this wish, but we need to say it exactly backwards together, okay?"

Ann nodded and, on Alma's directions, they did, but there was no change.

Syd came in through the door with what appeared to be authentic Anne of Green Gables clothes. Not a costume, but actual clothes. "Picked these up at Avonlea Village from some guy name Gilbert at a great bargain."

Alma handed them to Ann. "Put these on. Take off everything else."

The Wish Doctor nodded in appreciation. It was a good idea. Make the wish of being like Anne come to life without the need for green hair.

Ann disappeared into another room, and then returned to the kitchen. If you had entered the book of *Anne of Green Gables*, you would believe you had encountered Anne.

Except the green hair would be there for the entire story.

Alma turned to the father. "Aside from the green hair, does she look any different since she made the wish?"

"I think she used to be a little taller," he said. "And I don't remember the freckles."

So, thought Alma, Syd and the Doctor at the same time. There *was* more to the wish change than the hair. Was it the birthday wish alone that had made the changes? Maybe many wishes were at work.

Alma looked at the Doctor. A typical wish reversal wasn't going to work, she concluded. She needed to make a wish and wanted his permission.

He had given her an envelope with one of his wishkers to use. She delicately lifted the wishker from the envelope and gently touched Ann's face with it, wishpering, "I wish Ann was as she was before she was Anne."

She felt a tingling of excitement, as one would if they discovered a wish was coming true, but no one seemed to notice any difference.

Except her father. "Where are your freckles?"

It was true. Her recent, but very attractive, freckles were gone.

Could it be she had one hundred small changes from one hundred wishes to make her more like Anne? Would Alma have the energy to make that many wish reversals? Were there even enough wishkers on the Doctor's face?

"Tell me about the other wishes you made," Alma said.

"I made them almost every week for the last two years."

Alma could feel the Doctor's eyes go wide, yet he did not interfere, even as she struggled for a solution. "Did you use the exact same words, every time?"

"I did at first. But then I started changing the words, hoping I would be more likely to have the wish come true."

"I don't suppose you remember all the versions you used. You didn't happen to write them down, did you?"

Ann shook her head.

Alma's shoulders tensed. It would be near impossible to use the simple wish reverse technique on so many wishes when you didn't know what they were. She could see it in the Wish Doctor's eyes. To even try would be to invite danger.

"Can I make a suggestion?" Syd asked. "I feel the gathering of dreams and creaking imagination. I sense older people trying desperately to recover their childhood. I think we should go there."

Alma looked to Ann. "Do you know what kind of gathering could be near?"

"I came here because there is an Anne convention. Almost every person who ever played Anne is here for a celebration. They are supposed to be gathering at the Lake of Shining Waters."

Alma exchanged glances with Syd. It was too much of a coincidence.

It took only a moment in the Shelby Wishtang to arrive at a parking lot near a picnic shelter. Ann and her father were not far behind in a black Cadillac. There was a short trail, and Syd pointed the way.

Before long they could see the convention of Annes, a collection of all those who played Anne in the musical at the Charlottetown Confederation Centre or in the later production of *Anne and Gilbert*, a musical about their college years. There were a number of girls dressed as Anne, conjuring dreams and wishes and pulling on all the dreams and wishes of people who had read Anne over the years.

The lake was small, maybe more of a pond, but oh, how it sparkled in the sun. It was almost blinding. Alma could see many spectacularly coloured dragonflies flitting over the water.

In the distance, she could see the Anne of Green Gables golf course, a couple rustic houses and tall, firry spruce and pine trees. Arching over the greenery and touching the lakeshore, there was a luminescent rainbow. She knew there was some controversy whether this was truly the inspiration for the Lake of Shining Waters. There was another pond in a small hamlet of Park Corner close by that was also a possible candidate. Maybe it was or maybe it was both, but, true or not, the wishes of so many had turned this spot into a powerful focus of magic.

Alma felt the power of the lake. There was no doubt magic reflected off the sparkling surface. How many people taken with the story of Anne had stood here between the small lake and the sand dune on the other side of Alma and dreamt or felt their imagination take hold? How many had wished they had Anne's imagination or her red hair, or her pluck?

How many had wished they had a companion like Matthew, or pretended they were the Lady Cordelia. How many wishes had taken place here? Had Anne's author been the force that created the power of imagination here, or was it already here and she had been swept up in it?

On the other side of the dunes, Alma could sense the long stretch of sand that was Cavendish Beach. How many Maritimers had come here to relax and dream and wish for things that led them away from the poor economy of the Maritimes? How many had returned to vacation here, wishing they could stay forever?

How many Acadians had wished not to leave when deported? How many lingering, longing wishes to return here still existed in the Cajuns in her native New Orleans?

Across the island, Alma felt the power of wishes. People wishing their tee shot to go straight, others wishing to beat their brother in the game of golf just once, others wishing for their putt to go in. Still others wished they could find the perfect cottage to buy, while some wished for room in their stomach to have one more piece of the best strawberry shortcake in all the world.

This area was a cauldron of wish power.

There was a floating boardwalk across the water along the edge of the Lake of Shining Waters, separating the dunes. It bounced and swayed as Alma and the others walked along it, the dragon flies flitting alongside them.

Towards the far end, the bridge was clogged with women (and men) dressed as Anne, or Diana, or Marilla, or other characters from the Anne books.

They filed up the grass slope that led up to a beach parking lot with a crowd as big as, or bigger than, on the brightest August day, when the beach would be full.

It seemed almost folly to try to reverse a wish of being Anne here. It felt more like they should be joining the rest and wishing they were like her.

Syd grabbed Alma's hand. "Do you feel the power? Ron just sent me a message. He can feel it from back home."

Alma nodded. She had to resist wishing herself to be more like Anne.

Ann and her father huddled behind Alma. She looked at the Wish Doctor. Something was concerning him, but she didn't think it was his confidence in her. She swallowed. She didn't want to disappoint him.

"How are you feeling?" she said to Ann.

"It feels like my body wants to change. I'm scared."

Syd pointed at the girl's face, and Alma realized the freckles were back and suddenly the green locks were in braids.

Syd looked up with a strange insight. "She's going to be dragged back in time to when Anne was a girl if we don't do something soon."

More like Anne. To be more like Anne, she would have to live in her time.

Alma gasped as a current of data pushed into her intuwishin. They would have to make one hundred eleven wishes, and quickly. But how could you wish *not* to be Anne, when so many around were wishing to be like her?

She pondered. If it were true that so many were wishing to be Anne, wouldn't that almost create a vacuum? If all wish power close by was being pulled to do that, wouldn't there be an emptiness where wishes to be *not* like Anne would have power?

What better way to reverse 100 Anne wishes, then to use 100 Ann wishes? The wishker had not worked. Maybe because every wish was about being like Anne. What if she had Ann wish that she was more like Ann? Alma smiled.

But she needed wishes. What kind of wish would be most likely to make one be like oneself?

Birthday wishes of course. Birthday wishes were the most personal kind of wishes. Though problematic, they were best used on oneself.

The other kind of wish needed here was a wishing well. The girl had said she made about 100 wishes, but it had taken a long time for the full culmination. Alma's intuwishin told her the girl had made 111 wishes. Alma might not be able to make a pure wish, but she had studied wish lore so hard, her subconscious mind sometimes worked quicker than she understood.

The residual wish magic was feeding her intuwishin so she had a sudden inspiration. "How old are you grandparents?" she asked.

"All four of them are exactly 78 years old. My great grandparents all lived to be 94."

Math.

Those with mathematical coincidences were more likely to be susceptible to wishes. Selva had taught her that.

"How old are you?"

"Sixteen."

Sixteen. That meant she had 78 more birthday wishes left.

"How badly do you want to reverse this green hair?"

"Very badly. I'm starting to think thoughts that aren't mine. I think I will be sad to the depths of despair about Matthew and never able to marry if I don't change."

"Would you be willing to use up your future birthday wishes to help change?"

Ann nodded. "I will never use wishes again."

"I think I have a plan."

The Wish Doctor nodded. He had followed Alma's thoughts and agreed.

It was important to reverse Ann's wish, but there was something more going on than just the simple wish. The power generated from the Anne convention was overwhelming. Dreams and stuff that could be used to make wishes was almost palpable. The more the conventioneers became more like Anne, the more the power multiplied.

Some of it was hanging like ripe apples.

About to be harvested. The wish watch had brought them there to fix this wish for a reason.

"I need another 33 wishes," Alma said to the Wish Doctor. "Should I use the dragonflies?"

"No," he said vehemently. "They are not for you. We need to use 33 wishing well wishes."

"There is no wishing well here."

The Wish Doctor smiled. "There is a huge wishing well here, an extremely powerful one."

Alma couldn't help but scrunch up her face.

"Alma, concentrate. The answer is right in front of your face."

What did he mean, 'in front of her face'? She was leaning over the railing along the boardwalk. The only thing in front of her face was the Lake of Shining Waters.

"The lake is a wishing well?"

"Yes. It is now. There used to be a beloved little amusement park in the woods above, full of wonder. See where the rainbow is shining now? The park was just beneath that rainbow. In it was a wishing well. When the park was closed, the well was destroyed, but its water flowed across the park, pulling magic with it, into this lake, creating a giant wishing well."

"But I have no coins."

The Wish Doctor waved at her. "Could you please check behind your ear?"

Alma could feel the plush fabric of a velvet pouch behind her left ear. She grabbed it and opened it quickly. There were 33 strange-looking coins.

"Those are florins." Syd said with the confidence of a nerdy coin collector.

"Yes," the Wish Doctor said. "They will work. Trust me. I have used them before."

"We just need an agent provocateur to pull the birthday wishes here. Something that can't be tricked."

Syd looked up knowingly. "Ron has been wanting to come all day."

"Wish him here."

Syd closed his eyes. Suddenly, Ron was standing next to them, wearing sunglasses.

"Well wishes from a rainbow are blinding," he said. "Happy birthday, Ann. Nice to meet you, Ann's father." Even in a moment, of crisis, Ron could only be polite.

Ann's father stood in amazement. "Will this all work? Do I need to do something?"

"Guard your daughter from stray wishes. Go to the other side of her and let no one pass."

"And me?" Asked a game but confused Ann.

"When I say go," Alma said, "use your 78 borrowed birthday wishes. Say each as fast as you can, but with perfect enunciation. 'I wish to be more like Ann.' You must not add or pronounce an e at the end of your name."

"Of course not."

"Be sure. Make sure you picture in your mind your name as A N N. It's critical."

"Okay."

"Alma," the Wish Doctor said, "can you handle the rest? There is something else going on here and I need to be outside this reversal to discover it."

She nodded.

"One more thing. Divide the florins between you, Ron and Syd. Cast the wishes one after another, but do not overlap words or splashes. Make sure Ron goes last, okay?"

Everyone nodded, even Ann, who had banished the final e from her life.

"Ron, if you please," Alma instructed.

"I wish that all Ann's birthday wishes can be used today and cannot be reversed on her coming birthdays. I confirm that she will not try to use them on those dates."

Ann suddenly stiffened and began to glow. It was as if candles were flaming inside her.

"Go!" Alma said.

"I wish I was more like Ann. I wish I was more like Ann…"

Alma counted carefully, telling Ann when she had ten to go, five to go, one to go. She mustn't use one to many, or she would cease to exist immediately.

Ann stopped exactly as she should, and Alma threw her florin in the lake. It made a splash like a Shupershark breaching the water.

As she, Syd and Ron took turns throwing florins, Ann's hair slowly turned from green to red, then to darkest black. Her freckles disappeared and did not come back. Her body grew slightly taller, her shoulders hunched a little, but her face became more beautiful, almost as beautiful as the face of the lady in the painting.

As each florin hit the lake surface, a rainbow leapt from the water and descended upon Ann.

Alma had not really understood how much energy making several wishes took from you. Most of her other wishes had been one or two at a time.

She looked at Syd and Ron. It seemed like no effort for either of them, so she kept going until she had made her eleven wishes.

The rainbows drew attention from the crowd of Annes, and from someone else, too, just as the power of wishes was reaching its crescendo. The Wish Doctor pushed past Alma, Ann and Syd, and nearly had to jump on the railing of the boardwalk to bypass Ron.

There was a rush of wind on the other side of the lake, in no way connected with Her Splendiferousness. Not a real wind, either. Something was siphoning all the wish power here, taking it, holding it, storing it. Fully formed wishes, old wishes, spent wishes, budding wishes, the raw essence of power to form wishes. Dreams, and hopes and fantasies were all rushing into a receptacle.

A human receptacle.

The power was draining from the land, from the rainbow over the valley, from the convention of Annes. That group of people more than any other had the power to reject negativity, to hold onto their wishes and dreams, but that unnatural wind was pulling the dreams away like a vacuum.

Just as Ann's 111 wishes were completed, the cyclone stopped. There was a stillness everywhere. And not a wish to be found.

The crowd *en masse* swooned, light-headed, drained of all their wishes, weakened as if they had just drunk the last of the raspberry cordial.

~

There was one who did not swoon. A fairly tall man for the year 1500. It was a strange thought. The Wish Doctor thought he should know him but did not.

The man looked up and saw the Doctor. He seemed startled for a moment, but then began to grin and walk toward him.

The Wish Doctor whispered into Ann's father's ear as he passed, "Protect your Ann from further wishes. Get to your Cadillac and ride it down the highway like a big but fast old dinosaur."

"Thank you," Ann's father said. He led his daughter by the hand along the boardwalk to their car. The girl now looked like the Ann she was and not the Anne she had thought she wanted to be.

The Wish Doctor mounted the short green slope that rose from the Lake of Shining Waters toward the paved beach parking lot. The other man waved him forward. Ron was the first to follow, and then Syd and Alma.

They reached the road. The man was standing in front of a wooden pedestrian bridge that crossed a set of dunes to the beach. It was as if he was blocking the way.

The Wish Doctor's feeling that he should know the man was even stronger, but he couldn't place him. He just knew he was dangerous.

The man smiled. "It's been a long time, and a long way from our last meeting. I'm surprised to see you here, but I guess I shouldn't be. This part of the world has yet to fully harvest its wishes. And it's a good little corner of the world for you to run and hide in."

The Wish Doctor racked his brain. *Who is this man?* "What have you done here?" he said. "You've undermined nature, taken liberties with the will of people."

"Are you surprised?"

"Yes. I'm always surprised at tyrants. Who are you?"

The man was handsome, olive-skinned, and with immaculately coiffed curly hair with only a minor touch of grey that projected dignity. He was impeccably dressed in modern fashion, as if he had stepped off a Milan fashion runway. Even here in a beach parking lot, he was wearing gold cuff links that glinted in the sun. His smile could melt granite and his outstretched hands seemed welcoming. For all of that, there was a sense of menace.

To match the menace, behind them the rainbow dissolved and a dark cloud formed over the Lake of Shining Waters. There was a scurrying of creatures who created wishes out of the rainbow valley, their anger for what had been done to dissolve their park apparent.

Behind the Doctor, Ron, Syd and Alma formed a tired wall. The Wish Doctor knew he should send them away, but couldn't.

The man moved slowly in a semi-circle, leaving the bridge over the dunes, so that eventually his back was to the Lake of Shining Waters, and his body now blocked the entrance to the boardwalk. The Wish Doctor and his companions circled to face him.

"Hey, Edison," Ron said, meaning no disrespect. "This guy does not have our best interests at heart."

The Wish Doctor nodded, trying to figure out the puzzle. Why couldn't he remember this man? Something inside was struggling to tell him but the knowledge remained hidden. "Who are you?" he asked again.

"Who am I?" The man smiled lightly. "I thought for sure you would re-member. You once wanted to be better than me. My name is Ivelli.

"Mack Ivelli."

The man then grinned the evilest grin ever been seen by humankind.

30: Annes and quicksands

It was perhaps the most contrasting image the Wish Doctor had ever seen, the simple, dreaming beauty of the Lake of Shining Waters and the pure evil of his adversary. The heroine whose imagination had inspired so many others might have thought this a great adventure, but the Wish Doctor could only think of how out of place they both were. Their unsettled characters did not belong; the flaws that drove them stood in sharp contrast to childhood innocence.

And yet Anne's creator had in her later days been witness to the darkness of a priestly husband. He might have made fine company for the Doctor and his adversary. Was he, like they, a victim of petty hate and envy that had over time driven his entire future to darkness undreamt of in his youth?

As Alma watched the men take each other's measure, she tried to signal to the convention of Annes that they needed to leave, but the coterie of Annes were more attuned to each other than to the possibility of danger.

Until a rather large black bear appeared and chased them away.

Alma took a glance at Syd, and then Ron, who had a smile suggesting he was admiring some self-cleverness. She turned back quickly to look at the Doctor and Ivelli.

There was a connection between the two men, and despite the air of politeness, it was not civil. Surrounding Ivelli she could smell the same force that had prevented her from reversing the green hair. He had used some trick to stop wishes from reversing. Instead, he was absorbing both the power to reverse and to make wishes.

Grey tendrils of energy from the rainbow valley wafted toward him, saturating his body. There was something happening beyond her understanding. She grabbed Syd's hand. It was freezing cold, like a polar bear's paw. Syd's hand was never cold.

He was shaking. Scared. She looked to the Wish Doctor.

The Doctor's memory was returning. It had taken him a while, but now he recognized the man whom he'd gone to school with, the son of the great princely writer. So long ago, it didn't seem real.

He wondered if this could be a descendant, but the look was too cruel, too close to what he remembered. You did not forget such a look, not when it had set him to a lifetime of toil, 500 years and no end in sight.

But he *had* forgotten, hadn't he? How could he have forgotten the unforgettable? There was a powerful wish involved. He couldn't sense it but there had to be.

Ivelli was the adversary. The Wish Doctor had thought their enmity had ended 100 years ago with Ivelli's death, amid the tragedy that befell the Wish Doctor's own family.

Ivelli laughed. "Don't you recognize me? I must be your oldest acquaintance still alive. I know we haven't seen each other for a long time, but still. My face hasn't aged that much has it? If I can recognize you, with your much younger face, surely you can remember me. I think the grey gives me the sort of look of the intelligentsia from the 18th century, don't you?"

"Yes, I recognize you. You were the smart boy."

"The smartest boy. You remember that, right? You remember how I was the smartest there was, maybe the smartest there ever was until you stole my title."

"I wasn't trying to steal anything."

"You think making a wish to make you better than someone else isn't stealing? Isn't cheating? What kind of wish did you make to convince yourself of that? You won honours that should have been mine, took posts that should have been mine. You were always the favourite of kings and queens, judges and magistrates. And of course, princes. Let's not forget princes."

"It was never my intention to take anything from you."

"You never intended to steal Giselle? I could have understood the postings, the awards. But not that. In some ways, your success pushed me harder. It gave me the will to go on as long as you. I will not die first. I vowed that. Did you know it? Did you know that the right kind of vow can be more powerful than any wish? I have learned it is so, or I'd not be here now."

"It's not that simple."

"Isn't it? I could have lived with you becoming smarter, had you earned it. I know how hard you studied, how often you stayed up late, how you begged for coins to hire the best tutors, to buy the best volumes of knowledge, arcane and modern. But it didn't matter did it? You couldn't keep up with me. We did not know it then, but my mind is like a computer. I can draw conclusions from the scantiest data. I make your buddy Sherlock Holmes seem like a first-grader solving problems. I have insights into the way the world works, some that would scare the hell out of Socrates, others that would please Newton or Shakespeare. To be the smartest was my birthright. And you stole it. Ripped it from me, made my path ruthless and hard."

The Wish Doctor shook his head. "Do you think my life has been joyful? Do you think I wanted to live this way? If I did envy you, if I did hate you, I would not wish my life on you. It is a burden, and I carry it for the shame of what I have done, not just to you but to others."

Ivelli paused, as if maybe there was a spark of compassion within him trying to get out. "If those words came from an honest man, and not from a man more ruthless than my father ever observed, perhaps we could find a common term."

The Wish Doctor hung his head slightly. If you were not looking for the tell, you would not notice. The shame of his life stood before him. He could try to hide it with humour all he wanted. He could dedicate himself to curing wishes until the end of his life, and his shame would never end.

And yet, he too had been tricked. No doubt that Ivelli and his cursed cleverness had been the rationale of the trickster. Ivelli was born with cleverness that triggered rivalry. It was in him for a purpose, planted there, conjured there by who knew what powers. All to force the Wish Doctor to become what he had become.

"It is true," he said, "I made a little selfish wish in a bout of pettiness. I did not give myself a chance to become what I might have become naturally, but neither did the forces around me. I thought I acted of my own free will. Who would care if an artist's bastard wanted to pretend he was as great as his parent? But it was not of my own free will. The idle, selfish wish set me to do things that had to be done. Who would have done them, who will continue to do them if I had not, if I will not? Everyone before me, everyone after me has done their time, and pleaded 'enough!'"

If he thought there would be sympathy in Ivelli's face, he was mistaken.

"I think I was chosen," the Doctor continued, "because it was known I would not give up, even when all life drained from me and a new one was stuffed into me. Even now, when I would give anything to lay this burden aside, I will not, not until I know there is a successor, a line of succession.

I will not have another single person carry this chaos with them, and to know and remember all the torment for such a length of time."

He refrained from looking at Alma and Syd. It was too early, he told himself, too early to believe, and too early to take away happiness. And yet, he had seen the future and the possibility of that succession.

He looked straight at Ivelli, almost pleading. "If you are unhappy that I made an ill-conceived wish, consider yourself fortunate that it was not you."

Ivelli rubbed his jaw, as the Wish Doctor had seen Ivelli's father do when frustrated. "Despite all this, you have lived a life of wonder, as few others have. You have had a birthright, not your own, no matter how you've chosen to use it."

"Why are you here?" the Doctor asked, realizing there was no point to this conversation. It was too close to one that they'd had before a long time ago. If they went further, the words would lead to Giselle. And if they did, old wounds would spring to life and take actions neither of them could control.

Ivelli laughed again. "In a way, it does involve you. I'm not here for confrontation or to seize titles, though. I am here simply for personal pleasure. I had not expected to come in contact with you, though I had heard you had settled in this part of the world. I wasn't sure if you had a hand in the inventor's progress, or if you were just a cheerleader.

"This is quite a pretty place, even at this time of year, though I think we both agree the weather is unnaturally warm. It's almost as if someone wished it."

There was something in the Machiavellian Ivelli smile that sent warning bells through the Wish Doctor. This was not a visit for personal pleasure. The former smartest person in the world had no compunction about lying.

The Wish Doctor subtly tried to wave his hand to have Syd and Alma move away or at least hide behind Ron. Anything might happen.

"More importantly," Ivelli continued, "Why are *you* here? If you are so burdened with work, and angst, I cannot see that this is a pleasure vacation."

Ivelli's father might have been a shrewd observer, a clever advisor, but despite his reputation, no fox, no wolf. His son was a whole pack. His grin of realization came quickly.

He had once been the world's smartest man and was not very far behind the one who now was. His eyes pivoted to the protégés behind the Wish Doctor. "You're not just here to prevent some wish, or reverse one, or to steal one for yourself. You're here to teach others. You want to pass on your obligations." Ivelli laughed. "You want age to defeat you before I've had my chance."

The Wish Doctor knew it would be futile to deny such an obvious truth to anyone well informed of wishes, yet alone Ivelli. To do so would only anger him. "And you are here to collect the magic of wishes and dreams, to build your own house of dreams and wishes."

"Well, aren't we quite the pair," Ivelli said, "taking secrets from each other, as if plucking daisies on the Tuscan hillside in August?"

~

Alma wanted to say something, but she sensed that anything she did would be taken as an antagonism. She was sure now the force that had held her from reversing the wish was in this man. She didn't know if the Wish Doctor realized this, but she feared to say anything.

The tension between the two of them was ready to snap. Each had wish magic surrounding them, the most dangerous kind. If each employed it purely for the sake of harming the other, it would not only go bad, it would go really badly, harming not just them, but the land they walked on.

Ivelli took a step toward her and Syd. Syd tried to push her behind him, but she stood her ground, though she took his hand. If she could not heal the girl without an exhausting effort, she did not know how she could stop this man.

"There is something here that is new," Ivelli said as he took another step, though keeping his eyes fixed on the doctor. "A plan is in motion to aid your succession, one hidden in layers. I wonder what it is?" There was menace in confidence. He was radiating energy.

Alma could feel Syd straightening, growing taller. The bear was with him, but something else as well. The power of a pure wish was welling within him, unconsciously. She was useless, blocked from any source of power; too tired even to seek one.

The Wish Doctor came to them, not looking like he was running, but in a second of blur he stood in front of them, arms wide in protection.

Ivelli's sharp incisors flashed like those of a fox in the chicken coop. "I wonder if I were to stop the succession here and now, would we meet again six hundred years from now?"

His step was so menacing, Alma let Syd move in front of her. There was something happening to him. Was it a wish or...?

"I warn you," the Wish Doctor said. "I have a well of wishes at my disposal. Take another step, and you will know again the gift I was granted has not gone to poor use."

Mack Ivelli laughed. "I have had a long time to study, to work hard. I have learned that from you. While you have been distracted, I have gathered my knowledge and my wits. I may not be as easy to overcome as you think."

If Ivelli took another step, he would cross a line that should not be crossed. Alma couldn't hold Syd's hand any longer. It was shaking. He was shaking.

~

Syd felt the essence of his grandfather as he had felt it so often, and felt the words come unbidden. It was an old phrase his grandfather had used, now so out of date. It wasn't meant to be a wish but an oath.

Syd couldn't stop the old oath as it sputtered from his throat, animal instinct taking over. "I wish you were in quicksand," he muttered.

The Wish Doctor couldn't quite hear him, and thus had no way to easily counter. Ivelli always practical, always ready, always pretty smart even if he never had a wish to make him so, used the simplest way to deflect a wish.

Or any kind of magic if you believed in that kind of stuff.

He pulled a small mirror from his breast pocket. It seemed to grow larger in the blazing sun. Syd's wish hit the mirror, reflected backward, expanding, catching them all.

"*Arrivederci,*" Ivelli said. He backed along the boardwalk as Syd, the Doctor and Alma began sinking helplessly into the quicksand the ground had become.

31: The picnic basket

Ron retained many of the instincts of goaltender Ron Hextall. So when the wish reflected off the mirror toward the Doctor, Syd and Alma, he dived out of the way. A bear's speed was always underestimated, and he could move like a bear on goalie skates. It is a truism that the goalie is always the fastest player on the team.

Ivelli didn't notice Ron escaping, as Ron had activated a camouflage wish that made him almost invisible. If fact you could bearly see him.

Alma couldn't help panicking. She flailed her arms and legs, trying to swim, but that only made it worse. She was sinking through the water/ sand surface. The Doctor was spitting up sand.

The three of them turned to look at Ron. He was calmly opening a picnic basket.

"What the—?" Alma exclaimed. The Doctor looked similarly annoyed. Only Syd was looking relieved.

Ron looked back at them, his eyes creasing, disappointed they were disappointed in him. He pulled out three sandwiches. "You were expecting maybe Yogi Berra?" he said. "Quicksand traps are not over until they are over. How else do you expect to reverse a quicksand wish trap than with a sandwish?"

He had looked like he was going to swallow the sandwish whole, but instead he threw them in the air as he muttered a silent prayer.

The Doctor nodded as the quicksand began to solidify beneath his feet. He looked for a sign of Ivelli, but he was gone—and with him a whole lot of powerful wishes.

The island of PEI would seem a lot less magical for a period of time. It would be a year before there was a confirmation of new wishes.

~

After he returned to the School of Wishes from the encounter with Ivelli, the Wish Doctor seemed like a different man, younger if that was some-how possible, and tireless. There were fewer puns, mostly those related to a specific wish problem. He seemed less fatigued, as if he was a young man desperately trying to prove himself in the world.

The lectures now ran longer, with more information crammed in every one. The field trips became more frequent and the students were actively involved in fixing wishes gone wrong. There was more prepara-tion, and more protection wishes than ever. He had students going to the wishing well at the distillery to make and freeze and collect wishes.

Alma, as much as anyone, knew the seriousness of the problem. Ivelli was ready to attack her and Syd, which meant they were mostly left be-hind, allowed to collect wishes from the wishing well and not much more. The Doctor had made it clear: the one place they were safe was at the Lodge of Wonders. Nothing could penetrate Selva's defensive wish barriers.

"I'm not being mean," the Wish Doctor said. "He will harm me first if he can; but if he can't do that, he will harm you. I'll disguise the other stu-dents when I take them with me, but he knows you now, and no disguise I make could stop him."

"We're being benched," Syd had grumbled. "Worse than that, we're not even being allowed in the arena."

If the Wish Doctor had changed, so had Syd. He seemed older, crankier, and the expressions he had learned from his grandfather be-came more frequent. It was as if he had taken on the Wish Doctor's true age.

The encounter with Ivelli changed much for Alma. While she had en-joyed the whimsy of the School of Wishes, she now saw the deep serious-ness behind it. Deeper than she had ever believed. The danger she had seen in Ivelli was scarier than even Lavinia, when the crystal seemed to be whispering dark things to her.

Alma felt like a little dust ball caught in a great hurricane.

There was one ray of hope. Ivelli was jealous of the Doctor. If he was jealous, then the Doctor obviously was worthy of the jealously. How long had Ivelli been working to ready himself to attack the Doctor, while all the time the Doctor had been working selfishly for the world?

The next sense of danger came on Halloween, and brought the Doctor near to panic. "Halloween can be harmless fun," he said, "but there is a deadly undercurrent where dark wishes either come alive themselves or undercut good wishes. This year, I am afraid none of you are strong enough to face it, so I'm going to put you in the wish cellar. I've brought in candy apples, and apples to bob, and monster mash music, and plague masks, and other Venetian masks, so you folks can have a wonderful time."

It had actually been fun. The Doctor was clearly concerned about his students' well-being. Only Smaetag and Loretta stayed up with Selva and the Wish Doctor on All Hallow's Eve.

It was about the only remarkable event Alma could remember in that part of the year until Christmas. For the next several weeks, it was all serious wish work.

The snow came late in November, and the grounds were beautiful for walking. The Doctor gave longer lunch breaks so they could take advantage of it.

Alma needed the break. It seemed like the homework assignments kept the students up 'til ten every night. More students received their key to the wishmethere, as they went on field trips, but none of them had been as exciting as the meeting with Ivelli in the land of Anne.

By the time Christmas vacation came, which started December 22, Alma was too exhausted to do anything but sleep.

~

At four pm on Christmas Eve, Alma felt her heart flutter. The day had been peaceful. Many of the students had gone home for the vacation or had been invited to a party held by the triplets. Alma, of course, had not been invited. She didn't care really but was feeling left out.

The Wish Doctor was off on a personal errand. He had been gone since December 23, which he said was a lucky day for him. She'd been waiting for him to say that Wishmas was a magical time and to be careful of wishes, but he'd said no such thing.

She asked Selva about it and he said, "The real magic of Christmas has been gone for at least a century. There are no wishes anymore, just shopping lists, and dedication to rituals, and a need to keep the economy going."

Alma would have been bummed out by this negativity, but she still could feel the magic of Christmas. As annoying as it was, she would have liked to hear her father singing way off key, but with such joy, "Have a Holly Jolly Christmas." What would he think if she told him that she'd been to the Island of Misfit Toys? There was so much else she could tell him.

There was no sign of Bell or the caretakers or Syd, all gone to spend time with their families. She had snuck a small glass of wishkey and given a toast to the beautiful lady in the painting, who seemed to be in especially bright spirits, elegantly dressed in what must have been Christmas regalia in those days gone by.

Alma fingered the locket Syd had given her the night before, just before he left to visit his parents. He'd invited her, but she was feeling guilty about being away from her own parents. She was certain her mother could live with her being away at a school, but for her to hang out with potential in-laws would probably have been too much.

She'd wrestled for several weeks with finding a way home. On the rare evening when the internet was working, she'd exchanged words with her father. He had said he would find the money to fly her home, but she knew how much flights were, and how precious money was to her family, so she'd refused.

She'd spent most of the day looking out the lodge windows at the snow. It was falling lightly, with little breeze. So deep and crisp and even.

When a family of deer trotted across the lawn through the snow, she wondered if there were any more tranquil setting in the world. She would have liked her family to be with her.

The flutter in her heart made her stand up and start to walk, ending up at the room that Selva used as a workshop. There was clanging and banging, and then a yelp of satisfaction.

She opened the door. Selva, stood up covered in grease, almost like the day she had come to join the school.

"What are you working on?" Alma asked, "Shouldn't you be enjoying the day?"

"I *am* enjoying the day," he said. "Got some unexpected parts as a present. Just what I need to create a new edition of the wishmethere. It's a lot smaller, needs less wish power, and has some limitations, but we needed a second one, given how the old one is in use all the time."

"You know, I never had a chance to go in the wishmethere. It was broken when I went on my field trip."

"Yes, I remember. I was left behind to fix it while you guys met Ivelli. I need to give this one a field test. Would you like me to take you somewhere? I have it set to travel to a place that a person wishes they were at right now. I have a feeling you have such a place in mind."

"Could you? I'm feeling terribly guilty."

"Yes, but I'll need to take you then drop you off for 48 hours, as I've a few errands to run. I can make a preventative wish to shield you from Ivelli for that long. I will come back and get you. Is that all right?"

Alma didn't know what to say, so she gave Selva a big hug. He was startled somewhat at her strength. Of course, he didn't know she was now regularly hugging bears.

"That would be wonderful."

"Go pack. We are off in thirty minutes."

The most noticeable thing about the new wishmethere was that it was wishper-quiet. Selva beamed as they descended to New Orleans. What would have taken the old wishmethere many minutes, only took seconds for the new one.

"You must have wanted to get home really badly," he said as they settled soundlessly outside the row house her parents lived in. "This one travels according to the desires of the passenger. I hadn't expected to be this quick."

"It's the first time I've not been with my family for Christmas. I sent them all Christmas cards, but don't have any presents for them."

"Well, I have a thought for you. Why don't you give them this?"

Selva whispered something in her ear. The wishmethere made a sudden sound as it geared for his next errand. He did not have the same desire to go to his next destination and the wishmethere wasn't sure it should take him.

"Thank you," Alma said as she stepped out with her small overnight bag. "I'll see you in 48 hours."

As the wishmethere disappeared, Alma paused to catch her breath.

Her parents' row house with the grey shingles looked so simple now. She could smell the magic of New Orleans in the air. Part of her would always belong there. She could not wait for when she could bring Syd and show him the sights and watch him soak up the energy of the city. He'd told her that he'd always wanted to visit ever since he had read the Anne Rice novel *Interview with a Vampire*.

As much as she was glad to be home, she was scared. It had been an awkward time when she had joined the School of Wish. She had half expected that at any time Lavinia would come and pull her out. All the email she had received had been from her father. *What if I am not welcome? Where would I stay while I wait for Selva?*

Alma marshalled her will. She'd learned to deal with many difficult situations in the last four months. She'd come to understand that she was meant to be at the School of Wish. How could she explain that? How could she explain she had to abandon her duty to her family, all of whom held their own sense of magic.

She couldn't. All she could do was show she still cared.

It wasn't right for her to enter uninvited. She'd not had time to let her father know she was coming, so very delicately she pressed the doorbell and heard the buzz in the house.

She sensed someone gazing at her from the window, then at last someone opened the door. Her mother stood there, somewhat surprised, as if her crystal was not working at full mechanics.

"Alma," Lavinia said, her eyebrows raised straight as a ruler's edge across her forehead. "I thought you had forgotten us. Why are you here now?"

"Why," said Alma, silently invoking a bevy of protection wishes before she said, "I've come to wish you a merry Christmas."

32: The Christmas wish

The three New Orleanians sat quietly at the table, which was covered with treasured Christmas foods. There was a contemplative calmness among them that reflected an absence.

Pierre was not there. Alma's father, Jean, had not told her in advance. Could he be blamed, since he did not know that she would be coming?

They had sent Pierre to a boarding school. A magic boarding school. In Florence.

Her mother had not said a word about her brother, but his very absence was stronger than his presence ever was, just as Lavinia's silence was more eloquent than all her usual loquaciousness.

Alma's father had whispered to her as carefully as he could. Her mother had wanted Pierre to come home, but the boy had refused.

She knew her mother had not insisted that she be home, but she was long past expecting any more from her mother.

There was one unopened present under the Christmas tree. Addressed to her brother.

Nothing for her, nor had there been anything sent to the lodge in Baddeck.

Alma held her head high. She wasn't going to let it bother her that they wanted Pierre home and not her. She was going to leave this life behind. She had already left this life behind.

There was one oddity. She noted her Christmas cards to both parents had places of prominence over the small arch that separated the living room from the dining room. It was something, at least.

The family ate in silence except for the sound of chewing, and the odd exclamation of "Oh, that's tasty," from her father.

"Thank you for the food," Alma said. "I never had anything taste so good while I was away."

Her mother stopped chewing for a moment and looked at Alma, her eyes twinkling slightly.

"I'm stuffed," her father said after a while. "Time for a glass of whiskey."

Alma sat bolt upright. She had never paid attention to what her father drank before.

"Something wrong?" her mother asked.

"No. I just remembered something. We went on a field trip on Canadian Thanksgiving, and we stayed near a whiskey distillery."

"Alma, you are too young to drink. I hope you didn't have any."

"No," said Alma, "I certainly wouldn't drink whiskey." *Not when I could drink the taste of wishes instead.* "It's just that the place was beautiful. Really remote, with this cute stream and mountains in the background and hardly anybody around. There was a stone wishing well. I just thought you both would have liked the place."

Her mother nodded. "The scenery in Nova Scotia was certainly breathtaking, even if it was a bit of a wasted trip."

Alma felt a pang of hurt but tried to ignore it.

Her father sipped his whiskey, then seemed to recover his manners. "Mother, would you like some?"

Lavinia nodded. "I suppose I should. It would be nice if we made a toast. Here, Alma: you can have some sparkling cider."

She poured it for Alma, which was something her mother never did.

"Well, then," her father said. "To us all, and to Christmas."

There was another lengthy silence, but the whiskey seemed to be warming her parents.

"How about we play a game of Sorry?" her father suggested.

Isn't that what we have been playing at silently? Alma thought to herself, but then saw her father searching in a cabinet that held board games.

He plopped the game on the table. "We played Trouble last time. So now it's time to be sorry. Get it?"

Alma rolled her eyes. Her father was as good at bad jokes or as bad at good jokes as the Wish Doctor. Except the Wish Doctor never said 'get it?' He assumed you did.

Lavinia won the first move and paced her marker along the board. Jean took a turn, and pulled a card that said 12.

Each took turns as if growing accustomed to the game, before feeling comfortable for further social chat.

At her next turn, Jean said, "Alma, how is your school? Have you caught any wishes yet?"

Alma smiled mischievously. "One or two. I had to let them go as they were too small."

It was her mother's turn to roll her eyes, which Alma took as a good sign. If you rolled your eyes at an implied pun, you at least were showing some appreciation.

"Have you learned anything?" Lavinia asked.

"I've learned about mathematics and history and word puzzles. We study quite late."

"I hope you are getting some free time," Jean said.

"I did get to go to Prince Edward Island and attended an Anne of Green Gables convention."

"Really?" her mother said, as if forgetting for a moment that she detested her daughter. "That sounds interesting." Even crabby mothers like Anne of Green Gables, even if they secretly identify with Rachel Lynde.

"And the weather? Has it been too cold for you?" Jean said.

"I wouldn't say too cold. The snow has just come the last couple of weeks. It's been lovely."

A strange thought entered Alma's head. Neither parent had asked how she had come to New Orleans. Maybe they didn't want to know if she was going to ask for money for a plane ticket back.

Lavinia pulled a card that let her trade places with another player. Without hesitation, she sent Alma backward along the board. Alma didn't mind. She really didn't care if Lavinia won at being sorry.

"So," Jean said, "are you watching lots of hockey?"

Alma laughed. "We don't watch much TV, but I've made a good friend who could maybe have made the NHL."

"Wow."

"A boyfriend?" her mother asked.

Alma blushed and her father jumped in. "What's his name?"

"Syd. Syd Cowsby." She wasn't sure why she said that, but it seemed necessary to protect him.

"That sounds like a good hockey player's name. Does he treat you right? Is he really your boyfriend?"

"He's really sweet," Alma said. "I guess he is my boyfriend. He gave me the cutest teddy bear as a gift. He wanted me to go see his parents, but I wanted to come to see you."

There was an emotion on her mother's face, almost a smile. She stretched out her arm so that her hand lay adjacent to, but not quite touching, Alma's. It was not much, but it was something.

Alma looked up, and Jean was raising his glass to her. She smiled back.

"Merry Xmas," he said.

Then he got up and turned on the kitchen stereo, which was loaded with Christmas music. 'Holly Jolly Christmas', once named the world's worst Christmas song, began playing.

Knowing it was her father's favourite song, annoying ear worm or not, Alma felt an unexplainable flow of warmth.

Jean handed her a plate of Christmas candy, and that sent a further rush of sugar through Alma's body and another feeling. It took her a moment before she realized what it was.

Looking at her parents, who were both smiling, (though one more than the other), she realized they were all, for just a moment, feeling merry.

On Christmas Day, could anyone wish for more?

33: Boxed in

The Wish Doctor hated Boxing Day even more than he hated teddy bears coming alive. And that was saying a lot.

It had not always been so. The original Boxing Day had been about caring for others, about giving to the less fortunate, to the workers, to the servers. Before that, it had been a day for contemplation, for appreciation of art; a very powerful day indeed, when powerful, benevolent magic could live.

But commercialism and after-Christmas sales had turned a special day into something disappointing. More than disappointing: dangerous. And he had not been alert.

Now he was literally trapped in a box which was impervious somehow to his wish magic, a trap made especially for him.

He could think of only one culprit. Mack Ivelli. Had he ever thought that reversing the wish on that fountain in Florence would have left the world a better place, he would have done it, but it was clear now, if it hadn't been before, that Ivelli could never have taken the role as the world's leading Wish Doctor, not in the past, now not, not in the future. He would have been corrupted absolutely if he had.

The Wish Doctor felt it in him now, the power to overturn the wish that day when he had tossed the florin into the fountain. When Ivelli had trapped him, Ivelli left him that. It was the one wish he could still make within the trap.

Well, no way he was going to do that. His death would be less destructive than Ivelli amassing the power available with that wish reversed. Poor Selva, who likely would make a better Wish Doctor than he, would have to assume the mantle, undoing the great destiny that was otherwise ahead of him.

The Wish Doctor should never have used Lavinia's crystal the day he held it a hundred years ago to look at the future. He was pretty sure now it was the same crystal. There was too much resemblance to the original holder of the crystal in Alma for it to be a coincidence.

The Wish Doctor suspected it had been the girl's great grandmother who had loaned him that crystal for those precious seconds.

If he had not known what Selva was meant to do, he would have coerced Selva to take his place so he could seek the rest he so desperately craved.

He'd let sentimentality overtake him. Was it so wrong, though, to want to be with his family on Christmas, even so many years after their passing? He wasn't sure why he'd been so sad this year. Was it because his successor was in this current crop of students, or because she or he wasn't?

He should have been prepared. Boxing Day was always a dangerous day for wishes in the best of years. In the aftermath of Christmas not living up to expectations, and the greed of sales creating so many negative wishes, it was easy for Ivelli to harvest and twist those dark wishes to his purpose.

No need to panic, though. If this was the Wish Doctor's fate to die in a box, so be it.

But he had faced a lot of dangers in his life, especially in the first couple of centuries of facing wishes gone wrong, before he'd gotten the hang of the job. Now, with almost another 400 years under his belt, he had many experiences to draw on, as well as many ideas he'd yet not needed.

The simplest of course was to use one of his three power wishes, but it seemed a shame to use those on this trap when they really were meant for the end of civilization, or something similar. Besides, the power released would likely cause a lot of unintended damage. The power of creation was like that, needing an offset somewhere. And, of course, he wanted to save one at least for after his death, for, you know, in case.

There was not much room in the box, but he stretched his arms and legs, and relaxed as best he could. Rest now was the best thing for him. It would take time to sift through his experiences and see what plans he would make.

He didn't really care if Ivelli could outsmart him when he didn't know there was a trap being set. It didn't really prove anything. The Wish Doctor knew his edge in intelligence came unnaturally, so there was no ego involved for him.

Ivelli was, or might have been, the smartest natural person. But what did that matter? Was Ivelli responsible for his genes? It was a matter of how hard you worked. Ivelli would never have worked so hard if the Doctor hadn't given him a challenge.

After a couple hours, the Doctor began to grow more confident. He didn't have a solution, but his mind was working, cascading possibilities. There was at least one way out of the box.

The most likely way was that Selva would rescue him. The box was constructed by bending the laws of physics. That was a rookie mistake.

He didn't care how smart Ivelli was, or how smart he was. On physics, Selva was the smartest.

Smartness was such a hard thing to measure, of course, but the Wish Doctor knew he was not the master of every field. It might even be a good idea to wait and let Selva fix this. Might convince him that being the next Wish Doctor was the right career move. If he came to the duty willingly, his other destiny might still happen.

The wish that alerted the Wish Doctor when danger was at hand had come too late to prevent him from being trapped; his damn tears slowed his reaction time just enough. It was fully engaged now. If there was imminent danger, the wish would let him know.

To give Selva a head start, he touched the photophone at his hip and typed a message in Morse code. He wasn't sure where the box was, but at least Selva would know he was in a box.

He then snuggled against the walls of the box. Might as well get some sleep as he waited.

~

For many, Boxing Day was an integral part of Christmas. For the literal-minded tricksters of the wish world, it was most definitely excluded. The wish of a merry Christmas often trapped them, but as soon as Boxing Day struck midnight the wish was over.

Alma's wish was no different. The morning started with her hearing her mother sobbing.

Her father, as always, had left early for Boxing Day sales.

Alma tried to think of a way to comfort her mother. She could never make Lavinia smile the way her brother could.

She started toward the kitchen to see what she could do. A clanging in the small dining room interrupted her.

Two spoons were banging together on the table of their own accord.

Dot, dash, dot. Morse Code.

```
it's bell stop
urgent need for crystal piece stop
ask your mother if you can borrow it stop
emergency stop
```

Alma swallowed. She tapped back. "Understood."

But did she? Was there an urgent need? Bell had hinted at the crystal before. But if you couldn't trust the ghost of the inventor of the telephone, who could you trust?

She would at least ask.

"Mom," she said slowly as she walked into the kitchen, seeing her mother distraught, with red eyes and dark circles. "Are you okay? I hope you are not mad at me for coming home."

"No," Lavinia answered. "I'm mad for you going away in the first place."

The heartache of the days before Alma had joined the school of wish flooded through her chest. "I didn't ask to go. I wanted Pierre to go. I wished that he'd go."

Lavinia looked at her askew. There was some kind of realization in her mother. She could have done more to stop her daughter from going. All she would have had to do was not take her from New Orleans in the first place.

"Why are you so mad at me?" Alma said. "Why do I disappoint you? I know I am not like Pierre. I know you like him better than me, but I've never wanted to hurt you or do you harm."

"Yet you have. I'm sorry, Alma, I never wanted a second child. It's nothing against you, but the kind of magic I have is deplenished with every child after the first. I am weakened because you were born. It's not personal."

Not personal, thought Alma. *Not personal. Am I not a person?*

She didn't know what to say. The joy of the previous day was gone. Just like she wanted to be.

At last, she knew why her mother hated her.

"I will get out of your way. I just need one favour. Can you lend me the piece of broken crystal?"

Her mother stared at her for the longest time.

"Lavinia, it's important."

Her mother glared. "I should've known you knew the crystal was broken. I was trying to polish it and had a sudden vision of you in the future. It startled me so much, I dropped it and it broke. I don't think you know how much that crystal means to me."

Lavinia went to a rocking chair in the small living room, sat, and started rocking.

Alma knew better than to say anything more, and left her mother alone. Lavinia continued rocking past noon, her face becoming more morbid as the day went on.

Alma couldn't wait for Selva, who had said he'd pick her up at two. She slowly pulled her small bag together and wandered toward the front door. Selva was always precise.

Her father wasn't back yet and Alma was going to miss him. She didn't know whether to say anything more to her mother.

She didn't need to. As she zipped up her winter coat for the journey, her mother came into the kitchen. She held out her hand. "Here: take the crystal. Take the broken piece."

"Are you sure, mom? Are you sure? You seem so angry." Alma so wanted to take the crystal and run, but something in her mother's anguish held her back.

"Do I have a choice? The crystal told me it has to go with you if it ever is to be made full again, if I ever have hope of getting my magic back. Just know that I am lonely without it."

"I understand. I don't want you to be lonely." Alma knew how painful that could be. She looked into her mother's eyes and they were empty.

Lavinia blinked before finding her voice. "Take it, do your thing. But if you damage it or lose it, do me a favour. Never come back!"

Alma stood stunned, barely able to hold onto the broken piece of crystal. "Thank you, mother, Have a Happy New Year."

She walked out the front door, tears obscuring her view of the wishmethere.

Her merry Christmas wish had come true, but, as she had learned so many times, there was always a dire consequence to a wish come true. This consequence she might never recover from.

If she ever needed a bear hug from Syd, it was now.

34: The Chamber of Cooperation

Selva had one good reason for not wanting to succeed the Wish Doctor. He believed wishes were not sourced primarily by magic. He was sure there was a scientific explanation or explanations. He was sure mathematics was the key. If he could solve quantum mechanics, that unpredictable method of science that explored why electrons mysteriously showed up in a different spot from where you expected them, he was sure he would have his first best clue.

In the moments when he was uncertain of the whereabouts of the Wish Doctor, he felt the elements of pressured responsibility surrounding him. He was glad Mr. Bell had helped him find a way to locate the Doctor using earthly science. Mr. Bell's presence, he was sure, was also not a simple supernatural occurrence, but something else to be explained by science.

He hoped someday he could get the great inventor to sit down and discuss the matter. Maybe even help him solve the problem of quantum mechanics.

Right now, his focus had to be doing everything he could to recover the Wish Doctor so that, someday soon, he could be free to pursue his own interests.

When he saw Alma, fighting back tears, he was not as sympathetic as he should be. Every moment the Wish Doctor was kept captive might mean life or death for someone he might otherwise help.

He dared not even think the unthinkable. That the Wish Doctor was in danger himself.

He waved Alma into the wishmethere. "Buckle up quickly. Something unimaginable has happened. The Wish Doctor has been kidnapped."

Alma buckled her belt in shock.

"You and your friend Bell are going to help me get him out."

The Wish Doctor had overestimated Selva's skill and knowledge of physics. Or, at least, overestimated that his knowledge could help undo the trap. Fortunately, Selva was not alone.

As he and Alma clambered up the stairs after the wishmethere docked, Mr. Bell met them. "Mabel understands you need me. She's given me the go-ahead to stay here as long as we need to fix things. Alma, do you have the crystal piece?"

"Yes."

"Good. Follow me. The crystal will protect you. We are going to a spot that is dangerous, and you should never go unaccompanied."

A dangerous spot. One of the three places the Wish Doctor had warned about. She felt nervous and excited at the same time.

Bell led them up the stairs from the sub-basement she had descended just two days before. She had been so excited about travelling to see her parents that she hadn't thought much about her surroundings, yet something still seemed wrong. Bell kept floating up the stairs, except the stairs didn't stop where they had stopped before. They kept going, as if the roof that used to be there had disappeared.

Alma wasn't counting but she used her knowledge of geometry and spatial design to picture where they were.

They were higher than the Doctor's study.

They came to a dark iron door out of a medieval dungeon. "Selva, would you do the honours?" Bell said. "My current form is not much help in this kind of situation."

Selva obliged. The door swung open incredibly easily for a door into a deadly-secret place.

Alma followed Bell and Selva across the threshold. They were at the top of some great tower with windows on all sides, except for the medieval door. The views were magnificent, though the sun was coming low in the sky, night falling early this far north.

Alma couldn't understand. She'd studied the outside of the lodge carefully, knew every room. She had not seen the tower before. She asked the obvious, if nonsensical, question. "Is this tower invisible?"

"Yes," Bell said, "but unstable. We had limited invisibility cloaking material for it. Our theory suggests there is a way to use other material, but I keep getting distracted from the project. Still, there is more risk that this room can be seen while we are in it. Let me take a precaution: Privacy, please."

In a matter of seconds the windows darkened with a dense, forest-green tint.

Alma could see now the room wasn't all windows. There were narrow walls in between the large panes of glass. As the room darkened, a number of old photographs became visible on all the walls. In the adjusting light, the photos drew her eyes like a beacon.

Some were black and white. Some were square with large borders. None were in frames. There were small Polaroids.

There were mechanisms in half the photos, strange looking things, like prototypical inventions. In the other half were people and landscapes. There were maybe a hundred different people, some of whom appeared more than once.

What drew her eyes was that there were at least twenty people across different time eras and landscapes who looked exactly like Syd.

She did a double take. She looked more closely. There were differences. Some subtle, like hair colour or a mole, or a slight change in height. *Could these be Syd's relatives? Why are these photos gathered here?* She saw none of herself and only one of her other classmates.

Before she could think anymore, Bell waved his hands, and the photos on the walls disappeared. "Hard to concentrate with those things here. Photography. Just something I was toying with. One thing Edison beat me to."

Alma was lost. *What does it mean?*

Bell pointed at an onyx table with a single pedestal, and a small basin carved in the middle of its surface. It was almost exactly the same size as her mother's crystal when it was intact. "Alma, sorry to interrupt your daydreams, but the Doctor is in real danger. Could you put the crystal in this table? It will help us detect him."

Alma turned to Selva. "This won't hurt the crystal?" she asked, thinking of her mother's last words.

"No," he said with a smile, though the seriousness of his worry was clear. "This will enhance the crystal's power. It will also make it easier for this piece to rejoin its parent."

Alma didn't hesitate. Though she had a slight reluctance due to Bell's mischievousness, it was hard if, not impossible, to distrust Selva.

She slipped the crystal into the basin and felt a sudden shock. She jumped as electricity leapt into her hands, blistering her fingers. She was shaking.

"Am I in trouble?" she asked. "Should I be here?"

"You are safe now," Selva said. "The room has tested you and you have passed. This is the Chamber of Cooperation. It is designed for people to trust each other and work together. Only acts of selflessness to help others are allowed here. The room has no tolerance for selfishness. By loaning the crystal, which has meaning to you, you have earned the chamber's trust."

Alma didn't know what to say. Her fingers were hurting, but she understood that the pain was a kind of price. She felt oddly comfortable now that she could be trusted, and the danger was past.

There was little time for thinking as Selva dropped a tiny object into the basin beside the crystal. She looked closely, and felt a squeamishness climb up her spine.

It was too big to be a fingernail clipping. It had to be a clipping from the big toe. The Wish Doctor's toe. *Where did Selva get that?*

The crystal lit up; the basin shook. A red eye lit up on the front of the pedestal like that of a camera. For a long time, there was no sound, no movement, save for the humming of the basin. Everyone held their breath.

"The Doctor is separate from the Uniwish," Bell said abruptly.

"That can't be," Selva said,

"Can't it? Isn't it like your quantum mechanics, where an electron is in an impossible place? Is anything impossible for a wish done right? Remember, we still have to crack the science of what makes wishes work."

Selva looked at him. It gave him an idea he needed to explore, but not now.

"The Uniwish?" Alma asked, "What's that?"

Selva paused a moment. For what they were about to ask of Alma, he could at least tell her about the unknown.

"In wish lore, there is a theory that everything that is was made from one wish. Those who believe, say the universe was created from one wish, the Great Wish. That's why we refer to it as the Uniwish."

"Who made the wish? What gave it the power to do so?"

"It's not for us to know. It's part of the great wishtery," Selva said.

If their faces weren't so serious Alma would have been sure they were making this up.

"Some believe," Bell said, "that the great wish turned out wrong, and that all the terrible things we can't explain are because of this."

"We can have a deeper conversation about this another time," Selva said. "Even if he is outside the normal physical realm, he did get a message to me. So that means he isn't beyond our reach. He distinctly said he had been trapped in a box."

"I agree." Bell said.

"I think he was very literal about a box," Selva continued. "What kind of trap would be a box?"

"Don't they say, when some people die, they are going to put them in a box?" Alma said.

Bell and Selva looked at each other.

"You did say this guy called himself Machiavelli," Bell said.

Selva looked at Alma. "I think I know where he is. He's in the Medici chapel in Florence. The one designed by Michelangelo."

Alma looked shocked. "Why there?"

"You don't think he's actually from Scotland do you? He has a fascination with Gaelic culture, but that's not where he's from."

The Wish Doctor is from Florence, Alma thought, *the city that started the Renaissance, the centre of so many great artists.* She realized how little she knew about him. Her curiosity was heightened. Besides, who hadn't wished (herself included) they could go to Florence?

Maybe I'll see my brother.

"He won't be easy to get out," Selva said. "If he's in the tomb, it's either a trap or well-guarded. At least we know he is inside a box. So," he continued, channelling the Wish Doctor, "we need to think outside the box."

If the situation weren't so serious Alma would have groaned.

"Watson's readings indicate the box is being separated from normal space," Bell said. "We need to bring him into normal space."

"How do we do that?" Alma asked.

Selva looked worried. "I've been trying to locate him outside of space with a modified wish watch but can't. What if he isn't outside of space? What if this is one of DaVinci's theatrical tricks?"

"Don't know," Bell said. "Mabel was always into the theatre more than me. It's likely, though. He's outside known spaces where wishes can work. Probably why he hasn't been able to free himself already."

The inventor stared hard at nothing Alma could see. "Hmm. Would have to have been a prepared spell to allow the box to stay in place after the wish was cast, otherwise it would have dissolved being outside the Uniwish."

His focus came back to the room. "Selva, you need to go there promptly. Alma, I hate to ask it, but you need to go, too. The crystal will be critical in bringing the Doctor back into this universe, and it won't work if you are not near. It will be risky. If someone deliberately trapped the Wish Doctor, you know they are smart."

Alma nodded. The Wish Doctor had saved her from her mother. She couldn't abandon him, no matter the risk.

35: Out of this world

It was cramped in the wishmethere as they travelled to Florence. Besides Alma, Selva had recruited Smaetag, and Loretta, who had returned early from her holiday. And unfortunately, the triplets. That wasn't Selva's intention, but the wishmethere refused to take off without seven passengers.

"Harmonic distortion," he explained. "I expected the doctor's kidnapping and hiding place are causing the problem. Seven, you know, is a lucky number and helps wishes."

They rode the old wishmethere, which seemed to be insulted they were calling it that. Loretta and Smaetag were sleeping, and the triplets were playing Parcheesi, so Alma was left with her thoughts.

She was disguised now, so that Ivelli couldn't recognize her, or, at least, not as easily as without the disguise. Her hair was green. She had freckles, which she had pulled from the residual wish magic from the Island. She wore high heel boots and shoulder pads and had added hair extensions. She wore mock designer glasses that smouldered with designer style. She held a sketchbook with Michelangelo tracings so she wouldn't look out of place.

Alma held the shard of crystal tightly. It was so much easier to balance than in that jalopy ride when she first met the Wish Doctor.

Everything was happening so quickly; she had no time to think of her mother. She practised a number of wishes, both protective and pure. She had also rehearsed continuously so she could pronounce the words box and Uniwish in reverse.

One thought dominated her thinking. *Why does Bell have all those pictures that looked like Syd? Why did he turn them off so quickly?* She strained, thinking about it, and finally the vibrations of the wishmethere lulled her to sleep.

~

The Wish Doctor woke up in the dark box amazingly refreshed. He had slept more soundly than he had in Florence as a child. His thoughts were clear. He could remember the trap that had put him there.

He was going to have to do something about his fear of stuffed animals. It was time he faced the fact he just didn't hate them when they came alive, it was because he feared them. It was that fear that had caused the problem.

The boxing kangaroo had appeared out of nowhere, and he hadn't responded well to the shock of seeing a boxing kangaroo on Boxing Day. The kangaroo had hit him with an uppercut, knocking him to the ground.

He shouldn't have been surprised. It was one of those stuffed animals from New York. Ivelli had been behind the whole thing, and the kangaroo had escaped the Doctor's reversals. It was, after all, only a hop, ship and a jump for a kangaroo to get from New York to Florence.

He took a moment to face his fear. There had been two incidents, both from his rookie years as a wish apprentice. One was that bear that had come alive, but it was also the first kangaroo he had encountered.

Never having heard of that kind of creature before, he had assumed it was a mouse that had been enlarged by a wish, and thus his reversals had all backfired, causing many hardships. It wasn't until his friend Stallone told him it was a kangaroo that he realized what it was and how to fix it. The nightmares of that first kangaroo and his frustration stopping it had led to his shock in Florence.

He had now selected the three best ways to undo the wish trap. There was a little risk in each of the methods, but if he didn't hear from Selva shortly, he would have to use one.

He had been only able to get one communication to Selva. He hoped that was because Selva was on his way in the wishmethere. The Doctor hoped he had understood his message. 'I am outside the world.'

There was a reckoning to be had with Ivelli, but now was not the time. He just wanted to escape and get back to the lodge.

The rest had been doing him a world of good, though. He was remembering more of his memories, especially about Ivelli. It was odd that it had taken moments to recognize him. If he had remembered more about him, maybe he would have been better prepared and not trapped so easily.

"I should thank Ivelli when I see him," he thought as he returned to sleep.

~

With surgical precision, Selva piloted the wishmethere directly into the larger Medici tomb, the Principe. He had a momentary urge to disguise it as a blue British police call box, but that might be too obvious. Instead, he just wished it invisible. It was easy enough, for the paint job on it really wasn't that great and paled in comparison to the great art elsewhere in the tomb.

It was now early morning of the 28th, Florence time, long before anyone would be coming to view either of the tombs in Saint Lorenzo Church. Still, Selva worried that Ivelli or one of his acolytes, or worse, acoheavies, would be near enough to disrupt a rescue.

He led his group of seven into the smaller chamber. All tripped over themselves as they witnessed some of Michelangelo's lesser-known genius.

The dawn and dusk statues were unbelievable perfection. More than perfect, they evoked emotion, and symbolism as if they were magic. It was hard to believe someone so talented had not gained that talent through a wish. Or at least that was what the Wish Doctor had assured Selva.

Selva could not easily spot a box that might contain the Doctor, but then he hadn't expected to. Nor could he sense any wish protection. That only meant the trap might be more devilish.

He positioned the triplets across the door holding protection wishes against discovery. Loretta roamed the chamber neutralizing any wish she could sense.

Alma and Smaetag followed Selva as he searched for a box separated from regular spacetime. It had to do with the separation of life and death he figured. No one wanted to mention the box they were looking for was a coffin, even though they were in a chamber of tombs. The beauty of Michelangelo's statuary and monuments was so dazzling you couldn't help but stop to contemplate.

Selva did and began tapping around the tomb using one of his portable harmonics, which worked as an all-purpose sensor.

~

Alma could hardly pay attention, so awed was she by the statue of dawn. Was that what Artemis from myth would have looked like?

There were two statues languishing across the tomb, the marble as lively as flesh. An older man on the left, the younger Artemis on the right. Dusk to Dawn. There was no literal torch, but she could feel the transfer of power from older to younger.

For a second, Artemis seemed to lift her head to look at her. Did she wink?

Alma was torn away by Loretta's comment. "I've cancelled three wishes, but nothing of any importance to our mission."

The crystal was cold in Alma's hand. She mimicked Selva's motion, hoping that it would have some sensory capacity.

There was no response. Selva shook his head. "I can't get any reading of the Doctor."

"Is this a trap for us?" Smaetag asked.

"I don't know. I don't sense anything."

"I can sense a wish of a long time ago," Smaetag said, "Of people wanting to kill the Medici brothers, Lorenzo the Magnificent and his younger brother Julian. And then a wish for this to be their final resting place, but it was never completed. I can sense no active wish as strong as it would take to capture the Wish Doctor. Are you sure we are in the right place?"

Selva wasn't. The Wish Doctor was connected to one of the Florentine artists, but in today's lingo, that could have been literal, fine art, political artist, musician. The box made no sense. *Out of this world.*

He went back and checked his notes, which he kept scrupulously.

"Oh dear," he said. "I think I've mistranslated his code. He didn't say *out of this* world. He said *outside the* world. He's in Florence, but not here. Not outside of the world figuratively. Outside of the world literally. He's close. We can get there faster if we run. Smaetag, use your rook-key. Bring the wishmethere to Piazza della Signoria, where the replica David is."

The students followed Selva.

Alma stumbled, hearing an odd voice. "Your body is a canvas. Use it."

Something invisible had spoken to her.

It was just under a kilometre to the Palazzo Vecchio. Alma had a hard time focusing as they ran, unbelieving she was in Florence. Somewhere in the city was her brother. Would she have time to see him? Did he have anything to do with Ivelli? She was scared to know the answer.

Her eyes near boggled as she got her first glimpse of the Basilica di Santa Maria del Fiore (Saint Mary of the Flower), the duomo, one of the greatest engineering feats of humankind, in some ways the centre of the Renaissance. It was an effort not to stop to admire it, but she knew they couldn't wait. The great octagonal shape of the exterior dome with its red brick tiles beckoned her. She had to force herself to follow Selva down the Via Matelli.

There were signs directing her to amazing things in every direction: the Academi, where the original statue of David was on display; the Uffizi, where Botticelli and DaVinci had paintings, where the first museum in human history existed. They ran by a sign pointing to a sculpture by Donatello of St. George fighting a dragon.

Had someone wished that Florence be the greatest centre of art in the world?

~

Selva ran straight, his eyes not wavering, like he'd seen it all before. The street was relatively quiet, just a few people still trying to sell selfie sticks and some university revellers drinking into the dawn.

And there was the Palazzo Vecchio, surrounded by sculptures, the replica of David, its eyes giving a warning glance at Rome.

Selva closed his eyes and pulled from his pocket the one tool he saved only for special needs. His wish key. Not a drink, but a key that he could wish to unlock any door.

Not wanting to alert anyone in case of a trap, he used another electronic device to disable any security cameras. Still, it was only a matter of time before guards came. And whatever Ivelli might have prepared.

He had just undone the lock when Smaetag landed the wishmethere in the open plaza. He motioned her to join them. He had a feeling he would need her.

Without hesitation he sped into the interior and then up the staircase to the room of maps. He had to use the wish key again. It was less liable to detection than normal wishes, but Ivelli would be looking for any alerts. There would be not much time.

He hurried into the map room. The walls were decorated with maps depicting much of the known world, circa 1500. Near the centre was a giant globe.

Outside the world.

The box trap had to be just there. He couldn't see it, but maybe behind the globe. No nothing there. *Have I been wrong?* If he was, he might have doomed the Wish Doctor.

Alma suddenly yelped in pain. Her hand was burning. She pulled her hand from her pocket. "The crystal's on fire!"

"Hm." Selva said, maybe not as sympathetically to someone who's hand had just been burnt as he should be. But he did have other things on his mind. "This is the right place. Does anyone feel wishes here?"

"It's full of wishes," Dahlia said. "It's overwhelming. Most of them are old."

Selva couldn't sense them. Ivelli had planned well.

Smaetag had a thought. "What if these old wishes are concealing the new wish; could they be hiding it? Could someone have made a wish a long time ago that said 'I wish that any wish made in the future is not detectable?'"

"Yes," Selva said. *But then why can Dahlia sense the new wishes?*

He pulled out his harmonic sensor and it went crazy. It nearly blew a circuit.

"There were nine wishes at the door," Loretta said, "protection wishes, and only one wish. I've neutralized it. But I sense something else. There is a wish here I can't neutralize."

Selva nodded. There was an unknown danger, a wish outside of control. A wish outside the box.

"Okay, you guys try and figure it out. Alma, we need to find the box the Wish Doctor is in. I need you to make a wish on the crystal. Wish that the Doctor's hiding place is revealed."

"Should I make a protection wish first?"

"No. It's a pure crystal. In fact, I'm sure it's a wishtal. You don't need protection wishes. It can help you make a pure wish."

"It's still hot," she said. "Can I wrap it in something?"

"No, unfortunately, you will need to hold it with your bare hand."

~

Alma nodded. She made a silent wish. "I wish to withstand the pain."

She pulled the crystal from her pocket, held it in front of her face and said, "I wish the Doctor's hiding place was revealed."

She had a sudden panic. She hadn't said when or to whom. All her studying, and she had let a few first-degree burns distract her from carefully constructing a wish. As if to reinforce her concern, Selva had a stricken look on his face.

Nothing happened for what seemed the longest time, and then the air behind the globe began to shimmer. There was an anomaly in the floor.

Selva rushed to pull up a trap door, shaped too coincidentally like a coffin. Indeed, a box about the size of a square coffin was apparent, its lid just below the surface of the floor. It was simple pine, so not that heavy.

Although it looked like it was starting to sink. Had its revealing triggered another problem?

"Help me lift it," Selva said.

The triplets and Smaetag all grabbed ends and lifted for all they were worth. Alma, her hand still smarting, did her best with her left hand. They couldn't budge it.

It didn't make sense. The Wish Doctor was not a big man, and certainly not heavy. And while the narrator had not previously mentioned it, Selva was extraordinarily strong, and would be for five more years until a certain wish wore off.

"Somebody's wished it so heavy no one can lift it," Selva said. "I can't use a wish to lift it then, and likely not a wish to open it."

But why hadn't it been wished that no one could find the box? Because the Wish Doctor had been prepared.

There had to be a preeminent wish. A wish written or spoken preceding the trapping wish. Something that would undo the trap.

It would be hidden.

"We have to hurry," Loretta said. "I can feel a trap wish happening. It must have been set to activate. It's too strong for me to neutralize." The coffin was slowly sinking. It would be soon out of their reach.

~

Selva was perplexed. He silently said three protection wishes, then said aloud. "If the Wish Doctor had prepared me for this contingency, I wish I could remember it now."

No sooner said, then there was a smile on his face. He reached into the inner lining of his jacket and pulled a hidden thread. A secret pocket opened that he didn't remember.

From the pocket he withdrew a thick envelope, and opened it quickly to find several sheets of paper. In tiny handwriting, at the top of the first page, there was a single wish looking like it was living writing wanting to jump off the page.

The handwriting said, "I wish that I have a plan for every contingency my enemies may use to attack me."

Just below the handwriting, in italics, was written a series of protection wishes. Below this, the first thirty days of the year were listed and, on the following pages, the rest of the days of the year. Against each day there was at least one dangerous wish noted.

At the top of the page was the date the notes had been written, a date that was impossibly old. Selva had not known. Or he had known and been wished to forget. Wished to forget so that secrets could not be divulged, protections could not be unearthed.

He flipped to the last page, ran his finger down to December 27. There were two entries, one was about declawing a tiger, which made no sense, so he promptly read the second entry. "I wish that should I ever be trapped in a box, that that box become so light that anyone come to rescue me can lift it. This wish should be activated when read out loud by my rescuer."

It was not that simple. There were other wishes in play, and how long ago they were set in motion he couldn't not say. Selva said the wish.

And then more words appeared on the page.

> I wish a permanent wish that will activate when spoken and will undo any contradictory wish spoken after this wish. I wish that my friends can rescue me from any trap when they read aloud this wish.

The box began to groan, not because the Doctor was stretching inside, though he was, but because wishes were in conflict. Someone had wished the box to be too heavy to lift, but an older wish had anticipated this, and warred to make the box light.

The two wishes competed, partly on the source of their power, but mostly on the merits of their wish and their primacy. A newer wish could not overcome an older wish if the older wish was properly protected, except in the most unusual circumstances. You could not wish something to be heavier than the heaviest thing there was, already wished, or to wish something heavy, when it had already been wished light. There were, of course, forces of time that played into the equation that determined the primacy of the wish, but that was part of the curriculum for third year students only.

Slowly, slowly, the wish began to take effect. The box stabilized, no longer sinking, then lifted. There was a vibrating sound and the box began to float upward, almost as if it was made from helium.

Selva grabbed one end and Smaetag the other and heaved. The box came up easily, though the lid was still stuck.

Inside, a voice echoed through the wood, the voice of a grumpy teacher whose students had taken far too long to complete an assignment. "It's about time you got here."

"Back to the wishmethere," Selva said, "before any trap wish sets in."

He could move the box on his, own, but Smaetag helped, more to steer the awkward thing than because of its weight.

They hadn't gone far when Loretta said, "The trap wish is coming true, one I can't interrupt."

Selva kept running. But...

~

Ivelli had planned a wish that would go wrong but gone wrong in a way that the unintended action was just what he had unintendedly intended.

Suddenly there was an echoing voice, as if a wish had been made before but was now being said again. "I wish that the Tiger King was here to stop these meddlers from meddling."

And suddenly, he was.

Although not the crazed reality-show star of Netflix fame.

No, he was a large hungry tiger, with four large paws, sabreteeth, a tail and a jewel-encrusted crown.

Ready to earn his stripes.

There was no time to attempt the second planned contingency wish.

Even with a light box, they could not outrun the tiger, with his racing stripes flaring.

"Everyone, go," one of the triplets said. "We have this. Big cats are our specialty."

Selva hesitated, but heard Morse code from within the box.

```
let them save us stop
```

Selva resumed his flight, with Smaetag still helping with the box, and Loretta, and Alma following. The triplets formed a line blocking the way and met the eye of the Tiger.

"Why did you say we had this?" said one, shaking nervously.

"To prove we are trustworthy."

"We *are* trustworthy."

"See. We've proven it even to ourselves. Now, does anyone have an answer to stop this?"

"You are the one that said big cats were our specialty."

"Fine," one of them said as if watching almost any episode of *Brooklyn 99*. Our narrator would specify which triplet, but since they were quite close together, they all looked alike.

"Can anybody wish up catnip?"

"I wish for catsup."

But the cat stayed plainly on the floor. And sober.

"I wish for cataracts." The cat staggered maybe slightly, but his vision continued to be good.

"I wish you would abdicate," said the youngest triplet, but the crown stayed perched, if precariously, on the tiger's head.

"I wish for Catalan," but there was not a single thing that looked like Barcelona.

"Go back to your catalog."

But the cat remained. And no piece of timber fell from the ceiling to stop the grand beast.

"This is all very unsatisfying like that short story, 'The Lady, or the Tiger?'"

"What?"

"You know, that stupid short story they forced us to read in school where the person has to pick between doors. Behind one door is a tiger that will eat you. Behind the other door is a princess who will marry you, or a prince, depending on your tastes. But the story never tells you which door she picked and what was behind it. We really don't know if the tiger gets his or her meal. Totally unsatisfying."

Her sisters' eyebrows furrowed at the waste of time. Until one sister's eyebrows did an about face.

"What if we wished for a satisfying ending to that story? It's so far removed from the current circumstances it might work."

"You mean, you would change the ending?"

"I would. I wish the story 'The Lady or the Tiger?' had a satisfying ending before our eyes."

There was a flash of magic, as if every wish granter in the entire world wanted to bring a satisfying ending to that frustrating story that had once been forced on students in so many schools. Even those whose curiosity would now force them to google the story on the internet would wish for that ending.

There was no disappointment. A slight twist, the changing of two words, and millions of frustrated readers, and some very nervous triplets were satisfied and saved.

The triplets saw the outcome and backed away.

As narrator, we would not presume to humbly explain what had happened. (Since we had been forced to live the frustration known by *Lost* and *Westworld* fans everywhere, you should too.)

"Oh, but I will humbly explain," one of the triplets said to Alma later, since she was rightly proud of her use of wish magic, and of the final satisfaction of closing an open story. "We changed the title to 'The Lady *is a*

Tiger.' See, now behind the two doors were a lady and a tiger. The lady just happened to be a lady tiger. She had no need to marry a prince or a princess. She looked at the tiger king and roared a tiger roar that sounded very much like the satisfied yell you would give after eating a bowl of cornflakes, overly sweetened. We triplets had no fear of being eaten. You see, after being trapped behind doors for two hundred years with no companionship, they had better things to do then chase us."

At least two of the triplets were satisfied.

The group clambered into the wishmethere, Selva turning the box into a box kite which drifted up to attach to the top of the vehicle. The Wish Doctor was safe. It was time to go home.

~

Ivelli had not expected to hold the Wish Doctor trapped long. The Wish Doctor was smarter than he and would be as long as that one wish controlled him.

Still, there had to be a way to get the better of him. Ivelli had not yet thrown enough at the Wish Doctor to weaken him. If he tired the Wish Doctor enough, he was convinced he could defeat him.

Now he had learned one thing that would help his cause, and that was all he needed.

Ivelli stood in the plaza watching, sipping on an aperitif that magically appeared in his hand. He watched as the cursed Selva and his little troop of rescuers brought out the box he'd trapped the Wish Doctor in, or at least his agent had. He watched as they turned the thing into a box kite and mounted it atop the wishmethere. *Damn that the Wish Doctor had allied with an inventor who would live after death.*

Ivelli hadn't even tried to stop the rescue. It would have taken too much energy and been futile. The Wish Doctor or one of his pupils would have found a way to outsmart his trap and anything else he tried. He couldn't add much to stop the effort they were already putting into the rescue. Better for him to preserve his strength.

He would set his dangerous plan in motion, one that would threaten and maybe harm his secret weapon. Well, he couldn't worry about that. He had a new protegé, a very powerful one who would soon be able to replace his secret weapon, were she to be uncovered.

As the Wish Doctor's little band of rescuers climbed into the wishmethere, there was a moment when no one could see an exchange. Ivelli didn't want to waste a wish, so he said out loud, "Girl, I have a preference you look at me."

The girl, the straggling triplet, the one unsatisfied by the revised lady and tiger ending, swivelled around, already inclined to look for her long-time mentor. She tried to hide her smile as he winked, "Hello."

He then winked several times in quick succession. A code.

~

The triplet read the message loud and clear. It seemed innocuous, but she was sure the instruction to her was critical to Ivelli's master plan.

```
Kidnap the bear
```

36: Be it resolved

Despite his ordeal, the Wish Doctor was quite upbeat and filled with energy when they returned to the lodge. Being in a box for a while was not so bad. It allowed you to get in touch with your feelings and sort through a number of things you were thinking to get to the important bits. It also allowed you to really think about what meant the most to you, and what you would wish for the next time you had a totally guilt-free wish.

The Doctor was starting to remember something important, something he had wished some time ago that he would forget so that it would not be obvious to everyone else. He wasn't sure yet what it all meant, but he was sure that it was quite clever and would be needed before anyone else could figure out what he had planned.

He would need to put his students through some difficult paces over the next few months before the end of the semester. He would need all the help he could get from them before the next encounter with Ivelli. He was sure it would not be immediate, but would be soon.

The first half of the new year was shaped by special days of wish importance.

New Year's Eve was particularly spectacular on the magnificent lodge grounds. From almost all vantage points in and out of the lodge, you could see the silver of the frozen ice of the lake surrounded by the towering conifers with their icing of white.

It was the perfect setting to reflect the magnificent colour of a fireworks display. You have not seen a fireworks display until you have seen one created from wishes that would expire if not used before the next year.

Alma enjoyed it immensely, feeling satisfied with her part in the adventure to Florence. She tried not to think of the last words from her mother.

She was sad that Syd had not made it back yet from visiting his parents. She was glad, though, that she had seen no sign that her brother had anything to do with Ivelli. After being to Florence, and sensing the power of ancient wishes everywhere, she realized there could be many sources of wish teaching there.

"I know it's technically a holiday," the Wish Doctor said on January 1, "so I will keep the lecture short. I asked you here because today is a powerful day, perhaps one of the most powerful days in your life. On Thanksgiving, we talked about the power of thanks as an opposite view of wishes, but today, we have another alternative, perhaps the alternative that nature intended for us.

"Can anyone, and I hope almost everyone, say what I am talking about?"

There were several hands up, and, more importantly, recognition in many faces.

Venn, who had seemed to grow two inches over the break, raised his hand higher than any other. "Resolutions."

"Go on."

"You can make things happen by resolving to make them happen and then working hard to get them. This is a more foolproof way to accomplish things. It is more satisfying and less likely for things to go wrong than if you wished for them."

"Venn, you are invited to make this lecture the next time we hold this class. In fact, you can make all the lectures next time. If you resolve to do this, I will not be hurt."

Venn was taken aback. He had never diagrammed a future in which he would be a teacher.

The Doctor continued, "You have to be careful that your resolve doesn't become so strong that you do illegal or detrimental things to achieve what you want. So don't resolve that you will get a new Porsche 911 with all-wheel drive at any cost. That might lead you to steal money to help you pay for it, or, worse yet, hack into someone's computer and steal their identity and take out a fake loan. You should know by now that I have wished that all such perpetrators be tormented by demons like those painted on the ceiling in the Duomo in Florence. Resolve that you will work hard enough to earn enough money to buy that Porsche.

"And then, of course donate, it to charity. Porsches are far overrated. A Ford Mustang is much cheaper and will give you just as cool a vibe."

He winked at Syd, who couldn't keep his eyes open long enough to wink back.

"Resolve and hard work are intertwined, but they are not the only considerations. In fact, they can blind you to the true things you need to do or force you to work too hard. Consider a talented marathon runner getting close to her prime. She resolves to win the Boston Marathon and works extremely hard. Too hard. Every day in training she pushes herself to the limit. Her coaches tell her she needs to go easy in training on some days to let her body recover. She tries to, but she is so caught up in her resolve to work hard that every day she pushes herself close to the limit. She gets better, but her two greatest competitors take more rest and always beat her because their bodies have grown stronger with better recovery.

"I ask that you all spend the rest of the day contemplating and then, at 11 pm, make your resolutions ensuring your resolutions are achievable without undue costs."

He looked around to make sure they were paying attention. "Let me start with mine. I resolve that I will protect all of you in this room, or teach you to protect yourself, so that no harm can come to you." There was a shadow of seriousness in the Doctor's face that most didn't catch.

Alma surely did, after being in quicksand and seeing the Doctor trapped in a box. She looked at Syd. He looked tired from the early morning drive. He was so tired he hadn't had a chance to unpack Ron and bring him into the classroom, as he had been doing lately. As a result, Ron was not covered by the strength of the Wish Doctor's resolve.

Alma took her time contemplating but, from almost the moment she left the classroom, she knew what her resolutions would be.

> One, she would become a fully qualified wish apprentice and graduate to second year.
> Two, she would protect her mother's crystal.
> Three, she would find out what those pictures that looked like Syd meant.

She was sure at least two of the three would come true.

37: A short but important chapter

There was no class on January 2. It was a day the Wish Doctor liked to take for contemplation, and Selva knew the students needed a rest before the heavy workload of the second term.

Alma tried to talk to Syd at breakfast, but he was too tired. Looking at his weary face, she couldn't help thinking about those photographs. She had tried to ask Bell and Selva about them after the rescue, but both were elusive, so her best bet was to approach the Doctor.

Since she had been watching for him carefully, she noted that he had slipped off to the stairs that led down to the wishmethere. And once in a while up to the Chamber of Cooperation.

When no one was looking, she followed. But when she hit the steps, she saw a splash of tea on a step going up. He wasn't going to the wishmethere.

As she mounted, suddenly the steps became visible as they had been when Bell had led her up. She was a little nervous going toward this dangerous zone without Bell or Selva, but she had been there before. Maybe she would be safe.

Alma changed her mind when she got to the landing and noted the door was open just a little. Looking through the gap, she could see the Wish Doctor sitting. He seemed sad. *Is that a tear in his eye?*

"I miss you," he was saying to someone, as if looking at a photograph. "Even if you never missed me. You were the most beautiful woman ever without a wish.

"Everybody thought it was Giselle I was trying to impress the day I threw the coin in the fountain, but it was always you. I knew you admired genius and I was only trying to be as smart as my father. I'm sorry he was such a scoundrel to so many people.

"I wish you had never made that wish about him. And once it was made, I wished I had never learned to reverse it."

~

The Wish Doctor could not stop remembering what magic had once made him forget. It had seemed to him that she had once been gentle and unambitious, and maybe even kind. Why, then, had she been so cruel the last time she spoke to him?

She had said, "It is better for all of us. I wish never to see you again and that you forget all about me."

And he had for a very long time.

Until Scotland.

~

Alma realized this was too private a moment to ask about the photos of Syd, so she carefully backed away from the door as the Doctor lit a single votive candle. She quietly descended the stairs.

But not before hearing the Doctor say, "Happy birthday, Mother."

38: Rappie pie

It was to no one's surprise that the Wish Doctor was busy on Groundhog Day. If people would get it right, and understand they were supposed to honour groundhogs because it was their day instead of making wishes out of the weather, there would be fewer violent storms.

On this day, it was very clearly the Wish Doctor who was playing second fiddle to Her Presumptuousness, who was conducting a whole symphony as she tried to keep the shadows from disrupting the weather.

Smaetag and Alma accompanied Selva to Cleveland in the newer wish-methere. Feb. 2, always seemed to be a day of catch-22 wishes.

Smaetag and Alma were full. Selva had insisted they have a traditional Acadian meal for breakfast called rappie pie. It was different from anything they had tasted before, and must have had a bit of luck, since it was made from rabbit's feet and a savoury sauce. So, when they entered the Subway shop, Alma was sure she was too full for a sandwish.

Instead of placing an order, Selva asked, "Who is the one here who wished to be a rapper?"

A curly-haired youth packaging sandwiches rapidly nodded his head.

Selva put a small box covered in sparkly paper in front of him. "You need to unwrap this right now."

The sandwich wrapper and would-be rapper unwrapped the box. "Yo," he said, "getting a present is really rad

"I wish you didn't think my verse was bad."

Smaetag and Alma looked at each other. Not only was it a bad rap, but the boy's voice also seemed out of sync.

As he opened the box, which was unnecessarily over-wrapped, Selva whispered to the girls, "This is an important reversal. This boy was destined to be one of the world's great musical rappers, even more influential than Drake, if you can believe it. His poetry will one day be referenced to help end the race riots in 2222."

"And his wish went wrong. He wanted to be a great rapper, but was interpreted as being a great Wrapper?" Smaetag guessed.

"Exactly, and he made this wish on what day?"

"February 2," Alma answered.

"Right again. We need to get this reversed now. With Ivelli's interference we will not get another chance. And if you think 2020 was a bad year, you will never believe what 2222 is going to be like."

Before Selva could make the quip, Smaetag said. "Let's just say 2222 will be two, two much."

Selva smiled at her. He was so proud of her for how strong her character had become since her death wish.

The boy finished unwrapping the present. There were two large wishbones. His eyebrows furrowed. He picked up one of the wishbones and Selva took the other end of it.

"Now rapidly," Selva said, "you two unwrap his wish with a simple reversal. He and I will make a new wish."

Alma and Smaetag picked up the other wishbone and prepared to pull on it. "Wrapper great a be to want I," they chorused as the bone snapped between them.

Smaetag won the bigger half. Alma could feel Smaetag's wish power flow through the store.

The boy would be making no more sandwiches.

"I want to be a great rapper." The boy said, as the bigger piece of the wishbone snapped into his hand, Selva having taken a nick out of the bone so it would snap in the rapper's direction.

Suddenly the sandwich shop was alive with the sound of rapping. A smile of rhythm spread across the former wrapper now rapper's face.

The music he then made was so rapturous, it cannot be repeated here. Let's just say, that February 2, 2222, will be a day two remember.

39: Shark bait

January 1, in month-day format, was 1-1, a special day. February 2, 2-2, was a special day. It should be no surprise that March 3, 3-3, was a special day. Alma just couldn't think of the reasons.

She would not learn every aspect of March third's significance. At one time March 3 was the most powerful wish day in the year, when most granting agents were awakening in the feel of coming spring and full of power.

But also one of the most powerful in anger. Maybe because of interrupted sleep, one grantor had made a wish that March 3 would be a miserable day. It, of course, was, but that didn't mean that wishes made that day couldn't come true, just that it never felt like it on that day. You could never count on a March 3 wish coming true especially on March 3, though in the future a March 3 wish might come to fruition more powerfully than wishes made on any other day.

This was why a wish made on March 3, 1964 that a movie about Jedi Knights would be a box office smash didn't come true until May 19, 1977.

At the start of the day's lesson, all Alma knew was that this would be a special day. They were all invited to a special birthday presentation at supper.

She had a chance to google who was born on March 3, and at the top of list, there was a surprise that should be no surprise.

Bell.

The ghostly inventor had been born on March 3. She realized she had never seen the inventor and the Wish Doctor together; but clearly they were friends.

She suddenly felt unnerved. *What do you get a ghost for a present?*

~

For dinner, a special feast had been prepared on the beach. The ocean temperature was higher than normal and it was a blessed day for early kelp of all kinds, sauteed in special sauces.

At the back of the beach looking dapper, was Bell, shimmering brightly as if there were more of him than normal in the dimension of the living.

No one seemed to be looking at him often though, other than Alma. *Can others see him? Are they so used to his presence that they take him for granted?* She suddenly felt foolish for thinking she was the only one who had met him.

"A toast," the Wish Doctor said to settle things down, and motioned for the ocean waves to keep still so all could hear his barely disguised lesson.

"Today we celebrate a birthday of a very famous, very important person."

Bell straightened his jacket, smiling. But he lost some of his shimmer and sadness filled his face when the Doctor said, "Join me in wishing happy birthday to the Shupershark."

Out of the water jumped one not-so-fearsome shark that, on closer inspection, had a finely-carved set of false teeth. The student populace en masse laughed and whooped and clapped.

The shark in turn splashed the water with his tail, then jumped above the surface while touching fins to his nose, clearly showing off.

Bell, on the other hand, felt as if he had been ghosted. Alma saw his expression and felt for him. She knew how disappointing birthdays could be. While her brother's were always celebrated in outlandish ways, hers were always subdued, if not outright ignored.

"We have already talked about the danger of wishes on birthdays. But that doesn't mean there can't be a great celebration for each and every person who has a birthday, and that is a good many of us."

Alma looked over to Bell, who was trying to hold a solid face. Even a ghost could have his feelings hurt.

"If you help your friend or family celebrate their birthday, you will help them avoid taking a risk on a bad birthday wish," the Doctor said. "No matter if you have a beef or dispute with a person, and you have yet to forgive them, you must honour a person's birthday, for in so doing you honour the person. If they are your friend, and if you haven't yet, forgive them on their birthday. On a person's birthday more than any other day, they just want to be loved. The confidence your honour and attention give them will be more powerful than any wish.

"And so, having said that, I have a special gift for my friend Shupershark."

The Doctor unwrapped a small package and pulled out a silver object with the original insignia of the Bell Telephone Company on it. He tossed it in the water, and as the shark drew up to it, the cord on the bell moved as if by magic and attached itself to a tracking tag on the shark's fin.

"That will allow you to call me if you need," the Doctor said, "and vice versa." He said the last as if it wasn't as important as the shark calling him. "Oh, and it will also neutralize the stupid tracker on your fin."

The shark splashed the water, then said with all the might of his gills. "Thank you, Doctor! I was getting tired of being tracked! It's really quite a bore! Happy me day to all of you!"

While Alma was glad for the attention of the shark, and saddened by the emotions he invoked, she was also shocked by the nature of the gift. It seemed almost designed to insult Bell.

While the shark was swimming around, alternately ringing his bell and motioning students to throw him flavoured kelp, the Doctor made his way to the back of the beach. He strode to where Bell hung hovering, though slightly lower than he had when the evening began,

Selva came to Bell's other side. Both he and the Doctor were smiling.

"You didn't think we'd invite you here to your own birthday and not have something for you?" the Wish Doctor said.

"Well, I had no idea the Shupershark had the same birthday as me. He never mentioned it when I used my electromagnetics to pull the bullets from his scales."

"Well, he is a fish. Maybe he just assumed you'd realize you were both Pisces."

"Hoy, Hoy, you are a silly one, Doctor. I do appreciate the birthday celebration."

"Hoy, Hoy. We are not done. Do you want to do the honours, Selva? Tell Bell what we have discovered for him."

Selva leaned in and whispered in the ghost's ear. Bell's face lit up in enjoyment.

Alma, now watching, understood. What do you give a ghost like Bell, who could not stay dead because of his insatiable curiosity, and who could not hold a corporeal object?

Why, you give him the gift of knowledge.

40: April and May Days

Say what you will about the Wish Doctor and his corny jokes, he was no fool. If Alma hadn't expected a complete lockdown on April 1, she would have been a poor student, and undeserving of the crystal piece.

'Complete lockdown' was an understatement. The students had been ordered to pack dry food into their rooms the night before. The rooms were locked from the outside. Wishmethere keys had been confiscated. All types of communications devices were locked up, including old-fashioned pen and paper. Students had to trim their nails to the bone so they couldn't even attempt to scratch out words on a wall or their skin that might look like a wish.

All study material, all notes, all coins, all wishbones, all dragonflies, all clovers—everything was gone. They were asked to drink a Listerine type liquid to mildly freeze their mouths to prevent the temptation of talking.

"How are we supposed to entertain ourselves?" Wheatgrass asked.

"Get some sleep," was the answer.

Alma understood. What day could be worse for wishes to go bad than April Fools' Day, when trickery was the order of the day?

The Doctor explained that April Fool's Day was no recent cultural affectation. It had a long history of being the day when wishes went bad. If your birthday was April 1, and if you did not take care, your wishes could go bad and destroy the whole country.

Despite the Doctor's paranoia, he seemed to be comforted by his abundance of precaution.

Thus, it was the perfect day for Alma to escape and get the tattoo. The idea had been with her for months, since the wish gone bad had sent her to the Island of Misfit Toys. It had been emphasized by the voices in Florence. There seemed no other time she could get away.

She escaped the old-fashioned way, by planning ahead.

She had to get out early before the rooms were locked, as it was a long hike to where she had stashed the bicycle, but she easily made it into town. She hadn't been able to visit the shop ahead of time due to the exhausting schedule, but she had communicated ahead her need and wants.

She expected from the address that the tattoo parlour would be on the main street, but it was in a boat house, or a reformed boathouse, overhanging the water. There was a planked deck in front, though it had been added years ago, given its worn condition.

A young lady with an evil-looking nose held a series of cards in front of Alma as she approached. "Do you want me to read your future?"

Even if Alma didn't know the name of the community she was in and the date, she would have known there was danger in that request. She took a step to the side to avoid the woman and could feel the plank cracking a little under her feet. She looked down and could see the water. No way was she taking a tarot reading today. A bad deck on a bad deck in Baddeck was not to play with on April Fool's Day.

She was wondering if she had made a mistake. Her will was set, though, so she slid into the shop for her appointment with the not-so-young Goth tattoo artist.

"I'm Alma. I hope my stencil is ready."

"It is."

"We must finish at exactly 11:11."

"Ah, the morning wishing hour," the Goth smiled knowingly. "Don't worry. Selva figured out your little scheme and gave me a head's up. I once went to your school. Got trapped living with these bad decks when I made a wish about magic card tricks."

Alma felt a rush of excitement and danger as the needle with pigment set into her skin.

Lavinia will be royally ticked. The thought made her face all the brighter.

She had been extra careful that no wish was part of the whole endeavour. Just prudent planning. She held a mirror so she could watch as the tattoo was applied. She made sure every bit of ink was perfect; that there was nothing to upset the pattern.

It went so well that she felt a little too confident, confident enough to take a gamble. "Can you come outside with me?"

They went outside and the girl with the nose was still there.

"Hi," Alma said, holding out an American ten-dollar note. "I've changed my mind. Would you touch my back with your deck of cards, and then make the wish I ask of you?"

The girl nodded and listened as Alma whispered to her.

Then she touched the deck to Alma's back and repeated the words.

Alma smiled. It was a gamble, but it made sense. If most wishes with good intentions went bad, on April's Fool's Day, wouldn't a wish made to make fun, or cause trouble, or just be bad reverse and end up being a good wish?

She certainly hoped so. Or she was in a lot of trouble.

"You don't look like the kind of person who would get a tattoo, but this image suits you perfectly," the Goth said.

"I hope so. I think I'm going to need it."

~

For some, especially those who had seen a certain Jedi movie 12 or more times, May the fourth was the most powerful May day for wish magic. Alas, there was a long-running debate whether May 5 was the more powerful day. Logically, the 5th of the 5th month, Cinque de Mayo, powerful in many cultures, following the pattern previously set, must be a powerful day. (There is a reason April 4th was skipped over in the narrative, never fear for its purpose; It has something to do with the oddly-named estuary in Scotland, the Firth of Forth). Those who thought logically and tended to worship the more logical space spanning franchise, boldly saw May 5 as the more powerful day.

Thus, it was no surprise, given his background and interests, that Bell would more naturally align with May 5.

Even though he had been born and died before either franchise, the Trek communicator was certainly inspired by his own inventions, and its approach to problems was more along his own. Not to mention that the geographic mapping of the universe, led by interstellar geographic explorers, was similar to efforts he had led as the head of the *National Geographic Society*.

Bell appeared in the mirror in Alma's room at 5 in the morning on the fifth day of the fifth month, startling her as she rose with a yawn. Christine was sound asleep, as she had stayed up late, having unfortunately wished she was a Jedi Knight for a day, and having learned that a knight's responsibilities could be exceedingly exhausting.

Bell put a finger to his lips and stepped out of the mirror. He seemed slightly less ghostly than on his birthday, though he certainly had not been getting enough sun.

He sat down, hovering beside her on the edge of the bed. In a low voice, he said, "I know you have had bad luck on your birthdays, especially with presents, so I wanted to give you something."

Alma's pulse raced in excitement. She hadn't ever received a present from a ghost before. "But how do you know about my present history? I haven't told anyone."

"The Shupershark told me."

"What?"

"Oh, you probably don't know. As part of the wish that made him, he has ESP, ExtraSharkPerception. He read your mind."

"Oh." she said, hoping, horrified, she hadn't been thinking about Syd the day of his birthday.

"I got a special gift on my birthday, and it's allowed me to make some advances. I am not quite there yet, but I might have something ready for the day you'll need it."

Alma's eyes nearly crossed. *What is this about?*

He held out to her a small silver cylinder, with a curved lid on top. "Just take this. If I explain more at this point, it might make you count on this too much. Just promise me that if you hear my voice, you will take the lid off this device, press down and say, 'Okay'."

Alma nodded, realizing that he was holding something corporeal.

What had he learned from Selva on this birthday? Somehow they had learned to modify the laws of physics pertaining to ghosts.

"Gotta go now," he said. "Say happy birthday to your father for me."

Alma looked at his disappearing form in horror. She had forgotten it was her father's birthday.

41: The Age of Enlightenment

The rest of the semester was unexceptional, or unexceptional compared to the events Alma had lived through since coming to Baddeck. She anticipated something big still to happen before the semester end, but it was long in coming and she felt an underlying tension.

She studied long hours and practised her elocution reversals, so they were near perfect. She could do Morse code backwards and forwards and had become expert on every type of bear.

The tattoo on her back had stung for a while, and she kept it hidden from everyone. She was still concerned that somehow the April Fool tattoo would end up being a prank on her. Every day she twisted like a pretzel so she could get a glimpse of it in the mirror.

She was no clearer on the mystery of the photos of Syd. Was he a clone? Had he gone back in time on an adventure? Was he a robot that could live several generations?

It had put a little friction in their relationship, so that maybe they hadn't progressed as much as they should have. Still, they regularly spent time together, studying, eating, hanging with Ron and often joining the Wish Doctor on field trips.

All the students were now travelling with the Wish Doctor regularly to help fix wishtakes. Selva said there were still way more than normal, but they were expecting that, now they knew Ivelli was behind many. Many times, she thought they would meet up with him, but he was never anywhere they went, or at least that they could find.

The semester would officially end June 29, the day before the caretakers were officially coming for the summer. Alma was nervous about her final exam. She definitely wanted to return the next year. She did not want to return home, and she did not want to leave Syd. She had a lot more to learn, though she thought she had shown she had the talents for mastering wish magic.

She hadn't yet figured where she would spend the summer. She really did not want to go back to New Orleans, other than to drop off the crystal. She maybe should have done so earlier, since it had served its purpose helping to free the Wish Doctor.

There had been considerable progress with all the students in their ability to manage wishes. Most could line out all the protection wishes; most could reverse simple wishes. Smaetag had been in good spirits and was in fact more confident than ever, now that she knew she was going to live a normal life before she died at the right time, whenever that would be.

Late in June, just before the solstice, after Alma had helped on a field trip with a particularly nasty wish, she found herself alone in the lodge, the Wish Doctor having told her to rest. Selva had taken several students in the bus to Cape Smokey to smoke out bad wishes, while the Doctor had taken Smaetag, the triplets and Syd on an all-day trip across the globe.

One of the triplets had remained behind, an allergy acting up with all the pollen in the air. Alma hadn't seen her, though she'd heard her intermittently snoring and sneezing in her room.

As normal, she spent part of her study time reading from the *Encyclopedia Wishtannica*, but something nagged at her thoughts.

She was alone.

And she hadn't solved Syd's mystery.

At 9:09, Alma circled down the staircase to the wishmethere to see if the stairs to the secret chamber were open. They were not.

She tried to see if she could discover them by various means, by using mirrors, by going down to the wishmethere and coming up like they had that day with Bell. She called out Bell's name, and realized she hadn't seen him since May.

She lifted up her crystal piece, and there was a short, flurried sparking. She pulled in a step ladder and felt for a hidden latch. Nothing.

She went back to her studies in an alcove near the stairwell where she could watch for activity. She spent more time watching than studying.

At 10:10, she tried prying at the walls and the roof with a broom.

At 11:11, Alma carefully cleaned her glasses with over-priced lens cleaner so she could see better. Maybe it worked, or maybe there was something new to see. Or did she imagine the small drop of golden fluid was suspended where she knew the hidden staircase to be?

The air above her started to waver. The door appeared

She opened it but couldn't see the stairs. She felt with her hand. There was some kind of barrier, though she was able to push through it.

As she felt carefully for the steps, she touched a fat blob of stickiness. She lifted her finger and gently licked it with her tongue.

Honey.

Sweet testing, but with a tinge of guilt. Not guilt for eating the sweet, but guilt over something else, hidden knowledge.

From up above, another drip.

Someone is up in the secret room. Not the Doctor, nor Selva nor Bell.

Someone eating quietly. Who likes honey.

"Ron, are you up there?"

No answer.

Every time she had seen Ron eat, it had been with daintiness and care. He was gentlemanly and *bearly* all at the same time, a most perfect representative of the bear species. He also would not waste even a little bit of honey. He was either distraught or he was deliberately leaving her a trail, maybe to avoid the Wish Doctor's tricks to keep the room hidden.

"Ron," she called again, this time more tentatively.

He did not reply. She was sure she heard the sound of sobbing, the most painful sobbing she had ever heard.

Alma put a tentative foot forward and, though the step remained camouflaged, she could feel it soundly. As quickly as she dared, she went up the stairs. She worried what danger there might be in the room without any protection other than the crystal. Maybe it would protect her; she feared the bear needed help.

She had not been informed on her previously short visit that the Chamber of Cooperation had a second name. The secret room had a secret but sensible name: The Secret Room. It was a place to hide secrets, so that they would not be released. It was also a place to have secrets revealed.

She had not been at the school long enough to hear the Doctor's lecture on secrets. "Revealing a secret at the wrong time or the wrong place, or revealing a secret that should never be revealed, can cause more pain than any wish gone wrong."

Thus, though she looked for danger, she did not look in the right place.

She came to the upper door, which was ajar, just as it was the time she saw the Doctor and his candles.

This time, she entered quickly.

There was Ron, almost where the Doctor had been, his posture distraught, stiff. In his big paw, shaped a little too much like a human's hand, was a large black and white picture that appeared to be very old.

A picture of someone who looked like Syd.

"You, caught me," he said, blinking back tears from his red and puffy eyes. "Bear handed."

He tried to avoid her eyes and Alma looked away as well. As a result, neither of them saw the skinny threat sneak into the room and hide in the shadows behind Ron.

"Ron, why are you so upset?"

"Because you have asked questions and no one has given you those answers. It's coming to the time of denouement, when you must know."

Alma didn't know what to say. Ron looked so guilty, unlike his goalie namesake, Hextall, who always looked so innocent, even when he tripped someone with his goalie stick.

"I can grant you three questions," Ron said, as if they were in a fairy tale. "But only three. You must ask as carefully as you would make a wish. You cannot ask directly of the secret. You cannot ask who is in this picture."

Alma was taken aback with concern but also revelation. The right three questions could be as powerful as wishes.

She had already suspected the truth, but hadn't want to believe it. There was a dangerous reality, if it *was* true. She took a deep breath, let the taste of guilty honey swirl in her mouth. There was no such thing as protection questions, or no way to apply them that she could think of. She had to be precise.

"I hate to rush you," Ron said, "but things are spiralling to a conclusion. For the pieces to be in place, you must ask me quickly."

Alma grasped the crystal so hard she felt like she could crush it, then asked, "How long have you been a real live bear?"

She had wanted to add conditions and parenthetical comments and clarifications as if she were a lawyer laying a trap, but she could see the earnestness in Ron's eyes. He would not try to find a loophole in her questions if she asked correctly. A more complicated question might lead to a more complicated answer. She already feared the simple answer.

"Almost the whole time, he said. "One hundred years."

Alma caught her gasp. She really didn't need to ask the other questions, but she could not hold back now. There was still clarity and ramifications to be determined.

"Who made you into a real live bear?"

"Syd."

She did not need to ask the direct question. She knew now who was in the picture. *Ask the third question.*

"Does Syd remember the day he made you live?"

"There are many holes in his memory. He does not recall the real scheme that is played here, but he remembers the day he made me live. And the year."

Alma felt the world collapse on her. Syd was at least a hundred years old, clearly cloaked in illusion and camouflage. She had bared her soul to him, shared intimacy. Was his hidden form that of an old man?

He knew and hadn't told her. No wonder he knew so much without paying attention in class. What game were he and the Wish Doctor playing? Was this all a big joke? He had seemed so nice. Was he just a creepy old man? Her worst nightmare.

That relationship game she thought she had won. The wish she thought had gone right, after it had gone wrong, was wrong again.

"I'm sorry," Ron said. "It might mean trouble for us all, but I'm an honest, caring bear. I thought you should know."

Alma touched him lightly through her pain, and fled down the stairs, not realizing how vulnerable and weakened she left him. When the wishmethere arrived at 11:11 pm, Alma was waiting, arms crossed. As the Wish Doctor and students stepped out, the long tendrils of the wishmethere curled around itself as if huddling from Alma's anger.

The other students sensed it as well. There isn't anything more powerful than the anger of a ticked-off girlfriend.

Smaetag nodded and hurried past her while the two triplets deliberately smiled and giggled at Syd. The Doctor gave them a scorched look and they knew to give them space.

Alma stared at Syd, trying to understand what she had learned. *Is his body real? Is something keeping him young? Would he turn to dust the moment a wish wore off, like something from 'The Mummy'? Or is it an illusion, the same kind of thing that keeps the triplets looking alike, but only when they are near each other?*

"I have to talk to you," she said to him, flicking her shoulder so the Wish Doctor knew to vamoose. His memories, though returning, were not reformed enough to know that he should have stayed.

~

Syd stayed three feet from Alma, somewhat perturbed. After a long day of wish battling without either Ron or Alma, his favourite companions, he was looking forward to seeing both. Alma's attitude came as a complete shock.

"What is it?" he said, his weariness making his words sound rougher than he intended.

"Tell, me the truth. Have you been hiding something from me?"

Syd tried to hide the guilt in his face but couldn't. His memories were returning, but there was no context, no meaning. He hadn't meant not to share, but without context what did his memories mean? He had meant to share when meaning came.

"Okay, at least you aren't overtly lying. Tell me, Syd: how old are you really?"

The one fact Syd remembered. He hadn't when he first met Alma, or even when he had invited her for Christmas. Or at least he wouldn't admit so to himself. He had always known a little.

There was no point hiding now. The time was coming when the illusion no longer mattered. Events in the wish world had a way of catching up with you.

"I'm 122, I think," he said. "But it's not what you think."

Alma stood silently. She didn't think anything other than betrayal. She could not even remember the hundred other questions she had for him. When she had asked him if he was old enough to drive, he had hinted that he was, but not that he needed to be tested regularly to see if his health still qualified. He had definitely drunk more wishkey than Smaetag, who she realized now was much younger.

Maybe she could handle all of that. But the secrecy tore her apart. "You could have told me."

Syd hung his head. He could have, maybe should have, but there was a bigger game at play, a more dangerous one. He had not meant to hurt her. He loved her as much as Ron did.

There was a sudden tug at the connection he held with the bear. "Where's Ron?" he said in panic.

"He was here a moment ago," Alma said.

"Something's wrong," Syd said. "Something's happened to him."

He started to sprint up the stairs in panic, but turned just slightly. He had a tear in his eye, a tear that reflected the pain of a hundred years. "I'm sorry, you think I'm too old for you."

He had waited a hundred years for someone like her and knew now he had made a mistake of a very long lifetime.

~

Syd tore through the house, bringing a legion of stuffed animals alive to search with him. Edison had his lights out, a stuffed mole had a miner's helmet. Other students were roped into the search.

Alma, feeling bad, went up to the secret room, no longer hidden from her, but there was no sign of Ron, or honey, or the pictures of Syd.

As the night went on, Syd became more frantic and began showing his age, with creases on his forehead. Ron was not to be found anywhere.

The Doctor was worried that they might be facing the next attack from Ivelli.

Ron's disappearance was concerning. More of the Doctor's thoughts were coming back. Syd's age. Their plan. If the need was revealing that, then the danger so long planned for, so long anticipated, even in the Doctor's long life, was coming soon.

He didn't have to wait long.

Alma sat in the lodge exhausted, not far from the Wish Doctor. When the crystal started ringing, they both heard it.

Alma tentatively put it to her ear just as Syd came into the room, hair frazzled, eyes bloodshot.

There was a voice on the other line that chilled Alma to the core. She handed the crystal to Syd and said, "It's for you."

Perplexed, Syd held the crystal piece to his ear.

"If you ever want to see the bear again, tell the Wish Doctor to reverse the florin wish. I am quite serious. If you do not, Ron will be dead and bearied before you see him again."

Bell appeared suddenly, maybe because the crystal technology was infringing on Mabel's patents. He signalled with his hands that he was tracing the call.

"You understand?" the voice said.

"Yes," Syd said.

The crystal made a large noise like a click.

"It's a 506 number," Bell said. "New Brunswick."

Syd, stricken as if his worst nightmare had come true, repeated what Ivelli had said.

For a few moments they all stood staring at each other, but then a smile spread across the Wish Doctor's face. He knew where Ron was. And that Ivelli was with him.

"They are at the centre of the highest tides in the world. They are at Hopewell Rocks on the New Brunswick side of the Bay of Fundy."

Because where else would Ivelli be for the confrontation he had so long planned than at one of the greatest sources of wish magic in the world? For what else was a wish but a Hope Well made?

42: Foiled

There was no time for resolution with Syd, as events moved quickly. Despite the Wish Doctor's good humour, caused by knowing Ivelli's whereabouts, there was a deadly sense about his demeanour. They were heading toward climax. Alma knew things were happening above her ken.

She was glad, though, that at least she was one of the seven chosen to travel by wishmethere to Hopewell Rocks. Unlike Smaetag, who was furious she couldn't go.

"No," the Wish Doctor said. "That's part of this trap. Our foe wants to encounter you."

He didn't tell her that 'encounter' was a euphemism for his suspicion Ivelli was going to try and kill the most powerful students in the class, those most likely to replace him. He did not want to hope, but there was a sense that maybe his wish of finding a replacement was soon to come true. Unless Ivelli's strategy to outwit him worked.

If he was not smarter on his own, Ivelli had finally figured out you could outsmart someone smarter by surrounding yourself with other smart people. To counter Ivelli, they had to act quickly.

Selva went to unlock the wishmethere while the students gathered nearby. As he turned his wish key, there was a grinding sound that was not at all right.

Then the wishmethere exploded.

Debris and dust spread everywhere, choking the students. Venn, standing tall, was hit in the head with flying piece of metal. Brad came to help and was struck as well.

The Doctor issued a wish that sounded like an incantation and the debris dropped to the ground, but the damage had been done. He ran to the door of the wishmethere and pulled out a very damaged Selva.

Selva was barely able to speak, but muttered, "Sabotage."

The Wish Doctor barked commands and put Christine and Nola, the students most attuned to wellness, in charge of Selva, Venn and Brad.

Loretta was to stay behind and try to neutralize any future wish attacks.

The rest of the students gathered around the Doctor, feeling the magnitude of the coming crisis. Alma wondered who the two newcomers were until, she realized they were the twiplets, looking different without their triplet.

Where is their sister? Then she understood.

"I know who the saboteur is," she said so firmly that everyone stopped what they are doing. "It's one of the triplets."

The two remaining looked shocked, true ignorance in their faces. The ruse had worked. The likely suspect, Alfalfa, stood mortified. Her bad behaviour had been driven by jealousy and hurt, not menace.

In this time of crisis, no one, least of all the twiplets, took time to question what all now realized to be true. There was a traitor, and the danger to the school of wish was greater than it had been in a hundred and twenty-two years.

The missing Dahlia was the traitor.

The Wish Doctor swallowed. He would have to put some of the students at risk to save as many as he could. Glenda, Syd and Alma were coming with him. Though he thought he could trust the remaining twiplets, it was too much risk. Had he not been told that taking on the triplets would mean hardship, but that among them might be his saviour? It didn't matter now.

The students had varied reactions as he told each one who was coming and who was staying behind. When he came to Smaetag, he saw only resistance.

"No," she said. "I'm coming with you." Her tone was fierce.

"But," he said in a wishper so only she could hear, "Ivelli wants you more than anyone. He fears your power. He will stop at nothing to harm you."

He did not say Ivelli wanted her because she was the readiest to be his replacement, at least in terms of power.

"Then I wish a shield of protection," she said, "I know you are worried because I wished for my death and you fear it coming, but trust me, I am the one person who is assured not to die on this trip. I will die of natural causes. Those causes are not ready to call me. No wish will kill me. My wish, made with Wishkey, is a pre-eminent wish. It cannot be overturned. I felt the truth of it. I feel it now. I know when my death will come. It is the greatest gift I could be given. I will live my life to the fullest until that moment. To help you in this moment will make my life full."

She stopped and stared into his eyes with confident purpose. "Besides, I made a wish that I was the best hydrofoil pilot ever."

The Wish Doctor nodded slowly. With that logic, he could not argue.

None of this lessened any of Syd's panic.

Ron. His only true companion. Gone.

"What will we do?" he said. "Shall we take the Wishtang."

The Wish Doctor shook his head. He already knew it was sabotaged as well. As were the kites.

Smaetag had figured out the truth before all of them. At a place called Hopewell, on the end of the Bay of Fundy, the basin of the highest tides of the world, on the summer solstice, the zodiacal alignment meant subtle influences, not quite wishes, were at their greatest affect. The highest tides in the world would be at their highest level of two centuries, filled with the power of melting icebergs.

Ivelli was going to use the power of the moon's influence on tidal water to generate wishes.

"Don't worry, there is an even better solution. It's time for the hydrofoil. We have added all Bell's latest ideas. It's time to unlock her."

Because, after all, there is no finer vessel for disrupting wishes granted from water than a hydrofoil.

43: Hope Well

The province of New Brunswick is one of the, if not the most, under-appreciated places in the world. If the Wish Doctor had been born in this later day and worked as, say, an accountant to pay the bills, New Brunswick would be high on his list of places to retire. Not crowded, beautiful snowmobiling in the winter, reversing waterfalls (especially helpful with waterfall wishes gone wrong), magnetic hills, interesting tidal bores and the greatest number of covered bridges in the world, it is one magical place. No wonder there was a magical spirit trying to keep others out.

Of course, it is not easy to appreciate such things when you're trapped in quicksand.

The Wish Doctor sank slowly into the quicksand the ocean floor had become. He was up to his hips, but even at a slow rate he would soon be under the surface. It was not long before the highest tides in the world would start flowing toward him.

The soil was more clay than sand, but enough that the quicksand wish had worked. He was surprised that Ivelli had tried the same wish as in PEI, but that was partly what had caused him to be trapped. It wasn't a wish he had planned for.

He should have figured it out, given that all bread and all pre-made sandwiches had suddenly sold out just before they arrived in the hydrofoil, so there were no sandwishes anywhere to help against the quicksand.

That and the fact, that he intended to be trapped.

Ivelli's greatest flaw was his overconfidence. He often acted as if he were still the smartest man in the world.

The hydrofoil had travelled quickly. Smaetag was true to her work, captaining the ship as if it was part of her. They had travelled from Baddeck through the St. Peters Canal lock, and up the Canso Strait that separated Cape Breton Island from mainland Nova Scotia. From there they had travelled the Northumberland Strait, then hovered over land as they crossed the Chignecto isthmus. So many industrialists had dreamt of digging a canal across the isthmus, and many more romantics had wished there was a canal so that Nova Scotia could be that most romantic of things, an island.

As they arrived at Hopewell, Ivelli had sent the Digby fairy, whom he had recruited with guile, to tell the Wish Doctor to leave the hydrofoil and come alone to the ocean floor. Or they would not see Ron again.

There was little choice. For his plan to defeat Ivelli to work (and for the first time in a while he had some doubts), the Wish Doctor had to comply.

Ivelli stood on top of one of the Hopewell Rocks. The rocks were massive structures that had been carved by the power of the tides. At high tide, the water surrounded all but the tops of them, creating what appeared to be small islands, but at low time, they were tall structures that looked like flowerpots.

He called down to the Wish Doctor. "I repeat my offer. Reverse your florin wish, or let me reverse it, and I will return the bear to you or one of your proteges."

The Wish Doctor had learned over the years to keep his emotions from his face, but he could not hold back the conflict now. He knew how dangerous reversing his wish would be, and his easy answer should be 'never'.

Yet he had grown fond of Ron and Syd. The bear was very much a real being. Ivelli would destroy him if the Doctor could not release him. And the bear still had a very important purpose. The price to release him was just too much, wasn't it?

"Not an easy choice, is it?" Ivelli said. "I will give you until the tide is half-way to make a decision. Then I will do what I have to.

"I didn't come here just for this, as you will fathom when you are under water. And don't think your ally Her Presumptuousness will save you. I've seen that she is otherwise employed. I'm not sure your relationship will be so close, anyway, when she finds out what you do in the next book."

The Wish Doctor frowned. He did not like anyone but him breaking the fourth wall of his own story. Unless it was one of his proteges with the talent to be his replacement.

"Now, if you'll excuse me," Ivelli said. "I have a few chores to attend to."

The Wish Doctor heard the sound of metal clanging as Ivelli walked away. For a moment, he thought Ivelli would make the classic villain's mistake of leaving him by himself to make an escape, but atop the flowerpot he could see cameras capturing his every move. There was someone else up there. Ivelli had proteges of his own. Not everyone thought evil was a bad thing. Well, he hadn't expected his escape to be easy.

He felt a deep moment of melancholy. If possible, he would wish he could reverse that first wish. Hadn't he done enough? Maybe he should step aside and let things play out with Ivelli naturally. He was tired of the burdens.

But then the picture of Ivelli's face loomed, haunting his vision.

Ivelli had to be stopped and none of the possible replacements were ready. At least not yet.

~

Ron, meanwhile, was getting tired of all the chatter. Silly humans thought it was completely up to them whether he was freed. They should have learned by now that he was a very independent and right-thinking bear.

Now that he was in a place called Hopewell, it was time to make a wish of his own. Although the wellness he was hoping for was not necessarily his own, given the great capacity of his generosity.

He just had to figure out a way to escape the thick plastic bag that was suffocating his little teddy bear form.

~

The hydrofoil bobbed gently in the water as the others awaited word from the Wish Doctor.

Alma watched Syd carefully, concerned he would try to rescue Ron. She was right to be concerned, because Syd was thinking to do just that. The tension between them had been corporeal on the trip, but there had been no time to speak. The Doctor did not give them a chance to do anything but prepare.

She shouldn't be so angry. There was more to the story she was not understanding. *How can Syd be one hundred and look like he does? How can he be one hundred and act like he does?* He had played his role of student too well, like he was really a teenage student. Still the pictures did not lie.

Ron did not lie.

She held back her pride. They had to rescue Ron. He really was a fine bear.

~

Ron was continually surprised at how people underestimated him. When he was a live bear, they saw him as a circus act or a wild animal or some trick of a toy bear turned alive. When they saw him in his teddy bear form, they saw him as inanimate, unintelligent. He found it all quite insulting.

Those few who knew that Syd could bring him alive thought that was the only way he could change his form. No one had ever asked if he could turn himself into a bear.

It wasn't always easy, but when Ron set his mind to it, he could turn himself into any type of bear. After all, that was his true form. No one had ever considered that he was a bear, turned into a toy.

He unleashed his power, wishing to be a full-grown bear. His growing body would burst through the trappings of the plastic bag.

Only nothing happened. He tried turning himself to a baby bear, to a polar bear, but something was resisting him. The easiest wish for him, altering to become a real bear, was blocked.

Someone had anticipated how he might escape! He felt a bit ticked at himself for thinking so arrogantly that he could escape without help. He did not want help. His job was to be the helper.

The wish he held was potent. Since he could not use it to turn himself to a bear, he could still feel its power. It had not been spent. He had to use it in a different way.

His little glass eyes squinted, and the stranded threads of his little teddy bear cheeks grimaced. He didn't like it but he had to turn himself into something not like a bear, but something he could relate to.

He uttered the wish quickly.

And found himself growing, fur disappearing.

Until he turned into a full grown, if scrawny, human teenager. His growing body split the plastic bag that surrounded him. He gasped for air, feeling the sudden humility of being bare and not bear.

He snapped his fingers. Nothing happened. Whatever had stopped his bear wish was in complete control. He could make wishes but could not turn himself into a bear anymore. He groaned in frustration, realizing his greatest strength was gone. In fact, he was unbear Able.

He swore. It wouldn't be the first time someone being unbearable was a problem.

He couldn't dwell on the problem. There was still a doctor at stake at a stake, so he had no time to be shy.

Ron could feel Syd's presence and knew what to do next: uncover Ivelli's master plan.

There was a rough building so out of place on the flowerpot that Ron knew it was Ivelli's command post. It was really a shack, decorated with an odd flourish of symbols that appeared to have come out of a Da Vinci notebook. The wood was weather-beaten and partly rotten. It had been there awhile.

Whatever Ivelli was up to, he had been planning it for some time. Ron felt a deep chill only partly from the cold winds of the Bay of Fundy striking his bare body.

~

As Ron took action, freeing himself from the cellophane wish trap, Syd could sense it, feeling *déja vu*, just in a different time period. It was if they had rehearsed this moment so they could be synchronized. Then rehearsed it again and again. Even if Ron was forced to improvise.

Syd's stomach was in knots. He felt the hair on his arms stand up so thickly it was like Ron's fur. His lifelong companion was in trouble and he didn't have a way to get to him, despite being within a kilometre.

He looked over at Alma, whom he had so deeply disappointed. She had no right to help him, but maybe he could appeal to her feelings for Ron.

~

The Wish Doctor examined his captivity. Ivelli couldn't possibly expect him to drown, anymore than he could expect the box trap to defeat him. Ivelli had stated the Wish Doctor would be around for the next book. Thus, the quicksand was just meant to delay him if he didn't reverse the wish.

While Nova Scotia was the Doctor's adopted home, he loved all the Maritimes, and the Bay of Fundy in particular. If Ivelli was going to defeat him on his home turf, or in the turf about to be covered with surf, he was mistaken.

To help his cause though, he took a moment to send out a brief message in Morse code.

Nova Scotia is dotted with boulders everywhere. The Wish Doctor had made sure he was above a large chunk of granite when he felt the quicksand spell coming, so he could sink no further, his feet resting on solid rock.

He had time to find a way to escape, but that still left poor Ron in danger.

~

Ivelli was certainly disappointed the Doctor had not reversed the wish that angered him these last six centuries. Given the importance of the bear, he had thought the Wish Doctor would not be willing to sacrifice him. Surely, the Wish Doctor didn't think allowing a being to be sacrificed was worth the extra ability Ivelli would claim if that stupid wish was reversed? He wasn't after all purely evil.

Unless there was a plan for the bear to escape? He couldn't see it, not with the boy separated from the bear. Could his protege be wrong?

He glanced at the screen of camera feeds. The bear was still captive. Still, he'd send another agent to check. Since it was his birthright to be the world's smartest person, he didn't want to appear like a stupid Bond villain.

He could not rely on the bear's capture alone. He was playing a long game, and the main action was about to start. He couldn't keep the Wish Doctor trapped in sand any more than he had with the box. He just needed time to set his plan in motion.

The final preparations for what he was about to do would take unimaginable energy and use up some of Ivelli's best wishes. It would be worth it to create the most powerful wishing well ever. It could never be duplicated, once he'd harvested the power.

A hundred years of effort to make it happen and he had kept it hidden from the Wish Doctor. That in itself was a major feat.

Now the final wish to keep Her Presumptuousness away during the crucial moments. It was not easy making a wish that could upset a granter, especially when he intended to bend the laws of nature. It was a terrible risk, but a calculated one, and one he dared make. He just had to wait a little longer for the tide waters to come.

~

As Ron looked over the symbols on the walls, he noticed amongst the Da Vinci drawings odd references to two writers. There was the date of 1984, a farm with a bunch of animals. There were symbols indicating a clock going in a hundred directions, worlds warring at each other. There was a symbol of Fargo, but not North Dakota, the banking house.

What was the pattern he was seeing...? And then he knew. He had been hiding his intelligence for reasons unknown.

One of the factors of genius, certainly on IQ tests, was pattern recognition. And now he recognized the patterns.

Wells.

Edison, this is Ron. I know what he intends to do. He's going to turn the entire Fundy Basin into the most powerful wishing well ever made. He's going to harvest an unlimited number of wishes. He's been planning this for some time. He must have figured out a way to get around the prohibition of granting yourself more wishes.

He also intends to make himself well. For him, that means being the smartest man in the world. If he achieves this, he will cause unknown destruction.

Edison, also known as the Wish Doctor, gritted his teeth as he heard. He'd been distracted by Ron's kidnapping, while the bigger risk had been beyond his vision.

"Ron, you have done enough. That information will save the day. If you are free, swim out to the hydrofoil."

No. When first we met, you thought I was a dangerous bear. I can be a dangerous bear when needed, but more I am caring, contributing bear. My friends are on the hydrofoil and this battle will not be easy. I am the only one near Ivelli. I have to stop him if I can.

Plus, there is a rule where I come from that I would like to see enforced.

No one kidnaps the bare.

44: The Post Office

When the Shupershark heard the Morse code signal underwater, he turned from his vegetarian meal of kelp and salted algae off the coast of Massachusetts and swam as fast as he could toward the Bay of Fundy.

~

It was not as easy as the Wish Doctor had expected to escape the trap. It was as if he was in a wish-free zone. Ivelli had done this before. It took a lot of unwishes to do this, so the impact was only on a small area. He had to be careful, because any wish he used here would be stolen by his foe.

He murmured to himself as he worked. He had thought Ivelli overconfident to the point of arrogance, but perhaps it was himself who was overconfident. When he had made the wish to be the smartest, he had leapfrogged over Ivelli in intelligence; but in the intervening time the gap had narrowed.

Just because he had wished to be the smartest didn't mean that he had to be the smartest by much. Ivelli was catching up with him. That was dangerous, because if the Wish Doctor was smarter only because of some loopy skill like quick wit with puns, Ivelli might defeat him in other ways.

The Wish Doctor thought for a moment of Selva and some of the others he had known through half a millennium. Without his wish, they would have been, or be, smarter than he. Though his wish had been powerful, there was a tension that was unnatural.

Was his wish keeping them from reaching their true potential? Or was their potential continuing to push him to be smarter? He wasn't sure his heart could resist these contradictory forces much longer.

Maybe he couldn't trick his way out of this trap as easily as he had thought. If Ivelli had enough time to plan, maybe he had planted so many tricks it would take the Wish Doctor longer than the tide would take to rise to figure out how to free himself.

Still there was more than one way to escape. He needed to use that most potent force that could compete against wishing something to happen.

Hard work.

The ropes on the post were loose, and as the tide slowly came in, he was no longer mired in quicksand. He put his arms tightly around the post, the same with his legs, and started inching his way upward.

The tide was rising faster than he could climb and, unless he worked faster, he would be submerged.

He didn't panic. He had learned 300 years ago that panic rarely worked. He had to get a better rhythm, keep his muscles relaxed.

The Doctor had to admit he had come to rely too much on wishes and was not used to physical labour. It wasn't helpful that his true body was over 500 years old and had seen a lot of wear and tear.

If he survived this, he was going on a dedicated fitness program, maybe would even open a gym at the lodge.

The optimistic thought of the future brightened his spirits, spurred his energy. He felt lighter, moved quicker, found the rhythm he wanted. Hard work really wasn't so bad. He almost wished he could have more of it.

Except that he realized the tide was going to go much higher than the top of the post, and he had nowhere else to climb. Hard work had its limits. And he had used up his last underwater breathing wish.

No doubt, in hindsight, Ivelli had tricked him to use it.

In this, Ivelli might have outsmarted him, but the smartest thing anyone could do, was to make friends with and be able to call in a favour from a Shupershark.

The water was now deep enough for a supersvelt Shupershark, who had lost weight on a vegetarian diet to swim in and not scrape his dorsal fin. He gave his off-pitch shark whistle and soon enough was diving under the Wish Doctor's feet to lift him up.

"Doctor, whatever is going on here, there's a problem with nature. Her Presumptuousness doesn't have control and I should know."

It was the cause of the friction between the two. The Shupershark had borrowed what he had thought was a small, unmissable part of nature from Her Presumptuousness and held onto it. It was partly what allowed him to be a nice vegetarian shark and not a predator. He wasn't sure if he'd be able to free the Doctor without the power of that piece of nature.

The Doctor didn't have to think twice about what was causing the problem with nature. Ivelli was the source of the problem, naturally.

~

As the Shupershark carried the Wish Doctor from his post, the tide gained momentum, covering the solid sea floor around the flowerpots. The time was right for Ivelli's most important wish. He had to make a wish to subdue Her Presumptuousness also known as Gaea, also known as Mother Nature, or else his major wish would not work. He had to be completely separated from the world of nature for contact with nature would prevent any harm to nature itself.

He had tested and perfected the physics in Florence with the box. The Wish Doctor might have been friends with Bell, but Ivelli had Newton on his side. Who cares if Einstein refused to help? It also helped that his spy had stolen Selva's design for the wishmethere.

Ivelli stepped over to the fuse box inside the shack with the Well sym-bols and flipped a switch. No wish needed for this. Just pure technology.

Once outside of the realm of nature, he pulled out a shamrock formed from rock a billion years ago and made the wish he had spent so long preparing. You could not fool mother nature, but you could distract her.

"I wish Her Presumptuousness' craving for blueberry grunt comes to a peak."

Oblivious to all else, as if drunk, suddenly U Are Mother Earth sat on the top of Mount Everest, where she often came to view her domain, eat-ing blueberry grunt she had been saving. Blueberry grunt favoured with Iwish whiskey that predated the shamrock. Blueberry grunt flavoured with the most spectacular truffle-scented, hog-finding, grunt flavour.

Ivelli figured Mother Nature would be distracted for four hours. Drunkenness did this to even the most powerful of beings. Because everyone, even an immortal being, has a weakness.

~

The tides came into the Bay of Fundy unnaturally strongly. Smaetag used her expert skill to keep the hydrofoil in position. It would be needed shortly.

She felt oddly comfortable being the captain, giving orders to her small crew. She had worked through so many issues since Thanksgiving that her true self was resurfacing.

She would not have the long life of a Wish Doctor, but she would have

42 really great years, and another seven pretty good ones before the can-cer took her. At least by that time, pain medication would be universally free, and would not rob users of their energy.

She meant to use those years purposefully. She had an urgent mission. She would do as much as she could to ease the Wish Doctor's burden. If Alma and Syd and the remaining triplets would only do their parts, he might finally have peace.

She held her breath. If the right wish became available, she would use it.

45: The Duke of Wellington

Syd did not know how to apologize. Ron was the only one in their friend-ship to have good manners. In over a hundred years, Syd had not learned; no matter that hundred twenty years was the same twenty lived over six times.

He was selfish. He had never had time for a permanent girlfriend and in his 122nd year, he still felt as if he was 19. Maybe it wasn't that he hadn't had time. Maybe it was that he had. Time to wait for the perfect girl.

Alma was that, for sure.

Unless you expected the perfect girl to also like you. She had once, though.

At least when she thought he was living his first lifetime, when she thought he was a teenager for the first time, reading Anne for the first time, not a holder of a first edition.

The thought sobered him. If she did not want him, then he had no right to anyone else. He would worship her and serve her like no one else. He could not do the same for another, so if she rejected him, he was a bachelor for life.

There were very few beings who would accept a 122-year-old date. Those who would were either wish maniacs or ghosts. Those his own age were either satisfied with their life or were magical beings totally frightened of the strength he was gathering.

Maybe he should just turn into a bear. There were plenty of widowed bears who would not just accept him but would cherish him. Let's be frank: there is no one more genuine than a mother bear.

Nonetheless, Syd walked across the deck of the hydrofoil, amazingly stable under Smaetag's command. He was frightened Alma would walk away, but duty held her in place.

"I'm sorry," he said. "I won't bother you again. Please don't hold your anger against Ron. He needs your help."

"I know," said Alma, "I am just waiting for the signal."

Syd looked at her, confused. But then he could hear the Bell ringing.

~

Bell remembered the words he had used when his most famous invention had been found to work: 'Mr. Watson – Come here – I want to see you.' He was confident his latest would work now, so he simply said, "Come here, Alma."

He was atop a flowerpot, trying to ensure a bear's destiny stayed intact.

When she heard the words, Alma pressed the button on the little cylinder she had been given.

Suddenly she was transported to the kindly old ghost with a long grey beard. He smiled.

The physics had worked. And while his most famous work had inspired a Star Trek device, another Star Trek device had inspired his latest effort. The principles were amazingly simple and really didn't need a wish, though of course he had used one.

He had invented a teleport device, though it would have limited use because of the energy consumption. Still, he had had to make refinements to make the phone work practically, why not the teleporter? He didn't have Watson, who was certainly enjoying his celestial retirement, but he had Selva, and he was more than enough.

The technology allowed him a little more freedom to travel from the afterlife and so he was no longer restricted to the grounds of his lodge.

"Hoy, Hoy," he said as Alma arrived. "I sensed you kept both the crystal and my little signal device."

She nodded, only a little disoriented.

"Not much time. I'm late for an engagement, and don't have much power left in this corporeal world. You have everything you need to help Ron, most importantly your wits. Help him, and he will help you all."

Alma nodded again. It might take her centuries to understand all that was happening, but she had the essence of it.

"There is one last charge," he said. "It will return you to the hydrofoil when you reset the button. All you have to do is press it one more time. Just make sure the bear is a bear. Now, good fortune. I have to return, or I'll be in trouble with Mabel."

She nodded absently as he faded away.

It would be hard not to be distracted by the spectacular views from atop the flowerpot, but Alma had laser focus. She had to find Ron. No matter what was between her and Syd, Ron deserved it.

She looked for bear tracks in the soil atop the flowerpot, but the only footprints were those of a small human. *Where is Ron?*

~

Ivelli stepped out of the box annoyed the bear had escaped. Well, it didn't matter. The Wish Doctor was here, so Ivelli's most important wish would come true. The Doctor would either reverse his great wish, or his presence would allow Ivelli to draw three power wishes.

It had taken years and most of his intellect to formulate a conundrum that would allow him to create the ability to ask for more wishes. In the end it had been simple: "I wish that I could ask for zero more wishes."

Since zero was truly a number, as Selva's ancestor, had proved, the prohibition against asking for wishes was turned upside down. Because if your request for zero wishes was denied, that meant you could ask for an infinite number.

For a moment, Ivelli didn't care if he was the smartest person in the world. He was certainly the cleverest.

At the top of flowerpot, he spread his arms to embrace all of the Bay of Fundy as rushing water filled into the basin, and spoke authoritatively. "WELL, NOW!"

Immediately, he could feel the power coming. The power to make unlimited wishes for as long as the tide held strong. Six hours to draw power. One hour at peak to draw three power wishes, wishes that had no limitation.

The Bay of Fundy, filled with the rushing strength of the highest tides in the world, stronger than any time in the past five centuries, became the largest wishing well the world had ever seen.

46: Not just desserts

Alma was startled by the *plunk, plunk, plunk* sound of coins hitting the waters. "What the—?" she yelped.

Then she heard Ron's bearitone voice. "I know the enemy's plan."

Ivelli had turned the entire Bay of Fundy into a wishing well. A Hope Well. It was ingenious. The power of the moon creating the tides; the magical creatures of the maritime landscape. It was the greatest concentration of wish power in millennia, though she did not know that.

Ivelli was harvesting. Not making wishes now; harvesting, holding them for later.

Alma took a moment and wished a hope for well into the future.

She saw six of Ivelli's proteges, not unlike the students of her class, clinging to the steep sides of the flowerpot. Her hand was in her pocket, and she had to suddenly yank it free. The crystal was going hot.

She wasn't sure what that meant, but in her other pocket were six coins. Six chocolate coins. She flung them over her shoulder, making wishes as she went. She knew she needed all six wishes, but the first was most important: "Where is Ron?"

She felt the wish working, but all she could see was a naked teenager a few feet from her, unashamed and ashamed at the same time. She felt a moral obligation to look away, but couldn't for a variety of reasons. She was a teenager herself.

After a momentary distraction, she used another of her coin wishes: "I wish the youth is clothed."

Suddenly, Ron was dressed in a full Boston Bruin hockey uniform, including an old-style goalie mask with painted-on stitches. He looked much more fearsome than he ever had with fur.

"Help," Ron said. "I need some defence."

~

The hydrofoil began to shake. Although Ivelli's crew was mostly gathering wishes, they were also casting some to attack the hydrofoil.

Smaetag guided the vessel away from harm. It was not easy. There were so many powerful wishes being generated, the hydrofoil was being overwhelmed by them and the power of the tide. Smaetag struggled with the controls, but held on. If not for her skill, the hydrofoil would be buffeted against the cliffs.

She realized something, though. The boat was foiling many of the wishes, but not all.

Others were randomly reflecting off the boat into the water and onto the shore. For years to come there would be ramifications as those wishes came true foe creatures on land and in the waters of the Bay.

~

The creation of the massive wishing well was not a revelation for the Wish Doctor, nor for Syd or Ron, for that matter. It was a reawakening, the end of the wish loop.

The Wish Doctor one century ago had seen this time coming, not exactly involving the Bay of Fundy, but some ultra-powerful source of wishes that Ivelli would harvest. Somehow, he had known Ivelli would get around the prohibition of wishing you had more wishes. It wasn't a matter of Ivelli being smarter; it was a desperate effort involving great risks that a smarter man would not take. But an insane one would.

Fortunately, the Doctor had had some insight this would happen. He had needed a protection to fight it. One hundred years ago, Syd or Ron, one of them, had been his student with the most potential. Just as Alma, Smaetag, and the middle triplet were now: once-in-a-century strengths.

~

The details of his memory were still fuzzier than Ron's fur after a blow-dry. They had learned of the threat for the future, but Syd was not strong enough a hundred years earlier to do what needed to be done.

He was now.

He had lived through six sessions of the Doctor's school, his true potential hidden from Ivelli or anyone else. Each time he learned something more from the lessons. Each time he grew more powerful, more capable. If this session he didn't always seem to be listening, it was because he could remember the words exactly and was contemplating how better to apply them.

In his first semester of his first session at the School of Wish, he could not make a pure wish. He could of course even then bring a teddy bear alive, though he did need a well or a shooting star to make it happen.

In his second session, Syd could make a small pure wish. By the third session of the school, a pure wish was second nature to him; and by this time, he was as powerful as the Wish Doctor and Ivelli himself, just less experienced.

Ivelli could not have anticipated him. The cloak of secrecy over the wish loop had kept the knowledge hidden even from the Wish Doctor and Syd and Ron themselves, though he was pretty sure now that Ron was not his real name.

Syd readied himself for what was to come and, through the link they shared, sent Ron a message:

```
No matter what happens, you will always be my
best friend.
```

~

The Wish Doctor rode the Shupershark like it was a dolphin at SeaWorld, only much faster. They could not circle the flowerpot yet, as the water was not deep enough on the shore side, but they could come close.

The Wish Doctor watched and absorbed all. Ivelli had planned the Well well and The Wish Doctor was not sure he had planned his defence well enough. He definitely was getting too old for this. Still, he wasn't out of tricks just yet.

"Syd," he said. "As we planned, steal the first power wish."

~

Ron did not feel right in the scarred mask. Wearing a Bruins Jersey while being a Flyers fan was not cool, especially with the danger he was about to face.

He lifted his mask and turned to Alma. "I am very sorry about all that has happened. I have some things to do that are really important. I hope you can grant me a last wish."

"Anything. If I can."

"Will you give me a last kiss?"

"I have never given you a first kiss."

"A last kiss for me. There is more here than you know. It will be explained. Please, allow me this boon."

Alma didn't know what to say. It was definitely weird after seeing the bare-naked bear boy, given he was her former boyfriend's best friend. But she could feel the danger all around.

And Syd had lied to her. Still…

"Kiss him," said a voice in her head. A soft, huggable, motherly voice and not Lavinia's.

"Kiss him," the voice of URME said again. "I am somewhat occupied, but while I may have desserted you, I can't desert you."

Alma felt the warmth of nature and human companionship fill her. She leaned in and tenderly kissed Ron on the lips.

He responded, tentatively, gentlebearly. It was enough to create an electric shock.

It is a truism in the world that a true kiss is even more powerful than a true wish. Ron suddenly didn't need the Bruins jersey, because his fur was there again.

"Thank you, Alma," he said. "Now press that device and get back to the hydrofoil. I will join you shortly."

Alma would have hesitated, but she heard Bell ringing in her ear. It was the time for the bear to be the hero. Her time was not yet come.

Ron, looking rather grizzled from his long ordeal, lumbered across the jagged edge of the flowerpot where Ivelli was steadily throwing coins into the water. No telling how much magic was happening. The grizzly had to stop Ivelli.

Ron had absorbed some of Syd's wish magic and made the simplest of wishes. "I wish those coins would not hit the water."

Suddenly, a flock of loons were plucking the coins from the air, Canadian one-dollar coins with the monarch on one side, blank on the other.

Ivelli seemed mildly annoyed as Ron approached him, but suddenly rising or growing from the flowerpot was the triplet named Dahlia.

"So, you are the traitor," Ron said. "The one who kidnapped me and stuffed me in the plastic bag. Well played. Whatever wish you made, you sure made it look like Alfalfa was the trouble-making triplet."

Dahlia smiled. "You can't imagine what a thorn it has been in my side to be always mistaken for my sister. Now, *bear teddy alive come.*"

Reversed, Ron started to shrivel. But only because he pretended to, as he had cast his own wish.

"How? Why did the wish reversal not work?" Dahlia exclaimed.

"Has no one reading or living this book been paying attention? You can't reverse me back to a teddy bear. I'm a real bear."

There is no better way to deceive the enemy than to deceive yourself.

47: Outsmarted

The Shupershark delivered the Wish Doctor to the hydrofoil at the same time Alma returned. She felt guilty for the kiss she had given Ron, though she knew he had needed the power the kiss created. Thus, she did not notice the remarkable changes that were overtaking Syd.

The transportation, although a short distance, made her stomach sick. Without knowing it, she hit the device button again and this time it travelled alone.

The Wish Doctor needed a moment to clear his head, to allow the details of the long planning of the wish loop to come to fruition. And nothing helped better than a good draft of Scottish Wishkey. He opened up his flask with the thistle, the symbol of Scotland, where he had first met Bell in Bell's youth, and took a drink.

His senses came alert. He had not anticipated enough. He should not be here. His very presence gave Ivelli the opportunity for power wishes.

But it was too late to get away. He had to be ready to foil the rest of Ivelli's plan.

~

Ivelli had been mentoring Dahlia since she was a little sprout. She had flowered into such a promising girl. Yet she had been unable to stop the bear.

He had little time. He had to gather the first power wish.

He set his protection wishes. He had learned that well from the Wish Doctor. He set his obstruction wishes.

He waited as long as he could, as the tide came close to cresting, then said, "I wish for Power."

Ron had been waiting for this moment, without realizing it, for a hundred years. Nearly simultaneously, he said, "I wish for Ivelli's power."

It was the kind of wish that would not normally work, because it created a contradiction of wishes. Ron and Ivelli could not both have the power wish.

Yet Ivelli had set out to contradict the rules of wish magic. Which allowed Ron to say, "I wish to contradict Ivelli's contradiction."

It gave Ron his chance. He took the power wish and held it ready. He would need it before long.

~

Ivelli cursed and cursed again. He could only ask for power three times, and the first had been defeated. The water was almost to the top of the flowerpot now. He realized he might just have underestimated how important the bear was. He needed to get away. It was no longer necessary to be on the rock, anyway.

He took a step and jumped off the surface of the flowerpot, but not before wishpering carefully, "You wished for my power. Now let me grant it to you."

He pointed a device, and a stream of power made from a hundred wishes stolen from the arrogant, from lunatics corrupted by the abuse of power, coursed toward the bear. "May your next wish be bearren."

As Ron toppled to the ground of the flowerpot, singed, and hurt, fur scorched, an eye damaged, he called out one last time to the doctor.

```
Beware the power Wish!
```

Ivelli did not hear this as his feet landed on the deck of the Wishing Boat (because how else would you net all the wishes in the world's biggest wishing well?).

Nets overboard, with the hardiest looking crew ever seen in the seven seas. They did their work well, capturing the wishes like fishes. Which gave Ivelli time to ready for an attempt at the second power wish.

~

Smaetag piloted the hydrofoil on a parallel course with the wishing boat, keeping abeam of it. Both vessels were at the whirling centre of the giant wishing well, the location where wishes had their greatest chance of being granted.

The Wish Doctor looked across the rising waters. He had to time it perfectly if he was going to steal the second wish. Ivelli would be ready for a simple theft, so he had to be more clever.

He could see his former classmate's face and his confident grin. A grin that meant he had figured out something the Wish Doctor hadn't completely planned for. Nor, quite frankly, would have expected, given their long and bitter contact.

Ivelli looked over, and uttered a protection wish the Doctor couldn't hear, then said, "I wish the Doctor was one hundred times smarter than he is now."

The Wish Doctor looked up in terror.

His brain began to swell, pushing pressure against his skull that wasn't the real pain. The real pain was the overwhelming ability of the brain functioning at full capacity.

There was no brain bias, simplifying sensations. There was no ignoring any sensory input. Every piece of data around the Doctor was consumed, analyzed. He could feel his intellect reaching out, drawing conclusions from the data, forced without control to unravel knowledge of the nature of the universe.

He saw every decision he had made in the last six hundred years. He saw every single flaw with the new insight of his intelligence. It was hard to focus on the good things he had done. All he could see was the stupid things he had done. He also saw all the actions he didn't take that he should have taken.

A wish loop, for heaven's sake! Would any truly intelligent person go through such trouble, such gamesmanship, if there were so many easier and obvious ways to be prepared, or better yet, to stop them earlier?

Of course, some of those ways were quite ruthless. The Wish Doctor could feel a coldness within that he didn't like. The expanded intelligence ruled with less emotion. It was easier to see decisions as simple calculations, and side with the math despite the consequences.

As the tumult of knowledge and computation overwhelmed him, he could not get his brain to focus on the trivial outcome of a wish around him.

Thus, when Ivelli said, "I wish for power," his wish was granted.

~

"Oh my God," Syd said. "A hundred years of planning and we weren't quite ready."

He could feel it as Ivelli took the power wish. He had expected the Wish Doctor to do something, and Syd had been unprepared.

304

Since all his energy had been getting ready to stop the third wish.

~

Ivelli took a deep breath. A power wish is a hard thing to hold, not because it is dangerously ready to go wrong, but because it bequeaths a feeling of glory and temptation. The power wish *wants* to be used.

But a power wish grows in strength through time, and he was not yet ready to have a battle of power wishes with the Wish Doctor. Not until he had at least an equal number.

While he worked to recover his strength, Ivelli continued to bathe in the wishes being collected around him. Life for the next hundred years would certainly be very interesting.

~

Syd saw Alma staggering as she came back from helping Ron. "Is Ron okay?" he asked.

"Barely, but I helped him get back to normal."

"Are *you* okay? You look seasick."

"Not seasick. My stomach got upset travelling the way I did."

"Can you help the Wish Doctor? I have got to stop Ivelli from gathering a power wish."

Alma didn't know what that was and didn't have time to find out. She ran to the Wish Doctor, who certainly was not his normal self. "What's wrong?" she said.

"What's wrong?" he answered, irritated. "Isn't it obvious? I am too smart."

Her wrinkled frown irritated the Doctor, but, despite his emotions, the Doctor's new intelligence fought through the problem, and concluded that the smartest thing he could do was to get help.

"Get Smaetag," he said. "Tell her to put the hydrofoil on autopilot."

Alma did, and returned quickly with Smaetag, who immediately noticed two things. One, the Wish Doctor was clutching his head, unable to deal with anything. Two, Syd and Glenda were fighting like crazy to undo wishes that were being cast against the hydrofoil, trying to dislodge it.

Syd grew bigger every time he cast or deflected a wish, and was slowly gaining fur and claws.

Alma wasn't sure when he had crossed the line into becoming a bear, but there was no doubt now. He was a pure bear the size of a grizzly. She could not know he was draining strength from Ron.

There was no time to think. Smaetag was pulling on her shoulder, getting her to look at the Wish Doctor.

"Listen carefully," the Doctor said. "This is a lesson for year two, when we talk about more powerful wishes. There are types of wishes I didn't want you to know about until you were ready. But now I need to give you a quick lesson.

"A well-done wish can hold its effect forever, especially if it is in the flow of normal things. To wish to be a better waiter, when that is something that could happen—that wish can last forever. To wish to understand the lyrics of Cardi B, well, that's almost impossible, so that wish will not last long.

"Any wish that bends the laws of nature is unstable. It can be reversed easily. But it also can be dangerous. It can go terribly wrong."

He did not want to tell them of his wish in the fountain. That wish, to be the smartest in the world, was within the realm of nature. Someone had to be the smartest. Why not him?

But to be wished 100 times smarter than normal, that was outside the realm of nature.

He explained, "Ivelli played a trick. He wished I was a hundred times smarter, but to be so, my brain has swelled and is pressing against my skull. My heart can't take the strain. I can't undo the wish myself. I need you to do so. But you need to be careful."

If he wished his brain to be back to normal, then he would return to the state back in Florence so long ago, when he was no match for Ivelli's intellect. Ivelli would rule the world.

"Brain wash," Smaetag said. "We need to wash your brain of the wish."

~

Syd was stronger than he looked, even in his bear form. Those six cycles through the wish loop had given him a greater natural training than either Ivelli or the Doctor, though he was still an infant in the experience of wishes compared to them. He handled the wishes trying to harm the hydrofoil easily.

Yet Ivelli was now prepared for a wish steal.

Syd was not as clever as Alma, nor did he try to be. He had been too conscious of trying to control his strength. For that he was glad, for his strength was his greatest strength.

As Ivelli got ready to grab the power wish growing in the world's largest wishing well, Syd readied to fight with his bear strength. It was what he had worked so hard to do.

As it came time for Ivelli to wish for the third wish of power, Syd grabbed for it exactly as did Ivelli, like two dogs fighting for a bone.

It is a truism that if two equally opposite and equally strong forces contend for an object, and are strong enough, the object will break before either of the two can take control.

So was it true here. For though Syd was still a bear cub in the world of wishes, at 122, he was young and vibrant and fully willing to go wish to toe with Ivelli. He was full of youthful strength that nearly equalled the old-man strength of Ivelli. He had rehearsed this moment a hundred times, envisioned himself stopping Ivelli from grabbing a power wish.

Ivelli had never imagined this at all, not even after the convention of Annes, for the wish loop had suppressed the truth of Syd s power.

For a moment, Syd thought he might actually wrest the power wish for his own. In that moment, he thought what he might do with such a wish, a thought that relieved the angst he held within. But it was that thought that prevented him from doing so.

Yet, this part of the wish loop worked as written.

As the power wish tore asunder from the force of the two wish masters grasping it, it exploded in a kaleidoscope of broken dreams. Shattered rainbows, pummelled the bay with hardened moisture. Fragments were caught by bystanders, some naive, some tricksters, and others hidden, but Ivelli had lost what he wanted.

He once again screamed. If he had obtained one more power wish, he could have undone without permission the Wish Doctor's smartest wish.

The power of wishes was ever the battle of wills. To get what you wanted from the world of wishes, you needed to impose your will on the powers that created magic.

Syd had been well-prepared. The wish loop had hidden him despite Ivelli's best attempts to spy on that quirky lodge Bell had created in rural Cape Breton.

Syd had broken a power wish. An almost impossible task.

~

Smaetag gave Alma a little shove. "This is what I do best. There is some risk, and you extended my life."

Alma didn't want to say she had also convinced her to make a wish that had led to the death wish.

"My power allows me to see into the mind, into the brain, into wishes and the force behind them," Smaetag said. "It will be an invasion of privacy, but the Doctor needs help."

What Smaetag didn't say was that she had made such a wish once in the pursuit of solidifying her identity that allowed her to be expert in any kind of professional position, whether it be hydrofoil pilot or CPA—or brain surgeon from the 23rd century.

She let her senses enter his mind. She could feel the extra brain tissue, could feel the unnaturally large brain wanting to rebel against its unnatural existence.

In such a situation, there was only one thing a 23rd century brain surgeon could do. Hasten the process.

~

Ron continued to fight against the triplet. She was trying to gather wishes, but she also seemed intent on keeping him on the flowerpot so he could not return to the hydrofoil.

He had to find a way to get there. Everything she did seemed to be designed to counter the power of his bearness. She had clearly been studying him and he hadn't noticed.

Well, maybe it was time he stopped lying to himself.

He let go of the bear form to reveal again his true bare human self. Immediately, Dahlia's defences failed. She was just bearly prepared.

Before he could stop her, she was in the water on a small craft, heading to the hydrofoil. She would likely cause damage away from him, but at least now he could concentrate on getting back to the hydrofoil himself.

~

Smaetag had made so many wishes to improve herself when she was younger, before her power had overwhelmed her, it was hard to know where her natural self began and where her wish self took over. Of course, some of those wishes had also created deeply-dangerous problems.

Fortunately, there was no problem with her being able to focus completely on the problem in front of her. She placed her hands on the Doctor's head as if she was Mr. Spock doing the Vulcan mind meld.

As she probed into the Wish Doctor's mind, she was startled at the intellect she discovered. He could do almost anything. He could figure out any problem. He could have the moon. But necessity had led him to the world of wishes and protecting the world from wishes going wrong.

Part of that intellect guided her, guided her not as a brain surgeon, but as a wish expert, so she could reconfigure the wish Ivelli had made. It was too strong to completely undo, but she could alter it. The wish that had made the condiment lady confident, now made her confident as well.

~

Alma watched as Smaetag pulled her hands away from the Doctor's head. It took a moment for the Doctor to recover, but in that moment Smaetag turned to Alma and said, "When this is done. You and I have to have a long chat. I learned some things we both need to know."

Alma nodded. She thought she had learned a lot about wishes and life this year in the school of wish, but she saw now her education was just begun.

The Wish Doctor started to stir, becoming alert as if he had never had brainwash surgery.

"I had to leave a little behind," Smaetag said in response to the Doctor's curious expression. "If I had to estimate you are about 11.2% smarter."

"Hoy, Hoy," the Wish Doctor said with a grin, as he regained his senses. "That was the eleven percent I was wishing for. Now I can solve a few things that were eluding me."

He got to his feet.

"I hate to wish and run, but would you mind taking control of the ship again? Things are about to get unpleasant."

48: The bare truth of the shooting star

Ivelli had figured he would not gather all three power wishes he felt due to him, given the Wish Doctor's constant defiance, but he had hoped for two to add to the one he already had. Having gained only one on this day, after all this time of planning left him enraged.

He knew he should be satisfied that he had two power wishes, only one less than what the Wish Doctor held. He was gaining ground, but his six-hundred-year-old anger got the better of him.

He was gathering enough ordinary wish power, powerful in its own right, so he could spare enough to cause the Wish Doctor serious damage without impacting his future plans. Maybe if he could find the opportunity, he would still kill the Doctor.

He didn't want to. He wanted to see the wish reversed, but he was tiring of this game.

For any other foe, maybe one wish, with a couple protective wishes, would have sufficed. But the Wish Doctor was as crafty as ever, and this new group of acolytes was surprisingly strong.

He let loose a dozen wishes. A sudden whirlpool in the midst of the crazy tides. The Wish Doctor handled them all, as that boy-turned-bear assisted.

Thankfully, Ivelli had his own acolytes, even if some were recently joined. He nodded at the confident one, whose strange hatred of the Doctor intrigued him.

As Ivelli gestured another six wishes, the acolyte let loose the one that mattered: *I wish you were distracted.*

Ivelli followed it with another wish, and the rug was pulled out from under the bear. He landed on the back of his head, stunned.

In quick succession, Ivelli flung a pair of wish sticks, guiding their aim with another wish. The first went harmlessly by the Doctor. As he tried to avoid the second, he didn't notice that the first was in the shape of a boomerang. He was jumping away from the second, slipping on wish guts, the remains of the wish battle on the deck, when the wish boomerang struck him in the head.

Immediately reinstating the last wish. The Wish Doctor collapsed as the smartest wish took hold again. But not before he pulled a wishker and called for reverse.

~

Alma realized she was all alone for the moment as everyone else was hurt. She felt as if she was not doing her part, though she was the youngest, and had the least power.

She squeezed the crystal piece in her hand, and it gave her strength. She stood her ground and reversed the wish attacks. All her practising of using elocution to reverse wishes served her well. She could tell almost immediately what pattern she had to use.

She used other tricks as well. She turned the octopus into pies. She turned the giant humpback whale into a manageable-sized ogre when it tried to crush their boat. She didn't need a pure wish or an aid, even as she ran out of coins.

Alma turned the large leak in the hull into a giant vegetable. The huge wave coming toward her became a flow of hands for the fans of a soccer game being played somewhere onshore.

When she tired, she found an eerie strength, suddenly remembering the strength of URME's hug. The well Ivelli had created supplied the power of wishes. It was like plucking daisies from the ground.

She had tried avoiding his eyes, but their two boats were too close together, right at the centre of the powerful wishing well. She looked up and her eyes met his.

He was such a handsome, elegant, impeccably-dressed man that the horrific mask of anger his face had become shocked her. How he hated her teacher. Alma could see he considered her guilty by association, and that if looks could kill, Ivelli would kill her, just for a chance to strike at the Wish Doctor.

Not for the first time, she felt sorry for the Wish Doctor. Despite his jokes, he was hurting deep inside. She had to prove she was worthy to be his successor someday so he could lay down his burden.

Ivelli resumed his barrage of wishes. Alma stood her ground, wondering how long she could hold.

~

You might fool the Wish Doctor once, but never a second time (unless it had to do with quicksand). He would not be outsmarted by being made smart again.

This time he reversed the brainy wish without Smaetag's aid. He wished he had the ability to do what she had done, which allowed him to erase the extra intelligence with relatively moderate effort. His intelligence boosted by the same amount again, so he was about 22.4% smarter than he had been yesterday, enough to add to his psychological distresses, but not enough to incapacitate him as earlier.

As he returned to his normally above average self, plus the extra boost Ivelli had inadvertently given him, the Wish Doctor stood ready to resume the wish battle. He staggered as he stood up. He needed just a moment, and his students were holding their own.

Unfortunately, Ivelli was not in the habit of giving moments. He was growing more annoyed by the second, and he was a man who was born annoyed, his intelligence making it so he could not countenance the slow-thinking creatures around him. It was one thing to fight against the Wish Doctor, because, if he had to admit it, there was a certain of amount of joy in it, but to fight these young students, with whom he had no relationship or history, the battle was meaningless.

Still, this stubborn girl who had almost stopped his collecting of wishes at the Anne convention continued to thwart him. That she was coming close to making a wish that could hurt him made him even more annoyed.

Ivelli could not let the little girl defeat him. He gathered his wits and summoned a single powerful dark wish. "I wish you harm," he said.

A lightning bolt leapt toward her. It was no ordinary lightning bolt, but one of Zeussian power.

Syd, the bear, tried to turn into the motorcycle-riding Johnny Lightning, whose suit protected against lightning, but had only managed to don the gauntlets before he had to jump in front of Alma to protect her.

The gauntlets were not enough to absorb the lightning. His bear ears heard Ivelli's wish from a distance, and he countered not just with a pure wish, but with the power of the Fundy wishing well.

"I wish all harm aimed at Alma strikes me," he said.

The bolt of lightning hit Syd straight on and he had almost no protection. His fur alit with fire as his body shimmered with deadly energy, the electrical force of the lightning undoing the molecules of his body.

His body crumbled even as Alma vainly tried to catch him, knowing she might be crushed in the attempt.

Catch him she did, but in her arms was a shimmering body that transmuted briefly into the human teenager she had known as Syd, and then finally into his true form.

An orange, raggedy toy teddy bear no bigger than ten inches tall, with one eye missing.

The little bear, who would never harm anyone and had given so much comfort in a dreary world, raised its fur-singed little arm to its worn-out brow, giving a last salute. It then lay still, its breath gone.

Syd had never been a boy at all, but a teddy bear that someone had wished to life.

Ivelli did not give Alma any time to grieve. He cast another wish, and another.

But, the Wish Doctor, horrified at what had happened, was ready to counter.

Alma screamed in agony. She didn't know which was the more painful truth: that Syd was gone, or that Syd had been a bear all along. She might have felt betrayed if she didn't know this had all been for a purpose, all part of the wish loop, some long-time trap in the war between Ivelli and the Doctor.

She looked at the Wish Doctor in anger. He was busy reversing wishes as Ivelli continued casting them.

Ivelli was tiring. The wish that had killed Syd had been a very powerful and draining wish.

The Wish Doctor was distraught, but not distraught enough, Alma felt, about what had happened.

She had a mind to stop the both of them forever. For a moment, she felt she held the power to do so.

Then, unintentionally, she wished she knew the Doctor's true intentions. In a flash, she could see hope on his brow. There was more to the story, though he looked like he had taken as much as he could from Ivelli.

There was another trick to come, and she could not see it.

Ivelli tried the same wish of harm against the Doctor that he had tried against Alma, but the Wish Doctor wished for magical rubber-tree boots which protected him from the lightning.

Ivelli was relentless, casting wish after wish. His anger seemed to make him stronger, like some hulking monster. The Wish Doctor may not have looked old on the surface, but he was weakening toward the strength of his true age. He needed help.

Alma cast her own wishes, but they did nothing. Ivelli was well protected against her. Well wishes were not her specialty and there was no shooting star.

No shooting star…

She couldn't do it, but someone else could.

She felt a presence beside her. A ghost? "Bell?"

"No, not Bell," a voice she barely recognized said.

Slowly materializing, as if entering from another dimension, a small boy with a wizened brow and bruises on his face began to appear. She recognized him, but he was not the physical boy she had known. Nor the bear she had known that the boy had been disguised as, either. The boy she had kissed on the flowerpot.

He was close to a foot smaller than the Syd she knew, scrawny, nerdy, unconfident, unattractive.

Perhaps the most beautiful boy she had ever seen.

As kindred a spirit as she had ever known.

Alma could see the anguish in him and understood his need to make wishes to ease his pain, even if those wishes had deceived her. He had frozen his life in a wish loop, living through the agony of foster homes and harsh foster parents and bullies and abuse and loneliness through more than one childhood, so that he could at this moment do what was needed to help others.

"Syd?" she said tentatively. "Not Ron?"

She did not know this real Syd, but she instantly loved him despite the deceit. He may be 122, but he was still a teenager, a very caring teenager. His sacrifice was plain to see.

"Yes, it's me. The real Syd. I made a wish so that Ron and I could change places, so I could be here at the end of the wish loop. He was never supposed to die. I'm sorry I lied to you."

"There's time for that later. We need to stop Ivelli."

"How? My power is drained. Losing Ron has weakened me." He was holding back tears, fighting to find a way to do his duty.

"Wish upon a shooting star," she said.

"I can't. There's not a single star in the sky, let alone a shooting star."

"Touch my back and wish upon a shooting star."

He did, his hands much smaller than when he had been a bear.

She uttered a dozen protection wishes, then said, "Wish that the Wish Doctor has the power to stop Ivelli."

"I wish upon a shooting star that the Wish Doctor has the power to stop Ivelli."

~

You could not see it, but if you were trained even for a short time at the School of Wish you could sense the energy that transferred to the Wish Doctor, who did a mysterious thing.

He threw a florin into the Bay of Fundy. Then he looked Ivelli in the eye and said, "I wish you were well."

Ivelli looked stricken, then his face went calm as the bout of genius insanity that regularly took him over disappeared. Without the madness that drove his genius, he was not clever enough to avoid the next series of wishes.

The Wish Doctor wished the tide was changing quicker than the moon of nature would allow. He wished the wishing well a time of rest. He wished the wishing boats wish nets to dissolve.

Slowly the great waters of the Bay of Fundy began to subside, the tide beginning to drain.

The giant well was diminishing. Losing its power.

Ivelli's' craft held in place; its motors still strong against the tide.

The Wish Doctor took the time to study Ivelli. He could not make him well permanently because Ivelli did not think he needed curing, and even if he did would not have wanted it. The wellness the Doctor had given him would recede and he would try again.

The other students huddled behind the Doctor as Smaetag controlled the hydrofoil.

"How could I make that wish?" Syd asked.

Alma, blushing, turned her back to him and lifted up her blouse. There, on the bottom half of her back, was an immense orange and red tattoo of a star with a smiling face and two long arms holding pistols that were firing bullets.

It took Syd a moment, and then he laughed and laughed. He had never liked tattoos, but he liked this one.

A Shooting Star. Alma certainly was one, indeed.

If the creatures who made wishes could twist words around to make them go wrong, why couldn't someone twist words and images around so they could go right?

"Hi," he said. "My name is Syd, and I am real. I am not a bear. I remember all the things we shared when I traded places when I was a bear, but I can understand you will not find me attractive like this."

Alma shook her head, then turned and gave him a bear hug. So hard he almost fainted. "I didn't want to tell you, but Dahlia stole the teddy bear you gave me. From now on, you will have to be my teddy bear."

Syd smiled. He couldn't wish for anything better.

Alma, though scared, was happy, except for one more thing. A wish out of place in Ivelli's attack.

"I wish the crystal shard was dust."

The crystal's power had faded at the last, but Alma had hoped it would be restored when combined with the rest of the crystal. As she stared at the crystal dust in her hand, she realized a terrible truth. Her mother had warned her: *don't ever come back if you don't bring the crystal.* Tears were forming in her eyes.

Two of her resolutions were still on track. But the third, the resolve to protect the crystal, had failed. She could never go home again.

Alma looked at the new, scrawny Syd. He may have lived 100 years, but he was not old, nor was he truly jaded. He had the youth and energy of a teenager.

But also, a deep sadness.

Ron was gone, and whatever could be said of him, Syd had loved him. He was after all a real, thinking, polite bear.

Alma gently touched Syd's cheek, and said, "Other than you, I don't think I ever met a better man than Ron."

There was sudden splashing ahead of them and Alma and Syd turned to see what was happening. A dangerous tension separated The Wish Doctor and Ivelli.

The Wish Doctor was casting another wish. "I wish you would recede with the tide."

Ivelli's face was full of sane recognition and normal anger as he felt his craft moving, nudged, not so gently by a Shupershark and a group of ratfish.

"This is not the end," he yelled almost sanely. "This is never the end. I came closer this time than any time before. You grow older; I do not. I will be back, and I will take all your power. I will take back my birthright."

The Wish Doctor smiled. He had been tricked into taking Ivelli's birthright because Ivelli couldn't properly handle that power. If Ivelli had that level of smartness, and no one to stop him, he would have used his wish power to do untold harm. The Wish Doctor could not let that happen. He would continue to fight the rivalry as long as he could.

Now, he could not keep himself from taking one more jab at his enemy. He felt more confident than he had in years, for he was not alone anymore. He could feel the power of the students at his back.

He suddenly remembered all the plans of the wish loop he had designed and then wished he would forget. He already had other plans in place for Ivelli's next attack. And the one after that.

Then maybe it would be someone else's plan that would stop Ivelli. Surely the wish that kept his fatal heart attack at bay would not fade until then.

The Doctor could Well feel the Hope of the future in the students behind him and the one at the wheel and the least-expected one still at the Lodge. He quickly set out protective wishes in several languages, then crossed the middle finger over the index finger on both hands as he held them behind his back.

"I will be back," Ivelli yelled. "I will. And I will finally defeat you!"

"Well, then," the Wish Doctor said, smiling, keeping those fingers crossed as the tide and Shupershark pushed Ivelli away, Alma and Syd shivering behind him.

"I wish you good luck."

Epilogue

The ceremony was simple. They tucked the torn and ripped form of Ron the teddy bear into a protective plastic bag and carefully placed it prominently on a shelf in Syd's room in the Lodge of Wonders. Syd and Alma knelt, holding hands, fighting back tears as each made a silent wish.

"Let it be said that there was no better man than this bear," said Syd.

Alma nodded. It was the first day of the new school year at the School of Wish. She fondled the broken crystal in her pocket.

There was no going back home now. Especially after the terrible news that had come in the telegram about her brother.

Follow Mark E. Shupe @shuperdad on TikTok,
or on the adventuresofshuperman.com webpage, for news of the next
Wish Doctor book, *The Wishing Hour*.

Post pictures of you reading *The Wish Doctor*
on Facebook at 'Tales of the Wish Doctor'.
You could win a wishing rock,
with protection wishes already built in.

About the author

Every year on his birthday since he was 12, Mark Shupe has made a wish that someday he could share his overactive imagination through his writing. And now it begins...

On the outside Mark, looks like an everyday accounting clerk who has eaten too much pasta and forgotten to take his anti-hairline-receding medicine. But on the inside, he is a raging cyclone of imagination, romance, angst and awkward jokes. He never tires of his wife saying, "That's not funny."

He is not sure whether he is more comfortable atop a mountain peak, a beach at high tide, inside a Van Gogh painting, or browsing the shelves of a comic book shop. He is in all those places more frequently than his salary should allow.

A Bachelor of Journalism graduate, Mark gave up a career as a sportswriter (he hosted an international TV show, "Running") to write edgy and tightly-worded audit reports for a ginormous corporation. He and famous author Lana Shupe have Wishlight Cottage, at Sandy Point on Nova Scotia's South Shore, after years of living in Calgary, where Mark managed to walk all 15,000 km of its streets.

WishLight Cottage is a place of magic. If you ever visit there, and you really, really should, drop by and say Hi. If you time the tides right, you may even get to sit on the wine and sand bar behind their summerhouse, where only the grandest tales are told.